Peter Lovesey is the only living author in Britain to have received the two highest honours in crime writing – the Diamond Dagger of the Crime Writers Association and Grand Master of the Mystery Writers of America. He started with the Sergeant Cribb series set in Victorian London and later progressed to modern times with the award-winning Peter Diamond books set in Bath, his home for almost twenty years.

Now living in Shrewsbury with his wife Jax, whom he met at Reading University, he continues to reach and entertain new readers across the world.

Also by Peter Lovesey

Peter LOVESEY

DIAMOND AND THE EYE

sphere

SPHERE

First published in Great Britain in 2021 by Sphere

1 3 5 7 9 10 8 6 4 2

A CIP catalogue record for this book is available from the British Library.

ISBN 978-0-7515-8367-0

Typeset in ITC New Baskerville by Palimpsest Book Production Ltd,
Falkirk, Stirlingshire
Printed and bound in Great Britain by Clays Ltd, Elcograf S.p.A.

Papers used by Sphere are from well-managed forests
and other responsible sources.

Sphere
An imprint of
Little, Brown Book Group
Carmelite House
50 Victoria Embankment
London
EC4Y 0DZ

An Hachette UK Company
www.hachette.co.uk

www.littlebrown.co.uk

DIAMOND
AND THE EYE

1

'Mind if I join you?'
Peter Diamond's toes curled.

There's no escape when you're wedged into your favourite armchair in the corner of the lounge bar at the Francis observing the last rites of an exhausting week keeping a cap on crime. Tankard in hand, your third pint an inch from your mouth, you want to be left alone.

The stranger's voice was throaty, the accent faux American from a grainy black-and-white film a lifetime ago. This Bogart impersonator was plainly as English as a cricket bat. His face wasn't Bogart's and he wasn't talking through tobacco smoke, but he held a cocktail stick between two fingers as if it was a cigarette. Some years the wrong side of forty, he was dressed in a pale grey suit and floral shirt open at the neck to display a miniature magnifying glass on a leather cord.

'Depends,' Diamond said.

'On what?'

'Should I know you?'

'No reason you should, bud.'

No one called Diamond 'bud'. He'd have said so, but the soundtrack had already moved on.

'I got your number. You're the top gumshoe in this one-horse town and you're here in the bar Friday nights when you're not tied up on a case. What's your poison? I'll get you another.'

'Don't bother.' Diamond wasn't being suckered into getting lumbered with a bar-room bore who called him bud and claimed to have got his number.

'You'll need something strong when you hear what I have to say.' The bore pulled up a chair and the voice became even more husky. 'Good to meet you, any road. I'm Johnny Getz, the private eye.'

'Say that again, the last part.'

'Private eye.'

Against all the evidence that this was a send-up, Diamond had to hear more. '*Private eye*? I thought they went out with Dick Tracy.'

'Dick Tracy was a cop.'

'Sam Spade, then. We're talking private detectives, are we? I didn't know we had one in Bath.'

'What do you mean – "one"? I could name at least six others. The difference is they're corporate. I'm the real deal. I work alone.'

'Where?'

'Over the hairdresser's in Kingsmead Square.' An address that lacked something compared to a seedy San Francisco side street, which was probably why the self-styled PI added, 'The Shear Amazing Sleuth. Like it?'

There was a pause while the conflict in Diamond's head – contempt battling with curiosity – raged and was resolved. 'What did you say your name is?'

'Johnny Getz.'

'How do you spell that?'

'Getz? With a zee.'

Diamond sighed. 'Is it real?'

'Sure. You heard of Stan Getz?'

'The jazz musician. You're not related?'

'I should be so lucky.'

'It was his real name as far as I know,' Diamond said. 'Is yours your own?'

A shake of the head. 'In my line of work, you gotta make a noise in the world.'

'You play the sax yourself?'

'Nah. I'm talking publicity.' He took a business card from his pocket and snapped it on the table like the ace of trumps. '*Johnny Getz. Gets results.* How does that grab you?'

Diamond had a pained look, and not from being grabbed. 'What do you want with me, Mr Getz?'

'Johnny to you.'

'Mr Getz. I keep first names for my friends.'

Johnny Getz took a moment to reflect on that. He refused to take it as a putdown. 'What do I want? I want your help with a case.'

'Don't even start,' Diamond said, seizing his chance to end this. 'I'm a police officer. We don't get involved outside our work.'

'This *is* your work. It's got your name all over it.'

'What the hell are you talking about?'

'*Police, do not cross.* The break-in at the antiques shop in Walcot Street last Sunday night. The owner is away. You know about this?'

'I don't hear about every crime that happens on my patch.'

'The cops have sealed the place.'

'If it's a crime scene, they would.'

'Fair enough, except I need to see inside.'

'Why?'

'My client wants to know what was taken.'

'And who is your client?'

3

'The owner's daughter.'

'Has she spoken to anyone?'

'Several times. Your people tell her jack shit. They say they want to deal with her father.'

'That's understandable if he's the owner. Where is he?'

'Nobody knows. The best guess is he's buying more stock. From time to time he gets wind of a house clearance, hangs the "closed" sign on the door and goes looking for bargains.'

'No one else runs the shop while he's away?'

'He wouldn't let the Bishop of Bath run it.'

'One of those.'

'You got it.'

'Why isn't the daughter content to wait until he gets back?'

'You want the truth? She doesn't trust cops.'

'Careful what you say, Mr Getz.'

'I'm telling you why she hired me. She hasn't a clue how much was stolen. Not all of you are angels. Some are light-fingered and if it isn't a cop who walks out with a valuable item, it could be a scene-of-crime person. Who's to know if the thief took it?'

'I've heard enough of this horseshit.'

'I'm accusing nobody. I'm telling you what's on my client's mind. The longer this goes on, the bigger the suspicion.'

'The owner could be back today or tomorrow. He'll know what's been taken, I presume.'

'Sure – but he won't know who took it.'

'Neither will you, for that matter. There's more to this. Who reported the break-in?'

'My client. She came past the shop, saw it was closed, checked the door and found it had been jemmied, the wood splintered around the lock. She reported it right away.'

'This was when?'

'Monday afternoon. Two thirty-five.'

'She didn't go inside?'

Getz shook his head. 'She didn't know if the perp was still in the shop.'

'She'd heard nothing from her father about going away?'

'He wouldn't have told her. He's like that.'

'I'll tell you something for nothing,' Diamond said. 'I've known cases where the thief turns out to have been the person who reported the crime.'

'Now you're slandering my client.'

'You slandered the police. And here's something else for you to get your head around. The break-in may never have happened.'

Getz frowned and fingered his silver magnifier.

'The damage to the door could be a con, done by her father to defraud his insurance company. That happens.'

'We don't know if he was insured.'

'Find out, Mr Getz. Tell your client to quit racing her motor and leave us to do our job.'

A pious hope, but it ended the exchange and allowed Diamond to finish his drink.

2

Diamond had treated me like something he'd trodden in, but I expect no different from a cop. They can't take competition. I'd found the fat slob and he'd listened and there was a brain behind the bad-mouthing, no question. He was interested. I had a line into the pig pen.

Would he stir himself and get on the case? Not yet. Everything about him screamed idle bastard. We all know the police are cash-strapped and undermanned and only five per cent of burglaries get solved, so if you want action you need to kick ass.

Early Monday morning (early for me is around 10 a.m.), I called Ruby to fix another meeting. She offered to come at once. Tomorrow, I told her. Didn't want her thinking she was my only client.

When she showed up next afternoon, I made sure there was a shoulder-high stack of files on my desk and the red light on my phone was flashing. She wasn't to know I'd sent voicemail to myself.

I wasn't the only one putting on a show. She was in a long black dress more fishnet than fabric, matching tights and shiny pointed shoes. Her amazing red hair had turned black, or so I thought before I saw it was hidden under an eagle's nest of a wig. Velvet choker studded with jet beads. Murderous dark-rimmed eyes and purple lips like she'd just emerged from the bat cave. What was all this in aid of? The last time we'd met, she was dressed like Daddy's little helper.

'Do you want to get that, Johnny?' she asked, meaning the phone.

'They can wait,' I said, more laidback than a poolside lounger. 'This is your time, Ruby.'

Her eyes gleamed under the beetle-black lids. 'Have you got something for me?'

I didn't move my feet off the desk. 'You could say so.'

She waited and I kept her waiting. I let her take stock of the bookshelf behind. Funny how so many of my favourite writers have better names for sleuthing than their creations. Karin Slaughter, Ann Cleeves, Jonathan Gash, James M. Cain, Joe Gores, Martha Grimes, Will Carver, Christopher Fowler, Magdalen Nabb, Candace Robb. When any one of those guys advertises for clients, I'll be the first to hire them to find my missing Maltese Falcon.

'Speak to me, Johnny, for God's sake.' Today she was more hyper than ever. 'What's happened? I can take it.'

'Chill, babe,' I said. 'We're one step on the way, that's all.' I picked up my phone and thumbed in a number. 'Up to now, the break-in has been handled by the cops in uniform. You don't want that. This is a direct line to a chum of mine called Pete.' My thumb was poised over the green.

'Who's he?'

'The law.'

She turned whiter than a steamed plaice. 'A policeman?'

'Detective Peter Diamond. The chief of CID. This isn't his case, but I filled him in on the facts and he's our best hope of getting inside the shop.'

'No.' She raised both hands like I was Dracula moving in for a bite. 'I don't want the police involved. That's the whole reason I came to you.'

'Easy, babe,' I said. 'I'll be calling the shots, not Pete. I'll make sure of that.'

'You don't understand.'

'But I do,' I said. 'Think about it. You brought in the cops yourself when you saw the shop was broken into. They moved in and sealed the place. If I'm going to find your dad I need to see inside.'

'It's not the way I planned this.'

'Yeah, but get real. Trust me, Ruby, this is what we must do.'

She chewed on that for a moment and seemed to get the message. 'Are you going to speak to him?'

'Better if you do.'

'Me?'

Was I kidding myself when I thought for a moment the black wig stood on end?

'Call him "sir",' I said, passing the mobile towards her. 'He'll appreciate that.'

She wouldn't take hold of the phone. 'I won't do it, Johnny.'

'Tell him who you are. You're worried out of your skull about what happened, you think it's possible your dad was in the shop when it was raided and is being held by the robbers.'

'Is he? Please God, no,' she said.

Jesus, I thought. This dame is dumber than she looks.

'I made that up, about him being kidnapped. It's what you tell Pete. We need to ramp this up to get him on side. How's his health?'

'Daddy's? Okay, I think.'

'That isn't what you say. You say Daddy could die without his medication. You want to get into the shop to see if the pills are in the desk drawer where he keeps them. Is he on medication?'

'Not as far as I know.'

'Pete needs to be told how urgent this is, okay? Lay it on thick.'

Funny how fast the spooky goth turned into the virtuous maiden. 'I don't tell lies, Johnny. I can't. What you're saying isn't true. I could get in trouble, lying to the police.'

There was no changing her mind. 'Want me to make the call? No problem.' I touched green and got through to Diamond at once. 'Pete? Johnny Getz, about that matter we discussed in the Francis. My client is with me and it sounds like really bad news, I'm afraid.'

'Get lost, Mr Getz.'

Jerk. Good thing Ruby couldn't hear his end of the line.

'It's like this, Pete. Yesterday was her birthday.' I noticed Ruby's eyes widen in surprise. She had a lot to learn about the tricks of my trade. 'Her dad always calls her on her birthday, wherever he is. He's never missed. Yesterday, zilch. No phone call, text message, email. She's in a state of panic here or I'd put her on to speak to you. Between you and me, we have a wandering father job, to misquote the great Dash.'

I waited for his brain to crunch through the gears.

'If you haven't read Hammett, that's your loss,' I went on. 'I'm sorry for you. In words you understand, this looks like a misper situation.'

'You're talking bollocks, Getz,' he said.

'Have you been inside the shop yet?' I asked him, knowing how unlikely it was.

'Weren't you listening the other night?' he said. 'It's someone else's case.'

'It's yours if the old man has been topped.'

Ruby made a sound like an emergency stop.

'What was that?' Diamond said.

'My client. I'm speaking in front of her. I'm saying we should prepare for the worst.'

'Pure supposition,' he said. 'I've heard enough of this.'

'Hang on, squire,' I said. 'The young lady is talking about taking her own life.'

'I'm not surprised when you're feeding her this bilge.' A long, thoughtful pause. He wouldn't want to be responsible for a suicide after being warned it was coming. The police hate being caught with their pants down and I was giving him no choice. Finally, he said, 'All right, I'll put her mind at rest, but only to get you off my back. Ask her to meet me outside the shop at three this afternoon.'

'Cool. I owe you one, Pete.'

'You can start by calling me Mr Diamond.'

I put down the phone and did a mental victory roll. From now on, he was Pete and I was Johnny.

Ruby's eyebrows had lifted like a drawbridge.

I passed on the good news. Didn't get the hug I deserved, but she'd come round to my plan, in spite of all. 'I wish you hadn't told him so much that isn't true, like the stuff about my birthday and me threatening suicide.'

'Young lady,' I said, 'I'm a private eye, not the Pope. Truth-telling isn't in the job description.'

'But it wasn't my birthday and he could easily catch us out.'

'He won't even try. It's unimportant. We got what we wanted, didn't we?'

'Yes, and after listening to you, I'm dreading what we'll find.'

The antiques shop was at the end of Walcot Street, close to Beehive Yard, where the Saturday flea market pulls in the crowds. Other days it's quiet, if you know what I mean.

The traffic still makes one hell of a racket. I found Ruby waiting outside, checking her phone. She'd done another quick change, washed off all the black muck, liberated the do and put on tracksuit trousers and top. 'I'm thinking he may ask me to squeeze into one of those white forensic suits you see on TV,' she said, eyes gleaming.

I cottoned on. This lady got her kicks by dressing up.

'You can hope,' I said, 'but it's unlikely. They've had all week to lift the prints and collect the DNA.' I could have told her this was a simple B & E, not murder, but I didn't. You don't downplay a case to a paying client.

No sign yet of my new friend Pete. I'd be pissed off if he let me down.

The big shop windows and the doorway between them were boarded up and a police notice had been screwed to the front, like they expected a long closure. Already there was graffiti across the chipboard. Kids with aerosols can't resist a blank surface. This was a well-drawn burglar in mask, flat cap and striped shirt, with a bag over his shoulder marked SWAG. Being Bath, you'd call it street art.

'Daddy would hate this,' Ruby said.

'People knowing he's been done over?'

She nodded. 'He's a very private man. And so proud of his shop.'

'Who lives upstairs?'

'He owns that, too. It's where he keeps the stuff he hasn't valued yet.'

'Anything worth stealing?'

A frown spread over her pretty face. 'Mainly ceramics and fine furniture. He doesn't deal in tat.'

'Is this the first break-in he's had?'

'Small objects get shoplifted from time to time, but nothing as drastic as this.'

'Hold on, Ruby. Until we get inside, we won't know how much has gone.'

'I meant this is the first time anyone has forced the door.'

A cop car pulled up at the kerb and the back door opened for the big dick to heave himself out. Too idle to walk, obviously. He was in a light trenchcoat like he expected rain and he stuck a hat on his bald head, a brown trilby. One more fancy-dress freak, I thought. Join the club, pal. 'I agreed to meet the young lady,' he told me. 'I didn't invite you.'

Friendly.

I looked him up and down like he'd crept from under a stone. 'How would she know who you are? She doesn't talk to any hobo who comes up to her in the street.'

'Any more of that and you can wait outside.' He produced a key and poked it into the padlock. 'I didn't get your name, miss.'

'Ruby Hubbard.'

'And what's your father's first name?'

'Septimus.'

'Unusual.'

'He's Seppy to his friends.'

When he got the temporary wooden door open, we could see where the real lock had been jemmied. Nothing subtle about it. We stepped inside, all of us. Pete had said his piece about me being unwelcome and wasn't making an issue of it. In point of fact, he needed me. These days, it isn't smart for a senior cop to be alone with a young woman.

'Can anyone see a light switch?'

The boarded windows made the place darker than a beetle's ass. Ruby, who was no birdbrain, used her phone as a torch and found the switch.

As antique shops go, this was high class. Windsor chairs

in front to keep you at arm's length from the breakables. Chests and tables behind, covered with crockery, silver and glass, with a back row of display cabinets, big items like sideboards and grandfather clocks against the wall. Whoever had broken in could have had a field day. They hadn't.

Ruby walked towards the far end, giving the once-over to some funky items that probably appealed to diehard collectors: three shiny suits of armour; a rocking horse; a doll's house; an ancient Egyptian coffin half covered by a bearskin rug; a penny-farthing bike; several busts of Roman emperors; and a stuffed lion grinning like it had just made a meal of a stuffed antelope. She said she couldn't see anything missing. Her mood was improving. 'I was expecting mayhem.'

'Don't get your hopes up,' I warned her. 'It was still a forced entry. Something will have gone. Does he keep money here?'

'Very little, as far as I know. People pay by cheque or card.'

Pete had moved over to a corner formed by the bend in a wrought iron staircase. A massive ship's figurehead of a crowned Neptune was attached to the banisters and below was a mahogany desk topped by a land-line phone that was an antique itself, a wire in-tray filled with paperwork and a row of reference books arranged like a defensive wall. A magnifying glass. A china ashtray with two squashed cigar butts. A coffee mug with the words VINTAGE IS THE NEW COOL. The dregs had dried and left a stain inside.

'His lookout point,' Ruby said, stepping closer. 'He can see all he wants from here.'

'He sits here?'

'All the time. He doesn't go up to customers unless they welcome it. He believes in leaving them to wander until they find something that interests them.' She looked down at the only space left on the desk. It was the shape of a square outlined by dust. 'His laptop is missing.'

'Doesn't he take it home with him?'

'Not to my knowledge.'

Pete shrugged. He wasn't getting into a state about a missing laptop. 'Forensics will have taken it for checking. You said he takes credit cards. They'll also have taken his payment machine for evidence of recent transactions. I'm surprised he doesn't have CCTV.'

'He's against it on principle. He calls it Big Brother.'

The head of CID wasn't interested. Something had caught his eye. 'There's a safe here.'

I glanced down at a grey metal combination thing not much bigger than a microwave and still coated with some of the aluminium flake the SOCOs use to show up fingerprints. 'I wouldn't call that a safe. It's small enough to carry away.'

'I don't advise you to try. It will be bolted to the floor.'

I let him know I was no idiot. 'Is the report in from forensics?'

'You're joking. But I was told the safe was open and empty when they first got here.'

'It shouldn't be,' Ruby said, turning as red as her hair. 'He kept small items of value in there.'

'Such as?'

'Jewellery, for one thing.'

'Doesn't look like it was forced,' I said.

'They'd need the combination, wouldn't they?' she said.

For Ruby's sake I kept my mouth shut about some of the methods crooks use to persuade safe-owners to tell all. I bet the same thought was going through Pete's head.

'Do you know precisely what he keeps in there?' he asked Ruby.

14

She blinked nervously. 'No. Why should I?'

He sighed. 'It will help if we know what's missing.'

'I'd have said, wouldn't I?'

Probably not, I thought. Young Ruby doesn't trust the fuzz any more than I do. We only need them to do the donkey work for us.

'Want to look upstairs?' Pete said.

We followed him up, past a notice that said PRIVATE. Ruby had said this was where the spare stock was kept. Portable stuff mainly, pictures, toys, chairs, footstools, things like that. You wouldn't want to lug a sideboard up those winding stairs. The only big item I could see was a shabby old sofa with a back rest at one end.

'What's that?'

'The chaise longue?' Ruby said. 'Sometimes he works late and sleeps over.'

Almost everything else was covered in dust sheets or boxed up in cardboard. Most of the china and glass was in bubble wrap stored in tea chests and cartons tidily arranged in rows. An army storekeeper couldn't have made a neater job of it. I'm sure we all sensed right away that nothing had been disturbed up here. Thieves wouldn't go to the trouble of wrapping everything up again.

'I get the impression they knew what they were looking for and it wasn't any of this,' Pete said, speaking for all of us.

We returned downstairs.

I saw Pete looking at his watch. 'Seen all you want, Miss Hubbard?'

She thanked him.

I wasn't letting him off so lightly. 'Give us your two cents' worth, supremo. What's happened to Ruby's dad?'

'Who knows? I'm assuming he wasn't here when the break-in occurred.'

'So where is he?'

'Have you checked his home?' He turned to Ruby. 'Where does he live?'

'Odd Down.' There was a catch in her voice. 'He isn't there. I've been to the house several times and I can see the mail heaped up on the doormat.'

'He's away a lot, I was told.'

'Buying antiques, yes, but never for more than a day or two.'

'You reported the break-in a week ago, but you didn't tell us your father was missing.'

She shook her head. 'I thought he must be on one of his forages, as he called them.'

'No one will take any notice unless you report it officially.'

Hearing Pete talk to my client like she was twelve years old, I saw red. 'She's reported it now and you'd better get your finger out, pal, or we talk to the press.'

'Is that a threat, Mr Getz?' he said. 'If you want to help Miss Hubbard, you'll do well to keep your mouth shut.'

Ruby said, 'Please, Mr Diamond, I'm really worried about Daddy.'

'I'll inform the Missing Persons Unit.'

'Can't you deal with it yourself? I'd much rather put my faith in you.'

'Not my job.' He lifted his stupid hat an inch off his head. He was about to leave. But before turning away, he glanced down. 'What's that?'

'What?' I said.

'The white marks. They weren't here when we arrived.'

We all looked at the dark-stained floorboards, now marked with a trail of powder spots stretching all the way from the stairs we'd just come down to the stuffed lion.

'One of us trod in some chalk, by the look of it,' I said.

'It must be me,' Ruby said. 'Neither of you went right up to the end where the lion is.'

'Could I see under your shoe?' Pete asked her.

Holding my arm for support, she lifted each foot in turn, bending her legs behind her for him to see the soles of her trainers.

'Got it,' he said. 'Do you mind?' He curled his hand under the toe of her left shoe and prised out a chip of something wedged between the rubber ridges. 'Plaster, by the look of it, but where's it from?'

He released her foot and marched off, all masterful, to the end of the room where the lion and other objects were. 'Hey ho, someone clobbered Julius Caesar.'

Ruby and I hadn't a clue what he was on about until we joined him and saw for ourselves. The bust of one of the Roman emperors was lying on its side in a mess of dust and bits. Not much had broken off, mainly half the laurel wreath and part of the shoulder.

'How did we miss this?' Ruby said, and then covered her mouth with her fingers. 'Did I knock it over?'

'You'd know if you did,' Pete said. 'They're plaster of Paris and heavy, several kilos for sure.'

'It looks recent,' she said. 'The broken-off bits are really clean.'

'Must have been done by your cack-handed scene-of-crime people,' I told Pete.

He was quick to challenge that. 'They wouldn't have left it like this. It was the thief, more likely. Our people may not even have noticed. The three of us didn't when we came in.'

'It's their bloody job to check,' I said, and the blame game was well and truly on.

'Check what?' he said. 'Only the owner knows what's in

the shop and what isn't. Their job was to do the obvious stuff, lift any prints on the front door and the safe. They'll have taken the laptop away. Anything else is guesswork.'

'You're seriously saying they wouldn't make a full inspection of the place?'

'It's a pesky break-in, not a murder scene.'

Which was when both of us were silenced by Ruby giving a gasp and saying, 'Oh my God!' She was on her haunches, studying the damaged bust. 'Are these bloodstains?'

'Where?'

Pete and I both bent to look. She was pointing to a small crop of brownish-red stains near the base of the thing and smaller than ladybirds. I counted seven.

Not much doubt what Ruby was thinking. She was ashen.

'Is that all there is?' Pete said, trying to be the voice of calm.

'Anything on the floor?' I said. If there was, it wasn't obvious.

Together, we lifted the bust to one side. No more spots.

'He could have covered the stains with something,' Pete said. We pushed aside the lion, which was fixed on a wooden plinth the size of a door. No more stains.

'The coffin, then,' he said. 'Grab the other end, Getz.' He dragged off the bearskin and dropped it behind him. The man-shaped mummy case was solid considering it was so old, but the painting on the outside had faded and flaked off badly, which I guess was why it ended up in the antiques shop and not a museum. Originally the whole surface must have been covered in Egyptian symbols.

Mine was the top end. The lid had been carved into the shape of a lifesize figure, face up in a headdress and with crossed arms. Bits of paint remained, like the whites of the eyes. When I bent close to get a grip, an upside-down eye glared up at me. I don't easily get spooked, but this made my flesh creep.

'Heavy,' I said. I couldn't lift my end of the thing. Close to nine feet long, it must have been hewn from a single log.

'Try sliding it,' Pete said.

That almost brought on a hernia. With Ruby's help we shifted the brute a few inches. The floorboards underneath were a different colour from the rest, but there were no more bloodstains.

'Nobody's moved this bozo in years,' I said.

Pete stood back, hands on hips, like a bowls player studying the lie of the woods. 'It shouldn't be as heavy as this.'

'Something must be inside,' I said. 'Maybe they hid the loot here and meant to come back. Shall we look?'

He didn't need persuading.

We bent to it. The lid was solid and bulky, but easier to shift. Any fit guy could have done it on his own. What we hadn't decided was where the fuck to put it.

Naturally Pete wanted us to know he was in charge.

'This way.'

He tugged his end of the lid towards him and stepped back without looking and his heel struck one of the remaining Roman busts. The emperor rocked on his base like the tenth pin in a strike, toppled over and hit the floor with a mighty thump. Bits of plaster slid everywhere.

'Shit.'

I was pissing myself laughing.

Meanwhile, Ruby had stepped up to the coffin and used her phone to shine a light inside.

She took a huge breath and screamed.

You wouldn't have seen bigger eyes if a cartoon artist had drawn them. She backed off and couldn't find words. All she could do was point.

Pete and I dumped the lid, darted to the coffin and looked inside. The smell got to us first and then the sight of the dude lying at the bottom dressed in modern jeans and sweatshirt, socks and trainers, and as dead as last week's news. No mummy, for sure, but I had a nasty feeling he was someone's daddy.

3

Seppy Hubbard's antiques shop had a new identity as a murder scene. Outside in Walcot Street not much had changed except the temporary traffic lights allowing the police vehicles to park. But the inside was transformed. Everyone arriving signed a security log and squeezed into one of those white top-to-toe forensic suits reminiscent of an Apollo landing. To preserve the integrity of the scene (allowing that it was over a week old and trodden over by the first responders and everyone since), a sterile access pathway was created and the floor marked with crime scene tape. Then the Senior Investigating Officer did a slow walk-through with senior colleagues to try to arrive at some theories about the crime. The fact that the SIO was Diamond himself and he'd already wandered freely upstairs and downstairs with Johnny Getz and Ruby Hubbard made no difference. Procedure was observed. All traces left by the three were recorded as contamination of the original scene, every broken chip of plaster tagged and numbered, as were the prints and fibres left by all and sundry since two Mondays ago. The entire shop was videoed and numerous still photos were taken.

After the corpse had been photographed, Bertram Sealy, the forensic pathologist, zipped into his custom-made pale blue polypropylene overalls, stepped forward with a sense of ceremony and lowered himself inside the large coffin to voice-record his own first impressions. He wore a face mask that couldn't have insulated him much from the smell of decomposition. Nobody envied him his job.

At the other end of the shop, Peter Diamond stood with some of his team in a taped-off section where it was safe to lower the masks below chin level, briefing them on what he knew so far, and it has to be said that he was selective over detail. His own part in the discovery had been too humiliating to share in full, notably the damage to the second plaster emperor, so instead he stressed the deficiencies of the community support officers who had first dealt with the break-in and the duty sergeant who had followed it up.

'They have a lot to answer for. You'd think they would have noticed the broken bust and made a proper search of that area, but they totally missed it.'

'There are two broken busts,' his deputy, Detective Chief Inspector Keith Halliwell, insensitively pointed out.

'Nothing gets past you,' Diamond said. Sensing he wasn't going to get off so lightly, he added, 'One tipped over today by accident. We can ignore it. I was saying the first responders let us down by failing to make a proper search of the whole shop.'

'Do we have any idea what the thieves were after?' Sergeant Ingeborg Smith asked.

'Not yet. The owner has gone missing.'

'Isn't that his body in the coffin?'

'No.'

Surprised glances were exchanged. Everyone had assumed that the corpse was Septimus Hubbard.

'Are we sure of that?' Ingeborg asked.

'His own daughter Ruby confirms it isn't him. The victim has yet to be identified.'

Pause for thought.

'Isn't it obvious?' the junior member of the team, DC Paul Gilbert, said. 'It's the guy who broke in. He was caught by the owner, who took him on and killed him and then panicked and went into hiding.'

Ingeborg said, 'Whenever I hear someone say "Isn't it obvious" I think of the Flat Earth Society.'

'I'm not with you.'

'It's mutual, sweetie,' she said.

Diamond cut in. 'Let's not assume anything at this stage. Mr Hubbard is now listed as a missing person and we hope to find him soon.'

'Is the daughter reliable?' Halliwell asked.

'I've no reason to think she isn't, except she doesn't fully trust the police. She reported the break-in and was trying ever since to get inside the shop. Understandably, she's worried about her father.'

'And the victim? Don't we have any idea who he is?'

'Not yet. We may learn more when we run his prints and DNA through the system. If Paul is right, and he's the robber, it's likely he's a professional burglar.'

'Jemmying the shop door wasn't all that clever,' Ingeborg said. 'Someone in the street was sure to notice before long.'

'Yes, but he opened the safe successfully. It's empty, and Ruby, the daughter, says there were always items kept in there.'

'Cash?'

'Not much of that, apparently.'

'It would help to get an idea what the thief had come to steal. It doesn't sound like he broke in on spec.'

'We haven't searched the clothes on the body yet,' Diamond said. 'If he was the thief, he may have pocketed some jewellery. I won't even know how he was killed until

Dr Sealy's done his work. He's in the coffin with him as we speak.'

'Inside it?'

'They made them big in those days.'

'For the afterlife,' Halliwell said. 'A lot of other stuff had to be stacked inside as well. And sometimes one coffin was slotted inside another.'

Ancient Egyptian burial customs weren't of much assistance, as Diamond made clear by ignoring the remark. 'We need an incident room as close to here as possible and I've asked John Leaman to make enquiries at the Hilton.'

'That will cost an arm and a leg,' Ingeborg said.

'Headquarters turfed us out of Manvers Street, so they can foot the bill.' The relocation of his little empire six years ago to Emersons Green, thirteen miles from Bath, was still a running sore for Diamond.

'If headquarters have anything to do with it, a tent in the flea market is what we'll end up with,' Halliwell said.

At the other end of the shop, a voice spoke from inside the coffin. 'Will someone help me out of here?'

'Sorry, people.' Diamond tugged the mask over his nose and mouth, left the team and beetled along the access path to where Bertram Sealy was being hauled out, his on-site examination of the body completed.

'Is that the Michelin man I see before me?' the pathologist said when he spotted Diamond's large white-suited figure. Dislike between them went back a long way and amounted to more than the black humour the professionals use to mask their discomfort.

'Cut it out, Sealy. You know damn well who I am.'

'I do now. I should have guessed they'd choose an antique cop for an antiques shop.'

'Spare us the verbals. You're no spring chicken yourself. What's the story on the corpse?'

'Well-nourished male, forty to fifty at a guess, with little of interest in his pockets. No money, cards or ID in any form, but he was wearing surgical gloves, if that's any help.'

'Could be.'

'Nothing very subtle about the killing. Suffered a couple of blows to the back of the head that probably did for him. Impossible to say what was used.'

'The Roman emperor. You saw the bits.'

'That's a supposition. I deal in facts. I may have more idea when I've shaved some hair off. After death, he seems to have been dropped into the coffin from a height of about a metre. More abrasions. Some bloating is under way, confirming at least five days since death and probably several more. Does that fit your estimate?'

'Roughly,' Diamond said.

'You've been in the job long enough to know time of death is never better than rough. I'm bending over backwards to help you. You might show some appreciation.'

Diamond clapped his hands as if he was watching cricket and someone had scored the first run in twenty minutes.

Sealy rolled his eyes. 'We'll move him, then, and improve the air quality for you people. Do you have a name for him?'

'Sunny Jim at present,' Diamond said. 'When do you expect to . . .?'

'Tomorrow morning, early – but I won't see you, I'm sure. DCI Halliwell gets the pleasure, no doubt. Is this likely to interest the media?'

'At a local level.'

'I'm off home, then. Life goes on for us lucky ones who don't get their heads bashed in and don't have the task of

25

deciding who did it. Entertaining a couple of old friends tonight.'

Diamond was tempted to say he was surprised Sealy had any friends, but he saved his breath.

Soon after, the deceased was sealed in a body bag, wheeled to a mortuary van and driven to the Royal United Hospital.

John Leaman, the DI with an obsessive-compulsive personality, had delivered, as he always did. No one could ever fault him for efficiency. First, he phoned Diamond and broke the news that unfortunately the conference room and all four meeting rooms at the Hilton were booked for the week to come by the Bath–Braunschweig Association.

'What's that?' Diamond asked.

'A delegation over from Germany as part of the town's twinning arrangement.'

'That's a bummer, John. I had my heart set on the Hilton. Do we have a Plan B?'

'The Corn Market.'

'Where's that? I've lived here more than twenty years and I don't know of a corn market.'

'Where are you now?'

'Still in Seppy's antiques shop.'

'You must have seen it, guv, just across the street from there, even more convenient than the Hilton.'

He might as well have been talking about Timbuktu Town Hall. Diamond had no memory of any such place. A corn market, surely, was a large, significant building. 'You're telling me if I step outside I can see this place I've never noticed? I'm going to check right now.'

'At the entrance to Beehive Yard, the right side.'

Disbelieving, chuntering to himself, sweating in the

forensic suit, Diamond crossed the shop floor with the phone to his ear, lifted the do-not-enter tape with his free hand and pushed open the damaged shop door with his foot. He had to use his shoulder on the next barrier, the hinged sheet of hardboard. He was ready to blast Leaman if this was a hoax, but Leaman was the one member of the team who never joked about anything.

Across the street was the charmingly named Beehive Yard, where a curved entrance road led the eye to the brick-fronted tram shed, as everyone called it. After the trams had stopped running in 1939, the building had been converted to Electricity Board offices, later a covered flea market and now an upmarket furniture store with a terrace in front.

Not a corn market, by any stretch.

Diamond ground his teeth.

Only then did enlightenment dawn, or, more accurately, strike him like a sledgehammer. Much closer to him on Walcot Street itself was a narrow, quaintly proportioned four-storey building only two windows wide that he must have passed hundreds of times and ignored because it was such an eyesore. The stone-cleaners had ignored it as well. The doorway had been built to impress, with a classical portico now so weathered, chipped and stained with grime that you could hardly read the two words carved into the architrave.

Diamond read them and gave himself a mental kicking.

'I see it now,' he said into the phone.

'What do you think, guv?' If Leaman had been at Diamond's side he wouldn't have asked. If he'd seen Diamond's face he wouldn't even have spoken.

'Words fail me.'

'It's owned by the council, so we get it at a peppercorn rent.'

'I should bloody well think so. Is it safe?'

'It's stood since 1855. Don't be put off by the front. The bit you're looking at isn't where we will be. That's just the entrance. The Corn Market is the long building behind. From where you're standing it's difficult to tell the size of it.'

'Is it habitable?'

'Must be. It's up for sale. There's a glossy information pack. The council wants it brought back into beneficial use. I've talked to the people in the planning department and they agree that an incident room is beneficial.'

'How long has it been standing empty?'

'About twenty years.' Before Diamond could comment on that, Leaman added, 'There are some ground settlement issues.'

'What are they, may I ask?'

'The south side facing Manvers Street car park leans over rather a lot. It's shored up with scaffolding.'

'I've seen that scaffolding from the car park,' Diamond said. 'It's been there as long as I can remember. Are you sure this place is safe?'

Leaman ducked the question. 'We'll be upstairs. You'll enjoy the views.'

'We won't be looking out of windows, John. How soon can we get in?'

'Right away, on a short lease.'

'Better be short. I don't want this case dragging on for months. Affordable, you said?'

'A fraction of what we'd pay for a meeting room at the Hilton.'

'I'll look inside.'

'I'd rather you didn't. It's being cleaned right now by professionals. There's a certain amount of dust and debris.'

'Any wildlife?'

It was said in jest, but Leaman took it literally. 'There are bats. We're not allowed to interfere with them. And some pigeons got in through a broken window and made a mess. The gulls on the roof are another problem.'

'This doesn't sound like the palace I had in mind.'

'It will be fine.'

Leaman's 'fine' wasn't Diamond's, but time was at a premium. 'When will the cleaning be finished?'

'By the end of today. I'll get the furniture moved in tomorrow. The power is already turned on.'

'I can't wait.'

'It's better if you do, guv.'

'I'm saying I can't wait. We'll have a team meeting now.'

The team were suffering from what they called face-mask fatigue, so they peeled off their oversuits and moved to the Bell, just up the street. Renowned for its live music, the ancient pub was so quiet at this tail end of the afternoon that there was a risk of being overheard. Around a large A-frame wooden table in the old coachyard at the back, used as a beer garden, they had more privacy. Better still, the back face of the famous terrace called the Paragon dominated the skyline, creating a sun-trap this cloudless evening. A couple of palm trees in the garden were witnesses to the warmth. Somewhere on the rooftops a blackbird was broadcasting its territorial claim. The only other people present were staff preparing the outside pizza bar for the evening session.

Diamond bought the first round and then announced the duties in the incident room and out of it. 'Let's face it,' he summed up, 'we're handicapped from the start. A week and more has gone by since the break-in, giving the killer time to cover his tracks. We don't have a motive other than a guess that something was stolen and we don't have any witnesses. We don't even know who the victim is.'

'No pressure, then,' Ingeborg said, and got smiles from the team and a frown from Diamond.

He added, 'I was hoping we'd find something helpful on Seppy's laptop showing what's been going on in his life in recent days, but that's another dead end. The laptop wasn't removed by the SOCOs. It was missing when they got here.'

'Taken by the killer?' Halliwell said.

'That's the obvious inference. Doesn't help us.' Diamond spoke as if the chip on his shoulder had become a ten-ton weight.

'We should get some DNA,' Paul Gilbert pointed out.

'There's the blood on the Roman bust,' Ingeborg said.

'Prints on the safe,' Gilbert added.

'And who knows what the autopsy will show up?' Halliwell chimed in.

'I can put my feet up, then,' Diamond said, mellowing again. 'Is anyone here into detective fiction?'

Silence. Not one of them could tell what lay behind the question or what they might let themselves in for if they showed interest.

'Don't all shout at once. Dashiell Hammett mean anything to you?'

'*The Maltese Falcon,*' Gilbert said. Eager to please, growing in confidence, he was almost too easy a foil for Diamond's guile.

'Top of the class. Have you read it?'

'I may have. I saw the film for sure.'

'You're our Hammett expert, then. Someone was talking to me about him today and I didn't quite get it. Something about a wandering father job.'

More silence. The Hammett expert shook his head.

Ingeborg picked her phone off the table and googled the phrase. 'Did you say a wandering daughter job?'

'Father. I'm sure it was father.'

'A wandering daughter job is a line of dialogue from *The Great Lebowski*, the Coen brothers comedy. Jeff Bridges. Have you seen it?'

'No.'

She shared the essentials as she read them from the display. 'It didn't do all that well at the box office, but it's a cult favourite now. The screenplay is supposed to have been inspired by Raymond Chandler's writing. Chandler and Hammett both wrote private eye stories, didn't they? I expect there was some confusion.'

'I understand now,' Diamond said. 'This guy and I were talking about Seppy Hubbard going missing and he said it was a wandering father job – a play on words. Thanks, Inge. It never ceases to amaze me how much is stored on the internet.'

John Leaman, who hadn't spoken a word up to now, said, 'And how many people take it as gospel.'

'Stand by, everyone,' Ingeborg said. 'The fount of all knowledge is going to put us right.'

'The film wasn't the source. "It was a wandering daughter job" is the first sentence of a short story by Hammett. Offhand, I can't tell you which one, but it must have been written many years before the film was made.'

'So *you're* our Hammett expert,' Diamond said. 'Why didn't you say so when I asked?'

'If I was really an expert, I'd be able to tell you the title,' Leaman said. 'I don't normally read fiction unless I can't find anything more interesting. I must have seen it in some magazine. Hammett's name stuck and so did that sentence because I had to read it twice to understand what he was on about.'

'Makes a change from memorising the encyclopedia,' Halliwell said.

Ingeborg had been scrolling again. 'The story was called *Fly Paper.*'

Leaman confirmed it with a shrug and Diamond thanked them both. 'We got there between us.' At some stage he would have to let them know about Johnny Getz, much as he wanted to erase the man from his memory. Getz wasn't going to go away.

As if to mimic the pest that Getz was, a wasp started circling Diamond, making sorties towards his beer from all directions. Flapping a hand only encouraged the attacks. The other glasses on the table didn't seem of any interest at all. Diamond's was the attraction.

'Let it settle, guv,' Ingeborg said. 'You're only making it mad.'

'I don't want it ruining my drink. I don't know where it's been.'

'The sweetness attracts them,' Leaman said. 'I read in the *New Scientist* that researchers are asking people to trap wasps in beer for a survey. They drown, of course, and when you've collected several bodies you send them off to one of the universities to be examined.'

Nobody asked why. It was never wise to encourage Leaman.

Keith Halliwell nudged Paul Gilbert. 'Fetch a beer mat from one of the tables inside.'

'You're not going to squash it?' Ingeborg said.

Gilbert got up to do as he was asked.

Diamond, meanwhile, was still fending off the invader, reluctant to let it anywhere near his glass.

'Insect numbers are critically in decline,' Leaman started up again. 'They could vanish within the next century. Inge is right. They're vital to the ecosystem. We shouldn't kill it.'

'Encourage it to bring its friends, I suppose?' Diamond said, swaying back so far that he almost fell off the bench.

Gilbert returned with a handful of beer mats.

'Good man,' Halliwell said. 'Put a lid on the guvnor's drink. Has anyone emptied their glass?'

'Only you,' Ingeborg said.

'Okay. Cover everyone's except mine. Stop waving your arms, guv, and we can deal with this.' He slid Diamond's glass to the other side of the table and replaced it with his empty one.

The wasp didn't take long to fly inside and start supping on the dregs. Halliwell placed a beermat on top.

'I didn't hear you caution the prisoner,' Ingeborg said.

'Top result,' Diamond said. 'That's earned you another beer, Keith, and in a fresh glass.' With some difficulty, he manoeuvred his legs from under and over the bench and went inside to place the order.

'Make that five pints,' he told the barmaid.

He carried the tray to the table, his mind made up. He would tell them about Getz, the whole sorry tale, from the first approach in the Francis to the discovery of the body.

Awed, bemused or incredulous, they heard him in silence while the wasp performed drunken acrobatics inside the glass. High above them, the blackbird chirped its song of freedom.

'I thought I could put a stop to his nonsense by letting Ruby see inside the shop, but of course he turned up as well expecting to come in with us and it made sense from her point of view, me being a stranger.'

'Wise decision, guv,' said Ingeborg, his guide through the minefield of modern male/female situations.

'And as it turned out, I was glad of his help with the coffin. But we haven't seen the last of him.'

'He's way out of his depth now,' Ingeborg said. 'Private eyes don't investigate homicides except in books. A missing person case, maybe, but not a killing.'

'He hasn't solved his missing person case,' Diamond said. 'He'll want to earn his fee for that.'

'And what if his missing person has been murdered as well?' Gilbert said.

'I don't like "what-ifs",' Diamond said. He stared at the empty beer glass. 'What happened to the wasp?'

'Didn't you see?' Ingeborg said. 'While you were talking, I let it go to help the ecology.'

4

Diamond left his Weston home at seven next morning to be certain of arriving early in the city, yet when he reached Beehive Yard a furniture van had already been unloaded and was on its way out. Inside the Corn Market a hallway protected with plastic sheets led him to a large room with a high-pitched roof of dark-stained wood from which a few bare lightbulbs hung. Two rows of desks had been unloaded along with cartons that must have contained computers.

John Leaman was on his knees trying to disentangle a giant-sized knot of mainly white cable.

'This is above and beyond the call,' Diamond told him.

'You're early, guv.'

'Not so early as you. Don't you sleep at all?'

'I was planning to get the room into some sort of order before everyone arrived.'

'By "everyone", you mean me?'

'Whoever packed this cable stuffed it in a plastic sack without any consideration for the person who needs to use it next.' In the Leaman scale of iniquity the sin of disorder rated near the top. 'What do you think of the place?'

'I'm reserving judgement. Are there other rooms?'

'There are, but . . .'

'But what?'

'This is the one I had cleaned. Don't go through the door at the end.'

'Why not?'

'This one is ours.'

'What's below us?'

'A kind of arcade where they traded the grain. It hasn't been used as a corn market for a century or more. Farming practices changed.'

Any show of interest was sure to trigger the agricultural history lecture. 'What do you think? Can we get up and running by lunchtime?'

'That's the aim. We'd be better off using laptops than desktops with all this wiring.'

'Can't change over now. I'll help you.'

For a while they worked together on the cables like deep-sea fishermen mending their nets. 'It's had all sorts of uses,' Leaman said. 'During the last war, they made machine-gun parts here for Mosquito aircraft. It was a place of worship in the 1970s. The Seventh Day Adventists. Do you know about them?'

'Everything,' Diamond lied. Move this on, common sense urged him. You don't want to know about Leaman's religious beliefs.

'Really? Then you'll know they had their own organ in here.'

'They would. Is the power on?'

'The power of God?'

'Electricity, John, for the computers.'

'I understand you now. I told you last night. The cleaners needed it.'

'Look, I've freed one of the leads and an extension cable. We can make a start.'

'I'd rather get all the cables ready first, if you don't mind.'

If you persisted with Leaman – which wasn't easy – he had a lot to contribute. Diamond had long passed the stage of getting impatient. He understood the focused way the man's mind worked, employing higher-order thinking skills ordinary mortals didn't possess. The pity of it was that he was unable to relax and enjoy the company of colleagues.

'Quite right. We'll do it your way, John.' True, the Corn Market wasn't the Hilton. All things considered, it was a sensible choice.

In the next ten minutes, Paul Gilbert and Ingeborg Smith arrived and helped. In under an hour the disentangling was done and Leaman allowed them to get the computers connected. By then more of the team were at their desks. Three experienced civilian staff had joined them. On first entering, everyone sniffed the musty air and stared at the walls and the bare bulbs without needing to say any more about the incident room.

'Where's Keith?' Ingeborg asked and immediately remembered and answered herself. 'The post-mortem. We won't see him this morning.'

Diamond didn't expect much from Keith Halliwell. The crucial facts were already known: a fatal blow to the head two weekends ago and concealment of the body in the Egyptian coffin. The key thing was to follow up on the DNA sample taken at the scene and possibly, hopefully, ID the victim. Some fingerprints had been taken from the safe soon after the break-in, apparently with no result. Nothing was mentioned of them in the case notes. Unsurprising, since the dead man had been wearing gloves. Presumably any prints were Seppy's own.

DNA was definitely the best bet. Someone had once said the testing could be processed in eight hours, but it had never happened to any sample Diamond had sent in. His frustration with testers was well known.

'You seem to have forgotten something, John,' he said around mid-morning.

'Oh?' Leaman's face creased in hurt pride.

'Where do we get our coffee?'

Ingeborg had the answer. 'Didn't you notice, guv? That cafe across the yard. I'm sure it was in John's planning. Big improvement on that grotty machine in Concorde House.'

Leaman looked as surprised as everyone else and started to say so. He wasn't heard for the chorus of approval.

'Really?' Diamond said. 'Do they do snacks as well?'

Paul Gilbert was spared from his duties and instructed to fetch elevenses for everyone. Suddenly the new location wasn't so grim.

'Do they do lunches?' Diamond asked when he'd had a few sips of the best caffè latte he'd enjoyed in months.

'I thought you'd never ask,' Gilbert said, producing a menu from his pocket. 'I'll make copies for all of us. We need to check that the printer is working, don't we?'

Halliwell phoned from the mortuary before noon. There was more on the head injuries, one of which was secondary from being dropped into the coffin. The blow to the back of the head that had caused death had almost certainly been inflicted by the plaster bust of the emperor or a piece of it.

'Julius Caesar,' Diamond said.

'Does it matter who it was?' Halliwell asked.

It mattered to Diamond. The bust he'd knocked over had been Hadrian. He didn't say so.

Halliwell finished his report. Little else had emerged. The deceased had no scars or tattoos.

'But he was wearing the latex gloves.'

'Yes. Dr Sealy said he doubted whether he was a brain surgeon.'

'Sealy creases me up.'

'We're pinning our hopes on a DNA match, aren't we?'

'Yes, and I'm not holding my breath.'

The all-important call came soon after 3 p.m. Diamond held the phone to his ear, watched by almost everyone on the team. His expression gave nothing away. He said a couple of words of thanks and clicked off.

'They checked the database and . . .' He paused like a TV host announcing the winner of a reality show. '. . . we have a match.'

No one cheered, but Gilbert fisted the air in triumph.

'His name means nothing to me,' Diamond went on. 'Mark Rogers. He was collared by Wiltshire police after a break-in at a Westbury house in 2012. He's a peterman, to use an old term.'

'What's that?' Gilbert asked.

'Safecracker,' Ingeborg said in a weary voice, as if everyone in the room except Gilbert the rookie knew. 'Does he have much of a record, guv?'

'I gave it to you. A two-year stretch for the Westbury job.'

'That's all?'

'He's either not very active or so good he only got caught once.'

John Leaman wasn't letting that loose reasoning get by. 'There's another possibility. He's rubbish. He did one safe and messed up and now he's tried again and got himself killed.'

Diamond glared, thought about it and was forced to say, 'Fair point.' At risk of losing the initiative, he slapped his palm on the desk. 'Right. Your job between you is to flesh out the background on this guy. Everything you can find on the Westbury case and the trial. His prison record. Current address, family, occupation, any known contacts. The house he broke into was Veronica Lodge and the incident was in September. Get to it, people.'

They were under way.

The more he learned about this, the likelier it seemed that young Gilbert's first assumption had been right. Seppy Hubbard sometimes worked late in the shop and slept upstairs on the chaise longue, Ruby had said. If the burglar Mark Rogers broke in during Saturday or Sunday night and Seppy heard him jemmy the door, there was ample opportunity to get downstairs and hide. Rogers let himself in and got to work on the safe, unaware that the owner was watching him. Whatever loot he was after, he removed. Then Seppy broke cover. In the fight that followed, Rogers was no match for the enraged owner. The Julius Caesar bust was knocked over, Seppy grabbed a slab of plaster and bashed Rogers on the back of his head and killed him.

The shock of what he'd done must have panicked Seppy. Acting on impulse, he did what he could to hide the result of his actions, heaved the body into the coffin, closed the lid and draped the bearskin over it. Then he collected the precious contents of the safe and his laptop and headed off to some hideaway.

It made the most sense. However – and there's always a 'however' in a murder investigation – first suspicions don't often prove correct at the end.

5

R uby was having kittens down the phone line.
'Johnny, this is me. I don't care what other cases you're working on. You've got to help me. This is a fucking emergency.'

'Easy, babe, easy,' I told her. 'I'm listening.'

'The detective – your friend Pete – is on his way to see me. On his way *here*, Johnny, now. I don't know what I'm going to say to him.'

Typical cop, I thought, going behind my back. I looked at my watch. It was only 9.30 in the morning, for the love of Mike. No one in Bath is on the move before 9.30 except the shop-window cleaners. 'Where are you, my love? At home?'

'Yes. My flat.'

'He phoned you?'

'Not him. Some woman, five minutes ago. I didn't catch her name. She said Mr Diamond needs to go over some details and he'll be with me in twenty minutes.'

Go over some details, my ass. 'Didn't you say you had a doctor's appointment or something?'

'I didn't think. I was taken by surprise. Johnny, can you be here?'

'In twenty?'

'About ten now. Please.'

Ten minutes to get from my place to her pad in Oldfield

Park? Pigs might fly, but Johnny Getz hasn't mastered the art yet.

'Listen, Ruby. This is what you do. Have you got a Post-it note?'

'Somewhere, I think.'

'Find it now and a pen. I'm going to tell you what to write.'

Two more precious minutes passed.

'The only Post-it I can find is pink.'

'Pink will do. So here's what you write: "Sorry, Pete, had to pop out. Urgent. Back real soon, Ruby." Got that? Put a kiss after your name if you want. On second thoughts, cancel the kiss. Slap the note on your front door, grab your coat and hightail it to Oldfield Park station and I'll meet you on the bridge as soon as I can.'

'He'll be livid, won't he?'

'Apeshit, but there's sod all he can do.'

I ended the call. I could have used a whisky to oil my brain, but there wasn't time.

What was Pete's game? Think big: had they found Seppy?

Unlikely. If they had the main man, they'd be too busy questioning him to go visiting Ruby. They'd get on the blower.

Did they have some dirt on her?

Wouldn't surprise me.

I'm bound to say I had a gut feeling she was holding stuff back from me, so I guess Pete felt the same. Each of us needed the full story if we were going places with this case.

I got on my bike and started pedalling. Are you surprised the only independent private eye in Bath doesn't use an automobile? Think about it. Did you ever hear of the Continental Op driving any place? Sam Spade? Philip Marlowe? When those guys needed wheels, they hired a cab. Johnny Getz, with a slight cashflow problem, goes most places on a pushbike. I figured I could reach Ruby in under fifteen minutes and I did.

This time she hadn't dressed the part. She was in the same sports gear she'd worn for the antiques shop, pacing the bridge over the railway, talking to herself and fingering the zipper on the tracksuit top.

'He'll be outside my place already,' she said.

'Uh-huh,' the voice of calm said. 'That's why you wrote the note.'

'What does he want, Johnny?'

'We'll find out.'

We were a short walk from the street where she lodged. I lashed the bike to a stand in front of some shops. Didn't want sarcasm from Pete as soon as we met.

'Just as I thought,' he said when Ruby and I showed up. 'I could do you for wasting police time.'

He wasn't alone either. A tall, blonde dame was at his side, giving us the once-over.

'This is Detective Sergeant Smith.'

Smith? Tell that to the marines, Pete, I thought.

'Yeah?' I said. 'How about it, Ruby? Do you want these people in your home?'

'It's all right.'

I was as eager as they were to see her drum. It turned out to be a pretty basic walk-up, a large bedsit with a kitchen/bathroom, much of it taken up by wardrobes along two walls, which didn't surprise me. All the fancy clothes had to be stored somewhere. A generous-sized single bed. Dressing table, mirror. Scatter cushions, a large low oval table that you would only comfortably use if you were seated on the floor, candles stuck in wine bottles coated with molten wax. Sound system. Wall-mounted TV. Vintage punk posters pinned to the walls. The Clash, Bad Brains and The Damned. They were the only antiques in sight.

'Sorry, no chairs,' Ruby said. 'You're welcome to sit on the bed.'

Pete said they'd stand.

My legs were stiff from the bike ride, so I took up the invitation, flopped back against the pillows with my feet up. Ruby took her cue from me and sank into a giant bean bag.

And how stupid those two cops looked standing like waiters at a ten-course banquet while we relaxed. Put us at a clear advantage.

'So what's the problem?' I asked.

'I'm here to speak to Ruby, not you, Mr Getz,' Pete said. 'You're out of your depth here. We're conducting a murder enquiry now.'

'You don't have to tell me what happened, Pete. I helped you find the stiff, remember?'

Ruby, bless her little cotton socks, chimed in with, 'It's only through Johnny you have anything to investigate. Without him, we wouldn't have got inside the shop at all. He's my best hope of finding my daddy, so if you want to question me, I want Johnny here at my side. And I may be calling my solicitor as well.'

'You watch too much TV,' Pete said. 'You're not under suspicion. I simply want help finding your father.'

'We're all batting for the same team, then,' I pointed out – and got a cold stare for being matey.

He asked Ruby, 'Does your father ever discuss his business with you?'

'Not really,' she said. 'Antiques bore me. He knows that.'

'I'm interested in what may have been inside that safe. You said money in the form of cash didn't change hands

44

much in the shop, so whatever was taken must have been antiques of some value, such as jewellery, right?'

'You tell me,' Ruby said, growing in confidence by the minute.

'When we were in the shop you led me to believe he kept items of jewellery in there.'

'It's obvious, isn't it? He wouldn't leave them lying about.'

'Did he ever speak of anything especially valuable?'

'Not to me.'

'Is there someone he'd confide in if he came into possession of something rare, such as' – he paused for inspiration – 'a Fabergé egg? You know what that is?'

What a wuss! Even I know Fabergé wasn't a poultry farmer.

'Someone he'd confide in? Who do you mean?' Ruby asked.

'Like another antiques dealer.'

'Never. They're a cagey lot, friendly with each other on the surface, but giving nothing away. If Daddy ever gets an item worth big money, he keeps his mouth shut.'

'A practice that seems to run in the family,' Pete said.

'Lay off, Pete,' I butted in. 'You're only here by invitation.'

He didn't even look my way. 'You're being economical with the truth, Ruby. You were desperate to get inside the shop and see what had been taken. When we got there, you walked on ahead as if you knew what you were looking for.'

'I do have some idea what's in my own daddy's shop,' she said. 'Is that a crime?'

I was starting to admire my client.

Pete didn't let up. 'You know what the thief was after, don't you? You can't wait to find out what happened to it.'

'The thief is the dead man, I heard. He didn't get out with anything.'

'So what was the loot he was after? Something really small, like a rare postage stamp?'

If I'm honest, I didn't mind Ruby getting a little of the third degree if it led us somewhere.

'Daddy doesn't deal in stamps,' she said.

'What does he deal in?' Pete asked. 'Was the shop a front for something else?'

'I don't know what you mean.'

But I could tell she was on the verge of telling them something more and I'm certain Pete picked up on it, too, because of what he said next.

'Like drugs?'

'Oh, come on. You obviously don't know my daddy. Anyone will tell you he's straighter than a Roman road.'

Now Sergeant Smith joined in. 'It's vital that we find him, Ruby, and we need your cooperation.'

'You think he killed the thief and you want to arrest him.'

'Not if it was in self-defence. He may have gone into hiding thinking he's in trouble, but he isn't. You're our best hope of finding him and understanding what this is really about.' Sergeant Smith was obviously the nice cop to Pete's nasty cop.

Ruby softened a little. 'You'd treat him kindly, even though he hid the body?'

'Anyone can panic in a situation like the one he faced. Our job is to catch a villain, not a victim.'

The gentle persuasion started to work. 'I've no idea where he is now, but he did tell me a week before the break-in that he was excited about something he'd picked up recently. He said it could be the find of a lifetime.'

'Didn't you press him for details?'

Pete pitched in again. 'And how about you, Ruby? You must have been fascinated to hear this. Did you share the news with anyone else?'

She frowned and her face turned scarlet. 'Are you

suggesting I'm responsible for what happened? I resent that, Mr Diamond. In fact, I find it bloody offensive.'

Good for you, chick, I thought.

Cue the nice cop. 'We have to ask these questions,' Sergeant Smith said quickly. 'Do you have any idea at all where your father might have gone? Does he have a second home somewhere?'

'You're joking,' Ruby said. 'Anyone with a shop in Bath has so many overheads they're lucky if they can afford a poky flat.'

Even two of Bath's finest could tell they were getting nowhere in this session. 'We've got the picture,' Pete said. 'We'll need to talk more, but that'll do for now.'

'We'll be in touch,' Sergeant Smith said. 'If you hear anything from your father or anyone else, call us right away.'

After they'd left, I felt like opening the skylight for fresh air. 'You did okay, babe,' I told Ruby. 'Is there anything you can tell me that you didn't say to the cops?'

She shook her head – and I still wasn't convinced.

Some comforting words were wanted. 'They'll find him in the end, but it would be good if you and I got there first.'

'That's how you earn your fee, Johnny,' she said, cutting me down to size.

'What are your plans for the rest of the day?'

'A change of clothes for starters.'

Did I need to ask?

'Then lunch out with my best friend, Olympia. She's a true amigo, a tonic to be with at a time like this.'

'Be careful what you say, even to a best friend.'

'I'm not thick, Johnny.'

'No one could ever call you that.'

I left soon after, found my bike and took a more leisurely ride back to Kingsmead Square. I had heaps to think about.

*

This next bit is what I picked up later. I didn't witness it myself. I'm giving you the timeline to get the story in the right order. At 12.25 a train from Oldfield Park pulls into Bath Spa station and a load of passengers get out. A few make straight for the taxi rank in the forecourt, but most head north towards the main shopping areas. At 12.32, some loud bangs echo off the stone buildings in Manvers Street, panicking everyone in the area. In the screams and confusion, a young woman is seen lying on the pavement outside George Bayntun's bookshop and bindery. She is bleeding heavily from a head wound. Some think they saw a car rev up and move off up the street. When the first shockwave has passed, a group gathers round the victim, gawpers mostly. She isn't moving. Others rush out of nearby shops to see what is happening. Someone has the sense to call 999.

Back in the office at lunchtime, I treated myself to a bourbon and burger, a combination that never fails to inspire. I closed my eyes and listened to the *nee-naw, nee-naw* of emergency vehicles racing through a nearby street and in my head I was stateside in Nero Wolfe's brownstone on West 35th Street. I thought no more about the street noises until forty minutes later when my phone beeped and I heard Pete Diamond's voice.

'Mr Getz, I need to speak to you.'

Quite some turnaround after treating me like a bad smell.

'Fire away, Pete,' I said. I have no pride.

'Get to the Royal United Hospital now. Intensive care unit. Ruby has been shot.'

6

I'm a take-whatever-comes-and-sock-it-back-to-them kind of guy, as you must have worked out, but my head was reeling and I'd got the shakes. Ruby shot? How did that happen? The last I'd seen of her, she was off to lunch with Olympia, her amigo. If she was in intensive care, the wounding had to be serious. She could die.

Please God, no.

I cared about the kid and not only because she was my meal ticket, my only one if I'm honest. I'd grown to like her, even respect her. I loved the way she'd stood up to the cops and given them lip. I truly wanted to find her daddy and see her face light up – if she survived.

The RUH is a fair stretch out west, off Combe Road, so I took a cab and nagged him all the way to put his foot down.

With two armed officers on guard in the corridor, the police were taking no chances. One gripped the stock of his MP5 and told me to identify myself. I handed him my *Getz results* card. He squinted at it and called his oppo over for a second opinion.

A sticky moment.

Just then a voice said, 'It's okay, we're expecting him.' Pete's blonde sidekick, Detective Sergeant Smith, had appeared on cue and spared me from a pat-down at the very least.

'How's she doing?' I asked at once.

'We won't know for some while. She was shot in the head.'

'Christ!'

'. . . and the upper left arm. They've done a CT scan and are deciding whether to operate on the brain. They assess how much damage there is and whether she can survive surgery.'

'She's unconscious, I guess?'

'Must be,' the sergeant said. 'I spoke to a nurse and she asked me about next of kin.'

'This isn't good.'

'I couldn't help.'

'Next of kin would be Seppy.'

'He's missing – in case no one told you.'

'There's no need for sarcasm,' I said.

'Is there a mother?'

'Not that we can reach. She divorced Seppy a while back and moved abroad with her new man. Did the nurse say anything else?'

'She lost a lot of blood, but we knew that.'

'Is the bullet still in the brain? The scan will have told them.'

'No one is saying. The medics are far too busy to deal with the likes of us.'

'Where's your boss?'

'In a side room talking to a friend of Ruby's.'

'Would that be Olympia?'

She blinked in surprise. 'You know Olympia?'

I smiled in a superior way. I'd heard Ruby mention her best friend, but I didn't know enough to hold forth about her. 'Did she witness the shooting?'

'No. She was waiting nearly an hour at the top of Milsom

Street, where they'd arranged to meet before having lunch together. She knew Ruby was coming in on the 12.25 and couldn't understand why she was taking so long. Then she overheard a couple of women talking about the shooting and came straight here.'

'Where exactly did it happen?'

'Manvers Street, down by the railway station. The gunman seems to have been waiting in a parked car. Several shots were fired.'

'Waiting? So he knew her movements?'

'It appears so.'

'That's why Pete is questioning Olympia?'

'Pete?' she said, thrown.

'DS Diamond.'

'Ah.' She was in two minds whether to tell me to show more respect. Instead, she said, 'I'm Ingeborg.'

'Johnny,' I said, holding out my hand. I wouldn't say the cool Ingeborg succumbed to my charms, but they often do and the touch of a warm palm can swing it.

She kept her arms folded.

'What does he hope to find out from Olympia?' I asked.

'Isn't it obvious?'

I answered my own question. 'Who else knew about this lunch arrangement?'

I didn't get an answer because a door opened behind her.

A gorgeous black woman stepped out. Gorgeous, but tearful. She dabbed a tissue to the corner of each exquisitely made-up eye. Taller in her stiletto heels than I am – but most modern women are – broad-shouldered and with a figure curvy as a bobsleigh course, she was in a red coat with black fur trim over a peacock blue dress that must have needed an early wake-up call to squeeze into.

51

This cannot be a nurse, I decided.

'You must be Olympia.'

She eyed me through damp eyelash extensions. 'Are you Johnny? Ruby told me all about you.'

'Not everything, I hope.'

'She's sure you're going to find Seppy.'

'I was working on it. This attack puts everything on hold.'

'It mustn't.' She stepped closer, reached out with both hands and grasped me by the shoulders, her voice husky with emotion. 'Don't stop looking for him. It matters even more now.'

'Why?'

'Because the police are going to put all their efforts into finding the gunman. Someone has to find Seppy.'

Ingeborg had listened to this in silence and now put a firm hand on my sleeve. 'My guv'nor is waiting to speak to you.'

I can take any amount of being fought over by beautiful dames.

Before moving off I handed one of my business cards to Olympia. 'We must speak again soon.'

She responded with a card of her own. 'I'll help any way I can.'

I entered the room she'd just left, some sort of waiting room for visitors. Pete was in there alone, sitting at the end of a row of chairs under a poster with the heading BRAIN INJURIES AND WHAT TO EXPECT.

I didn't comment.

He pointed to the seat beside him.

So we sat next to each other under that poster, two prime examples of what to expect.

'Anyone told you what happened?'

I nodded.

'It doesn't look good,' he said. 'Have you been to the scene?'

'I came straight here.'

'Keep away if you don't like the sight of blood. They're giving her a massive transfusion to keep her alive. You were with her this morning after I left with Sergeant Smith. Did she tell you about the lunch date?'

'Only that she was meeting her best friend Olympia.'

'Did she say what it was about?'

'No.'

Sharp sigh of annoyance. 'Olympia insists it was purely social, a girlie gossip session. I don't believe that.'

'You think Olympia is holding back?'

'She might be more relaxed speaking to you.'

'Pete, that's the nicest thing you've ever said to me.'

He didn't exactly melt. He made a sound in his throat like a biker kickstarting his vintage Harley. 'Against my better judgement, I may need to work with you . . . Johnny.'

For the head of CID, this was a huge helping of humble pie.

'But you'd better be open with me,' he added. 'To my knowledge, only three people knew in advance about the lunch date – Ruby, Olympia and you,' – deep breath to get up strength and speak the word – 'Johnny.'

'In advance?' I echoed. 'Not much in advance in my case. Barely an hour.'

'Plenty of time to spread it around.'

As his new partner, I let him know what a piss-poor remark this was. 'Bollocks. What am I supposed to have done – flagged all my contacts to say Ruby and Olympia are going to lunch today? They'd think I was crazy.'

'I'm not saying it was deliberate. You could have said something casually.'

'Well, I didn't, maestro. Satisfied?'

'Up to a point.'

I'd heard all I wanted of this horseshit, so I threw him something else to chew on. 'The restaurant.'

'What about the restaurant?'

'A reservation in Ruby's name could have been seen on their computer by any number of flaky people on the staff, not to mention hackers.'

He was unmoved. 'They didn't make a reservation. I asked Olympia. All they agreed was to meet at the top of Milsom Street. There are any number of eating places along George Street.'

'So it comes back to the two women,' I said. 'What do we know about Olympia and the circles she moves in?'

'She's some kind of journalist, works for a posh magazine, glossy, expensive, publishing only three times a year.'

'Would I have heard of it?'

'Probably not. It's called *Exorbitant*.'

'Strange name. I don't get it.'

'Neither did I until she explained. Their readers are the super-rich – we're talking zillionaires – looking to invest some of their ill-gotten gains. They run features on items like Shakespeare first folios. Most people would look at the price guide and say, "But that's exorbitant" – and that's how the magazine gets its name. It's an in-joke among fat cats who own Pacific islands and Premiership football clubs.'

'Is Olympia the editor?'

'God, no, just a junior reporter.'

'How did Ruby get to know her?'

'You'd have to ask one of them. Excuse me.' Pete's phone had buzzed. He got up and crossed to the other side of the waiting room to take the call out of my hearing.

So much for the Pete and Johnny partnership, I thought.

When he came back, he told me he'd heard from the crime scene. They'd found several discharged bullets and not a single shell casing.

'Must have used a revolver,' I said, airing my expertise.

'Unless the casings are in the car,' Pete said.

'What do we know about this car?'

'Nothing. Nobody remembered the reg or even the colour and make. In broad daylight. I despair.'

Was he always like this?

'We're not used to shooting incidents in Bath,' I said. 'People in this town cross themselves when a dog barks. Maybe a CCTV camera will have picked up the vehicle.'

'We won't know which vehicle.'

'We know the time. She came in on the 12.25. You have to check everything that drove by.'

He bristled. 'Let's get one thing straight, Johnny. Don't tell me my job.'

'You asked,' I said, 'and I answered.'

My logic was not appreciated.

'What I don't understand is why,' I said.

'Why what?' He was barely listening, already having second thoughts about teaming up with me.

'Why anyone should want to rub out Ruby. Is it connected to the break-in?'

'Must be a possibility.'

'She doesn't appear to be a threat to anyone. She's worried about her daddy and she made sure you and I got on the case, but that's done. We found the corpse and we know who he is. Ruby was only the whistle-blower. Where's the sense in it?'

'I can't answer that,' Pete said, 'but the shooting looks like a professional job.'

'Sure,' I said. 'This is bigger than either of us thought when we took it on. Is there a syndicate behind this?'

He gave me a pained look. 'Bath isn't Al Capone's Chicago, if that's the way your thoughts are going.'

'I don't live in the past, Pete.'

'I've yet to be convinced of that.'

Ingeborg looked in. 'Okay to come in now?'

'Be my guest, Inge,' I said, and got another glare from Pete for using her first name. 'Do we have any idea how long this is gonna take? Three key people sitting in a waiting room for hours on end isn't the most productive use of our time.'

She nodded. 'I asked a nurse the same question and wished I hadn't. They'll take as long as they need.'

'Makes sense. And we won't be much wiser when it's done,' I said. 'She'll be under sedation for some time after.'

'You're right,' she said. 'I don't mind staying if you two would like to get back to the action.'

That was what happened. We parted, but not before Pete had laid down some ground rules. 'Your job is the same as it always was, Johnny. Find Seppy, if you can. Leave the major incidents to me and my team.'

You can stuff that, Pete, I thought. I insisted we exchanged our personal mobile numbers. Would you believe it? – he treated me like I was a Russian spy. He expected me to contact him by way of the incident room. I won that battle with some subtle support from Ingeborg. She seemed to know how to handle the brute.

I took another taxi ride to the station. We had to go by St James Street West because Manvers Street was closed to traffic, the driver told me. 'They say some woman was shot. Jealous boyfriend, if you ask me. It's always sex behind these things. You wouldn't believe how many women I've had in

56

my cab in fear of their blokes. I know where all the women's refuges are, right across the county.'

He put me down in the forecourt and moved off to join the rank and spread his theory among the other drivers.

I crossed the street to check the scene. Some flatfoot in uniform stopped me at the first police tape, so I flashed my card and said I was a ballistics expert called in by DS Diamond. This got me closer, but I couldn't get past the next tape without a forensic suit. I had a good view of where the main activity was. Even from twenty yards away I could see the bloodstain on the pavement.

What puzzled me was where the gunman was supposed to have parked. Ruby had been felled in front of the railings outside Bayntun's bookshop. Across the street was the recessed front of Debenhams store behind a row of massive columns with, true enough, a pull-in right in front.

No way was that pull-in a parking space.

It was a bus stop. And for several different routes. The poles and signs told everyone as much – if they couldn't read the big white lettering on the road. You wouldn't be popular with bus drivers or traffic wardens if you parked your car there. My guess is you wouldn't last two minutes.

I smoked a fag and thought about it. No one had seen the car drive off. No one remembered the make, the colour or the reg.

So what if the car didn't exist? Suppose some boob had said the first thing that came into his head?

I eyeballed that building across the street. Three floors and plenty of windows. Could the gunman have fired from there? Unlikely. You don't use a department store as your gun emplacement. If you aren't noticed setting up, you'll get some attention when you fire the thing.

At the street level I counted seventeen large pillars in front of the shop, each broad enough to hide behind.

Two problems with that. Customers coming out would surely spot a guy with a gun. And even if he wasn't noticed, there was no guarantee a bloody great bus wouldn't pass in front just as he was pulling the trigger.

Forget the shop front.

I looked up again, sixty feet up. From here, the building seemed to have a flat roof. I knew it didn't really, but there was a broad ledge right along the front where a gunman could lie unseen. He'd need a weapon with a telescopic sight. Not impossible, I decided. There had to be a way to get up there. A fire escape, maybe.

My theory was as good as any other, but I didn't fancy scaling the building to check. The angles of any bullets in Ruby's body would confirm whether the shooting had been done from above. Even a plodding Bath detective superintendent would then work out where the gunman had stationed himself.

I stubbed out my cigarette.

7

'I can't tell you. I don't know. Nobody knows.'

The atmosphere in the incident room had changed since Diamond had returned from the hospital. Up to then, everyone had been absorbed in the challenge of chasing up information on Mark Rogers, the man found dead in Seppy Hubbard's shop. Between them, they'd put together a pretty useful profile and they expected the boss to ask for an update. This was the routine whenever he got back after a few hours away. Instead, he'd stayed silent, preoccupied until Keith Halliwell had enquired what news there was of Ruby's condition.

The force of the reply silenced everyone.

He was obviously strung out, troubled by what was happening.

Normally Ingeborg lightened his moods with a few well-chosen words, but she was still at the hospital.

Halliwell moved across to Paul Gilbert's desk and quietly instructed him to visit the cafe next door.

No more was said until a cafe latte with two sugars and a large chocolate brownie were put in front of Diamond.

'You wanted more background on the victim,' Halliwell prompted him.

'Did I?'

This was so unlike the boss. 'That was the last thing you asked for.'

'Who do you mean?'

Halliwell's eyes crinkled in disbelief. 'Mark Rogers, the safecracker.'

'Got you.' Each man rebooted mentally. In Diamond's troubled mind Ruby Hubbard was the victim, and unlikely to survive. He stared into the untouched coffee. 'Has Ingeborg called?'

'No.' Becoming testy himself, Halliwell pressed on with his summary. 'Rogers was unmarried, forty-five, registered as a job-seeker. Do you want to hear this?'

'I'm listening.'

'And living modestly in a council flat in Keynsham. He wasn't a regular criminal unless he used other identities we don't know about. He seems to have come out of retirement for the Bath job.'

'Must have been promised a good payday,' Gilbert chipped in when Diamond failed to react.

Their boss rubbed the side of his face. He noticed the coffee and drank some. Transparently, he made an effort to tear his mind away from the hospital. 'How about associates? Did you get any names?'

'The gang he worked with on the Veronica Lodge break-in – the Wiltshire job when he got caught – has dispersed. Mr Big was almost certainly a villain called Dave Dell who lives a charmed life. He planned the robbery, recruited a gang of expert housebreakers and was smart enough to stay away from the action.'

'What went wrong?' Diamond's eyes were focusing better. Either the caffeine or the sugar rush was starting to work.

'Someone tipped off Wilts CID and they knew exactly when to move in.'

'Why wasn't Dell arrested?'

'Not one of the gang would finger him and there wasn't enough evidence to prosecute. He and his wife live in style in a villa in the south of France. They failed to turn a profit from the Veronica Lodge job, but they're well fixed from other heists. He won't need to work again.'

'Toe-rag. Can't they extradite him?'

'No chance. All they have is whispers. The others who were caught that night were Bernard Harvey, known as the Bellman, and Dave Bartholomew, the break-in specialist. Harvey disabled the alarm system and Bartholomew forced the window without breaking any glass. He had previous and is still serving out his sentence. Harvey got religion while he was inside and now sells Bibles in the Good News shop in Shepton Mallet.'

'Who was the driver?'

'A smart woman called Maggie, smart enough to get the hell out when our lads moved in. She was never traced.'

'Do we know what they were planning to steal?'

'Five gold ingots worth three million.'

Diamond whistled. 'From a private house?'

'This is what made the whole case so messy. The loot was stolen property already, handed down through the family of a crook involved in the Brink's-Mat robbery at Heathrow back in the 1980s.'

'What happened to the ingots?'

'Rogers opened the safe and removed them and the gang were caught red-handed a few minutes after.'

'I mean after the case was over.'

'They weren't restored to the owner, that's for sure.'

'So they had sat in the safe for nearly forty years and no one profited?'

'I guess knowing they were there brought peace of mind.'

'We could all use some of that.' Diamond checked his phone again for a message.

'We also did some research on Seppy Hubbard,' John Leaman said.

Diamond looked up, fully alert.

'He's owned his shop for six years. Before that he dealt in antiques in Devizes and ran a stall at the Saturday flea market for about ten years. He gets a lot of his stock from deceased estate.'

'What's that – house clearances?'

'Yes, but he doesn't do that himself. It's a specialised job. He has arrangements with the guys who do it and buys pieces he thinks he can sell at a profit. He's well known in the trade and popular. Never got rich from it. Each time he makes a sale he's already thinking of buying something else to stock up.'

Diamond revealed where his true interest lay. 'What of his family?'

'He was married and divorced. Just the one daughter, Ruby. She's Bath born and bred. Attended King Edward's.'

'Hefty fees.'

'Someone paid them – her mother, perhaps. Ruby wasn't academic and left school at sixteen. The rest you know.'

'She'll have plenty of contacts locally. I wonder where her best friend Olympia went to school.'

Confusion bordering on panic spread over Leaman's face at a name he hadn't processed yet. 'Who's Olympia, guv?'

'Haven't I told you? Of course not.' Diamond shared what he'd learned about the ill-fated lunch date.

'Which one of them suggested meeting?'

'Ruby, I believe.'

'What was her reason?' To the literal-minded Leaman, every social arrangement had a purpose behind it.

'I expect she simply felt like unwinding with her closest friend. She's suffered a lot recently.'

Leaman was unmoved. 'Is that what you were told?'

'No. It's bloody obvious, John. Olympia strikes me as a well-adjusted young lady, more stable and mature than Ruby.'

'Do you have a reason for saying that?'

'She has a job with connections to some of the richest people in the world.'

'Go on!' Leaman needed tying down, he was so excited.

Diamond explained about the job with *Exorbitant*. 'I don't know if she's any good as a journalist but she looks and dresses like a fashion model. No doubt she'll hook one of the fat cats they feature and get on the rich list herself.'

A female voice from behind said, 'If you don't mind me saying, sir, that's unworthy of you.'

He swung around to see who had spoken. She was the newest member of the team, DC Jean Sharp, who had made herself indispensable on a recent case by analysing hours of CCTV footage. She was blushing now, looking as if she wished she hadn't spoken.

'You'd better explain,' he said.

She took a sharp breath. 'What you just said about this woman came across as sexist as well as cynical.'

Diamond frowned, blinked and then reddened as deeply as Jean Sharp had. 'You're right. I was out of order. It was a cheap remark. If Inge had been here she'd have shot me down in flames.'

The moment passed, but it would be remembered by the team for weeks after.

Leaman hadn't finished his cross-examination. 'Do they see each other regularly, or was this a reunion after a long interval?'

'I've no idea,' Diamond said, becoming weary of this. 'I'm not sure why you're banging on about a meeting that never took place.'

'Because we haven't got a motive for the shooting. One possibility is that somebody wanted to stop them from meeting.'

'I can't think why.'

'You've already made up your mind that it was purely social, and you may be mistaken, that's why. It could have been such a threat to this third person's plans that Ruby had to be stopped at all costs.'

'You're assuming there's an agenda behind what happened.'

'Behind what happened today and the break-in at the shop. There ought to be a connection.'

Diamond was weighing the suggestion when he was galvanised by his phone ringing. The call was from Ingeborg.

'Guv?'

'I'm listening.'

'She's in the recovery ward. They took a bullet from her left upper arm. The other shot drilled the top of her head. That's good news.'

'Is it?'

'The site of the injury. Any lower and it would damage brain tissue and vascular structures and almost certainly kill her. The bullet made a groove along the scalp and didn't penetrate. There's bleeding on the brain from the jolt she got, the surgeon says, but she has a chance of surviving.'

'Thank God for that. Was anything said about the wound to the arm? The size, the angle of entry?'

'The entire operation is on video, I was told.'

'Get a copy for our people to study. And make sure the bullet is sent to forensics. Are the armed police on duty?'

'Yes.'

'We must keep the guard going day and night. When word gets out that the wounding wasn't fatal, someone may have another try.'

'What's she done to deserve this, guv?'

'When we can answer that, Inge, we'll get a handle on this case.' He ended the call and updated the rest of the team.

'Are you going to ring the private eye?' Halliwell asked after the briefing ended.

'Why?'

'Keep him on side.'

'He'll stay on side without encouragement from me.'

'He won't have heard from Ingeborg.'

'He came to the hospital. He knows Ruby was shot.'

'He hasn't got the latest bulletin. She's his client, isn't she? He's sure to start pestering them, saying he's working with us.'

Bowing to the inevitable, Diamond took Johnny's business card from his pocket.

8

That evening Paloma served up a chicken pasta bake. Since Diamond had moved in with her, his diet had undergone a transformation. All the years he'd lived alone in Weston, he'd managed with meals from the freezer, the same traditional British fare – cottage pie, sausages and mash, roast beef dinner, whichever of these three came to hand first. Sometimes he had the same two nights running. If the food became too boring to stomach, he'd go to the Crown and order a steak and kidney pie. Never anything else. What more could a man want? Paloma took pride in showing him. She surprised him daily with a freshly cooked treat and didn't always tell him what it was. In a two-week span, no dish was repeated and not one was wasted.

'I like to unwind after a day in the office,' she would say. 'Gives me something different to think about instead of dressing Daniel Craig.' She worked from home, advising film and TV directors on how to bring the authentic look to whichever period setting they needed to create. Her collection of fashion illustrations was a legend in the business.

Diamond wasn't encouraged to enter the upstairs room that was Paloma's office. His veteran cat Raffles was welcome to stay all day and usually did, curled up in the best armchair, but it was written in the stars that a large, notoriously clumsy policeman would trip over the bowls of dry food and water left out for feline snacks.

'Can I get your expert opinion?' he asked in the safer area of the living room, where they relaxed after their evening meal.

'On what?' Paloma said.

'A case we're working on. It hinges on an unknown item that came into the possession of an antiques dealer, the guy who owns the shop opposite Beehive Yard.'

'Seppy Hubbard?'

'You know him?'

'He's one of the local characters. Straw boater, blazer and cravat, shiny shoes and you could cut your hand on the crease of his trousers.'

'If your hand happened to be anywhere near his trousers.'

She laughed. 'We're not that well acquainted. I've met him a couple of times at social events. His shop was broken into recently.'

'You know about that?'

'Everyone in Bath must have seen it boarded up. There's a picture being tweeted showing the damage to the shop door. I don't know what was stolen.'

'Neither do we. Possibly nothing. The thief was found dead in there, so he didn't get what he was after. Our suspicion is that Seppy was staying overnight in the shop, as he sometimes does. He heard the door being forced, bashed the guilty party on the head and panicked when he saw what he'd done. He's disappeared and so has whatever was in the safe – which we found open.'

'Money, I expect.'

'Not according to Ruby, his daughter. There was never much in the shop.'

'What size is this safe?'

He made a shape in the air with his hands.

'Quite small, then?'

'She also told me Seppy was really excited about some item he'd picked up recently. He called it the find of a lifetime.'

'Intriguing. What was that?'

'He left her guessing.'

Paloma shook her head. 'Didn't she demand to be told? I would.'

'He clammed up. He's like that, she said.'

'And you think this precious object is what the thief was after?'

'Something small enough to stow away in a safe no bigger than your average hotel fridge.'

'Jewellery, I should think. Does he specialise? Dealers usually do.'

'Couldn't tell you.'

To a professional researcher like Paloma this wasn't good enough. 'Can't you find his phone or his laptop? He'll have made searches online to check the value.'

'Nice idea, but his laptop is missing and he uses an old-fashioned phone.'

'You can still check the records with his phone company.'

'We did. He orders takeaways and speaks occasionally to his daughter. That's about it.'

'Where does he live?'

'Odd Down.'

And now Paloma laughed. 'This whole thing is odd. Have you searched his house?'

'We have to work within the law. I can't get in without a warrant and I don't have enough to put to a magistrate.'

'It's obvious something is wrong. His shop has been broken into and his daughter doesn't know where he is.'

'That won't wash, unfortunately. We have to make a case

that a search warrant is necessary. He could be taking time off somewhere, on holiday or visiting friends and knowing nothing about the break-in. If he comes back and learns we entered his house, he could file a claim for compensation, and rightly so.'

'Have you put out an appeal?'

'A missing person alert? That's easier to arrange. It goes out tomorrow. We had to allow a reasonable amount of time to pass in case he reappeared.'

'But you're already on the lookout?'

'Someone is working full-time at finding him.'

'Who's that – the youngster, Paul?'

'No.' He gave a sheepish grin. 'We, em, have a private eye working with us.'

Paloma gripped the arms of her chair. 'A *what?*'

'I know it sounds ridiculous. He's being paid by Ruby.'

'I can't get my head around this. A private detective? But if Ruby hired him, he'll report to her, not you.'

'Correct, but unfortunately someone gunned her down in the street today and she's in the RUH.'

She caught her breath. 'Poor soul! Will she live?'

He nodded. 'But they meant to kill her. She took a bullet to the head. There's no knowing if she'll recover fully.'

'This gets more and more weird. A shooting in Bath. And you're thinking there's a link between the break-in and the shooting?'

'Got to be.'

'What would anyone gain from killing Ruby?'

'I've no idea yet.'

'Kidnapping her would make more sense if some villain wants to find Seppy and his once-in-a-lifetime antique, but killing her achieves nothing.'

'It could bring him out of hiding.'

'There are smarter ways of achieving that.' Paloma leaned back, trying for a rational explanation. 'Whoever did the shooting is not very competent and not very bright. You've met Ruby, I gather? What did you make of her?'

'Early twenties. Flame-red hair, if that says anything about character.' He left Paloma to pronounce on that.

'A bit of a tearaway?'

'That's a shade too strong,' he said. 'Typical of someone that age, yet to settle into her personality, dealing with conflicting emotions, trying to appear in control but living off her nerves, hugely committed to finding her father, yet no daddy's girl. She isn't interested in his business and doesn't often visit the shop.'

'You've really weighed her up. Some contradictions there. What sort of company does she keep?'

'We haven't investigated that yet.'

'You must.'

'She has a friend called Olympia.'

'Good name. I like it.'

'Another millennial who is much more grounded than Ruby. A career girl with a job in journalism.'

'Perhaps Olympia can tell you whether she's mixed up in anything dodgy.'

'We'll be asking. I had the feeling there are things Ruby wasn't keen for us to know about, but serious crime I doubt. Undesirable company, possibly. Big-time crooks, no.'

'And you won't find out any time soon. I think I need a dessert while I'm trying to make sense of all this. How about you?' Paloma went out to the kitchen and came back presently with two portions of lemon meringue pie and a jug of cream.

After it was eaten, she served rosehip tea, a delicacy he'd never gone near in his Weston existence. 'All right,' she said, 'here's what I suggest.'

'I'm up for anything.'

'I'm talking about Ruby, Peter. You won't thank me for this. You have a soft spot for her, I can tell.'

He frowned a little, but she was probably right.

Paloma set out her stall. 'My theory is that Ruby is behind all this. She's in with a bad crowd and owes them money or needs money to keep face with them. Serious money.'

'That's not impossible.'

'And then her dad happened to confide in her that he was on the brink of something big with his find of a lifetime.'

'That part is fact,' Diamond said. 'She told us he did.'

'Okay. Ruby sees a way out of her troubles. She hires a break-in man to steal the precious item from Seppy.'

'Ruby?' His mouth sagged at the edges. 'From her own father?'

'Sweet little Ruby. The crook she uses is an also-ran who jemmies front doors badly.'

'To be fair to the guy,' Diamond said, 'his skill was opening safes.'

'Makes sense. Did you find his name?'

'Mark Rogers.'

'Mark Rogers, then, was a flaky character who'd never had a big payday.'

Impressed, he said, 'True. He was a nearly man. Spent time in jail for a heist that went wrong.'

'This all fits in. His life was a mess. I'm guessing here, but probably he was in hock to some powerful and dangerous crooks. He told them he'd soon clear his debts because he was about to do another job, a big one. Part of the deal with Ruby was that he would fence the stolen goods and split the money with her.'

Diamond was thinking Paloma had a worrying grasp of the way crimes were hatched.

'But when the day of the break-in came and went and Mark Rogers didn't reappear, his criminal masters got suspicious. And when word got out that the safe had been emptied and Rogers was dead, they asked themselves who ended up with the swag. They decided it must be Ruby.'

'Ruby? How?'

'She'd never intended to share the takings with him. She'd joined Rogers the night he broke in, waited for him to crack the safe and then bashed him over the head.'

'What are you saying – that she murdered him?'

'It's what the crooks believed. She may not have intended to kill him, but that's what happened.'

He was confused. 'Let me get this clear. Are you suggesting Ruby really did take part in the raid?'

'I'm beginning to think she did. It would look like a casual break-in and no one would suspect that the real thief was Seppy's own daughter.'

'You've given me a whole new angle on this. You're saying Ruby came away with the find of a lifetime?'

'It fits the facts.'

'And then what?'

'Naturally the Bath mafia wanted the prize for themselves. They watched Ruby for days and she played a blinder. To deflect suspicion from herself, she hired the private eye, who was another chancer like Rogers. How am I doing so far?'

'I'm all ears.'

'It's smart. Anyone would think she's worried about her missing father and that's what she tells the eye.'

'His name is Johnny Getz.'

'I don't believe that for a moment.'

'You're right. He made it up.'

'Johnny – we'll call him that – is marginally smarter than

the break-in man. He quickly realises he won't get into the shop without police permission, so he contacts you guys.'

'Dead right. He cornered me in the Francis and I wasn't pleased.'

'The crooks weren't pleased either. Ruby is a loose cannon. She's going to get found out at some point now she's playing this dangerous game with the private eye and the police. They don't know how much Mark Rogers told her about his links with them. They decide she must be silenced, so they send a gunman to eliminate her.'

'Neat.' Diamond clapped in appreciation. 'I was hoping you'd give me some advice about the antique that was stolen and instead you've dissected the entire plot and solved the mystery.'

'Say it. You don't believe a bloody word of it.'

'No, no, no. It's given me a whole new insight and I've got to think how much of it I can take on board. You summed up Rogers and Getz as deadbeats and I agreed with you.'

'But you can't see Ruby as a scheming hussy?'

'Well . . .'

'Of course you're not influenced by the fact that she's a stunning redhead.'

'I said she's unstable, didn't I?'

'But not dodgy enough to steal from her own father?'

He used a long pause to reassess Ruby. 'I've heard her speak about Seppy and she comes across as genuinely fearful for him. She'd have to be a brilliant actress to fake it.'

A faint smile formed. 'I'm not going to change your mind.'

'You've shaken it up, and that's no bad thing. I'll sleep on this and see how it holds up in the morning. You've answered most of the questions, Paloma. Nobody else has come up with anything so complete.'

'And now you'd like me to tell you what was in the safe.'

'Please.'

'I haven't the foggiest.'

He was up early next morning, but not too early for Raffles, who was waiting on the landing where Paloma had installed a padded cat-bed in the shape of an igloo, a small fridge, feeding station and litter tray filled with expensive bio-degradable wood pellets for the most pampered pet in Bath. The stairs were too much for an elderly cat to manage.

Ocean fish the evening before. A fresh pouch of gourmet beef this morning.

'You've got it made, haven't you, old friend?' Diamond said when he placed the bowl on the floor.

Raffles already had his face in the gourmet beef.

Diamond's morning routine was established in this new setting. Downstairs with the litter tray before seeing to his own breakfast. In Weston he would have opened the back door and sent the cat into the garden.

Empty the tray and clean it. Refill it. Carry it upstairs.

Halfway up and his mobile went. It was early for a call. He gripped the tray with his left hand and took the phone from his right pocket.

The screen showed it was from Keith Halliwell.

'This is bloody early.'

'Sorry, guv. I thought you'd want to know. Someone broke into Ruby Hubbard's bedsit last night and turned the place over.'

The litter tray fell out of his hand and slid down the stairs, scattering biodegradable wood pellets over Paloma's Axminster stair carpet.

And the day would only get worse.

*

When he arrived at the Corn Market incident room, there weren't the usual shouts of 'Hi, guv' and 'How you doing?' All of the team were there, but unusually subdued. He saw the reason at once. Two visitors were seated in front of his desk at the far end. Middle-aged women in hats, one a police hat, worn by his boss, Assistant Chief Constable Georgina Dallymore, the other a light brown fedora. It's remarkable how much you can tell about people from the backs of their heads. The pair had been waiting some time and were resolved to remain. Out of their sight, Ingeborg raised the palms of her hands at Diamond and swayed back in her chair as if to say prepare for battle.

'We came at nine expecting to find you here,' Georgina began when he reached the desk.

'I would have been earlier than that, ma'am, if it weren't for a minor accident.'

The second woman spoke, the face under the brim of the fedora creased in sympathy. It was a pretty face, made prettier for Diamond by her response to his excuse. 'Oh my word. You aren't injured?'

'No, no, ma'am. I'm fine.'

'Was anyone else hurt?'

'Happily, no.'

'But they could have been?'

He was being drawn into details he didn't want to give. He avoided telling a white lie. 'It was my duty to stop and do what I could.' Which was true. In all conscience he couldn't have left the house without sweeping up the cat litter.

'You did the right thing and made sure.'

This woman he'd never met seemed to be batting on his side already. He tilted his head and smiled at her. 'You do what you can in a situation like that. It was more messy than harmful to life.' To draw a line under the double-talk,

75

he added in the same breath, 'If I'd known you ladies were waiting to see me, I'd have phoned in, of course.'

Georgina's expression was showing she hadn't swallowed the story at all. Fortunately, she chose not to wade in. 'We don't have much time. Lady Bede is one of a number of lay members of the ethics committee, and before you say another word, allow me to remind you that this committee exists entirely to support officers such as ourselves to make good decisions as we grapple with ethical dilemmas thrown up by day-to-day policing in a rapidly evolving society.'

Some mouthful, even for Georgina. He'd heard of this committee at some stage and decided not to go within a mile of it. Committees are like traffic jams, worth going out of your way to avoid. As for ethical dilemmas, he hadn't been troubled by them up to now in his long career and he had no reason to expect any were coming his way. But if the charming Lady Bede got off on them, who was he to object? He said, 'Good morning, my lady.'

'Please call me Virginia,' Lady Bede said. 'Let's start on a friendly footing and stay that way. You won't mind if I call you by your first name?'

'It's Peter.'

'You look like a Peter. Suits you better than mine suits me. And don't be put off by what you just heard about the committee. We're just local people like you doing our best to ease the bumps and strains the job throws up. Your little episode this morning is a case in point. You had an ethical dilemma. Should you stop and help in a minor accident, which would make you late for work? It can be as simple as that.'

'So what's cooking?' He was about to add another 'my lady' and changed it in time to 'Virginia'.

Georgina winced at the blunt question. She was fundamentally incapable of being informal. 'Lady Bede has asked to observe a real investigation in progress, and she's interested in this new case of yours.'

The lady's large blue eyes shone as if she was a child on Christmas morning. 'This is the first time I've been inside an incident room and I'm so excited.'

Georgina told her, 'This is far from typical. We generally find better premises than this. We tried for the Hilton, which is equally close to the crime scene, but it wasn't available.'

'Pre-booked,' Diamond said and enquired casually, yet nervous of the answer, 'Will you be with us full-time, Virginia?'

'I wish I could. I'd learn plenty from you, I'm certain.' The eyes twinkled, showing that she, too, could wrap extra meanings into words. 'My difficulty is that I have my fingers in too many pies. I can only visit you when my schedule allows.'

'Pity,' he said, thinking the opposite and getting a glare from Georgina, who was watching him through narrowed lids. 'But you know where to find us now. Do you live nearby?'

'I'm often at my London house, but I have a home in Bath as well and a driver who'll see I get to whichever places your enquiry takes us. Don't you worry. I'm good at merging into the background.'

Really? he thought. In your chauffeur-driven car wearing your fedora and a purple designer suit that looks as if you were sewn into it? Some chance. She was liberally perfumed, too, bringing a heady fragrance to his end of the room that would linger for hours and need explaining to Paloma at the end of the day.

Georgina rose from her chair. 'Duty calls as always. Now that you have met, I'm going to leave you in Superintendent Diamond's capable hands.' She took a sharp breath as if she regretted the words she'd just used. 'Virginia.'

'That will be divine.'

'He'll show you round and introduce you to his team, and I'm sure he'll be fascinated to learn how the ethics committee operates.' With that, she quitted the scene faster than an actor who forgot his lines.

Virginia was more attractive and friendly than he expected a titled lady to be, but a hanger-on of any kind would still be an infliction. Saddled with this new responsibility, Diamond asked, 'Do you know anything about the case?'

'Only what I've seen in the press,' she said. 'It's a murder, isn't it? I do love a murder mystery.'

'We're calling it a homicide at this stage. And a missing person enquiry. Plus a gunman taking shots at witnesses. So my team have plenty to occupy them. If you have time, I'll show you round.'

'I can make time for you,' she said playfully. 'Shall I take your arm?'

'It might give the wrong impression here.'

In the next twenty minutes, they did the tour of the room, with Lady Bede lavishing fragrance and charm on everyone and insisting even the lowest ranks called her Virginia.

Finally, she said, 'I'm going to leave you now, Peter. There's so much more I want to hear about, but I've taken up heaps of your valuable time already. Here's my card. When you have an hour to spare, give me a call and I'll send my chauffeur to collect you and bring you to my house for a glass of something and a briefing, or a debriefing, or whatever it's known as.'

A debriefing with Lady Bede. He wasn't ready for that.

After she was gone, the perfume lingered. He told Paul Gilbert to open some windows. Then he sank into his chair, head in hands. The lady was charming, and trying her best, but he could do without a groupie.

'Guv.'

He looked up and saw Ingeborg standing in front of his desk.

'I thought you were sure to ask me to run a check on Lady Bede, so I did.'

'Already?'

'The main facts were easy to find. I'm sure there's more if you want a full search.'

'The main facts are all I can take right now.'

'She's forty-seven, originally Virginia Perkins, a builder's daughter from Mile End. Attended Our Lady's, a convent school for girls, motto "Ever better", then Wimbledon College of Arts, followed by a short spell in advertising. Married the managing director at twenty-one and divorced the next year, after which she doesn't seem to have had any career except more marriages, first to a North London garage owner called Norris, which lasted eighteen months. Then a merchant banker called Bergson. Four years. Finally a peer called Lord Clifford Bede. Six years so far.'

'How many marriages was that? I didn't count.'

'Four. Each to a richer guy and each divorce netting a generous settlement.'

'She took the school motto to heart. And she ends up with a title.'

'If she's ended up,' Ingeborg said. 'Lord Bede is seventy-five. When he goes, she'll be free to find number five. Watch out, guv.'

'No concern. She'll be looking for a duke.'

He called Keith Halliwell over. The big development overnight needed to be discussed. 'What exactly do we know about this break-in?'

'At Ruby's? She has this walk-up flat in Oldfield Park, as you know, with her own entrance. The old couple downstairs

79

are the owners of the house. They had the place converted a couple of years ago when the stairs got too difficult for the old man, who is disabled. Ruby is their first tenant. They heard somebody moving about upstairs late last night, around eleven, but didn't think anything of it.'

'Why? Didn't they know she was in hospital?'

'Nobody had told them. Early this morning, the old lady took something out to the wheelie bin and noticed Ruby's door had been forced. She called 999.'

'What's it like inside?'

'Not too bad. Drawers pulled out. Some stuff on the floor. They didn't take her bits of jewellery or a couple of credit cards still left in one of the drawers. Impossible to tell what they did get away with until Ruby recovers enough to check the place.'

'Whoever broke in was quick off the mark. This doesn't sound like an opportunist burglar,' Diamond said. 'Who would have known she was in hospital?'

'It was all over social media soon after it happened and it made the early evening news.'

'Not her address?'

'Her name got out during the afternoon.'

'So a lot of people will have known the flat was unoccupied last night. We'd better assume there's a connection to the break-in at Seppy's. Send Paul Gilbert to inspect the place and make sure it's marked as a crime scene. We don't want the plods treating this as a nuisance-value offence and forgetting about it.'

9

Say what you like about me. Johnny Getz is no quitter.

My client was fighting for her life in intensive care and if she won that battle there was no certainty she would get her brain back and no certainty I would ever get paid. Worse than that, a gunman was on the loose. I could be next.

Did I go into hiding?

No way.

But I'm not stupid. Not wishing to take a cut in my lifespan, I decided to leave my partner Pete and his team to follow up on the street shooting. I would focus on the line of enquiry we'd agreed from the start – finding Seppy Hubbard.

The smart move was to pump Ruby's buddy, Olympia, for more background. As a source, she was the next best to Ruby herself. The two must have talked about their families.

I took out her business card. *Olympia Ward, Journalist, Petunia Cottage, Limpley Stoke.* An email address and a mobile number. I thought about turning up at her door and surprising her. Questioning a witness is always better face-to-face. Then I remembered the cute-sounding Limpley Stoke is deep in a valley four miles out of town, scenic, but a muscle-buster. Even if I could get there on my bike, I wouldn't fancy the ride back.

I picked up the phone.

Straight away she knew my voice. 'You're Ruby's private detective. We met at the hospital.'

'Right on,' I said, 'and I heard from Pete that they operated.'

'Yes, I called them myself. I hope to God she pulls through.'

'She will,' I said as if I did brain surgery in my spare time. 'She's a fighter. And she's counting on me to find her dad. I'd like to ask your advice on that. You know her better than I do. Any chance we can meet in Bath for a cuppa?'

'As it happens, I'm on my way there shortly,' she said. 'I have an appointment.'

An appointment. Because I work over a hairdresser's, I hear that word and think shampoo and set. 'Tell me which salon and I'll find you.'

She laughed. 'It's the Royal Crescent Hotel. My boss is visiting Bath and invited me for a drink.'

'Lucky you.'

'We could meet in the lobby if you like.'

Pause for a rethink. Tea at the Royal Crescent would cost me an arm and a leg. They'd bring us fancy cakes and smoked salmon sandwiches on a three-tiered stand. A get-out was needed.

'After drinks with your boss you may not fancy that cuppa I offered.'

It worked. 'You could be right about that. I should be free about twelve thirty and I don't suppose they serve tea at that hour.'

They serve lunch, I thought. Even more alarming. Both arms, both legs and my torso.

She must have read my thoughts because she added, 'As

long as I'm not keeping you from your lunch. I never eat at midday.'

I breathed again.

So it was fixed. We'd meet outside and go for a walk.

I was there in good time. The drinks overran by twenty minutes and when Olympia emerged she looked a little unsteady. She was in a tailored white suit and matching shoes with heels that made her four inches taller. Her shoulder bag was patent white leather. There's only one doorstep at the front of the hotel, but she didn't take it well and almost ended up sitting in the geraniums to the right of the doorway. Her companion steadied her and she laughed and said something to him. Then she spotted me and waved. What could I do but step forward?

'Jock Scoular, meet Johnny Getz,' she said. 'This may be giving away a secret, but Johnny is a private eye.'

'Sweet.'

I disliked Jock from there on. Short, overweight, with curly black hair that covered his ears and reached below his twee velvet collar, he had eyebrows like a pair of hairy caterpillars that meet on a pink twig and refuse to give way to each other. His puddle-brown eyes dissected me from either side of a fleshy nose crimson from the drink. The mouth, what there was of it, was small and disapproving.

Olympia must have felt the frost because she said, 'Jock has a train to catch, so we can't linger. Did you call a taxi, Jock?'

'Sorted,' he said. Not much of a talker, it seemed.

'So you edit the magazine for the super-rich?' I said to fill the silence.

'I own it.'

He'd just tripled his word count.

'I'd like to see a copy,' I said, getting more and more narked. 'I've never come across one.'

'You wouldn't find it on the shelves of WHSmith.' He was eyeing my trousers. They pick up mud from all the cycling and I forget to brush them. 'Are you employed by Olympia?'

'Where did you get that idea?' I said, not wanting to say any more to this prick than I needed.

The champagne, or whatever, had loosened Olympia's tongue. 'Johnny is helping my best friend, Ruby,' she told him. 'She's in hospital, unfortunately. Somebody shot her yesterday.'

'Falling down on your job, Johnny,' Jock said.

'I'm not her bodyguard,' I said.

'Sounds like she needs one. More use to her than a private eye.'

'She needs all the help she can get.'

He looked away at a car approaching over the cobbles. 'My transport. Keep at it, Olympia. Do a good job and I'll have you between the sheets before the end of the year.'

She looked startled before twigging that he was talking about her journalism. Supposedly. Except of course it was a well-planned try-on. I'm no prude and I thought it was coarse.

Olympia gave a faint laugh and thanked him. They exchanged a token meeting of cheeks.

I didn't get so much as a farewell nod. He'd blanked me out.

'Don't mind him, Johnny,' Olympia said after the cab had turned the corner. 'His sense of humour takes some getting used to. I struggle with it myself.'

'Still want to do the walk?' I asked her. The white stilettos weren't made for walking.

'I've been looking forward to it.'

The obvious route to take was Gravel Walk, a few steps

to our left. Sounds like a yawn, but for my money this lovers' lane is a secret treat, fantastic value in this overpriced city. Designed by eighteenth-century toffs as a cut-through for sedan-chair users heading downtown, the path offers sunlight, shade, handsome trees and cheeky views of the backsides of Brock Street, The Circus and Gay Street. Even better, it's free.

'Is Scoular a good payer?' I asked Olympia when we'd started along the path. There had to be a reason why she put up with the jerk.

'The job will never make me rich, but I get to meet interesting people,' she said.

'Fabulously wealthy interesting people,' I said. 'Play your cards right and you could hook one.'

She laughed as if I'd cracked the best joke ever and leaned against me. She was well lubricated. 'That never crossed my mind.'

'What are you working on right now?'

I was only making small talk, but she backed off and reacted like I was the inquisition. 'I can't possibly tell you.'

'Why not? I might be able to help. I have hidden talents. Are you researching some amazing work of art?'

She drew her arms across her front as if a force-nine gale was blowing along the walk. 'Wild horses wouldn't drag it from me. I've invested so much of my time and energy in this, I don't want anyone else muscling in on it.'

'I wouldn't do that. I'm a private eye, not a journo. Did Jock assign you to it?'

'It's my baby, not his, not anyone else's except mine. Let's talk about something else. Why did you want to meet me again?'

I'd touched a raw nerve, bringing up her research. She was desperate to sidetrack me. I didn't want our meeting to end yet, so I played along. For now. 'You're Ruby's best friend. I'm hoping you can give me some background on her father. You must have met him.'

'Seppy? Yes. He's nice. Under fifty, I think, but he dresses and talks as if he's seventy. A gentleman, through and through, charming and very knowledgeable about antiques.'

'I get the impression Ruby doesn't see much of him. Is that her choice or his?'

'There's no bad feeling between them. They're very different people, that's all. He's rooted in the past and she's up with everything that's going on now. I think her mother was similar, which was why the marriage broke down.'

'Have you met the mother?'

A shake of the head. 'She moved to South Africa with her new man when Ruby was ten.'

'Tough to deal with at that age.'

'She doesn't often talk about it.'

'How did you two meet?'

'At school.'

'King Edward's.'

'Why ask me if you know already?'

'I know Ruby went there.'

'We clicked. She felt rejected after her parents had parted and so did I, a long way from home.'

'Her dad is not too well off, I get the impression.'

'That's true. Every time any money comes his way, Seppy buys more antiques.'

'I'm beginning to understand why she stays away from the shop. After school, you went your separate ways, I expect.'

She nodded. 'I had this dream of being an ace reporter. I went to London and got a degree in journalism, which sounds all right if you can find a job after. I didn't. Not as a journo, anyhow. I was too highly qualified. I should have left school at sixteen and joined the local paper. I did a whole lot of things, telling myself I was getting useful experience.'

'Like what?'

'Oh, anything I could find. Manicurist, hotel receptionist, croupier, waitress, programme-seller, childcare. The only thing I can say with any pride is that I didn't sell my body.'

'But you left London and came back out to the sticks. Why?'

'If you think of Bath as the sticks, I don't. There are several online magazines here. I decided to go freelance and work in a city I know well.'

'Back to your roots?'

She treated me to a flash of perfect teeth. 'I was born in the Caribbean, but I know what you mean.'

'And what career did Ruby follow?'

'Fashion, as if you couldn't guess. She stayed in Bath and worked for a top designer.'

We were more than three-quarters of the way up the Gravel Walk when I heard a rasping noise, the buzz of something mechanical. We both turned and watched a rider on a moped rattling along the path towards us.

'That's not allowed,' Olympia said.

'Some people,' I said.

At one time, the walk was an unofficial car park for the locals and anyone else who knew about it. Handy for them and sod the rest of us who wanted to enjoy the scenery. I'm glad to say the council put a stop to the parking by placing a bollard at either end. That doesn't keep out bikes and the occasional scooter.

We both moved to the side to let this scumbag through. No point in waving him down and telling him he was a danger to pedestrians. I didn't suss the real threat until he was level with us and stopped.

He jammed a foot on the ground and kept the engine running. He was wearing a helmet and leathers like a real biker.

When he tugged open his jacket zip and reached inside, I reacted quicker than hell would scorch a feather. I'd seen in the nick of time what this was about. Before he took out the gun and levelled it, I turned and shoved Olympia in the chest with both hands.

She screamed and tipped backwards on her high heels. A holly bush cushioned her fall, if that doesn't sound stupid. In the same movement, I swung around and threw myself at our attacker.

What I did was crazy at point-blank range. Crazy but heroic, if I have to say it myself. Faced with sudden death, you don't stop to think. I made a grab for his shooting arm, only my hand couldn't get a grip. My fingers slipped off the shiny leather sleeve. I did just enough to spoil his aim. The shot passed somewhere over my left shoulder. I fell so hard against the back of his scooter that the whole thing skewed across the path.

He didn't fire a second shot. I guess he thought I was better placed to grapple with him than I was. He shoved the gun in his jacket, revved up and rode off, leaving me grounded and with a lungful of exhaust fumes. No one else was close enough to have witnessed any of this.

Dazed, eyes watering, deafened by the gun, I picked myself off the ground and went to help Olympia. She was stuck in the holly – not the best place in a thin white suit – legs going like a kicking colt, yelling something I was too deafened to hear, which was probably a good thing. I grasped her wrists and hauled her upright. A holly bush is dusty and dirty as well as prickly. She tried brushing herself down and didn't improve things. She looked more shocked than angry.

I mouthed some sort of apology and she shook her head. Her ears were as useless as mine.

When I picked her bag out of the bush, the strap was hanging loose from one end.

Two or three minutes passed before we could make each other understand.

'He tried to kill you,' I finally heard her say over the rock band in my head.

She'd suffered enough, so at this stage I didn't tell her she was the real mark and not me.

'I messed up your clothes,' I said. 'Are you okay?'

'I think so. You did the right thing.'

'I'll call a taxi. We can have one waiting at the end of the path to take you home.'

'Thanks, but what I'd really like is a strong coffee. My head feels as if it doesn't belong to me.'

The nearest I could find was Colonna and Small's in Chapel Row. They welcomed us even though we looked like dropouts from a commando course. Olympia said she'd go to the ladies to clean up. I offered to mend the broken shoulder strap, so she took out her comb and lipstick and left the bag with me. The D-ring had been forced apart. All it needed was to re-attach the strap and twist the metal back into place.

When the guy came to the table he brought some pliers. I thanked him and told him he didn't have to tell me the coffee options. 'We'll have a two-shot Americano twice over, a jug of milk and two glasses of water.'

Olympia smiled her thanks when she returned. She was getting her mojo back.

'Pity I can't fix your clothes,' I said.

'They'll clean up all right. We're lucky to be alive. What's behind this, Johnny?'

'I'm thinking he must be the same gunman who shot Ruby.'

She summoned up a brave smile. 'He's not having much success, is he?'

'That's one way of looking at it.'

The water arrived. 'Good thinking,' she said and gulped most of hers down. 'Was that what you'd call a hitman?'

I nodded and waited. I knew what was coming next.

'How could he have known we'd go along Gravel Walk? It was a spur-of-the-moment choice, wasn't it?'

She needed to be told the truth now. Her life was under threat. 'He must have been keeping watch earlier.'

'Are you saying he followed you to the Royal Crescent?'

'Not me, Olympia. I'm nothing. I'm out of this equation. He was tailing you.'

'Me?' Her eyelashes flapped like a flamenco dancer's fan. 'Why? I've done nothing to him.'

'If I'm right and he's a hired gunman, someone has put a contract on you and Ruby. Two shootings in two days. There's got to be a connection. Do you understand what I'm saying?'

'Yes, but I can't think what's behind it.'

'Everything points to the break-in at Seppy's shop.'

'I had nothing to do with that.'

I was watching her keenly and believed what she was saying. More important, I could see she believed it herself. She couldn't think how she had become a target.

'Maybe the lowlife behind this thinks you and Ruby know too much.'

'About what?'

90

'About Seppy's so-called find of a lifetime. I'm thinking the break-in was staged to rob him of whatever booty it was.'

'I don't know anything about that.'

'Rightly or wrongly this jerk believes you and Ruby need to be silenced.'

She shuddered. 'Horrible. What can I do, Johnny?'

'Stay off the streets and make sure your home is secure. Is it isolated?'

'Kind of. There are other cottages a short walk away.'

'Is there anyone you can stay with while this goes on? It's not going to last for ever. The police are going to nail the villain sometime soon,' I said modestly. I could have added that they wouldn't get far without help from me, but my status was sky-high with Olympia already.

'I'll think about it,' she said.

'Don't just think. Do it.'

'Okay.'

'And let me know where I can reach you.'

'You can get me on the mobile. If I go into hiding, it's best I tell no one, not you, not the police, not anyone. Speaking of the police, shouldn't we report what just happened?'

She was right. Pete had to be told, damn him. The crime scene needed to be taped off and searched for the bullet. Forward the plods.

10

'We can't go on meeting like this.'

The pair stood together at the crime scene in Gravel Walk. In their forensic suits, you wouldn't have known the freelance sleuth from the salaried policeman.

Peter Diamond wasn't amused by the tired old quip. 'It's not my choice,' he said through his teeth.

'Don't blame me,' Johnny Getz came back at him. 'I'm the innocent party here.'

'I blame you one hundred per cent.'

'You can't mean that,' Johnny said with such passion that his mask puffed out like a frog's vocal sac. 'I was almost totalled.'

'From all I hear, it was your idea to come here. Don't expect sympathy from me.'

'Do you want to be shown what happened or not?'

'I'm waiting.'

Johnny pointed beyond the verge to an undistinguished patch of holly at the side of the path. 'That's where Olympia ended up.'

'What use is that to me?'

'It's the proof of what happened. You might at least get a photo taken of the dent.'

'Let's hear this properly from the beginning. You meet her outside the hotel.'

Shaking his head at the poor police procedure, Johnny recapped as Diamond required. 'With her boss Jock Scoular, who owns that magazine. He caught a taxi to the station.'

'Straight away?'

'A few words got spoken, mostly by me. He's more of a killjoy than you are, if that's possible.'

The insults no longer made any impression on Diamond. He'd pick his moment to return them with interest. He'd become distracted by one of the figures in forensic kit who was standing close enough to hear what was being said. Clearly a woman, she seemed to be making a fingertip search like the others, but she looked up once and widened her eyes, apparently in recognition. He couldn't place her and couldn't understand how he would know one of the scene-of-crime people. They were all privately employed, not attached to the police.

He forced his thoughts back to the job. 'Did you watch him get into the taxi?'

'Scoular? Yes. And then Olympia and I chose to walk along here. And it wasn't only my call. We agreed on it together.'

'Were there people about?'

'In front of the Crescent? There always are. It's the main tourist attraction after the Roman Baths. You should know that.'

'You're there waiting for her to come out.'

'No I'm not.'

'You just said you were.'

'I moved on in the story, if you were listening. She's left the hotel, kissed her boss goodbye and we already started our walk.'

The man was a pain in the butt Diamond had to endure.

'Let's rewind. Didn't you look around you at the other people in front of the Crescent?'

'Why would I? I wasn't expecting a gunman.'

'He must have been among them.'

'You bet he was, but if I'd seen him I had no cause to be suspicious.'

How dense was that? Diamond said with disdain, 'On a moped, the day after Ruby was almost killed in a drive-by shooting?'

Johnny's voice leapt an octave in surprise. 'Is that what it was – a drive-by? Nobody told me. I was thinking the gunman must have fired from the roof of Debenhams.'

'That's ridiculous.' But as he was saying this, Diamond realised he had knowledge he hadn't shared with his so-called partner. 'The bullet wound in her arm showed the trajectory was horizontal and some of the smoke had soiled her clothes, suggesting the range was close up. The shots weren't fired from a car as we first supposed. The shooter was level with her. Either he was standing in the middle of the street, which is unlikely, or he was seated on a bike.'

'How do you know this?'

'The report was in my inbox this morning.'

'You could have told me.'

'I've told you now. It's police intelligence. You don't have an automatic right to be told anything. Anyhow, you're supposed to be looking for Seppy Hubbard.'

Johnny spread his arms. 'It's not going to work, is it, dividing up the case?'

'It's not divided. The deal is that you do what you're being paid to do and don't interfere with my investigation.'

'I'm central to it now, chum. Do I have to keep reminding you I was almost plugged an hour ago?'

Diamond grinned behind the mask. 'Shame he didn't make a better job of it.'

'You can't mean that.'

In all truth, he didn't. He wouldn't say so, but he was enjoying the verbal sparring. None of his team would have dared give him the lip he was getting from this deluded fantasist and there was no need to hold back on the counter-punching. Bashing Johnny Getz was his new sport. 'I was never more serious.'

'Do you want to hear the rest?'

'Not unless you remembered something new. Tell me what you got from Olympia before the gunman appeared.'

'Not much. We talked about Seppy and how crazy he is about antiques, how the trade was a turn-off for his wife, who left him, and Ruby, who keeps her distance mostly.'

'Except when there's the prospect of big bucks.'

'That's only human,' Johnny said in defence of his client.

'I've got my suspicions, as I made clear,' Diamond said. 'There's more to Ruby than she wants us to know. What else did you discover?'

'She and Olympia were at school together.'

'As early in life as that?'

'Yeah – and they found something in common. They both felt their families had given them the big E.'

'Rejected them? I can see that. So it threw them together. Are they just friends or . . .'

'What are you hinting at now, chum? No, Olympia is straight. They both are, far as I know.'

'But the ties are strong, obviously. Could they have hatched something between them?'

Johnny's eyes widened above the mask. 'Like what?'

'Like the break-in that went wrong.'

95

There was a pause. 'That's a long shot, Pete. Are you saying they hired the safebreaker, whoever he was—'

'Rogers,' Diamond said. 'Mark Rogers.'

'You know his name? *Now* you tell me.'

'It didn't come up. He was a professional criminal, a peterman. We put out feelers to our underworld sources, but nobody knows anything about this job, or so they say. They sometimes clam up when a killing occurs. Did you probe any more with Olympia?'

'There you go – wanting me to tell you everything. Where's the give and take in this arrangement? You keep me in the dark about the ballistics report and Mark Rogers and expect me to tell you every last thing I learned from Olympia. There wasn't any more time before the gunman appeared.'

'And afterwards? She was in shock, I expect. That could have loosened her tongue.'

'We went for a coffee and I calmed her down. It was no time to rake over the past.'

'Where's Olympia now?'

'With a friend. I told her not to go home. She's obviously a prime target, so she's gone into hiding.'

'Who's the friend?'

'Someone she trusts.'

'You didn't even ask?'

Johnny looked down his nose at Diamond. 'Have you ever heard of the need-to-know principle?'

'I need to know. I must get her first-hand account of the shooting. I can't rely on yours.'

'Thanks for the vote of confidence.'

'A good detective never takes anyone on trust, Johnny. You're too naive for your own good. Where is this place?'

'She wouldn't say.'

'You can tell me.'

'Scout's honour, I don't know.'

'I don't believe you.'

They were interrupted. A scene-of-crime officer who had been part of the backdrop to all this gave a shout and waved her hand. She'd found the bullet the gunman had discharged. It was under a box hedge in the Georgian garden behind number 4, The Circus.

Diamond stepped over to where the yellow evidence marker was being positioned. 'Looks in good nick to me. We'll find out if it matches the bullet they extracted from Ruby's arm.'

'And look at CCTV footage?' Johnny said. He was already at Diamond's side, not wanting to miss anything. And so, also, was the scene-of-crime woman Diamond thought had been eavesdropping. She was close enough now for a whiff of perfume to invade his nostrils.

Lady Bede.

She'd claimed she was good at merging into the background. He didn't know whether to be annoyed or pleased that he'd recognised her. How she'd got here so quickly was a mystery that could only be explained by someone at the nick tipping her off about the shooting.

He put her out of his mind and picked up Johnny's point about CCTV footage. 'I don't see any cameras here.'

'Right here, no,' Johnny said. 'There must be some in front of the Royal Crescent. Did we catch any of the Manvers Street shooting?'

'The film is still being checked. The cameras outside the train station picked up Ruby arriving. There's nothing on film of the incident itself, but we're studying the traffic heading that way.'

'If the bullets were fired from the same gun, who do you think is behind this?'

'Someone who believes these two young women know too much.'

'About what – the killing of the break-in man, Mark Rogers?'

'Sometimes a serious crime can set off a chain reaction, one murder leading to another.'

'Except he failed twice over.'

'True.'

'What does that tell us? That he's no damn good?'

'That's one way of looking at it,' Diamond said. 'We've been assuming up to now that someone hired him. If they did, they wasted their money.'

'He could be the main man.'

'Who do you mean?'

'Seppy.'

'Seppy?' Diamond shrilled in disbelief.

'He's the crap gunman. He's been keeping tabs on what's going on and his big payday is under threat.'

'How?'

'Ruby has hired me. There's a danger his secret will be blown before he can cash in.'

'So he shoots his own daughter? You're off your trolley.'

'He didn't shoot to kill. He meant to miss. It was a warning. But he's not used to handling a gun and she ends up in intensive care. He shut her up, but not the way he planned. And then he remembers she shares everything with her friend Olympia, so he needs to put the frighteners on her as well. This time he makes a better job of it. He misses. Nobody is hurt. Neither of those young women is going to blab now.'

Diamond was unimpressed. 'It doesn't wash with me, matey. We're thinking Seppy is a victim. We put out a missing person appeal this morning. One of my team was on TV while you were chatting up the gorgeous Olympia.'

'Let me know what you get, if anything,' Johnny said without enthusiasm. 'What's your take on this, then?'

'The obvious one. It's far more likely that our man is some professional criminal who got wind of the deal and hired Mark Rogers to break into Seppy's shop and hijack the booty, whatever it is. His problem was that there isn't a half-decent burglar or hitman to be found in Bath. Rogers made a mess of the break-in and was killed. And the gunman paid to blow away Ruby and Olympia couldn't shoot for toffee. Did you ever hear the one about the short-sighted gunman?'

'I'm going to hear it now, for sure. Tell me.'

'What's the difference between a short-sighted gunman and a constipated owl?'

'I give up.'

'The gunman shoots but can't hit.'

'And the owl?' A slow grin spread across Johnny's face. 'Okay.' He let a few seconds pass. 'Seriously, if some Mr Big was after the loot, why did he want Ruby and Olympia shot?'

'For the same reason you mentioned. They knew too much.'

'Both of us can't be right,' Johnny said. 'And who knows? What if there's another scenario?'

'Go on. I'm listening,' Diamond said. 'Can't be more half-baked than the one you just spilled.'

'I didn't say I have one.'

11

And now you're going to hear how the private eye in this snaggy saga got ahead of the game and outsmarted the cops. I left Pete Diamond at his crime scene bogged down in forensics bullshit. He'd be there another hour at least and go home knackered and slump in front of the TV.

Not me. Before the day ended, I aimed to find out where Olympia was holed up. She was my best hope of cracking this case.

Okay, you're thinking, how could I do that when milady refused to give me the address?

Here's how.

Every PI worthy of the name knows about surveillance. Ninety per cent of our business is following people – two-timing husbands, wayward wives, insurance cheats, fiddlers, fixers and frauds. For this, we use the tools of the trade, devices for listening, locating and recording. Modern stalker-ware is amazing. Unless you're in the game, you won't believe how small a camera can be. No shit, there's one the size of a grain of sand that takes colour pictures. So you're shaking your head. Look in the *Guinness Book of Records*, my friend, and see if I'm right. Too bad I can't afford one like that. But mine is no bigger than my thumbnail. It's always ready in my pocket and if only I'd been quicker I would have got a shot of the Gravel Walk gunman as he rode away. His bike reg would have been useful.

As well as the mini-camera, I carry a wallet stuffed with bugs and trackers for listening or locating. Now do you see where this is going?

Cast your mind back. If you remember, I repaired Olympia's shoulder bag while she was in the restroom at the coffee shop. This is going to sound sneaky to my women readers. I make no apology. Sneaking is my living. That's where I take issue with Raymond Chandler, who famously wrote that the sleuth needs to be a man of honour striding through the mean streets.

You don't say, Ray?

Is that the man of honour who bashes a blonde with his gun in *The Big Sleep* and asks her, 'Did I hurt your head much?'

While working on the shoulder bag I had to empty it in case something got broken, didn't I? That's how I found Olympia's moleskin credit-card holder. The GPS tracker I tucked inside was a beautiful piece of engineering as flat as a card and one-hundredth the size. It would emit a signal that would give me her location whenever I chose to tune in.

What happens if she changes her bag, you're thinking. A woman as chic as Olympia is going to have a different bag for each outfit. Yes, but she'll transfer the card case, won't she?

When I checked my phone, the bug gave me a reading south of the river in Westmoreland Street, off the Lower Bristol Road, so close to my office that I wouldn't even need to get my bike out.

I was in no hurry now I knew where she was. I hadn't eaten for hours, so I ordered a takeaway, returned to base and turned on the TV in time to catch an item on *Points West* about the shooting in Gravel Walk. You had to feel sorry for the reporter. She had sweet FA to work with except some footage of the scene-of-crime people doing a fingertip search. She tried to interview my chum Pete and he was as approachable as a chain-gang boss, refusing to confirm or deny that the incident had anything to do with the shooting in Manvers Street the day before. He wouldn't even comment on suggestions from bystanders that the gunman had appeared to target a black woman wearing a white suit and a white man wearing a black suit.

My suit was dove grey, so they got that wrong.

After eating, I checked the location again.

Definitely Westmoreland Street.

The light was still good, so I took a stroll.

Needing to cross the river, I headed towards Midland Bridge. I was halfway across when I had a tickle in my bones that something wasn't right. I checked the phone and sure enough it gave me a different reading.

She was on Wellsway, moving out of town.

If she'd been going the other way, I would have been happier. This was the time when people are going out to eat. I don't know of any restaurants at the top of Wellsway. There are pubs, but would you go all the way up there when pubs and restaurants are on your doorstep?

From the speed the cursor was moving across the screen, she was in a vehicle.

Ugly thought: what if she'd been abducted?

Getting alarmed, I sprinted the rest of the way across the bridge and looked for a taxi on the busy A36. The first I tried to hail was filled with laughing teenagers giving me the finger. Three more minutes went by before another stopped for me.

'Where to, squire?'

'I'm not sure yet.'

'Are you serious? I need a destination.'

'I'll tell you as we go along. Up Wellsway, for a start.'

A discussion took place about the method of payment. Understandable, considering that the journey was open-ended. Perish the thought, but we could be travelling seventy miles to the south coast for all the driver or I knew. Finally I convinced him I would pay the fare no matter what, and we moved off.

By now, the little arrow was level with Entry Hill golf course. At the foot of the screen, Wellsway merged with the ancient Fosse Way and got a name change. Roman Road headed over Odd Down roundabout towards open country.

Odd Down was where Seppy Hubbard lived.

Various scenarios sprouted in my head:

1. Seppy is back home, knows nothing and has called Olympia to see if Ruby is with her.
2. He is a hostage and Olympia is dealing with his captors, fetching something from the house as a ransom.
3. He's dead and she wants to have a root around.

'Want to tell me what this is about?' the driver asked.

'No.'

'Is it, like, a treasure hunt?'

'Can we speed up?'

'I'm on the limit already.'

My day to pick a law-abiding driver.

Olympia (or her transport) left the main road and turned right at the Odd Down roundabout. I didn't know Seppy's address, but it seemed likely she was heading there.

Good deduction. The cursor had stopped.

'Okay,' I said, widening the map on the screen. 'We're looking for Bloomfield Road.'

'Want me to pull over and put it in my satnav?'

He was a pain. 'No. Keep going. I'll tell you.'

I don't know how long it took us to cover the distance, but it felt like the whole week. Although the streetlights had come on, it's sod's law that they never position them near a road name. We had to find Frome Road first, which was easy, then Bloomfield, which wasn't. Raymond Chandler's mean streets were neatly divided into blocks. Mine were designed by idiot town-planners. We drove straight past once and had to do a U-turn.

'Take a right where the church is.'

Nineteen-thirties council housing. No one ever mistakes Odd Down for a beauty spot, but the gardens are generous-sized and if you can afford a north-facing one, you get a view of Bath.

'Want me to wait?'

Perish the thought.

'No, I'll settle with you now.'

The house the cab had stopped outside wasn't the one the GPS showed. Any half-smart private eye knows better than to show his hand before the game is under way. The satellite indicated a house fifty yards away on the other side of the street, a buff-coloured stone-faced semi like all the others. Some had cars outside. This had a white van.

I waited for the cab to disappear before crossing.

Standing up close to the frosted-glass window above the letter flap, I could just see the whiteness of a spread of mail on the floor and I remembered how Ruby had learned her daddy hadn't been home for days.

Round to the side, then, through a wooden gate to the kitchen door. More frosted glass. Six small square panes of it.

Except there were only five. The one nearest the door handle had been smashed. All an intruder had to do was reach inside and turn the key. I didn't even need to do that. The handle let me in.

I stepped inside, crunched broken glass, eased the door shut and listened.

Voices, too muffled to make sense.

The place was darker than a Frenchman's beret.

Hands in front, blind-man's-buff style, I shuffled closer to the sound, crossed the kitchen and started along a passage, following the voices until I could eavesdrop at a partly open door with a faint, shifting light behind.

Olympia was speaking.

'This will take too long.'

'I'm in no hurry, babe.' A male voice, deep and laidback, so far back that I pictured a sunbather who has just woken up.

'I can take the whole thing home and study it there.'

'Want me to carry it?'

'Okay. Catch. I can't see much else, can you?' Olympia said. 'Ruby told me he has a laptop, but we're not going to find it here. The calendar will help.'

'Want me to look upstairs?'

'What for?'

'The laptop.'

'If you like. I'm not optimistic.'

Neither was I, but for another reason, standing the other side of the door. When it jerked open, I caught no more than a glimpse of a large man holding a Rolodex which he swung at my head. Everybody for miles around must have heard the steel framework connect with my skull. I toppled back like a skittle, hit the wall behind me and slid down it like something I'll leave to your imagination.

'Who the hell is that?' Olympia said, shining a torch that dazzled me.

My attacker didn't wait to find out. He put the boot in hard, a kick in my side like the end of a nine-iron swung by Tiger Woods in his prime. Any PI expects to be done over in the course of solving a crime. It comes with the territory. It's easy to read about. On the receiving end, it's no picnic.

I bellowed in agony, certain three of my ribs had snapped like dry spaghetti.

'Lucky,' Olympia said.

This wasn't my idea of luck. The big man had drawn his leg back for another go.

'Lucky, stop! I know this guy.'

So his name was Lucky.

Lucky couldn't stop the next kick from making contact, but there wasn't quite so much welly behind it.

He grunted.

I groaned.

He was the biggest black guy I'd seen outside a boxing ring. His body-builder's torso was squeezed into a red singlet. Olympia's torch behind him outlined his figure and obscured his features. His right hand still gripped the Rolodex he'd floored me with. The impact against my skull had broken the thing, because bits of card were dropping from it – the Rolodex, not my skull.

'Look what you've done,' Olympia chided him.

Fuck that, I thought. God only knows what he's done to me.

'He was outside the door,' Lucky said.

'I saw. He saved my life today.'

She had an early chance to return the favour.

'I need those cards, every last one of them,' Olympia said, 'and now they're all out of order. Pick them up, for God's sake.'

The big goon played the old soldier lowering himself to the ground, like he'd injured himself kicking me. Serve you bloody right, I thought until I caught sight of his ankle – or what should have been his ankle. The frayed jeans had rucked up and revealed the shiny metal of a prosthetic leg. No surprise, then, that my ribs were giving me grief.

Olympia now turned her anger on me. 'Johnny, you idiot, what are you doing here?'

'Same as you,' I managed to say, each word hurting so much it was punctuated with a groan. 'It's my job.' I handed Lucky a couple of cards that had fallen in my lap. I didn't want him groping for them. He had difficulty bending, so I scooped up a few more. Best keep on the right side of the punk.

'This will take all night,' Olympia said and stooped to join in.

Slight overestimate. We took ten minutes.

Between us, we collected every piece of card that should have been attached to the Rolodex, including the grey dividers, and put them in a carrier bag. Seppy's contacts would have filled three Rolodexes. They would have filled the Albert Hall on the last night of the Proms.

Olympia hadn't finished with me. 'Were you following us?'

Careful here, Johnny boy, I thought. She won't appreciate being told about the bug in her bag.

'Great minds think alike,' I said through the pain.

'What does that mean – you fetched up here by chance?'

'Something like that. We're on the same side, aren't we? I'm trying to find out where Seppy is. Maybe we should pool information.'

She wasn't attracted by that suggestion. 'Come on, Lucky. Let's get out of here.'

'Is that your van outside?' Dumb question, I thought as soon as I spoke it. A high-flyer like Olympia owning a van?

'Lucky's.'

'Can I hitch a lift back to town?'

'How did you get here?'

'Cab – but he's gone.'

So I rode in the back of the white van wedged between a bath and a hand basin that nudged my injury each time we passed over a bump. Lucky was a plumber, I gathered. One thing soon became clear. He was a faster driver than the taxi man. I didn't care to think how he managed the controls with his artificial leg.

Seated as I was with my back to the driver, I couldn't tell where they'd brought me when we stopped.

Lucky opened the rear doors, Olympia at his side.

'Where are we?'

'Kingsmead Square,' Olympia said. 'Isn't this where you live?'

'Thanks. I thought I'd need to walk home.'

'Are you still in pain?'

I made light of my injury. 'Nothing a drop of whisky won't cure. Can I offer you guys a bevvy in my local?'

'Not for me, man,' Lucky said. 'I'm drying out.'

Only Olympia joined me below street level in the Dark Horse bar, a place I consider my living room. We sank into black leather below one of Mishka Westell's sensational 'Heartless Bastards' posters. Where else, in the circumstances? I ordered Manhattans. They use genuine Bourbon here.

'It's spot on,' Olympia said, taking it all in, eyes glittering.

'What is?'

'The bar, the drink, the company. Just where I'd expect a private eye to bring me. We could be in LA.'

I grinned. That remark made up for a lot.

'Are you really okay, Johnny? Nothing broken?'

'Only my pride, and that mends quickly. It's always taking knocks.'

'Not always from a metal leg.'

'That was a first, I gotta say.' I took a long sip. 'How did he get to be called Lucky?'

She laughed. 'It's not funny at all, but it amused me when he told me. That was from the accident. He was just a kid then, riding his first motorbike, and crashed into the back of a lorry. The surgeon who did the amputation told him he was lucky and he asked why and the surgeon said you still have one good leg. The name stuck.'

'How much does he know?'

'About the accident?'

'About Seppy.'

'Oh – almost nothing. He has other interests. But I needed his help to get into the house.'

'And collect the Rolodex?'

'I didn't expect him to use it as an offensive weapon.'

'You're on to something big, aren't you?' I said, and I didn't mean Lucky.

She tensed. 'I don't know for sure.'

'Something Ruby tipped you off about?'

'You're probing, Johnny. I thought we came down here for a relaxing drink.'

For me, this meeting was a breakthrough opportunity, my first real chance to find out what she knew. Turned out it was like stealing meat from a lioness.

'Funny.'

'What is?' she asked.

'You and me – like two trusted agents sent on a mission to deliver a top secret. Each of us is given half the wording,

109

encrypted. Alone, each half makes no sense. But if we both get through, the two halves can be united and the world is saved.'

'You're talking in riddles,' Olympia said.

'It's like that. You know stuff about Seppy that I need to know before I can find him. Equally, I can make your mission a success by tracing him to his hideaway. We should trade with each other.'

She found that amusing. 'What have you got to trade?'

'My skill as an investigator.'

'Which has got you nowhere so far. You have no more idea where Seppy is than I do.'

'With your help I can find him. He's essential to your story for the magazine, isn't he?'

She looked down into her drink. 'Did I say anything about a story?'

'You didn't deny it when we spoke on Gravel Walk. You called it your baby and said you didn't want anyone else muscling in on it.'

'You don't miss a trick, do you? The whole point of a journalist getting a scoop is that no one else gets a sniff until the news breaks. If you think I'll be divulging it to you or anyone else, Johnny, you're deluded. This is a million-to-one opportunity.'

You see what I meant about the lioness?

'And bloody dangerous,' I said, trying a new tack. 'Someone else must have a sniff of it.'

'I'm taking care of myself.'

'Famous last words. I'll make sure they put them on your tombstone.'

'What a comfort you are.'

'What did you do with the Rolodex?' I asked, still sparring for an opening.

'Don't you dare make me nervous. It's still in the van, I hope, along with all the cards and the calendar I took off the wall. It's safe with Lucky. No one messes with him.'

'I did. And look at me now.' I offered the cheap laugh to relax her.

She gave a sympathetic smile.

'Now that you've got all those names and details,' I pressed on, 'what will you do with them apart from putting them back on the roller?'

'I'll start with the calendar, find the names of everyone he's contacted lately.'

'Antiques people? Dealers, buyers and sellers?'

'I expect so.'

'Aren't they the very people he'll avoid if he's on to something big?'

'Mostly, yes, but not all.' Her lips tightened. She'd said more than she intended. I needed to offer something in return, but what?

'Wouldn't it be safer to use a neutral like me to check them out?'

'Johnny, you're no more neutral than I am.'

Which was true.

'Call me a third party, then.' Thinking the shutters were about to come down, I made a bad mistake by issuing a veiled threat. 'Pete Diamond is going to take a poor view of you and Lucky breaking into Seppy's house and stealing evidence.'

She pushed her unfinished drink towards me and stood up. 'I'm leaving.'

The last I saw of her that night was her high heels disappearing up the stairs.

Shit for brains, I'd destroyed any trust she had in me.

111

12

Already this case was stretching Bath CID. Too many strands were under active investigation. The forensic test results from the crime scene at Seppy Hubbard's shop were still coming in and showing little more of real assistance. The killing of the safecracker Mark Rogers had required an operation to trace his underworld contacts, who so far were silent about his actions. Seppy's disappearance couldn't really be left to Johnny Getz to follow up. The shooting in Manvers Street and the break-in at Ruby's flat were new crimes requiring more legwork, not to say brainwork, and generated officers' reports, witness statements and forensic examinations of scenes and exhibits. There was no certainty that everything was linked, but at this stage it all had to be indexed and prioritised in the incident room – an almost impossible juggling act.

The missing-person appeal for Seppy produced the expected trickle of attention-seekers. Diamond recognised the names. These people were mostly fantasists wanting to be involved in some way in police matters, just like Mr Getz. After that bunch were discarded, twelve genuine informants remained. DC Jean Sharp had taken time out from her main task of studying CCTV footage and spoken to everyone who had left a phone number. She'd made helpful short notes for Diamond.

It was obvious at once that no one had seen Seppy since the break-in. But on the Saturday before his disappearance he'd been spotted early in the morning in the Beehive Yard flea market with the other professionals scouting for bargains. Anything of real value is always snapped up by dealers before most tourists arrive. Dressed in his boater and striped blazer, Seppy had been unmistakable. Normally he would also have been seen on Sunday before 7 a.m. working his way through the offerings at the car-boot sale on Lansdown racecourse, but not that weekend.

'Did any of these people speak to him?' Diamond asked Jean Sharp.

'No, guv. It was just sightings.'

'He should be obvious dressed like the Dick Van Dyke character in *Mary Poppins*.'

'Yes, he was also seen early Saturday in the coffee shop.'

'*Our* coffee shop.' He was about to add 'Small world', but it wasn't surprising that Seppy used the cafe closest to where he worked.

'And there are two witnesses who looked round his antiques shop during the Saturday morning,' DC Sharp added.

'He was in there?'

'At his desk, yes. They didn't buy anything and didn't speak to him. He's not much of a communicator.'

'Don't I know it? Nobody has heard from him since the break-in. What else have we got here?'

'Earlier sightings.'

'Any worth following up?' He glanced down the list. 'What's this about? "Lansdown car boot. Sunday the eleventh. Informant Mrs Elspeth Bickerstaff. Do not contact husband Douglas."'

'What it says. Mrs B doesn't want to involve her husband. I felt sorry for her.'

'You spoke to her?'

'Yes, and she made that clear.'

'Does she have anything helpful to say about Seppy?'

'It's going back some time, guv, five or six weeks before the break-in. But she did take the trouble to get in touch and she and her husband did at least speak to him. In fact, they sold him some of their stuff.'

'Namely?'

'A china jug, a fossil and a picture.'

'Fossil of what?'

'I'm not sure if I heard properly. It sounded like anthracite.'

'Can't be that.' He played the word over in his head. 'Ammonite?'

'Yes.'

'They're two a penny. I'm surprised he wanted one of those. Sometimes a dealer will pick up extra items as a distraction from the thing that really interests them. Did this woman tell you anything about the picture?'

'Only that it was modern art.'

'Abstract?'

'She didn't say.'

'Seppy would have known if it had any value. How much did he pay?'

'I didn't ask.'

Possibilities stirred in Diamond's thoughts. Could this modern picture be Seppy's find of a lifetime? An undiscovered Picasso? A Jackson Pollock? A Bacon? His knowledge of bankable twentieth-century artists stopped there. If you found a valuable painting, you'd need to get it authenticated. Experts don't like to be rushed. Five weeks may well have gone by before Seppy confided in Ruby that he'd acquired a masterpiece. 'I need to speak to Mrs Bickerstaff.'

'But not her husband,' DC Sharp insisted.

He reacted testily. 'If I need to see him as well, I will, don't you worry. Did she say why?'

'I got the impression he's the controlling type.'

'Bit of a sergeant major? I can't understand men like that.' Jean Sharp didn't comment.

Diamond called Mrs Bickerstaff's mobile.

The lady answered at once, as if she had the phone in her hand. 'Who is it?'

He'd barely finished saying his name before she said, 'Thank you. It isn't convenient,' and ended the call.

'The husband was breathing down her neck, I expect,' he said to DC Sharp. 'I'll try later.'

So he breathed down the necks of everyone in the incident room until a reasonable amount of time had gone by.

He pressed the recall key. 'Mrs Bickerstaff? Is it okay to speak now?'

'I may need to cut you off at any time.'

'Is it better if I meet you?'

'That would be easier. I'm about to go to yoga. I do three sessions a week. The one time I can call my own. It helps to relieve the stress.'

This sounded like an invitation. Visions of himself relieving the stress on a mat in black singlet and tights. No. Not even in the cause of justice.

'Where do you go for this?'

'The Hive.'

'Where's that?'

'Do you know Beehive Yard?'

'Do I know Beehive Yard?' He grinned. 'That happens to be where I'm speaking from, ma'am.'

She paused to take that in. 'Do you do yoga?'

115

'No, ma'am, I catch lawbreakers. I work in the Corn Market building at the entrance.'

'The Hive is in the Foundry at the far end, by the river.'

'Shall I see you after you finish?'

'At twelve thirty would be good. For a few minutes only. My husband will be waiting in the car looking at his watch. But I don't have much to tell you. It won't take long.'

He was there in good time to see the ladies emerge with their rolled-up mats and backpacks. Mrs Bickerstaff was easy to spot: the loner with eyes swivelling left and right to be sure the husband wasn't in sight. Dark hair turning silver. In a loose top and shorts, she seemed pathologically slender and vulnerable.

He introduced himself. 'I know you don't want to hang about. Following up on your phone call, I'm interested in the job lot Mr Hubbard bought.'

'There was nothing special,' she said. 'A fossil we found years ago on the Dorset coast, a milk jug I never liked because it doesn't pour nicely and an old picture.'

'Old? I was told the picture was modern.'

'It was old to me. It was a long time waiting for a buyer.'

'I get you. We're not talking about an antique, right?'

'Impressionistic. Is that the word?'

His interest quickened. 'Depends. What was the subject?'

'No subject. Just a daub, I'd call it. Nothing but splodges.'

'An oil painting?'

'Yes.'

'When you say splodges, do you mean brushstrokes?'

'I suppose.'

'Like a Van Gogh?'

She managed a sad smile. 'Definitely not. It wasn't anything you could recognise.'

'An abstract, then?'

116

'I wouldn't have it on our wall, whatever it was called.'

'Tell me, did Mr Hubbard ask where you got it from?'

'I don't know. Doug made the sale. I was busy showing someone else the jigsaws.'

'I must speak to Doug, then.'

She put her hand to her throat. 'I was promised.'

'Rest assured, ma'am, I'll keep you out of it.'

'I can't see how. He's sure to ask how you found out.'

'Do you do the car-boot sale every Sunday?'

'Saturdays at Greenhill and Sundays at Lansdown. It's Doug's hobby.'

'So you'll be at Greenhill tomorrow morning. Where's Greenhill? I've never heard of it.'

'Greenhill Farm at Southwick, off Bradley Road. It covers three fields, but please—'

'Don't fret,' he cut in. 'I won't look anything like a copper. I'll blend in with the scene. How will I find you?'

She bit her lip. 'I don't like this.'

'Believe me, he won't have a clue – and I know more about clues than most people.'

She wasn't amused. She took a long interval to think it over while Diamond did his best to look trustworthy and implacable. Finally she said, 'I've got to leave now or he'll come looking for me.'

'Where do I find you at Greenhill Farm?'

'Our pitch is always near the entrance. We've been doing it for years so we've earned a good position. Ours is the yellow Vauxhall Corsa.'

'Should be easy to spot. I'll see you there.'

'Please don't let him know we've met. Treat me like a stranger.'

'No problem. I ignore my colleagues on a daily basis.'

*

He sought out Keith Halliwell and asked for a progress report on the hunt for the gunman.

'We're confident we have him on CCTV now,' Halliwell said. 'DC Sharp has trawled through hours of footage and one of the cameras in the station yard the day Ruby was hit picked up a moped rider shortly before the shooting.'

'Did we get the reg?'

'Unfortunately, no. The rear plates should have been in view, but he was wearing a loose jacket that hid them.'

'Deliberately, no doubt. Can we tell anything at all from the film?'

'Very little. The helmet was a full-face job you can buy at Halfords. There are hundreds on the streets. He wasn't wearing gloves, presumably so he could grip the gun when he needed it. That's one reason we think this was our man.'

'Okay. Is there anything on video from the Gravel Walk shooting?'

'No cameras there, unfortunately. Jean Sharp is looking at everything from in front of the Royal Crescent. If it's there, she'll find it.'

'I'm impressed with her. Keep beavering away. I suspect the gunman is only a hired hand – and a piss-poor one at that – but if we can collar him we'll find out who is behind this. What's the latest on Ruby?'

Halliwell sighed. 'No change. She's expected to recover, but she's in an induced coma for the present. I wouldn't get up your hopes of learning any more from her.'

'Stay positive, Keith,' Diamond said. 'It's a pig of a case, I know, but we're about to make a breakthrough.'

Unheard by Diamond on the other side of the incident room, John Leaman murmured, 'In your dreams.'

13

A rare and possibly never-to-be-repeated sight: Peter Diamond in shorts. And only Sergeant Ingeborg Smith from CID was there to bear witness to the corpse-white shanks on display.

'I know,' Diamond said, 'but I want to mingle.'

Ingeborg was lost for words.

'My suit wasn't right for a car-boot sale,' he explained. 'What do you think?'

She knew what she thought and it was best not to say.

'Is the shirt okay? I don't possess a T-shirt.'

Transfixed by the shorts, she hadn't noticed the shirt. Now that he mentioned it, she could see it was one of his striped office shirts. 'Perhaps if you fold the sleeves . . .'

'Like this?'

'No. To just below the elbow. On second thoughts, you might do better to buy a T-shirt when we get there.'

'What a good idea. I'm glad I asked you along.'

Ingeborg knew she'd been asked along as his chauffeur. If they went anywhere together, it was always in her small Ka.

'I made the effort out of chivalry,' Diamond explained while they were on the road to Southwick.

'How is that?'

'Doing the right thing for a nervous lady.'

Who is going to be even more nervous when she sees those legs, Ingeborg thought. 'Who's that?'

'Elspeth Bickerstaff, the wife of the man we're going to see. She's anxious – well, desperate really – that I shouldn't behave like a cop and let the husband know she got in touch with us. I'm honour-bound to act like an ordinary mortal.'

'Quite a challenge,' Ingeborg said, straight-faced.

He smiled. He'd fed her the line and she'd not missed the opening. He was genuinely thankful for her support. 'So I'm relying on you to play along.'

The car progressed to the next roundabout before she spoke again. 'Who am I supposed to be, guv?'

'My companion. Other half, or whatever the term is. Don't look concerned. You fit the part.'

'Thanks,' she said with more than a touch of irony.

In a stiff silence, they travelled another mile.

'You should definitely get a different shirt,' she said. 'And you shouldn't be wearing socks with sandals.'

'But the shorts get the seal of approval, do they?'

'Fashions have changed, guv. Men's shorts reach down to the knees.'

'Are you serious? This is getting expensive.'

She laughed. 'I haven't thought about my own outfit yet.'

One look at the people emerging from other cars in the buyers' parking area dispelled all doubts in Diamond's mind. His fashion adviser was right. He tugged off the socks right away and slung them on to the back seat of the car. 'I won't forget about them, promise,' he told Ingeborg.

When eventually they got to the real business of the morning and approached the Bickerstaffs' cluttered folding table, he was a changed man, in a red polo shirt and black jeans. He'd gone to the extra expense of buying a belt that cost more than the other things together. But he did feel as if he belonged.

Ingeborg suddenly said, 'Take a look to your left, guv.'

All he could see was a woman in a straw hat, blue T-shirt and white jeans that must have been a struggle to get into. She was eating an ice cream and looking towards the Bickerstaffs' table without really focusing on any of their wares.

'The woman in the hat, you mean?'

'Don't you recognise her? It's Virginia.'

Lady Bede shadowing him again. The last time, she had been in a forensic suit. If he hadn't known she was here on behalf of the ethics committee, he'd be getting paranoid. He'd done nothing unethical so far. Changing your clothes wasn't unethical if it was done discreetly in the back of a car.

'Pretend you haven't seen her.'

Professional as always, Ingeborg gave her mind to the job. She asked Mrs Bickerstaff if she had any jigsaws without missing pieces. Some were on the table and the twitchy little woman was only too willing to turn her back and search for more in the cartons behind.

Diamond got straight to the point with the controlling husband, who appeared affable enough, tanned like a golf professional, with faultless teeth that must have paid for a dentist's holiday. 'I was hoping you might still have a modern painting I noticed one Saturday a while back.'

'What's it like, my friend?' Bickerstaff asked.

'Smallish. Sort of impressionistic. Mainly brushstrokes.'

'Too bad.'

'Gone?'

'Long since. Mind you, I didn't get an offer in six months. It hung about here because the locals don't go for that sort of thing. A seascape or a hunting scene is what Bathonians like.' The face he showed the world was all bonhomie, but there was a meanness about the eyes and lips that didn't deceive.

'Do you remember who bought it?'

'A dealer. He eyed it up for weeks and finally took the plunge. I was pleased to be shot of it. He picked up a couple of other things as a job lot, but I could see it was the painting he wanted. Now you're going to tell me I sold him an unknown masterpiece. I know damn all about art.'

'If you did, that's egg on my face as well,' Diamond said. 'I should have snapped it up when I saw it. Where did it come from – if it wasn't the National Gallery?'

'Funny you should ask that.' The look he gave Diamond was anything but amused. 'The guy who bought it asked me the same question.'

'Art is all about provenance, isn't it?' Diamond had done his homework on the internet.

'So I'm told.'

'What did you tell him?'

'Only what I heard second-hand. Back in the 1940s someone was clearing out a mews building in Bath that must have been used by some artist to store his junk. A bunch of frames, some canvases, bits of an easel, and someone took a liking to an abstract painting that had been discarded with the rest. He had it framed in an art nouveau frame. Totally wrong for the picture, but he probably got it on the cheap, like the painting. He gave it to his wife as a birthday present. Fast forward to 1990 and that young wife was now an old lady, widowed and living in Bennett Street. She died intestate and left a load of possessions, some of them rather juicy, as we say in the trade. Various distant relatives had a claim and the lawyers sold everything by auction and divided the spoils.'

'Making sure they took a large cut themselves,' Diamond said.

'Name of the game, isn't it? The picture was bought by an artist who liked the art nouveau frame but never did anything more about it and the thing sat in his studio with a heap of other stuff until he got senile and his daughter did a clear-out. She knew I'm a boot-sale fanatic and asked me if I'd take a crate of junk off her hands.'

'May I ask how much you paid?'

Now that money was mentioned, a new expression dropped over Bickerstaff's face like a visor. 'Why? Have I been done?'

'Don't you remember?'

'I'm a soft touch. I probably gave her thirty.'

'And how much did you get back when you made the sale?'

'For the picture?' Pause for thought. This canny character wasn't going to admit to a profit. 'Twenty-five, no more, and he got a milk jug and a fossil thrown in. This is a mug's game. If you chase him up, he'll be happy to make a small rake-off, no doubt. He's often nosing around here with the other dealers early in the day. Dapper guy in a blazer and straw hat. Haven't seen him this morning.' He turned to his left. 'Ellie.'

The jittery wife dropped the jigsaw she was about to show Ingeborg. Fortunately the box had been resealed with a Band-Aid.

'Careful, my love,' Bickerstaff said in an icy tone that made the endearment a rebuff. 'All breakages must be paid for. Do you remember the geezer in the boater who bought the modern picture in the art nouveau frame? Has he been by?'

She turned as pink as if Seppy had been her secret lover. 'I haven't seen him for weeks.'

'And that's a woman who misses nothing,' Bickerstaff told Diamond as if his wife had left the scene. 'The only other art we have on sale this morning is Van Gogh's sunflowers and that's a jigsaw. Take a good look at the rest. I've often wondered if the Chinese vase at the end is Ming. I might be persuaded to part with it for fifty.'

'I'm strictly into paintings,' Diamond said.

'Sensible fellow. A smart buyer knows what he's looking for.' And now he produced a libidinous grin. 'Does your interest extend to photography? There's a seller called Anton in the next field who deals in tasteful shots of ladies wearing very little and professionally framed, and if you ask to see his portfolio he'll show you something that may appeal even more.'

Diamond made clear with a cold stare that he wasn't looking for porn. 'Where can we get a coffee?'

'Don't get me wrong. I was about to add that a few weeks ago Anton persuaded some of us traders to join in.'

'In what way?'

'As models.'

'The mind boggles.'

Bickerstaff beamed. 'So now there's a permanent record of my pride and joy.'

'I can do without seeing that,' Diamond shut him down, stretched to breaking point to stay civil with this waste of space. He owed it to the victimised Elspeth not to trigger an outburst. 'A coffee place?'

'I don't think you follow me,' Bickerstaff said. 'He photographed us as you see us now, fully clothed and standing proudly in front of our stock.'

'Aha.' Rapid rethink. 'I get you now. Pride and joy. All this.' He gestured at the objects displayed on the table. Out of nowhere, the smutty chat had taken a more promising turn. 'When was the photo taken?'

'At the end of last year. We had ours printed up as a Christmas card.'

'Do you still have any?'

'No, we ran out. Anton will have the original.'

'We may take a look after all,' Diamond said, masking his sudden hope that the pride and joy included the picture Seppy had bought.

'And the tea and coffee van is nearby.'

'We're obliged to you.' He turned to Ingeborg, so encouraged that he became quite skittish. 'Picked your jigsaw yet, love of my life?'

She wasn't fazed. 'Are you treating me, honey bunch? In that case I'll have the thousand-piece Sherlock Holmes.'

When they turned to leave, Lady Bede had already moved off.

Anton the photographer was a small, smiling man with curly black hair about as controlled as a teenage rave. He had two cameras hanging from his neck. Before anyone said a word he was holding a light meter in front of Ingeborg's face. She shook her head. He'd convinced himself they wanted a picture together, but Ingeborg said she hated being photographed and Diamond said his fans (a fabrication no one could challenge) wouldn't want to see him with a stroppy woman. They were enjoying their little feud. The photo session didn't happen. Diamond explained what they'd come for.

When the portfolio was produced, displaying sheets of 8x10 colour prints of various stallholders standing beside their wares, hope blossomed.

'Can you find the one of our friends the Bickerstaffs?' Diamond asked Anton, to avoid the tedium of looking through the lot.

'I can – and it's a beauty.' Anton pulled it out with a flourish. 'Don't you agree?'

Diamond gave it a glance, nodded and didn't agree at all. His blossoming hope had withered on the branch. Sharp and well composed as it was, the photo was no help. The Bickerstaffs were standing so close to the camera that almost everything on their sales table was blocked from view except the (possibly) Ming vase.

'If you'd like a print, I can send you one,' Anton offered.

'That won't be needed. It's a fine picture, but not what we were expecting.'

'Your friend Doug is proud of it.'

'I'm sure. Thanks, anyway.' Diamond turned to leave. He'd been in this game long enough to know that not all hunches bring results.

Ingeborg touched his sleeve as if in sympathy. Then her grip tightened. She turned back to speak to Anton. 'That one can't have been the only photo you took of the Bickerstaffs.'

Anton had lost interest in them. He was doing an imitation of Achilles in his tent.

Ingeborg tried flattery. 'It was the prize pick of a very good session, obviously.'

He mellowed a little. 'I used several viewpoints. It's the way we work to capture the perfect shot.'

'What happened to the others, the ones you didn't pick? Did you delete them?'

'Delete them?' Upset again, Anton tossed his head and the curls reared up in horror at the suggestion. 'I don't work in digital. I use film. The result is always superior. I will have shot at least one roll and probably more to get one as good as that.'

Diamond saw where this was going. Smart thinking by Ingeborg. 'So did you keep the film?'

'I'll have it at home with hundreds of others, yes.'

'Could you find it for us?'

'Why? It's no use to anyone else.'

At this minute the temptation to get heavy and say this was a police enquiry was strong, but Diamond resisted. Anything like that was sure to get back to the Bickerstaffs and put the hapless Elspeth at more risk of domestic abuse. 'I'll be honest with you. We're not interested in the people in the picture. We're hoping to get an image of an item they had on their table.'

'The Ming vase? It isn't anything of the sort. It's chinoiserie.'

'No. A small abstract painting, framed.'

'That?' Anton squeezed his eyes shut at the memory. 'I remember it, but not with any pleasure. I'm no philistine. I enjoy modern art. I have some on my walls at home. That specimen didn't do anything for me. I wouldn't give it house room if they offered it to me tied up with a blue ribbon.'

'Art is subjective, isn't it?' Diamond said. 'We all have our preferences. Is it possible you snapped the painting in the background when you were taking the photos?'

'*Snapped?*'

'No offence. You know what I mean.'

'It's not impossible it was in shot. In fact, I'd say it's quite likely.'

'Could we borrow the piece of film? For a fee, of course.'

'Strictly for private use? I can't sanction any of my work being published without my authority.'

'I can guarantee it won't. What time do you finish here?'

'At one. You *are* keen.'

'We'll pay you well. Would you be willing to sell any rolls that show the picture clearly?'

127

Anton looked happier than he had through the whole encounter. 'Every man has his price.'

'This is the sort of challenge John Leaman enjoys,' Diamond said to Ingeborg on the drive back to Bath from Anton's studio in Bradford on Avon. For twenty-five pounds they'd bought a strip of six frames of exposed film that each had the mysterious modern painting in the background.

'Does John know much about art?'

'He will, once he gets started.'

First, the film had to be delivered to the senior photographer on the SOCO team with a request for as sharp an image as he could obtain. Claude was at home enjoying Saturday sport on TV, but didn't need informing how urgent the job was. The head of CID on anyone's doorstep was alarming. Nobody was better at getting things done. Claude took to his darkroom in the loft like a vampire at the crack of dawn, leaving his two visitors to treat themselves to pork pies and beers while they watched the racing.

The result was worth the wait: a blow-up 8x10 colour print of the detail they needed and a promise that the image was also scanned and online, ready for Leaman to access in the incident room.

Outside in the car before driving off, they studied the print.

'What do you think?' Diamond asked.

'Fantastic.'

'The painting?'

'I mean the definition,' Ingeborg said. 'I never expected Claude to bring it up so sharply.'

'I was asking what you think of the painting.'

'Is it up the right way?'

'Hard to tell.' He turned the print top to bottom. 'Any better?'

'I have to say I'm underwhelmed.'

'Me, too. Mrs Bickerstaff called it a daub and I think I agree with her.' He gave it another turn. 'No better.'

There was no sense of design in the painting and no resemblance to anything. The paint seemed to have been applied indiscriminately in blobs and smears, the colours running into each other – and not attractive colours.

'Like something the cat threw up,' he said.

'I expect it takes a trained eye to appreciate it,' Ingeborg said, trying to be positive. 'When I first saw a Jasper Johns I couldn't see why people admired it, but I've learned to appreciate him since.'

'Jasper who?'

'Guv, it would take too long to explain. Maybe if we could see the original of this, we'd get it.'

'Now you're asking for the moon. Come to think of it, some of these splodges look like craters.'

'I'm wondering if John Leaman is the right person to research this,' she said.

'Why?'

'He'll want to please you, but if he can't get a handle on the task, he'll worry. A sense of order is important to him and I can't see any here.'

'You think it might push him over the edge? All I want from him is to give the painting a context. Is it an early work by some well-known modern artist? He'll happily sort through thousands of images comparing them for style.'

'Do we really need to know who the artist is? If Seppy bought it, he liked it. Isn't that enough?'

'Seppy saw something in this that makes it a life-changer. It's got to be a major work of art and I must know why. I'm backing John to find out. Let's get started, Inge.'

129

14

If Olympia thought she'd dumped me, she was in for a surprise. It would take more than our spat in the Dark Horse bar to put me off. With Ruby out of it in the RUH, who else but her best mate could lead me to Seppy? She knew stuff I didn't. And I had one trick up my sleeve she didn't. For 'up my sleeve' read 'in her bag'.

The bug.

I checked my phone every few hours to see if she'd moved from Lucky's place and she hadn't. Not a serious move, anyhow. Short trips for shopping, a manicure and a takeout. Nothing to excite me. I was waiting for the one that mattered. I pictured her in the flat with that damned Rolodex, sifting through hundreds of names for the one that would lead her to Seppy.

The whole weekend went by.

Monday I got edgy. Checked the tracker at the end of each hour until I fell asleep and then found I was waking up on the hour to check again. About three, my banjaxed brain agreed there wouldn't be any action that night.

Tuesday I surfaced much earlier than usual, reached for the phone and found she was already on the move, travelling east along Lower Bristol Road towards Churchill Bridge.

Jeez, I moved fast. Dressed, dashed downstairs into the street. Found a taxi dropping a client at the salon, dived inside and said, 'Station' before he could say, 'Where to, mate?'

How did I know Olympia was heading for the station? I didn't. I'm not a mind-reader and neither is my phone. When someone invents the mind-reading app, we're all in deep doo-doo. I picked the station because if I was wrong and she was walking into town, I could deal with it. If she got on a train and I didn't, my chance was gone.

'Late for work, are you?' To add to the stress, my driver was a talker.

'Something like that.'

'Which one are you hoping to catch?'

'The first I can.'

'Traffic's bad this morning.'

'Do what you can. I'll pay.' I almost said, 'I'll pray.'

We took to the side roads, me watching the little arrow on the GPS all the way.

The driver put me down in the station yard just as Olympia was entering the ticket hall. Good thing she wasn't carrying an overnight bag.

She was wearing a yellow coat that would be easy to follow. Her hair was hidden under a matching yellow turban.

You may be interested in what I was wearing. Sorry. Not for publication. Did Mike Hammer ever tell you he was in a grey pinstripe and spats? Get away.

Tricky. I didn't want to be seen in the booking hall, so I couldn't get close enough to overhear her destination. My best guess was London. Then Bristol, Reading or Swindon.

I watched from behind a pillar, figuring that the platform she chose would help me. She picked up her ticket and went down the subway to Platform 2, the London line.

Bristol and all points west were eliminated. I bought my own ticket at the machine. Lashed out more than fifty quid on a London Travelcard. I'm not made of money, but the freedom to follow her anywhere was a must.

The departures board told me the next one in would be the 8.43. Incredibly I had time to buy breakfast. So much had happened since I'd got out of bed, I was sure it must be past nine already.

Clutching my bacon and egg sarnie and a black coffee, I made it on to Platform 2 as the train rolled in. I looked for the yellow turban and made sure she boarded. Then I did the same, two carriages behind.

The 8.43 is laughingly called 'off peak'. It's always full. I was lucky to get a seat next to an old guy in an expensive suit who gave my breakfast such a filthy look I opened the pack and treated him to the full aroma.

I could relax as far as the first stop. My hunch was that she would go all the way (think what you like, reader – I'm talking transportation here). The trouble is that hunches are mostly your brain telling you what you want to hear. I needed to know for sure. The four stops before Paddington are Chippenham, Swindon, Didcot Parkway and Reading. At each, more passengers squeeze on board. Not many leave. Whenever we stopped, I stepped briefly on to the platform and looked for the flash of yellow leaving the train two carriages ahead. No-show was fine with me, so I climbed aboard again each time and scythed a way back to my seat.

Ten minutes from Paddington, I got up and walked through the carriages as far as the one Olympia was in. I needed to be close behind her when up to a thousand passengers got off and massed at the ticket barrier.

Bad moment. She'd gone.

I had a sight line of all the seats. No yellow turban showed above a headrest anywhere.

Philip Marlowe never panicked in a situation like this

and neither did yours truly. This cool dude knew she hadn't left the train. She had to be doing what savvy commuters do: moving to the front to be ahead of most of the others when she got off.

How wrong I was.

The toilet door at the end of the carriage slid open and who do you think stepped out? I should have known a smart dame like Olympia would refresh her make-up before we reached the terminus.

Now I *did* come close to panic. She was facing me no more than fifteen yards away.

My sharp left-turn would have made a drill sergeant's day. A bunch of people had collected near a set of doors and I used them as cover, nudging so close to two large women that they stopped their chat and eyeballed me like I was a groper.

Olympia hadn't spotted me. She was busy keeping her balance in the swaying train and looking for her seat. I was one more passenger, no more.

Safe again. Even so, I kept my hand against my face as if I was suffering a migraine.

Official announcement: 'The train is now approaching Paddington and the time is 10.05. Please remember to take all your personal belongings with you. The doors will not open until the train has stopped. Please be careful as you alight.'

Unspoken announcement for private eyes: 'Pull your hat as far down as you can. Get within fifteen yards of the mark and hold that distance at all times, but use other people as cover. Keep alert in case she stops or looks round. And don't forget to have your ticket ready to use at the barrier.'

The brakes squealed. The doors opened. The keenos with their noses against the doors stepped out, followed closely by Olympia and me. Then we were in the thick of it, almost carried along. Impossible to hold the fifteen yards.

Thank Christ for that yellow turban.

Through the ticket barrier and on to the main concourse, busy as always, squeaky clean under its glass canopy roof.

Question: would she join the taxi queue?

Answer: no, she beelined for the tube. Helpful, because I didn't want a 'follow that cab' situation. Unhelpful, because you can't use your mobile in the tunnels except bits of the Jubilee Line with the new 4G coverage. My tracker wouldn't track.

This lady was a quick mover, even in heels you could have mistaken for the stalks of fresh-cut tulips. She didn't just stand to the right and ride the moving stairs. She stepped down with the people in a hurry, making me ever more certain she was keeping an appointment. Down in the underground she made for the Bakerloo line with me on an invisible tow rope. At times I needed to jog to keep up. But it was action. Hell, I told myself, I'm chasing a beautiful dame. I could be Travis McGee tracking a broad through the New York subway.

Was it too much to hope she was leading me to Seppy? Could it be as simple as that? I'd been patient. I'd lost sleep. I deserved the payoff, didn't I?

She picked the southbound line, heading through central London. Okay with me, babe.

Enough people stood on the platform for me to stay close and not be noticed. Strange how helpless I felt without a phone signal. Keeping her in sight was essential down here. To any out-of-town guy, the Underground is enemy territory, the soundscape so different, the hum of approaching trains mounting to a roar, the sizzle of sparks and the shriek of brakes.

The trains come every three minutes on the Bakerloo line. She boarded the next to arrive and picked the row of seats near the exit. Two seats opposite her were vacant. I didn't make that mistake. Unless you have something to read, the only thing to do is stare at the people facing you. I found a seat farther along the carriage on the same side she was. After that, it was a matter of staying alert. Not many left the train at Edgware Road or Marylebone. Baker Street was a popular stop that earned a brotherly nod from me to the wall tiles depicting its most famous resident. Regent Street came next, and then Oxford Circus, and the game was afoot and so was Olympia. I made it to the doors just before the next set of passengers streamed in.

Troubling thought. Oxford bloody Circus. Was this just a shopping trip?

So here we were, riding the escalator up, passing through the barrier, taking the steps, blinking in the sunlight and being shunted willy-nilly up Oxford Street by the press of shoppers and tourists. But was this the direction we wanted?

Like me, Olympia had her phone out, checking our location. You know where you are, sweetheart, but where are you going?

Evidently she had it right. Even so, chunks of my confidence eroded with each step. Was Oxford Street the place Seppy would choose to meet his daughter's friend? I couldn't see it. All I could see was a beautiful black dame striding out as boldly as a suffragette on her way to throw eggs at the prime minister.

In no time at all she turned left.

New Bond Street, for crying out loud.

I crumbled to dust. Shouldn't I have known all along that this fashionista was hellbent on visiting the most expensive shopping street in Europe? Will I ever understand the mindset of a woman?

I was ready to call time and slink back to Bath a wiser and poorer man. But I noticed she didn't even glance through the windows of Fenwick, Dolce & Gabbana and Armani. She marched on, unmoved.

Increasingly, we were passing ultra-posh shops with foreign-sounding names and banners hanging over the entrances. The windows were starting to show one or two pictures in gilt frames displayed on small easels. I'm no more a connoisseur than your average PI, so forgive me if I say it dawned on me only when we came to an awning stretched across the pavement with the name Sotheby's written on it that we'd come to the centre of the capital's art market, stuffed with auction houses and galleries.

My sunken spirits soared again. Seppy had talked about the find of a lifetime. If it was art, we'd come to the place he'd look for a buyer. You could go bail on that.

High on this big idea, I didn't notice Olympia had stopped walking and was stock still in the centre of the pavement. When you're trailing someone all day, it's easy to be lulled into thinking you're just an observer, not part of the action. I found myself so close behind that if I'd reached forward I could have grabbed the yellow turban. I came to my senses in the nick of time, veered right and darted behind some people who were also standing still and staring ahead.

Like they were playing the party game of statues.

I checked right and left and others were doing the same, unsure what was going on. Nothing I could see was going on.

Spooky.

Then, forty yards ahead, I saw the reason. A horse-drawn

hearse was waiting at the roadside. Four sleek black horses with plumes on their heads. Two guys in top hats and long black coats.

You don't walk past a solemn scene like that without some show of respect, which was why everyone had stopped.

And presently a white coffin covered in flowers was carried out of one of the galleries. And so was a wreath arrangement of white carnations that formed the name CARLA.

A funeral, New Bond Street style.

The coffin was loaded into the glass-sided hearse by guys in frock coats overseen by the head honcho, a blonde woman in plumed topper and all the gear and holding a silver-topped cane. She and her team formed the front of a procession. Behind were two black limos for the mourners. Some private cars as well.

People were leaning out of upstairs windows to watch this silent show.

The cortège moved off slowly, and the wait was over for us bystanders. I looked towards Olympia expecting her to rejoin the flow, but she seemed in two minds, first glancing back at the hearse and then forward to the gallery the coffin had been collected from. Then she spoke to a man in a dark suit who had stepped outside to see the hearse leave and was on his way back into the gallery he worked in. I wished I could lip-read. The guy did most of the talking while Olympia listened, shook her head and pressed her fingers to her mouth. To my eye, this was more than a polite show of sympathy. She was upset at what she was hearing.

The man finished answering her questions and returned to his shop. Still Olympia was undecided what to do next. She took out her phone as if that might have the answer. Looking for cover, I backed a short way into a gallery

137

entrance and was immediately approached by a security guard.

Instead of asking what the fuck a lowlife like me was doing in their doorway, he said, 'Can I be of assistance, sir?' In Mayfair even the doormen talk as if they went through Eton and Oxford.

Quick off the mark as always, I said, 'I'm just getting myself together. Upsetting sight, a funeral.'

'True,' he said, giving nothing in return.

'Who was Carla?' I asked him. 'She was obviously much respected round here.'

'A lady well known in the art world,' he forced himself to say.

'Seller or buyer?'

'Neither.'

'Artist?'

He shook his head.

'Model?'

Now he rolled his eyes. He'd heard more than enough dumb questions.

I made one last try. 'If she didn't paint, sell, buy or model, how did she get to be well known?'

'If I tell you, sir, I'll require you to move on,' he said. 'One of the rules of my job is that you don't get into long conversations.'

'Okay, it's a promise.'

'She was the best conservator in London.'

I played the words over and didn't understand them. 'She was what?'

'You heard the first time and that's all you're getting, my friend. On your way now.'

I wouldn't get any more out of that tosspot if I stayed all day, so I stepped outside.

And did my nut.

Olympia was gone. In that short interval she'd quit the scene.

What would Lew Archer do at this juncture? In his day, electronic surveillance was limited to the CIA and the Russkis. Private eyes had to wait a few more years. Lew used brain-fag and boot-leather. Me, I took the phone from my pocket.

Up came the street map and the arrow told me she was heading back the way we'd come. Mission aborted? If so, I couldn't think why.

I stepped out sharply, knowing those long legs of hers moved at a fair lick. Didn't need to keep my head down while she wasn't in sight. Smartphone in hand, I kept checking her position and dodging the shoppers coming towards me.

She reached Oxford Street when I was crossing Brook Street, all of two hundred yards behind. She was going like an urban fox.

Then the little arrow stopped.

What was she up to now? Hailing a taxi? Waiting for a bus?

I started running.

When I reached the junction with Oxford Street the cursor still hadn't shifted, but Olympia wasn't in sight. My first thought was troubling: Oxford Street is notorious for bag-snatching. Someone had nicked her handbag, removed any cash she had and dumped the purse in the gutter.

Second thought, not just troubling, but alarming: she'd found the bug in her purse and got rid of it herself.

I stepped to the pavement edge and looked along. Nothing to be seen in the gutter except screwed-up leaflets about sales that are thrust at you all the way along Oxford Street.

The idea of sales and shopping revived an earlier theory. The GPS system I was using isn't pinpoint. It's accurate to about twenty metres. Possibly I was right and she'd come to London to shop. I was standing outside the flagship branch of Next, the fashion chain, where a freelance journalist like Olympia would find the prices easier on her budget than the Bond Street boutiques. She'd had her fix of window-shopping and now she was buying. Was that it?

If so, it was no help to me.

I could see the store was huge inside, so I didn't go in. It's on the corner of Bond Street and Oxford Street, with entrances from both sides. I posted myself where I thought I could get a view of both. Some chance.

She came from behind, tapped me on the shoulder and said, 'What the fuck are you doing here, Johnny?'

'Olympia?' I died inside, my cover blown. I dug deep for something to say and all I could dredge up was this corny old line: 'Of all the gin joints in all the world, she walks into mine.'

She was entitled to look confused. 'I don't follow you.'

I could have quipped, 'But I followed you.' I didn't. I do have a head on my shoulders. I collected my thoughts enough to say, 'I'm on an enquiry. How about you?'

She frowned.

This was when I noticed she'd changed her outfit. She was now entirely in black: dress, coat, tights and shoes. Even the large Next bag she was carrying was black. It must have contained her yellow outfit. She said, 'I'm on my way to a funeral.'

'Anyone I know?'

'I doubt it. Her name was Carla.'

My brain buzzed like a bee in a foxglove. 'I saw a hearse go by with a flower arrangement spelling that name.'

'Horse-drawn?'

'Yes.'

'That will have been her cortège.'

'If it was, you're late.'

'I'm not going to the service,' she said.

You could have fooled me, dressed like that, I thought, but I had the sense to keep my mouth shut.

'I'm planning to show up for the refreshments at the Royal Academy. I just bought these clothes. I didn't know she'd died until I saw the hearse. It came as a massive shock. When I'd got my head round that, I realised what I was wearing was unsuitable.'

'Was she a close friend?'

'No. We've never met. One of Seppy's contacts.'

I played my trump card, the only one I had. 'And the best conservator in London.'

The big eyes climbed all over me. 'You know about Carla Denison?'

'She's why I'm here,' I bluffed. 'Like you, I didn't know she was dead. Now I'm thinking I should crash the wake as well.'

'Dressed like that?' The eyes made another slow tour. 'Don't you think you should do what I did and find something suitable to wear?'

She was right. An artist might get away with a funky get-up, but I'm not an artist and can't talk like one. I wouldn't know a Pissarro from a Jimmy Riddle. A black tie was sensible.

'There's a men's department in Next,' Olympia said.

More outlay. In truth, I couldn't see myself marching into the Royal Academy dressed like I was. But I was quietly chuffed that Olympia was acting friendly again and willing to let me tag along. We'd be more plausible as a pair.

141

I couldn't stretch to a new suit, so Olympia suggested a waistcoat in a purple and grey check, black trousers, white shirt and grey cravat. As my fashion guru, she said black ties were only for undertakers and old men. I changed into the new gear and stuffed my other things into a big plastic carrier like the one Olympia had. The bill hadn't broken the bank.

She'd learned that the funeral was out at Golders Green – quite a stretch for those horses. It meant we had time in hand before the rave-up at the Royal Academy. I suggested a drink and Olympia shook her head and said coffee. There would be plenty to drink at the RA.

In the Hanover Square Starbucks, she told me more. Back in Bath, she'd gone through Seppy's calendar noting all the appointments since the start of the year. One of them, last month, was with Carla Denison. The name was one of fifty-odd she needed to investigate. But when Olympia had looked among the Ds in the Rolodex, Carla wasn't there. Just a fleeting contact, she had decided, and moved on to other names. Some were so well known to Seppy that he'd written the first names only on the calendar, requiring hours of work with the Rolodex, only to find that they were his barber, his dentist and a cleaning woman. Driven near to despair, she'd returned finally to Carla Denison and googled the name. Up had come any number of hits showing Carla was well known in the art world as a restorer of paintings.

'And conservator,' I joined in, not missing another chance to buff up my one and only credential.

'Well, yes,' Olympia said. 'Seppy wrote a time beside her name that made me think he must have made an appointment, so I phoned Carla and got through to her and asked if she remembered him and she did, but she wouldn't tell

142

me anything about the reason for the meeting even when I said he'd gone missing and his daughter was critically ill in hospital.'

'Fair enough. You were just a voice at the end of a phone line.'

'Exactly, which was why I asked to meet her. She said she couldn't deal with anything right then because she was on a ceiling.'

'I'll need time to think about that.'

'Yes, it puzzled me until she said something about a scaffold tower.'

'Decorating?'

She smiled. 'In a way, but conservation describes it better. Restoring a painted ceiling in a church.'

'Okay. And you got in touch again and explained what you were on about?'

'Only superficially. I thought it best to meet her in person. I wanted every detail and photographs if possible. That's my training as a journalist.'

'Restorers keep a record of their work,' I said.

'Exactly.'

'Where did she work when she wasn't on the ceiling?'

'New Bond Street. She had a studio above one of the galleries on the same side as Sotheby's.'

'That's where I saw the hearse.'

Her voice shook and she rubbed her arms as if the air conditioning needed turning down. 'At the very time we were due to meet, she was being driven to her funeral.'

'Spooky,' I said.

We both stayed silent for a while.

Then she asked the question I'd seen coming. 'I'm curious to know how you found out about Carla.'

Tough one, even so.

'Detective work,' I said. 'Pursuing enquiries.'

'Because I thought Ruby and I were the only people in Bath apart from Seppy who knew about the painting.'

Catch that, Johnny. The find of a lifetime is a painting.

I put on a wise expression and spoke like an archbishop. 'Never underestimate the grapevine.' And while that piece of hokum was sinking in, I switched the questioning back to her. 'How did Seppy come across the painting? There was a previous owner, obviously.'

'He found it in a car-boot sale.'

'I've heard stories like that before and never believed them.'

'The seller didn't know it was valuable, but Seppy was smart enough to snap it up.'

'Is he an art expert?'

'He's been in the trade long enough to know a good thing when he sees it. Ruby told me he was treating it like a state secret until he was certain it was the genuine article.'

'He would,' I said.

She was back to her main gripe. 'So how did you get to know so much?'

By listening to you, babe, I thought. I took this as my chance to chuck her a red herring.

'In the art world everything has to have a pedigree.'

'Provenance,' Olympia said. 'So?'

'Seppy needed to go back to that car-boot salesman and discover all he could about the previous history of the painting.'

'The guy who sold it to him. Is that how the story leaked?'

'It's one possibility. Another is that Seppy will have wanted to get the picture to an expert to give it the green light as the real thing and not a forgery. People blab. A find like that won't stay secret for long. But I don't need to tell you this.'

She pushed her coffee aside and leaned across the table. 'Quit flannelling, Johnny. Who told you about Carla?'

'Sorry,' I said. 'Can't divulge sources.'

'Selfish prick.' But she smiled as she spoke, a smile that said she, too, wasn't telling everything she knew.

And that was the meat of our conversation. Soon after, we returned to Bond Street and took the short walk south to the Royal Academy to find out how the art world paid its last respects to Carla Denison.

15

John Leaman had brought in two display boards that normally stood in the foyer of Concorde House covered in police posters about knife crime and weapons amnesties. They were now filled with forty-eight freshly printed A4 sheets of abstract art. You might think the CID team would have welcomed some colour in the incident room, but not everyone was pleased.

'We're going to need more cartridges for the printer,' Keith Halliwell said.

'Lighten up,' Ingeborg Smith said. 'He's bringing some art into our lives.'

'Call that art?'

'Actually,' Leaman said, 'it's abstract expressionism.' There was no answer to that, so he went on, 'And after searching the internet for these, I'm starting to take an interest.'

'What's it for?' Paul Gilbert asked.

'I'll leave the boss to explain.'

A briefing was scheduled for 9.30. Diamond arrived early carrying an A2-sized drawing board and folding easel. Claude, the forensic photographer, had supplied an even bigger enlargement of the picture that had become the main focus of the investigation. A mere detail from the photo of the Bickerstaffs and their wares, it was now almost the size of the board it was clipped to. He stood the new exhibit in front of Leaman's art show.

'Can everyone see this?'

Nobody complained.

'Seppy Hubbard called it the find of a lifetime. With your help, I intend to find out why.'

'Because he was two sandwiches short of a picnic,' Halliwell said without a hint of a smile. This usually amiable man was in a foul mood this morning.

'You know better than that, Keith,' Diamond said. 'He's not stupid. He manages a shop on his own and he's well known in the trade.'

'So how could a dog's dinner like this be valuable? Do you seriously think it's by a famous artist?'

'That's what I want to explore,' Diamond said, surprised by the force of his deputy's reaction, 'and as culture isn't our strong point in CID I asked John to do some research. The floor is yours, professor.'

Brimming over with importance, Leaman stepped up and first took a long look at Halliwell, almost daring him to interrupt. 'When I started this I kept an open mind and I recommend you all do the same. The painting is an abstract, obviously, unusually free in style even by abstract standards. If you look closely, you can see the artist used several different techniques – brushstrokes, smearing, flicking and dropping paint on the canvas. Lots of paint. From what I can tell from the photo, the surface is covered thickly in places as if it was squeezed from the tube. And there's a thumbprint in the corner rather than a signature.'

'Which could be a clincher,' Diamond said.

'So I looked for well-known artists whose work is similar,' Leaman said, 'and the results are pinned up.'

'Are they, like, a group?' Gilbert asked.

147

'Roughly speaking, yes. They're known as action painters.'

'Call them what you like,' Halliwell said. 'None of it is art.'

'The best of it sells for millions.'

'Doesn't mean it's any good. How can you tell what's best when they're all the same?'

'Let him speak, Keith,' Diamond said. 'Some of us agree with you, but there must be more in this than you can see at first glance, which is why I asked John to look into it.'

'The most famous action painter was Jackson Pollock,' Leaman motored on, undaunted. 'You can see one of his on the right-hand board, top left. I don't think ours is a Pollock, but he made action painting famous, pouring and splashing household paint on to huge canvases on the floor of his studio. There's a film clip of him riding a bike over a canvas while dripping paint from a bucket. Some smart journalist called him Jack the Dripper.'

Ingeborg clapped, pleased of a chance to break the tension. 'Love it.'

'See what I mean?' Halliwell said, red-faced. He wasn't backing off.

Leaman smiled in a superior way. 'Not everyone shares your opinion. One of his sold for a hundred and forty million dollars in 2006. At the time, it was the highest price ever paid for any painting.'

'Do we have it here?' Diamond asked. 'As a printout, I mean.'

'The one I pointed to. It's called *Number 5, 1948*. And there's a story about it. After the picture was sold privately to a wealthy Filipino and they were packing it up to ship it, a chunk of paint fell off. They told the artist and he said he'd patch it up and the owner would never know. But when it arrived, there was still a smear the new owner spotted, so Pollock offered to make it good. He did more than that. He actually repainted the entire picture, saying, "He won't know the difference. No one knows how to look at my paintings."'

'I can believe that much,' Halliwell muttered.

'Anyway, the owner was satisfied, even though it wasn't the picture he bought.'

'Crazy,' Halliwell said.

'You think that's crazy?' Leaman went on, enjoying himself. 'Wait till you hear this. An action painting called *Interchange*, by another guy, Willem de Kooning, raised the world-record price to three hundred million. It was only bettered when a Leonardo da Vinci came on the market.'

'When was this?'

'The sale? 2015.'

'I mean when did he paint it?'

'1955. Action painting peaked in America in the 1940s and '50s. People call it modern art, but it's not all that modern.'

Ingeborg said, 'Are we seriously suggesting that a painting by one of these top-selling guys turned up in a car-boot sale in Southwick?'

'They're the biggest names, but there are others,' Leaman said. 'Clyfford Still, Franz Kline, Robert Miskines.' He pointed to examples on the boards. 'An undiscovered work by any of them would fetch a hefty price at auction.'

'Why?'

'Interesting question. The art market is strange. Some of the top work is sold to private collectors who don't want anyone to know who they are, so it disappears. The Jackson Pollock I was talking about has vanished from the scene. There weren't all that many of his paintings to start with, so if they come on sale they fetch astronomical prices.'

Ingeborg was checking details on her smartphone. 'There's a problem here. The A4 printouts on your boards give no idea of size. Most of the work you're talking about was done on a big scale. The Jackson Pollock was 2.44 metres by 1.22 and the de Kooning was 2 metres by 1.75.'

'What's that in old money?' Diamond asked.

'Eight feet by four, and six feet seven by five feet nine. The one Seppy bought was not much bigger than a place mat.'

'So it has a rarity value as well,' Leaman said.

Ingeborg laughed. 'Nice try. Sorry, I don't buy it.'

'You couldn't afford it.'

But she'd made a telling point and the room fell silent.

This was when Diamond noticed an extra face at the back of the room, female, well made up, certainly no one from CID. He was about to challenge her, but just in time he saw who it was, and was forced to concede she had a right to be there.

Lady Bede.

Remarkable how she had the knack of showing up at critical moments. He couldn't object. Officially she was shadowing the investigation. But why? Had anyone questioned her motives? She professed to be starry-eyed about police work. There was more to it than that, he was certain. Maybe someone should be shadowing *her*.

'Getting back to your point about car-boot sales,' Leaman said, needing to take centre stage again, 'I watch the *Antiques Roadshow* every Sunday and there's nearly always something found in a charity shop or a car-boot sale that turns out to be worth a mint of money.'

'Yes, and the owner always insists he wouldn't dream of selling it.'

Diamond steered the meeting back to Seppy's painting.

'We know this has been in Bath at least eighty years and probably longer. An old lady in Bennett Street owned it until she died about thirty years ago. It was put on sale and someone bought it because he liked the frame.'

Attention switched to the frame shown in the photo, about two inches wide, dark blue and decorated with what looked like curved, interlinked tendrils of vine.

'I was going to say it's a pretty frame,' Ingeborg said. 'Is that art nouveau?'

'Does it matter what it's called?' someone said. Tempers were getting frayed.

'It's all wrong for the picture,' Leaman said, grabbing the chance to take over again. 'Far too busy. You don't need a frame for an action painting. Let the image make its own statement.'

'Can it speak, then?' Gilbert said. 'No wonder it's valuable.'

'Can't you people be serious for a moment?' Leaman said. If the asides went on much longer, he'd get as bitter as Halliwell.

In reality, no one was comfortable. Abstract art was way outside their territory and humour was their way of dealing with it.

Diamond called his squad to order. 'Thanks, John. This is a good point to break off and bring you all to the front for a closer look. See if you can spot similarities with any of the paintings on display. The style, the colour, the brushwork. None of us are experts and we don't need to be. This is about observation, which is what we do. John has numbered all the prints and I'll be interested to see if there's any agreement.'

During the general movement to the front, Keith Halliwell went over to Diamond. 'If it's okay with you, guv,

I'll step outside for some fresh air. I'm a mud-slinger here, no use at all.'

'I'll join you presently. Let's go for a coffee.'

First, he wanted to catch Lady Bede before she slipped out of the room. Her appearances at critical times were distracting him when he ought to be one hundred per cent on the job. She was already making for the door. He called her name and several faces turned to see who this Virginia was.

She stopped at the end of the room and flashed her charm-the-birds-out-of-the-trees smile.

'Spotted you a couple of times recently,' he said when he caught up with her. 'In a forensic suit at the scene of the shooting in Gravel Lane and out at the car-boot sale. You're as good as your word, merging with the scene.'

'I'll take that as a compliment, Peter.'

'And now you turn up here for John Leaman's presentation. You must be getting inside information to be on the spot so fast. Do you mind telling me who your source is?'

'I keep my ear to the ground.'

'No, Virginia, someone tips you off.'

'Does that bother you? We're on the same side.'

'I'm trained to be security conscious, that's all.'

'And I'm the soul of discretion.'

'You're not going to say?'

'Tell you what. Why don't you take up my offer of a drink and whatever with me at home? You'll find me more amenable on home territory. I must dash, Peter. My life isn't all about Bath police.'

She mouthed a playful kiss and went through the door.

Over coffee in the Provenist, Diamond switched his attention to Keith Halliwell. He was troubled to see his normally unflappable deputy in such a state. 'Feeling calmer now?'

'I'll be okay, thanks. I shouldn't have sounded off at Leaman like I did. That was out of order.'

'I'm sure there was a reason.'

'A raw nerve.'

'Want to tell me about it?'

Halliwell seemed reluctant. He hesitated.

'Get it off your chest.'

'I'm not looking for sympathy, guv. Spare me that, please.'

Diamond shrugged. 'Fine.'

But it became clear that Halliwell was ready to say more. 'I don't know if I ever told you about my dad.'

'No.'

'He worked at a racing stable on the Marlborough Downs when I was growing up.'

'A jockey?'

'Stable lad. Groom is the posh word, but it's mucking out, whatever name you give to it.'

'There's more to it than that.'

'Okay, looking after the feed and grooming the beasts. He was one of those people who wanted to work with horses and he joked that it gave him the chance to meet girls because most of the stable lads were lasses. If you're wondering what my mother had to say about that, she'd long since died. I don't remember much about her.'

'So your dad brought you up?'

'He was a good father, allowing that not much money was coming in. There was even less when he was forced to retire early after getting kicked by one of the horses. His knee was smashed and he lost all sensation below it. They thought about an amputation and decided against it. His left leg was useless after that and he couldn't do the work. He wore a metal brace that allowed him to stand and move about stiffly, but he was restricted. He went on the dole, as he called it.'

'How old were you when this happened?'

'Seventeen. I was already training for the police.'

'Didn't the stables help him out financially?'

'I think there was a one-off payment, but it didn't amount to much. He supplemented his income by painting. He'd always had a talent for sketching. His speciality was horse pictures and he could sell them at local exhibitions and through a shop in Marlborough for about a hundred after he paid for the framing and the commission. I expect I'm biased, but I thought they were wonderful. He'd visit the stables and they let him sit there with his sketchbook. He did a few on commission for owners because he was so good he could catch the likeness of each horse as an individual.'

'Were these watercolours?'

'All sorts, but the oils sold best. He was given an exhibition in the Marlborough shop and sold five and that was a big deal. I wasn't living at home then. I visited when I got time off. He told me his ambition was to get one accepted by the Royal Academy for their summer exhibition. It means a lot in the art world.'

'Did he have a go?'

'Plenty of goes. He'd been trying for some years before he told me about it. In this computer age you can send them an image online for the first round of selection, but in his day it meant lugging the picture up to London yourself, which was no easy job for a handicapped man travelling by train with a large framed painting, and then going back to collect the damn thing when it didn't get selected. I pitied him when I heard. Rejection many times over is hard to take.'

'But he kept trying?'

'At least four years' running. Maybe more. Some well-meaning friend told him his style was behind the times.

He'd do better with a cubist version of a horse reduced to geometrical shapes. But he couldn't change. We talked about it once. He had an article from a weekend colour magazine showing some of the top picks for that year's summer exhibition and there was a whole page of what I might call patterns if I was generous. To a twenty-year-old plod, which was what I was, they weren't even nice patterns. They were daubs, not much different from the stuff Leaman showed us. Dad said he couldn't get his head around modern art. He wasn't repelled by it, like I am, and he didn't hold any grudge against the artists, but he still believed there ought to be recognition for painters who caught reality and put it on canvas with a personal touch better than any photograph.'

'He's not alone thinking that, Keith.'

'I know.'

'The Royal Academy do take some work you and I would consider normal, don't they?'

'To tell you the truth, I don't know and I don't care any more and here's the reason.' He clasped his hands under his chin and the knuckles were white. 'This is just between you and me, guv.'

'We agreed.'

'In the fourth year into my police career, I had a job that took me close to Dad's village and I decided to stop off and see him afterwards. When I got to the cottage there was no answer at the door. I knew he kept a spare key in the shed, so I found it and let myself in, thinking he was out and at least I'd make myself a coffee before going back to my flat in Swindon. I was wrong about him being out. Dad was there. He was in the hallway facing me, hanging from the banisters. He'd been dead at least two days.'

'Keith, that's dreadful.'

155

'He left no note. The only thing I found was on the kitchen table, a letter from the Royal Academy saying – the words still burn in my memory – "The members of the summer exhibition committee regret they will not be able to include your work." And before you say another word, guv, we agreed no sympathy, right?'

'All right,' Diamond said, and he didn't speak for some while. 'Let's say I understand where you're coming from.' But he *did* sympathise. He ached with pity for his colleague of more than twenty years. He thought of the many testing situations Halliwell would have faced as a young policeman, including suicides. Not once had this loyal colleague ever backed off from dealing with death. The trauma of his father's suicide had never before been spoken about. For years, he'd been the go-to man for attending autopsies, a duty Diamond shrank from and delegated.

The petulance in the incident room was nothing compared to the hellish discovery this quiet, dependable man had kept to himself for so long. And the hurt that could never be forgotten.

They paid their bill and left.

Back in the Corn Market no consensus had emerged except that the picture was unlikely to be by Pollock or de Kooning. A handful of other artists on display had been listed as possible, but without any conviction. Two or three votes for one little-known painter didn't amount to the breakthrough that was so desired.

Diamond thanked Leaman for all the research and said he'd take note. Then he sent his focus group back to their desks to focus on other things.

Towards the end of the morning, while he was still troubled by memories of the treatment he'd given Halliwell over all the years, he heard a female voice asking for a word with him. DC Jean Sharp was standing by his desk, hands clasped in front of her. She looked as nervous as a prisoner when the jury returns.

He told her to pull up a chair. 'I'm listening.'

'It's about the painting, sir.'

'Before you say anything else, we don't do "sirs" here. Remember? What about the painting?'

'I couldn't match it up with any of the pictures on the board.'

'That's okay, you're not alone,' he said. 'We all failed that test.'

'The more I looked at it, the more I thought it may not be a picture at all.'

'What?' He sat forward. 'How do you make that out?'

'I know it's in a frame, but that could have been fitted by someone who thought it was a picture when it wasn't.'

'You're losing me, Jean.'

'The paint marks are so random and messy . . .'

'I'm with you there.'

'. . . that they look as if the painter was using the canvas as a palette.'

'That's a new angle.' He scratched his head. 'A palette? It's small enough to hold in your hand, I give you that. We were looking at an enlargement.'

'A lot of the marks could have been made by a palette knife.'

'Let's not jump ahead of ourselves here. Some painters use the knife to paint with, don't they?'

'But I think the artist was mixing colours.'

'How can anyone tell?'

'There are lumps of paint squeezed from the tube and worked with the knife in a criss-cross motion.'

157

'I must take another look.'

She took that as encouragement and said with more verve, 'The thing that really makes me wonder is the thumb print in the corner. If you look closely, there are faint traces of more thumb prints around the same area. That's where the artist would have held the canvas in his free hand while he used it as a palette, mixing colours and dipping the brush into them to use on his real painting.'

He was warming to this theory. 'You say there's more than one thumb print? I didn't notice any others.'

'Very faint. I shone my phone on that corner. It would be easier if we had the real thing rather than a photo, of course.'

'If we had the real thing we'd know a whole lot more,' he said and then, having interrupted her flow, did his best to restore confidence. 'I'm glad you mentioned this. I know what you're getting at. He'd grip the framework underneath with his fingers and only his thumb would show on the canvas.' He got up from his chair. 'I'm going to check. Come and show me.'

The easel and its subject still stood in the centre of the room beside the boards with John Leaman's display of prints, but was no longer a focus of everyone's attention. He carried it to a place where the light was better. With the evidence in front of him, he soon saw that Jean Sharp's suggestion made some sense. Not only were there indications of more marks made by a thumb, the moon craters, as he thought of them, could well be paint squeezed from the tube and mixed with a knife to get the colour the artist needed.

'It would be good to study it through a magnifying glass,' Jean Sharp said.

'We wouldn't have one here. They went out with Sherlock Holmes. What would that tell us?'

'You can't see enough with the naked eye. I'd like a closer look at the individual marks. The flat ones made by the knife seem to be mostly crosswise compared to the brush marks which all go upwards, away from the thumb. Under a strong lens you'd probably see small deposits of extra paint at the top where the brush was lifted off.'

'You're quite an expert.'

She gave a shy smile. 'I wouldn't say that, guv. I do a bit as a hobby.'

'Using oils?'

'Yes.'

'And I bet you have a proper palette?'

'Yes, and I sometimes wipe off the excess paint on an old canvas.'

He leaned so close to the easel that his nose was within inches of the photograph.

She asked, 'What do you think, guv?'

He took a step back and turned to face her. 'What do I think? I think you've cracked it.'

She deserved a hug, but you don't do that and she'd jump out of her skin if he tried. His estimation of Jean Sharp had shot up. He understood the effort this had been for a shy young officer quite new in the team, approaching her peppery boss with an idea he could have rejected, or ridiculed. He wanted to reach out with appreciative words, but he'd always found displays of emotion difficult. In the end, he fell short. He settled for the brusque statement he'd just made.

In mitigation, he was conflicted, his enthusiasm undermined by the human problem her discovery inevitably caused. One person's triumph was another's disaster.

He found more words, but they were all about somebody else. 'Don't say anything yet to John Leaman. He's invested so much of himself in this it could tip him over the edge.'

16

A local hobby shop lent them a saucer-sized hands-free magnifier on a stand with built-in LED lights. Jean Sharp had been right. The photo yielded more. If the artist had held the canvas by one corner to use as a palette, as she was suggesting, the natural direction of most brush-strokes would be upwards, away from the thumb, and so it proved. The 'craters' were in the other corners and showed signs of being flattened with the blade of a palette knife. Where the paint had run a little, the movement was all towards the bottom corner.

'I don't need any more persuading,' Ingeborg said after seeing it. 'Are you going to break it to John?'

'I'm trying to break it to myself,' Diamond said. He felt shot to bits.

'Someone should tell him, guv.'

'I will in a sec.'

'He'll take it badly. He was up all night putting his lecture together.'

'Don't keep on,' he snapped. 'I heard you the first time.' And immediately wished he hadn't spoken. Ingeborg had said nothing that deserved the rebuke. She was rightly concerned about Leaman – a sentiment rare in the team. He had a moral duty to speak to Leaman before the others were told and tore the poor guy to shreds. He muttered the nearest thing to an apology to Ingeborg he could concoct. 'You're right, of course. I'll get this out of the way now. It matters.'

Ingeborg shrugged and said nothing.

He crossed to where Leaman was at his computer making a search for action painters he might have missed on the first trawl. Even by the standards of an obsessive-compulsive, the man had overworked. A cloud of desperation hovered over his desk. Handled badly, this revelation could damage his mental health.

Trying to radiate calm, Diamond said he had something of interest to pass on.

The fingers lifted from the keyboard. The red-lidded eyes were wide in expectation.

In as gentle a way as he could, Diamond set out the reasoning, explaining each element in the thinking: the several thumbprints, the marks made by brush and palette knife, the concentrations of pigment and the downward creep of the excess paint.

Leaman listened without reaction except a slight rocking movement. Towards the end, when it became obvious where this was going, his eyes squeezed shut. Finally he opened them, sat back, loosened his tie, eased the collar away from his neck and gave Diamond the biggest shock of the day, by smiling. 'Now I understand.'

'You do?'

'This is such a relief, guv. It makes complete sense to me. I was up a blind alley here, looking for more action painters.'

'Aren't there any?'

'No big hitters. Apart from Pollock and de Kooning, there aren't many you could call bankable. Anyway, none of their styles match the marks on Seppy's canvas and now I know

161

why.' Against all expectation, his entire face was freed from stress. He didn't seem at all concerned about being fed to the jackals. The transparent truth of the new explanation disposed of any embarrassment. 'Who was it who spotted this?'

'Jean Sharp.'

'I must thank her. She's saved me hours of extra work.'

'Before you do, take another look with a magnifier like we did. I want to be certain you agree.'

Leaman beetled across the room to check for himself.

Crisis over, it appeared. Leaman's brain functioned through logic. He'd needed to be persuaded that the new theory was based on good observation. Diamond's painstaking explanation had worked.

Across the room, Ingeborg nodded her approval.

Harmony restored for the present, Diamond returned to Ingeborg's desk and thanked her for helping him sidestep another flashpoint. But a bigger problem remained.

'If it was only a canvas used as a palette, why did Seppy believe it was so special?'

'I'm thinking the same thing,' she said. 'Let's face it, we're a bunch of plods who know damn all about art, but he's an antiques expert. He should have known what it was straight away.'

'He did, I expect.'

'But there's no way it can be the find of a lifetime.'

'Unless he can prove it once belonged to a really famous artist by matching the thumbprint to the right person.'

She nodded. 'Just what I was thinking, guv. When I saw that thumbprint, I checked the internet for major artists who have left prints on their work. It can happen, usually by accident, like when they think paint is dry and it isn't. Some really big names. Leonardo da Vinci, Rembrandt and our old buddy, Jackson Pollock.'

'Really? So Seppy could have found Leonardo's palette in a car-boot sale.'

That drew a smile. 'Leonardo is stretching it. Someone more modern might fit.'

'We have the resources to find out. An interesting challenge for forensics.'

'Yes, and they'll say you can't tell anything from a photo.' She slapped the back of her hand. 'It's catching. I'm turning cynical.'

'Don't,' he said. 'We need at least one clear head in this team.' He was trying to put himself in Seppy Hubbard's shoes. 'Where would you start with this? There are so many famous artists.'

'The colours ought to give a clue. An expert will know the pigments favoured by certain painters.'

'Ours aren't all that colourful. Shades of brown mainly. Some blue. That's about all.'

'Seppy will have taken it to an expert, I'm sure. He seemed certain he'd got something special, so he must have had it authenticated.'

'The thumbprint?'

'The paint, the canvas, the wood it was made from. The full deal.'

He shook his head. 'Even if it belonged to some old master, a palette is only a tool of the trade. Is anyone going to pay top dollar for that?'

The question wasn't answered because Diamond's phone sang out. He checked who was calling, gritted his teeth and put it to his ear. Georgina, his boss, said, 'You're needed at the One Stop Shop. Can you get there in the next ten minutes?'

Needed at the One Stop sounded risible and it was. Ever since the Manvers Street nick had been moved out of town, the hole in the wall in the One Stop was the only police presence in Bath. What did they want now, someone to do a stint at the counter while the duty sergeant had a comfort break?

'I'm on a murder case here, ma'am.'

'There's been another drive-by shooting.'

That put a different slant on things.

'Where? The One Stop?'

'Actually, no. A cottage in Limpley Stoke.'

'Shouldn't I be going to Limpley Stoke, then?'

'Don't argue.'

'It's only a suggestion, ma'am. I'm capable of driving out there.'

'A response car is already on its way and so is the scene-of-crime team. The only witness is at the One Stop, waiting to give you his statement.'

'Who is he?'

Georgina hesitated. 'I don't want any of your so-called humour. His name is Lucky.'

'Is anyone hurt?'

'Thankfully no. The gunman missed.'

'Shoots but can't hit.'

'What did you say?'

'This sounds like the gentleman we're trying to nick.'

'I'll tell them you're on your way.'

The One Stop Shop opposite the former police station was the go-to place for a range of council-run services like housing, citizens' advice and Shopmobility. The police counter was manned by a white-shirted woman officer who pointed to the tables opposite where a large black man was holding a bottle of water with both hands and jigging his legs to whatever was playing in his earbuds. His legs were so long that the table was rising and falling with the beat.

Diamond went over, trying to think of a greeting that wasn't cheesy. 'Are you Lucky?' 'You must be Lucky.' Or just, 'Lucky?' It didn't matter because the drumming would have drowned the words. He stood opposite and brandished his ID.

The man switched off, removed the buds and held out a large hand. 'Lucky Andrews.'

'You came in to report a shooting, Mr Andrews? We appreciate that.'

'Doin' my civic duty. And I go by Lucky.'

'What happened, Lucky?'

He sat back, remembering. 'Concerns Olympia.'

'Miss Olympia Ward? Charming young lady.'

'My house guest.'

'You're Lucky in more than one sense,' Diamond said and immediately wished he hadn't.

Lucky was performing a windscreen-wiper motion with his forefinger. 'Don't be making any 'sumptions with me, inspector. House guest I say and house guest she is, house guest and no more. She have the bed, I have the sofa. Separate arrangement, understan'?'

'Got you.'

'So here's what went down. The lady leave my place early today for London. Business meeting, she say. High-powered woman is Miss Olympia. Next thing, she call me from the train.' His voice rose an octave or two. '"Lucky, darling, will you do me a favour and go to the cottage and feed the fish?"'

'She has a fish?'

Lucky found that amusing. 'Two hundred tropicals, man. And seein' as no one has fed them for a couple of days she figures they must be eatin' each other.'

'Can we backtrack a minute? Olympia is your house guest, but she has a cottage of her own?'

'Petunia Cottage, Limpley Stoke, but here's the thing. The lady is scared to be there after some lowlife take a shot at her the other day. True. So she move to my place and want to bring the fish. But it's a five-gallon tank, man. No way. With all the clothes she bring, my van is fuller than a stuffed chicken.'

'I'm with you now,' Diamond said. 'I can picture this. What happened this morning?'

'Okay. So I drive to the cottage and see a moped outside the front door. Visitor, I'm thinkin', but why stop by when Olympia isn't here? I step round to the back and find this sawn-off guy in a black balaclava standin' on a stack of logs tryin' to see in the window.'

'"Sawn-off"?'

'Low rise, man. Knee-high to a gnat.'

'Got it. Go on.'

'What's your business, junior, I think, and that's exactly what I say. No answer. Jumps down and is off round the side. Too damn quick for me.'

'Why is that? You look like a good mover.'

The big man laughed. 'Hey, man, I ain't no Usain Bolt.' He leaned over the side of the chair, lifted his trouser leg and displayed six inches of metal. 'And this thing don't make me no blade runner.'

Colouring up, Diamond said, 'My mistake.'

'Easily done, bro. The 'sumption thing again. I follow quick as my tin pin allow me. Then the shit gets real. I see the dude is back on his scooter. And when I shout somethin', he turn and pull a goddamn piece from his jacket and fire at me. Misses, thank God.'

'How many shots?'

'One was too many, b'lieve me.'

'How close were you?'

'Ten yards.'

'You were lucky.'

'I hear that joke a million times, man.'

'I wasn't joking. Do you think it was a warning shot?'

'Think? I don't think. The weasel pops a cap at me, I thank the Lord and I'm off on my five good toes behind the cottage, heart thumpin', ears ringin'. I can't hear shit and scooter boy is already off up the lane.'

'You said he was short. Did you notice anything else about him?'

'Balaclava with eye holes, black bomber jacket, blue jeans and white trainers.'

Reeled off like that, it sounded a useful description, but it didn't add up to much.

'Do you have any memory of the scooter's number plate?'

Lucky's grin answered that question. It had to be asked.

'What did you think when you saw him at the window? Was he trying to break in?'

'Look that way to me. But he won't have found nothin' unless he was after fish.'

'Did you remember to feed them?'

A depth-charge of a laugh. 'Sure. Those guys had a feast.'

'Are you expecting Olympia back tonight?'

'Hey, I'm not her pop. She do what she want.'

'Did she speak to you about her reason for going to London?'

'What for? We stay out of each other's faces. She have her life and I have mine.'

Diamond didn't prolong the interview.

17

You might be thinking the trail had gone cold now that Carla Denison was dead and unable to tell us about Seppy and where he might have ended up, but Olympia and I had our noses to the ground like bloodhounds, in there sniffing for any remaining traces. We weren't leaving London without finding something.

The hospitality bit of Carla's final shindig was in the Keeper's House at the Royal Academy. 'Keeper' sounds grim, echoes of the workhouse. Trust me, it isn't. The keeper is the top banana in the Royal Academy Schools, and until modern times lived in this grace-and-favour townhouse tucked away in one corner of the courtyard at Burlington House in Piccadilly. And there were extras like a wine cellar in the basement, a models' staircase with private access to the keeper's studio (don't ask) and any number of ginormous rooms hung with world-class art. Whoever put a stop to the perk of living there has a lot to explain to the keepers who came after.

I'm not complaining. The house had now been converted to bars, restaurants, meeting rooms and lounges. Ideal for a funeral feast. Hiring any one of those rooms costs an arm and a leg. Carla must have been a superstar of the art world because the entire building was freed for the evening to host the mourners, if you could call us that. It seemed like all the artists in London and their mates had come to enjoy the free booze and food – or should I say pay their respects?

Olympia and I got in without trouble, swept in by the crush, and dropped our Next bags on a heap of coats, shoes and bags in the hallway. Down a marble staircase we located the basement bar, a quick fix for two thirsty gatecrashers. I can't tell you much about the décor because we barely had elbow room to raise the champagne to our mouths. Real champagne. None of the cheap Prosecco they palm you off with at most weddings and funerals. And the eats weren't peanuts and sausages on sticks. There was caviar served on points of toast. Quails' eggs. Spare ribs with a five-spice sauce. I was hungry. I got stuck in.

We needn't have bothered about the dress code. I was jammed against a woman in a pink feather boa and not much else. Over Olympia's shoulder I could see a bright green hairdo back-combed and held in place with dragonfly hairclips studded with pulsing LED lights. *At a funeral?*

Early on, we stood together wolfing the food and drink. I soon sussed that the basement bar wasn't the place to pick up information. All the talk around us was gossip competing with the music (anything but funereal) and damn all about Carla. As if this was just another jolly, they yak-yak-yakked about recent parties they'd enjoyed, what they'd snorted and smoked and who they'd slept with. Not knowing any of the names made it boring.

'Shall we move upstairs?'

'I can't think of anything I'd like more,' Olympia shouted back. 'Some lech keeps grabbing my bum and I can't turn round and clout him.'

I bulldozed a route to the stairs. Getting up them was difficult because people were sitting on every step. We followed a waiter with an empty tray who moved like a ferret through a warren.

The ground floor was a mite less crazy. We found ourselves in a large clubroom with armchairs and sofas bagged by wrinkly old gits who must have got there before dawn. Most of the standing space was taken up by younger folk willing to squeeze up to let us past. We could just about move in there.

'Is the man in the padded shoulder dress Grayson Perry?' Olympia asked me.

'I wouldn't know,' I said. I could see four or five men in frocks.

'I've seen people gawping at him.'

'You're probably right then.' I grabbed two glasses of fizz from a passing tray and handed one to Olympia. 'This cravat is making me sweat. I'm going to take it off.'

'I wouldn't mind taking my dress off,' she said.

'Don't,' I said, never more serious.

'Nobody would turn a hair.'

'If you do, you're on your own.' Impossible in the circumstances, but she knew what I meant.

She held my champagne while I pocketed the cravat. 'I like it better here. Is it normally a lounge, do you think?'

From a nearby armchair an old tosser with a Father Christmas beard said, 'It's the Academicians Room, strictly for members only. Sit on my lap, gorgeous, and I won't say a word to the keeper.'

To my surprise, Olympia played along with him. 'Are you famous? I'm choosy which laps I sit on.'

'World famous,' he said. 'I'm on the committee.'

'Did you paint any of these things on the wall?'

'No, my dear. I practise the plastic arts.'

'What's that – Tupperware?'

'Ha-ha. I'm a sculptor.'

'In plastic?'

'In a variety of materials. Sit on my lap and I'll show you my magic hands.'

'I can see them from here, thanks.'

'Have you done any modelling, sweetie? You should. You really should.'

'I have better things to do with my time.'

To help Olympia get shot of him, I touched her arm and reminded her there was another floor upstairs. She ignored me and allowed the chat-up to continue. I suppose she expected to hear something helpful. All I could hear was this old tomcat yowling, 'I haven't seen you before. I'm sure I would remember. Were you a friend of Carla's?'

'Johnny was,' Olympia said without a word of warning to me. 'He can't get over it.'

'Who the fuck is Johnny?' It took an effort, but the old skirt-chaser removed his eyes from Olympia. His tone turned drier than a martini when he spoke to me. 'Are you an academician? I don't think we've met.'

'No,' I said. 'We haven't.'

'If it isn't a state secret, what's your connection to Carla?'

'That's private,' I said.

'I was like an older brother to her,' he said. 'I'm heart-broken. It was so sudden.'

'So were you at the service?' I asked, knowing full well he couldn't have been or he wouldn't have bagged an armchair here.

'Too distressing. Did you get to it?'

'We came in on the train. Just too late. But at least we can raise a glass to her.'

Which we duly did. And I added, 'May she rest in peace.'

'Well said. She was a charmer. And irreplaceable. Dealers

171

all over Europe are going to be looking for someone as good as Carla and they'll be wasting their time.'

I started to probe, trying not to show my ignorance. 'When you said it was sudden, was it heart?'

The sculptor stared at me as if I was from another planet. 'What do you mean?'

'Or a stroke?'

'Stroke of misfortune, if you ask me. Broke her neck, didn't she? God only knows why she fell. A moment of absentmindedness? A fainting fit?'

Olympia rescued me. 'We heard she died, but we don't know how it happened.'

'I thought everyone in London knew.'

'We're from out of town.'

'She was restoring the dome in St Mary Abchurch, one of the city churches, working alone forty feet up a scaffold tower. She's done ceilings before, heaps of times. Nobody knows why, but she fell off and was killed.'

We caught the last train back to Bath. The carriage wasn't crowded, so we had a table to ourselves.

'Do you believe in jinxes?' Olympia asked me suddenly.

I had my eyes closed. I was squiffy from the champagne and didn't catch on immediately. 'Jinxes?'

'Like fate.'

'What about them?'

'Oh, come on, Johnny. I've taken one body blow after another. My best friend Ruby is shot in the head when she's on her way to meet me for lunch. You and I meet and are shot at and I'm forced into hiding. And now Carla Denison is dead – the woman who was my best chance of understanding what's behind this. It's too much.'

'Like the mummy's curse?'

172

I'd taken off my shoes under the table. She jammed the point of her heel between my toes and made a hole in my sock. I was lucky she didn't hit flesh. 'Don't you dare mock me. I want a serious answer.'

'At this time of day, it's a big ask,' I said. 'You want my opinion? You can forget about the jinx.'

'Can you explain it, then?'

'The shootings? Obvious, isn't it? Some evil schmuck is out to get you.'

'I worked that out for myself. I can't even use my own home.'

'You did the right thing, moving out.'

'I don't need your approval of something that was blindingly obvious. I'm talking about Carla falling off the tower. People at the party seemed to think it was an accident.'

'And you don't agree?'

'Coming after everything else, I'm not sure.'

I couldn't resist trotting out the obvious. 'Did she fall, or was she pushed?'

Olympia didn't appreciate my wit. She thought it was sarcasm, which it wasn't. I got a look the like of which hadn't been seen on Network Rail since the conductor asked the Queen to show her ticket. 'I want your opinion.'

'I'm a private eye, so I have to be suspicious.'

'But she was working alone, the man with the beard said.'

'How does the old buzzard know? How does anyone know? Nobody knows except the killer, if there is one.'

Her dark eyes fixed on me in awe, unblinking. The lights of buildings flashed across them.

Buddha-like, I stared ahead. What I'd said about nobody knowing except the killer was pretty damn cool, I have to say.

And now Olympia frowned. 'But how was it done? Have

you seen one of those scaffold towers? There's no way anyone else could climb up secretly without Carla hearing.'

'When I said "was she pushed" I wasn't speaking literally. There are other ways.'

'Such as?'

'Giving the tower a shake from the bottom, so she loses balance.'

'They secure them with struts.'

'Cantilevers. Easiest things in the world to unfix. The tower itself is rickety and top-heavy. Get the thing rocking from the ground and it soon builds up a momentum and she topples off.'

'There are safety rails she could grip.'

'While holding a brush and paint pot? Okay, if you don't like that scenario, here's another. The killer spikes her drink with some drug that brings on dizziness.'

'Such as?'

'Anti-seizure medication.'

I'd surprised her again. A gumshoe who knew how many beans make five.

'They're well known for their side effects,' I went on, talking like a medic. 'My epileptic sister needed to take the stuff and was warned about attacks of vertigo.'

'Poor girl.'

'You asked.'

The train hurtled through a darkened station before she spoke again.

'If they really planned to kill a person up a tower, wouldn't shooting be more straightforward?'

I smiled. 'If the gunman was any use. His success rate so far doesn't give much confidence.'

'Will there be an investigation?'

'An inquest, you mean? Sure to be.'

'I mean by the police.'

'I doubt it. A coroner's jury is almost certain to say the death was accidental. End of story.'

'Detective Diamond should be told.'

'London is off-limits for him. It's policed by the Met.'

'He could ask them to investigate.'

'It's only speculation,' I said. 'They'd want more evidence. Are you willing to make a witness statement?'

I'd silenced her. The clatter of the train wheels took over.

I knew she wouldn't want to reveal why she'd got in touch with Carla. There was still plenty Olympia wasn't willing to say to the police or me.

18

After finishing with Lucky, Diamond called Ingeborg and asked her to meet him outside the station. Time for a quick bracer in the Royal Hotel. He sat alone at a table looking on to the street in case she arrived early. A chance to collect his thoughts. Early on, Paloma – if only to tease him – had named Ruby as her number one suspect. Paloma was often a shrewd helpmate, but she had been wrong this time. Ruby was definitely a victim, almost murdered and now in a coma. But her father, Seppy, was firmly in the frame – if he wasn't also a victim. Who else? Johnny Getz had muscled his way into the case. Was that in order to create confusion at the heart of the investigation? If so, it was a high-risk strategy. Then there was Bickerstaff, the car-boot salesman and likely wife-abuser. Could he have sold the find of a lifetime to Seppy and bitterly resented doing so? Last came Olympia, aided by her muscleman, Lucky. That young lady certainly had secrets she wasn't prepared to reveal. Any from that list was capable of hiring burglars and hitmen to do the dirty work.

Then – an extra, troubling thought – there was the charming Lady Bede, not exactly a suspect, but far too involved in the case for his comfort.

*

When Ingeborg arrived in the Ka, he was waiting near the taxi rank looking as if he'd been there for the past half-hour.

He offered her a peppermint since he was already sucking one.

'No thanks, guv. Where to?'

'Limpley Stoke.'

'So what's new?' she asked when they were heading down the stretch of the A36 that follows the course of the River Avon.

'Another shooting and another miss, from ten yards,' he said and told her briefly what he knew about the incident at Olympia's cottage.

'The same guy?'

'Almost certainly. I'm starting to wonder if this gunman has a heart of gold.'

'And misses deliberately? I don't buy that.'

'He hasn't killed anyone yet.'

'Not for want of trying. He hit Ruby.'

He didn't want to be reminded about Ruby. She was on his conscience already. 'How's she doing? Any change?'

She shook her head. 'I called the hospital first thing. She had a comfortable night – the phrase they use each time I ask.'

'Comfortable for the nurse because she didn't press the call button. It means nothing. If she dies, they'll tell us she was comfortable at the end.'

'Are we going to the scene of this shooting?'

'Yup. Olympia's cottage. She isn't living there, as you know. Her friend Lucky visited the place to feed her tropical fish and found this guy at a window round the back.'

'Trying for another shot at her?'

'Possibly. He'd arrived on a black scooter and fits the

177

description of the first gunman. As soon as he was spotted, he hared off. Lucky has an artificial leg and couldn't catch him. The shot was fired at the front of the cottage.'

'Just a warning, do you think?'

'It's hard to miss at that range.'

In another mile, Ingeborg glanced at her smartphone in its holder on the dashboard. The GPS wasn't much help in the labyrinth of lanes.

'Do you know where this cottage is, guv? Limpley Stoke spreads over a sizeable area.'

'We may need to ask.'

Originally, the village was known as Hanging Stoke and the reason is clear from the steepness of the valley side. Scattered cottages are built on cut-ins and natural ledges accessible by the narrow lanes that only the locals use with any confidence.

They left the main road and asked for help from the first person they met, a woman on a bike who had dismounted to let them squeeze past. 'Petunia Cottage?' she said. 'Would that be Lower Stoke?'

'We're hoping you can tell us, ma'am. It's owned by a young woman of colour.'

'That will be Olympia. She's in Middle Stoke.'

Spoken with certainty. They'd asked the right person.

'You're headed the right way, but the roads can be confusing. I've lived here twenty years and I still go wrong.'

Maybe not the right person.

'The best I can tell you is try and keep on this level as far as you can. Don't be tempted by anything on your left because you'll end up in Lower Stoke and you don't want to go there.'

The phrase *Here Be Dragons* crossed Diamond's mind.

'Olympia's cottage is definitely Middle,' the local expert

said. This was the bit of knowledge to hang on to. 'It's one of the oldest hereabouts and you can just see it on your right behind the trees when you're driving by. Don't drive by, of course, whatever you do. It's easy to miss. Be sure to keep your eyes peeled. I wouldn't bother with your satellite thing. I heard of a man last year who came looking for his own mother's cottage and gave up in despair and left his car blocking the lane. He was found half a mile off in Upper Stoke sitting by the roadside in tears. He'd got so angry he smashed his phone.'

'We won't do that. How far ahead is Petunia Cottage?'

'I wouldn't care to say.'

'At a rough guess?'

She shook her head. 'It's a long time since I saw it. But I'll give you a bit of advice. Watch out for the beer lorry. About this time he finishes delivering to the Hop Pole in Lower Stoke and drives up here like a maniac. He takes no prisoners.'

After they'd started again, Ingeborg said, 'What did we learn from that, guv?'

'Keep going, but dead slowly.'

'I'm starting to realise why you didn't use your own car.'

He stared ahead as if he hadn't heard. Cars were a necessary evil for Diamond. He avoided driving them whenever possible and he wasn't comfortable being driven.

She added, 'I've seen some narrow lanes, but these beat everything because there are so few passing points.'

'There's a reason for that.'

Ingeborg didn't say a word. She wasn't giving an easy feed line for a Diamond downer.

He delivered one, even so. 'If there's room for a passing point on the right, they've built a cottage on it. If it's on the left we fall two hundred feet and end up in Lower Stoke.'

'What if we meet the maniac lorry-driver?'

'Slam on the brakes and start reversing.'

In less than five minutes, Ingeborg did exactly that.

'Is he coming?'

'This is it, guv.' She halted the car.

All Diamond could see were trees and bushes.

'The stone,' Ingeborg said.

A slab of limestone to their right had the words Petunia Cottage painted on it in white.

'Hold on. There's a pull-in.' She turned the wheel hard right and forced the car up a bank and under a low branch that brushed the windscreen and roof. They stopped on a parking space of sorts behind another car. 'This hasn't been used much.'

'I expect Olympia owns a bike,' Diamond said.

Ingeborg smiled. 'In her stilettos? Interesting picture.'

A small, stone-built cottage with a tiled porch was now visible. Pots of geraniums were ranged in front.

They got out and were met by a uniformed constable. When he saw Diamond, he touched his cap in deference.

'Is that your car?' Diamond asked him.

'Yes, sir. I'm the only one here. I was about to leave. I thought everyone had been by.'

'Did they recover the bullet?'

'It wasn't in good shape, sir. It hit the stonework on the cottage and ricocheted into the turf. We found it eventually.'

'So it's mangled?'

'Rather. It's being sent off for a ballistic check. I can show you the chip it took off the wall and where it was dug out.'

'Won't mean much to me. Any tyre tracks?'

'They couldn't find any. The gunman seems to have left the scooter on the hard surface by the front gate.'

'They checked the back of the cottage, I hope?'

'Certainly did.'

'And?'

'They spent most of the time studying an interesting set of footprints they said must have been made by someone with a gammy leg.'

'The man who was shot at.'

'Is that a fact?' The constable shook his head in admiration. 'Bloody brilliant, if you'll excuse my language. They told me how they worked it out. Sherlock Holmes stuff to do with the drag of the shoe.'

Diamond rarely had a good word for the people in paper suits. 'No use to us at all. I already knew about the leg. It's artificial. He showed it to me. I want evidence of the gunman.'

'What about the bullet?'

'What about it?'

'Isn't that enough evidence?'

'We'll need to compare it with the bullets found at the other scenes, but you just told me it's in poor condition. Ballistics experts work mainly with the tiny marks made when the bullet is fired through the barrel. I'm not confident we'll find out anything of use to us.'

They walked around the side to the back and looked at the stacked logs Lucky had mentioned. The window had been dusted for prints, but there didn't seem to be any. It wasn't all that high off the ground. The 'sawn-off' gunman was indeed short if he'd needed to stand on the logs.

'I've seen enough,' Diamond said. 'We can all return to base.'

Before going into the incident room he treated Ingeborg to tea and cake in the coffee shop. She didn't want the cake so he added her slice to his plate.

'One thing bothers me,' she told him.

'Only one?'

'Where was Olympia when all this was happening?'

'In London. Didn't I tell you? According to Lucky, she phoned him from the train. A moment of panic. She'd remembered the fish needed feeding.'

She was frowning. 'She sent him out to Limpley Stoke to feed her fish? All kidding aside?'

'And he came under fire from the gunman for doing a good turn – if it really happened the way he told it. I've got my doubts.'

'What was Olympia doing in London?'

'A business appointment, I was told.'

'To do with her journalistic work?'

'Who knows? Lucky didn't ask. In his own words, "She have her life and I have mine." They're not sleeping together. He made that clear.'

'He's just a friend doing her a favour? She's going to feel bad when he tells her what happened.'

'He'll make light of it.'

'Even so, she'll be in no doubt she's the real target. That's scary.'

'And debatable. I'm not sure anything scares Olympia. She looks after number one, which is why she moved in with Lucky. Olympia has her own agenda and tells no one what it is.'

'That's the measure of a good journalist.'

'I'd forgotten about your previous career. You should meet her.'

'I'd like to.'

In the Corn Market, he made the call that would stop the nagging doubts about Virginia Bede, he hoped. Her ladyship made the prospect of drinks next morning at eleven sound like an invitation to an orgy.

That done, he started the chore of writing reports of his trips to the One Stop Shop and Petunia Cottage. Every interview had to be logged to the satisfaction of the office manager, who was John Leaman. Whoever you were, Leaman made sure you didn't duck that duty.

'Working on it,' Diamond called out when Leaman approached his end of the room on one of his regular patrols. 'You'll get it soon, John.'

He still felt guilty about the effort Leaman had put into researching the action painters. That lecture to the team had misfired horribly. Policemen aren't noted for their interest in abstract painting. After the whole thing proved to be a washout not much had been said, but the poor guy must have known they were laughing up their sleeves. He'd taken the humiliation stoically, suppressing the pain. A delayed reaction would be understandable.

'I'm not here about your statements, guv.' Leaman glanced left and right to be sure he wasn't being overheard before lowering his voice. 'Can I have a word in your ear?'

'You've got it.'

'I want to show you something.'

'What's that?'

'Can I bring it over?'

'Depends. What is it – you haven't written a poem?' Immediately Diamond came out with this, he wished he hadn't. Shooting off at the mouth was one of his biggest flaws. The unkind thought had popped into his head and amused him, literal-minded Leaman waxing lyrical.

The man deserved more respect.

Fortunately he didn't answer and may not have heard. He'd stepped across to the centrepiece of his talk to the team, the drawing board with the enlarged photo of Seppy's 'find of a lifetime', now no longer rated as a work of art. This embarrassing item was still on its easel but mercifully someone had moved it from the middle of the room and propped it face inwards against a wall. The magnifying glass had been returned to the hobby shop by Paul Gilbert.

Diamond's legs flexed under the desk at the sight of Leaman lifting the board from the easel and bringing it over.

He didn't relish going through the minefield a second time.

Leaman looked with disfavour at Diamond's overloaded desk. 'There isn't enough room.'

'Never is. We'll make space. Load as much as we can on the armchair and anything else on the floor.' The upheaval was in a good cause, a way of atoning for the cruel thought about the poem. Leaman deserved better. Diamond helped shift the unread directives from headquarters, folders and notes. Each stack thumped on the floor was a conscience-salver. Even his computer screen had to be moved. The desktop was now bare. A box of tissues had been buried under the stacks and he used some to wipe away the dust. 'How's that?'

No answer. Leaman had no time for social niceties. Busy as a stagehand moving props, he planted the drawing board flat on the desk, checked it for position, stepped away again and came back with a tin that could have contained biscuits and surely did not. He took out his phone and positioned it squarely between the board and the tin. This was serious business. Only when everything was in place did he pause.

'You haven't had second thoughts?' Diamond said, expecting the worst.

'About it being an action painting? No, guv. Jean Sharp is right. It's a canvas used as a palette.'

Big relief. Yet Leaman plainly still had something to prove. 'The light isn't much good in here.' He seemed to have forgotten he was the one who had found the Corn Market in the first place.

'It's an old building, John, and the windows could do with a clean.'

'I'll need to use the flashlight on my phone. There's a section of the photo I want to show you. It's such a pity we don't have the canvas itself.'

Which was basically what Jean Sharp had said when she set out her theory.

Leaman switched on. 'It's towards the top.'

The light picked out some diagonal strips of brown where the artist seemed to have unloaded excess paint from the brush before using it on the real canvas.

'It's layers of thick paint as far as anyone can tell,' Leaman said, 'but if you look here, between the bands of brown, there's an area about a centimetre and a half wide with some pink showing through. Can you see?'

Diamond was thinking it was a long time since he'd had his eyes checked. He was supposed to have twenty-twenty vision. 'Pink? Yes. I see that now.'

Leaman reached for the tin and took out an object wrapped in black velvet. 'Now would you mind putting this on? It's a headband magnifier.'

'You must have been reading my thoughts.' The gadget he'd been handed was a circular band of steel with an attachment incorporating eyepieces. 'Where did you get this?'

'From a friend who uses it for jewellery making.'

Diamond was trying to be amiable, even in a lost cause, but this could quickly descend into farce. Nobody else in the incident room seemed to be paying attention so he lifted the magnifier over his pate, peered through the two lenses and fiddled with them until he could see details in sharper focus.

'Are you on the deep pink bit?' Leaman asked.

'Yes.' He'd have said so just to get this over quickly, even if he could see nothing.

'Stay with it. I'm going to turn the board through ninety degrees.'

Trust Leaman to make a production number out of this. 'Go on, then. Now I've lost it. The whole thing is a blur. No, it's coming back.'

'What does it look like to you?'

'The pink? From this angle it could almost be an ear.'

'Excellent,' Leaman said, sounding like a carer with a stroke victim learning to use a spoon. 'That's what I saw, too. If you look at the lower part, it's a touch lighter in colour and comes to a neat curved end. That's the lobe, and the darker bits above are the folds of the ear. Now look at the light brown either side. Does that look like hair to you?'

'Now you mention it, yes.' He was uncertain, but he had the good sense not to dispute anything.

'They're not random strokes. They're carefully worked. You can see some individual hairs if you look closely. The sideburn is on the right and the main head of hair to the left hangs more loosely. The rest is painted over.'

Diamond turned one of the eyepieces and the image sharpened. Suddenly he could see what Leaman was on about. This tiny section was like a glimpse through curtains of a slender section of a painting.

'The canvas was used as a palette for sure,' Leaman said, 'but there's a portrait underneath, or at least a part of one.'

It appeared that originally someone had painted a human

186

face – or at least part of a face – and later discarded the canvas and used it for mixing colours.

'I think it's a study for a larger work,' Leaman said and recovered his confidence enough to go into lecturing mode again. 'They often did this in the past, making a likeness and copying from it rather than asking the model to pose for a painting that could take weeks to finish.'

Diamond felt a flutter of excitement. Now that the picture had been turned through ninety degrees there could be no question that he was looking at the image of a foreshortened human ear slightly obscured by hair. Leaman had made a discovery that could galvanise the investigation.

'You've convinced me, John,' Diamond said, lifting the magnifier off his head.

Leaman grinned. It was a moment to savour. In spite of everything, he'd been vindicated. His fists were clenched in triumph.

There was a pleasing sense of justice in this. It was fitting that Leaman himself had discovered the secret of the picture that had threatened to be his undoing.

Diamond grinned back, nodding his approval and at the same time thinking through the implications. 'No disrespect, but if you spotted this, you can bet Seppy did and I can understand his excitement. If this was painted by anyone really famous, it could be an unknown work, worth a fortune.'

Leaman was ahead of him. 'I've thought about that, guv. Do you remember visiting Bickerstaff, the car-boot salesman?'

'All too well.'

'You wrote a report for me – for the investigation, I mean. I've been looking at it again. Bickerstaff told you the recent history of the painting and it belonged for a long time to an old lady who died intestate in 1990. She was given it back in the 1940s by her husband, who had it fitted into the art nouveau frame. They probably thought it was an abstract like we all did. We don't know their name, but we know where they lived.'

'Bennett Street. How does that help us?'

'It may not be significant, but . . .'

'But what?'

'Bennett Street leads to The Circus. And that's where Bath's most famous artist lived.'

'Gainsborough?'

'Thomas Gainsborough, whose paintings sell for millions if they ever come on the market. Ten years ago one came up for sale at Christie's. They valued it at three million and it more than doubled that. It went for six and a half. Guv, it wasn't even one of his best.'

19

Diamond's senior people, Halliwell, Leaman and Ingeborg Smith, had grouped with him among the debris from his desktop to talk about the latest discovery. Halliwell and Ingeborg had taken turns with the magnifier and agreed that a fragment of painted canvas was visible between the layers of paint. Carefully painted with soft, feathery strokes, it was unlike any of the other marks.

'But it's a huge jump from this to Gainsborough,' Ingeborg said. She made it her mission to challenge any assumption that couldn't be proved.

'Seppy Hubbard called it the find of a lifetime, and that's what this would be,' Leaman said. 'He's a dealer and no fool.'

'A dealer in second-rate antiques. Doesn't make him a Gainsborough expert.'

'Agreed, but he'll have shown it to an expert.'

'He'd need to. Even if it looks authentic, it's probably a forgery.'

Leaman was unwilling to give ground. 'And he will have gone to a reliable restorer to get all the excess paint removed and reveal what's underneath.'

'Already?' Diamond said.

'He wouldn't be crowing about the bargain he'd found without seeing it in full.'

'So what's under all that paint?' Ingeborg said. 'A full face?'

'Head and shoulders, I expect,' Leaman said. 'The canvas is the same size as one Gainsborough used for a portrait of his nephew painted in Bath about 1768.'

'You've done your homework as usual.'

'I was up late last night checking everything I could. He lived in Bath for sixteen years and painted some of his best work here.'

The look she gave him was like a cold shower. 'But you as a logical man will have heard of the *post hoc* fallacy.'

Leaman reddened, and it was clear he knew what she was talking about, even if no one else did.

Ingeborg didn't spare him. 'This is a good example. Gainsborough lived in Bath and a painting turns up in Bath, so it must be one of his. *Post hoc ergo propter hoc.* You don't need me to tell you the danger in this sort of thing, linking events that mistakenly suggest causality.'

'Hold on,' Leaman said with more animation than a logician ought to employ. 'I never claimed I had proof. It's a hypothesis, if you want to bandy terms. A starting point for more investigation.'

Diamond stepped in like a boxing referee. 'You're both right. Honours even. For now, I'm willing to go with John's hypothesis. You said Gainsborough lived in The Circus.'

'For thirteen years, from 1766. He watched it being built and he and his family were the first tenants. He kept up two other places, in Abbey Street and Lansdown Road, but this was his main residence.'

'Where exactly?'

'Number 17, on the Bennett Street side.'

'Let's take a look.'

'How will that help?' Ingeborg said. 'He hasn't lived there in two hundred and fifty years.'

'I'm not expecting him to show us round. Who's up for it?'

Halliwell was only too happy of a break and made his feelings clear. Leaman couldn't be excluded. So Ingeborg, the disbeliever, held the high ground at the cost of being left in charge of the incident room.

Bennett Street was only a few minutes' walk.

'Have you been there already?' Diamond asked Leaman as they strode up Lansdown Road.

'No, guv. All my research has been online.'

'Do you good to get out. Computers aid the brain and screw up the rest of the body.'

They arrived at The Circus as a tour bus crawled between the parked cars surrounding the circular lawn with its five majestic London plane trees. The address system was explaining to the passengers that this was the last master-piece of John Wood, the architect of most of the city's greatest buildings. 'Sadly, he never lived to see it. He died within a few days of the first stone being laid. He was only forty-nine. Another fifteen years passed before his son, John Wood the Younger, completed the work.'

'What they never tell you,' Leaman said, 'is that the ground plan is a perfect match with Stonehenge and there are all kinds of references to the Druids in the carvings along the frieze.'

Diamond gave Leaman his Sonny Liston stare and the lecture on John Wood's Druidical connections stopped in its tracks.

Number 17 had a plaque above the door recording its first and most famous resident.

'Shall we see if anyone's in?' Halliwell asked.

'I'd rather not at this stage,' Diamond said. 'We don't want the story breaking in the media. Let's look round the back. He will have had his studio there.'

'How do you know that?' Leaman asked, surprised.

'I thought everyone knew an artist likes to work with a north light. The front is south-facing.'

Leaman exchanged a glance with Halliwell. It was never wise to underestimate their boss. They'd forgotten he now shared a house with an expert on art.

Off Bennett Street, behind the Museum of East Asian Art, they found Circus Place. What once had been coach houses were now garages, most of them rebuilt.

'Can we see 17 from here?'

They studied the backs of the houses. Typically of Georgian building, the rears were an eyesore, constructed with uneven stone now heavily stained with centuries of grime. All the plumbing and drainage was on view and few of the windows matched.

'You can't see enough from here,' Leaman said. 'Apparently his studio was upstairs and he had the window enlarged. I'm trying to work out which one it is.'

'Climb on the wall,' Diamond said.

'Do you think I should?'

'Give him a foot-up, Keith. Walk to the end and you can stand on the garage roof. You'll have an excellent view from there.'

'Is that an order?'

'You're better built for climbing than I am or I'd be up there already.'

Leaman used a wall support to get up to chest level and then hauled himself up and did a neat balancing act along the top of the wall to the garage roof and easily got up there.

'You see?' Diamond said to Halliwell. 'He's enjoying himself. He needs to get out more.'

They didn't notice the police patrol car that drove slowly

past and up Circus Place. But they saw it after it turned round and came back because it stopped and the window was wound down. Diamond didn't recognise the boyish face staring out at him.

'Are you two with him?'

'We are. We're CID and it's a covert operation.'

'Oh, yes?' The disbelief couldn't have been clearer. 'Got to hand it to you. That's a new one.'

'Want to see our IDs?'

The cop was in two minds. 'You know what this building behind you is?'

'Are you joking? Of course we know.' But only now did it dawn on Diamond that suspicious behaviour behind the Museum of East Asian Art was going to get attention.

'And you know it was burgled in 2018 by professionals who broke in through a first-floor window and took items worth a small fortune?'

'Of course we do. Show the officer your ID, Keith.'

Halliwell had it ready.

There was deference in the next comment. 'It's not for me to tell you what to do, sir, but we're going to get calls about this. The residents won't know he's one of us.'

'He won't be there much longer.'

Leaman, oblivious, remained another ten minutes on the garage roof and had to be called down after the cops had driven away. Diamond confided in Halliwell: 'I was tempted to hand him in and find out if these stories of police brutality are true.'

They helped Leaman off the wall.

'Well, Spiderman. Did you get a sight of Gainsborough's window?'

'That's not all,' Leaman said, his voice unusually emotional.

'He didn't wave to you?'

'I could see right to the bottom of the garden.'

'And how does that help us?'

'You get a view from up there of the mews at the far end, the only one that's survived. All the rest are gone. It's still there, a barn of a building in the original eighteenth-century stone with a one-up one-down attachment that must have been where the groom slept.'

Diamond thought he knew where this was going. The mention of the mews had got Leaman excited. 'You're thinking about my report of what Bickerstaff, the car-boot man, had to say? An old mews building belonging to an artist. That's as far back as he could trace the picture.'

'No, I'm thinking of what I read last night in James Hamilton's biography of Gainsborough. He calls it "a unique and miraculous survival". He says the artist's horses and carriage were kept there and – more important to us – it was used for extra storage.'

20

The first person Diamond met next morning in the incident room was Georgina Dallymore, his boss, all black serge and silver buttons. He'd been hoping she wouldn't trouble him here. No such luck. She was becoming a regular visitor. He had an uneasy feeling this would be about yesterday's surveillance trip. Those cops in the patrol car weren't going to miss a chance to put CID in the wrong.

But Circus Place wasn't mentioned.

'Just passing through,' she said without a hint of censure, 'keeping abreast of the investigation.'

'You're always welcome, ma'am.'

As if this smacked too much of bonhomie within the ranks, she said, 'You should tidy up your end of the room. I almost tripped over those files on the floor.'

'I will. Busy day yesterday.'

'So I gather. I've had a walk round and chatted to some of the team. You've moved on from the modern art theory, I gather.'

'True.'

'Keep me informed, then.' She looked at her watch. 'I must dash.'

And she was gone.

'What was that about?' he asked Ingeborg.

She smiled. 'I can't say for certain, but I think she's on

her way to Quiet Street. She had a few minutes to kill, so she called here first.'

'What's going on in Quiet Street?'

'The Dressing Room sale. Upmarket lingerie. Regular customers get first pickings if they come early. I saw her yesterday looking in the window.'

'Good observation. I would never have thought of that myself. Georgina's underwear is the one great mystery I have no inclination to solve.' He placed a small Styrofoam box on her desk. It was tied with a pale blue ribbon. 'But just to show how much I appreciate you . . .'

Ingeborg reddened. She frowned. He'd never seen her so uncertain how to react. As if it might contain a tarantula, she kept it at arm's length and loosened the bow.

It was a slice of cake.

'What's this – a peace offering for yesterday?' she said, fully herself again.

'Angel cake,' he said, 'and I won't say the obvious.'

'You've been to the Provenist already?'

He shook his head. 'We ended up there last night.'

'So it's yesterday's cake?'

'Kept fresh in my fridge.'

'Kind of you to remember me, guv, but I thought you knew I don't eat cake.'

'Not a problem.'

She moved it out of his reach. 'I'm sure Jean Sharp will appreciate it. How was your Circus trip? Worth doing?'

'We don't know for sure,' Halliwell told her. 'John climbed a wall and saw Gainsborough's original mews building at the bottom of the garden.'

'John Leaman climbed a wall?'

'And stood on a garage roof.'

'I can't believe this.'

196

'When he's really into something, there's no stopping him.'

'That I *can* believe. Where is he? I must ask him about this.'

'Not in yet. He's in the library mugging up on Gainsborough.'

She gasped and snapped her fingers. 'Guv, there was a call from the hospital. Sister somebody-or-other. Yesterday they started bringing Ruby out of the coma. The swelling on the brain has reduced to a safe level. She's recovered enough for you to visit for a short time.'

'She's conscious? Marvellous. I'll go right away. Want to come? She'll appreciate having another woman there.'

'I think I'd better,' she said.

But when they got to the RUH and found the ward, they were told by the sister they'd have to wait because the patient already had another visitor. And if she was tired, they might need to return another time.

'Who's the visitor?' Diamond asked, displeased, to put it mildly.

'She calls him her agent, so it must be to do with business. She asked us to contact him and he came at once. A Mr Getz.'

'Him?' He made it sound like a four-letter word.

Ingeborg touched his arm. 'Careful, guv. Your blood pressure.'

The sister eyed him in a professional way. 'Why don't you sit down for a moment? I'm sure you won't have long to wait.'

'He's in the right place,' Ingeborg said half joking to the sister and steered him to a seat.

'There should be an armed officer here,' Diamond said. 'What the fuck was he doing, letting Getz inside?'

'Moderate your language, please,' the sister said. 'Getting yourself in a state won't help you or anyone else. The guard is just along the corridor and I can assure you he checks everyone going in.'

He asked Ingeborg to speak with the officer. Mindful of frequent warnings about his hypertension, he remained seated. But muttering.

When Ingeborg came back, she was suspiciously silent. She took the seat next to him.

'Well?' he said.

'From the description, it's Johnny all right.'

'There's something else, isn't there? I can tell.'

'Someone else.'

'Tell me, then.'

'I don't know if you're ready for this. Before Johnny went in, there was an earlier visitor, a young woman of colour, the constable said.'

'Olympia?'

'Ruby asked to see her first, so the sister phoned her an hour before she called us.'

'We know where we come in the pecking order, then.'

'It's understandable,' Ingeborg said. 'Olympia is her best friend and Johnny is the gumshoe she hired to find her father.'

'If she had the sense to know, we're far more use to her than those two.'

'She'll find out.'

No more than five minutes passed before Johnny Getz emerged with a grin like a dolphin. He didn't walk towards them so much as strut. 'Wouldn't you know it? The old bill, last on the scene. How you faring, Pete?'

'No better for seeing you,' Diamond said. 'More important, how's Ruby doing?'

'A little tired now. She wanted bringing up to date. I was doing most of the talking.'

'That would be tough for anyone to bear.'

'So don't be surprised if you don't get in today.'

'Did you see Olympia?'

'Sure. We arrived together and we'll leave together. She'll be waiting for me in the Atrium coffee bar.'

'I want a word with you both, and that's as good a place as any. Don't leave before I do.'

Johnny smirked. 'That's an order, is it?'

'If you don't want me knocking on your door at home.'

The sister appeared and said, 'Ruby is rather tired now.'

The veins throbbed alarmingly. 'That's not our fault, sister.'

He was given the look usually reserved for probationer nurses who can't fold hospital corners. 'I was about to add that she's so anxious to speak to you that I'm allowing you five minutes. And don't distress her. She has a buzzer to press if needed.'

The armed officer outside the ward recognised the two detectives and gave some sort of greeting and got a glare from Diamond in return.

Ruby was alone in a side ward, her pallor matching the bed linen. Her head wound was dressed with a bandage that covered the top half of her head and was kept in place with a mesh skullcap. Some of her red hair must have been shaved, but plenty was visible emerging from under the bandage and spread across the pillow.

'Do you have any news of Daddy?' she asked.

'I wish we could tell you something positive,' Diamond said. 'You should have given me the full story when we first met. We're still piecing together what this is about.'

'The damned picture. That's what it's about. He didn't want anyone to know.'

'Your friend Olympia knows.'

'Yes, and I feel so bad about that, breaking my promise. I thought I was doing her a huge favour, giving her a scoop for the magazine she writes for, and she's been shot at and so has Johnny. Is Daddy safe? That's what worries me. I hired Johnny to find him and he doesn't seem to know.'

He resisted commenting on Getz's sleuthing skills. 'How's your memory, Ruby?'

'Aren't you going to answer me? You've had days to find him. What can you tell me?'

'I need your help.'

'I don't think you know any more than the others.' Her right hand felt for the buzzer lying on the bedclothes and failed to find it. Diamond had moved it out of easy reach.

'Without your help,' he told her, as gently as he was able, 'we're wasting our time. Will you relax for a moment and listen to me?'

She was tight-lipped, but she made a small movement with her shoulders that seemed to be an affirmation, so he went on, 'You just said this is all about the picture and I believe you're right. Tell me why your father calls it the find of a lifetime.'

No answer.

'I'll make it easy for you,' he said. 'I'll say what I believe happened and you need only nod to confirm, or do nothing if I'm wrong. Got that?'

'All right.'

'Your father noticed part of the canvas that led him to suppose a portrait might be under all the surplus paint. Right?'

Ruby's only reaction was to blink several times.

Perhaps he should have started with something less direct to get her confidence, but he was up against time. 'Can you confirm what I just said?'

200

The dip of the head she gave was so slight it might not have been noticed.

Diamond nodded himself to show how it should be done. 'He took it to an expert to have the paint removed.'

This time there was a definite nod.

Encouraged, he added, 'It's a portrait, head and shoulders, most likely a study for a bigger painting.'

So far, so good.

'The expert identified the painter as a famous artist who lived in Bath.'

Her teeth pressed on her lower lip as if she was reluctant to go on with this game.

Now for the clincher.

'Thomas Gainsborough.'

A five-second hesitation before she confirmed it, but she did with a quick, unmistakable nod. A moment that deserved the cannon and bells from the *1812 Overture*.

John Leaman would go into orbit when he was told.

'And then your father needed to prove it was genuine.' The patient fact-finding exercise had worked. Any more he could extract from her would be a bonus. His questioning took on the force of an interrogation. 'He will have got the painting checked for age. The canvas. The wood it was made from. And the paint. Were they the pigments Gainsborough worked with? Some paints artists use today weren't around in the eighteenth century.' In his keenness to press on, he was overwhelming her, wasting precious time speaking the obvious. 'Was it signed?'

No answer. She didn't seem to know.

'Did your father go to London?'

She found her voice again and made clear she wanted to end this. 'I've told you all I can. I don't know any more than you do.'

'Have you seen the painting yourself, Ruby?'

She didn't answer.

The sister appeared in the doorway. 'That's more than enough for now. Time's up.'

21

I found Olympia sitting alone studying her smartphone. She took six months to notice I was there and then gave me a look she might have given a cleaner called to clear up a mess.

The atrium in the Royal United Hospital isn't Trump Tower, but it's tall, light and airy. The sun through the bars of the skylight windows fifty feet above was patterning the terracotta-coloured wall with a cat's cradle of shadows. To my eye (now I'm into art) it was like some graffiti genius had got busy with a broad brush and splashed out a modern masterpiece in black paint. I thought of a neat title: *Looking for Seppy Hubbard.*

The designers of the coffee bar had done everything in their power to combat the straight look of everything else. Round tables, curved chairs with circular seats and a drum-shaped serving area.

'I don't know why I waited for you,' Olympia said without looking up.

Where had I got the idea she thought I was Britain's answer to Sam Spade? Well, if she hadn't succumbed to my good looks and one-liners, maybe some bonding would help. 'I thought we'd exchange information.'

'What about?' Her eyes hadn't left her smartphone.

'What's new from Ruby.'

'I've got nothing to tell you.'

I could be just as stubborn. 'Snap.'

'What did you expect? She's bombed by the drugs they gave her.'

'Pete is with her now.'

She continued scrolling. 'Remind me who you're talking about.'

'My buddy and co-investigator, Detective Superintendent Peter Diamond.'

'He'll get nowhere with Ruby.'

'He wants you and me to wait here for him.'

'Just to be pumped? No thanks.'

'I'm going to switch roles. I plan to pump Pete,' I said. 'We haven't spoken for a while. Who knows what he's turned up with all the forensics he can call on?'

She ignored that piece of wisdom. 'I've finished my coffee. I'm leaving.' She opened her bag and put the phone away.

'Not a good idea,' I said.

'Why?'

'Pete said if he doesn't get to see us now, he'll come calling. I don't know about you, but I don't want my door battered in with the big red key at four in the morning.'

'He doesn't know where I'm living.'

'Don't count on it, babe.'

'Don't you dare "babe" me, Johnny Getz. I have a perfectly grown-up name you can use.'

'What's that – Ballbuster? I was telling you the fuzz will know where you are. I found Lucky's house, no problem.'

'I was going to ask you about that.'

'Professional secret.'

She rolled her eyes, but I'd got through to her about Pete and she didn't move from her chair. 'This place depresses me.'

'It's not the comedy club.'

Patients in dressing gowns and slippers, some in wheel-chairs, were passing our table regularly, heading for the exit. One was sitting up on a trolley pushed by his wife. It looked like a mass escape, but they were all smokers forced to leave the building to light up. I was tempted to join them.

Pete appeared through a swing door with his blonde sidekick and came straight to our table. 'What's the plat du jour?'

Olympia looked away, unamused.

He turned to Sergeant Smith. 'What's your choice, Inge?'

She said, 'Perhaps one of these good people would like a refill.'

'Where are my manners?' he said. 'You ladies haven't met. Ingeborg is my detective sergeant but in another life was a journalist like you, Olympia.'

'Oh?' She ran the eye over Ingeborg. 'Who with?'

'I was freelancing, specialising in crime,' Ingeborg said. 'I believe you're a staffer.'

'A magazine you won't have heard of, called *Exorbitant*.'

'But I have. You're on our radar. It's my job to know about everybody with a connection to Seppy. Are you on a story right now?'

'Several,' Olympia said. 'Whether I get into print is another question. The editor-in-chief has high standards.'

'Is that Jock Scoular?'

No question: Ingeborg was on the button.

Olympia clocked her with more respect. 'He's the owner.'

It was agreed Ingeborg would have elderflower cordial and Pete a caffè latte. He ambled over to the counter.

'You've got him well trained,' Olympia said.

'I wouldn't say that,' Ingeborg said with a laugh. 'He'll

205

bring back cake for himself. He puts away two slices a day, to my certain knowledge, so he knows I wouldn't order it for him. We wouldn't have any other boss in CID, and we do what we can to moderate his cholesterol level, but it's a battle.'

'If that's policing, I can't think why you gave up journalism.'

'I can ask more questions than I could in a press conference. And I'm closer to the action.'

'Just like me,' I chipped in. 'My job beats everyone's. Right in there. No rules. No boss.'

'And no income,' Olympia said, razor sharp. 'Whoever heard of a private eye with a wallet?'

Which I have to admit sums up my profession.

Well and truly skewered.

Pete came back with the drinks and a slice of Dundee cake, which went in three bites. 'Cards on the table, people. What did Ruby tell us that we didn't know already?'

Nice try, but we'd already decided not to be pumped.

'She told us nothing,' Olympia said. 'I was updating her.'

'On what?' Pete said. 'Did you tell her about the break-in at her flat?'

She ran the eye over him as if he was rat-arsed at a funeral. 'What sort of monster do you think I am? I didn't come here to distress her when she's barely out of the coma.'

'Same goes for me,' I said. 'She's my client. I brought her a bunch of grapes.' Then, quick on the draw as Wild Bill Hickok, I fired one at him. 'How about you, Pete?'

'I'm well satisfied,' he said. 'She confirmed what I didn't know for certain until now – that this is all about Gainsborough.'

Olympia tensed as if volts were passing through her. 'She told you that?'

'I told *her* and she gave the nod.'

'What do *you* know about Gainsborough?' Olympia demanded. She was livid her secret was out. She'd guarded it like her pin number at a cashpoint in Soho on a Saturday night. To be truthful, the name of the artist was news to me, too. Even I felt my nerve ends tingle.

'What do I know? Not a lot,' Pete said, underplaying his hand in the way I was starting to recognise. 'I'm a film buff and Gainsborough Pictures made some of my favourite black and white movies. They gave starts to some of the great directors: Hitchcock, Carol Reed, Michael Powell.' He seemed to have lost the plot.

'That's immaterial,' Olympia said.

'Ah, but the opening logo was a Georgian lady in an enormous black hat. The first time you see her, you think it's a still and then she turns her head and smiles and you realise she's a model dressed to look like a famous Gainsborough painting.'

'Mrs Siddons.'

'I wouldn't know the model's name.'

'I'm talking about the original. The sitter was a well-known actor.'

'A bloke? Never.'

Ingeborg exchanged a sisterly look with Olympia and said to Pete, 'Women on the stage prefer to be known as actors, guv.'

'The portrait is in the National Gallery,' Olympia said.

'You sound like an expert.'

'I wouldn't say that.'

Ingeborg buttered her up some more. 'You're a serious journo, so you do your research.'

Olympia mellowed a little. 'I do the best I can.' She turned back to Pete. 'Who told you I'm researching Gainsborough?'

207

'One of my team made an informed guess and now we know he hit the mark. Seppy was smart as a whip to buy that canvas. I wouldn't have spotted it in a million years.'

'He's a bright guy.'

'You've met him, of course.'

'Many times. Ruby and I went through school together.'

'You must have a theory where he is.'

'I'm not optimistic. He's been silent so long. Even if he's holed up, he will have been too worried about Ruby to stay hidden for long.'

'I thought they kept at a distance from each other.'

'They're not estranged. She can't stand his shop, all those dusty old objects. He's made antiques his life, but he's fond of her.'

'When exactly did he discover he'd acquired a Gainsborough?'

'Only after all those layers of paint were removed.'

I've got to hand it to my friend Pete. Hardly a minute had passed since we'd agreed to give nothing away to the guy, yet here he was pumping Olympia like she was a lifeboat shipping water. I was learning stuff, too, so I didn't try to muzzle her.

He pumped her some more. 'He will have gone to a top professional to get it cleaned.'

'He did,' she carried on blabbing, ignoring our pact to stay silent. It was a wonder her teeth stayed in. 'There was none better than Carla Denison.'

And I couldn't resist airing my only bit of artspeak. 'The best conservator in London.'

'May she rest in peace,' Olympia added.

Pete had been processing all this like a calculator, but now his jaw dropped. 'She's dead?'

Olympia gabbed on regardless. 'We went to the funeral. The wake, to be accurate.'

'How come? You didn't know her, did you?'

'We crashed it,' I said, loving every second of this. Pete was almost foaming at the mouth. He couldn't believe anyone else was better briefed than he was.

Ingeborg had to take over, her boss was in such a state. 'Really? And if she did the work on Seppy's picture, she can't have been ill for long. How did she die?'

'She fell.'

'Do you know what happened?'

Olympia said, 'She was at work on a church ceiling. She was found on the floor beside the scaffold tower she'd been using.'

Pete looked at Olympia. Then he looked at me. He could tell we weren't bluffing. He couldn't have been more blown away if we'd just sung the love duet from *Madame Butterfly*.

He made a huge effort to sound cool. 'Unfortunate.'

Olympia didn't spare him. 'That's a crass understatement only a policeman could make.'

'What age was she?'

'Does it matter?'

'It does if she was too old for that kind of work.'

'We didn't ask. I got the impression she wasn't old.'

'The papers will have given her age,' I said. 'She was famous in the art world. Like I said, the best—'

'We heard the first time,' Olympia closed me down. 'I was shocked by her death. I had an appointment with her.'

'Which is why we were in London,' I put in, refusing to be silenced. 'We were hoping she could tell us where Seppy is.' I wasn't passing up the chance to rub Pete's nose in it, letting him know how a lone private eye can go places and learn stuff an entire CID team doesn't have a clue about.

'You were together?' Pete said.

'Johnny followed me from Bath,' Olympia said, making clear that this had been no pleasure.

I resisted the urge to wade in. I didn't want my professional secrets compromised.

'What else did you learn at the wake?' Pete asked.

'Very little,' Olympia said, but her tongue still wagged like the south end of a goose. 'This was the Royal Academy and it was full of freaks and geeks, most of them claiming they knew Carla when it was screamingly obvious they were only there because they wanted to be seen.'

'We stuck out because we were normal,' I said.

'Dressed in mourning,' Olympia added.

We'd coughed up far too much already, so I slammed the door on it. 'And now we'd like to hear what you've found out.'

'Not much,' Pete said, still trying to get his act together. 'Ballistics confirmed that the bullet that hit Ruby was fired from the same gun that missed you two.'

'And Lucky, outside my cottage?' Olympia said.

'You heard about that? I guess he will have told you. We haven't got the results from that incident yet.'

'What's this?' I said, ears flapping. 'Another shooting? Nobody told me.'

'We shouldn't need to tell you,' Olympia said. 'You're a dick.'

'Do you mind?'

'Any half-competent shamus would have found out for himself.'

I felt like she'd chewed up my balls and spat them out.

Pete asked Olympia, 'Do you have any idea why you're a target?'

'No,' she said, 'and I didn't waste time thinking about it. I moved out of my cottage fast. Can you make sense of it?'

'I'm starting to. You're right to be careful. You shouldn't be here. You took a big risk coming.'

'I had a call from the hospital. Ruby was asking to see me, mainly, it turns out, because she's still worried sick about her father. Is he dead, do you think, or is he behind all this shooting?'

'That's the question none of us can answer yet. How did you travel here?'

'Taxi.'

'Did you arrange a pick-up?'

'No. I'll call one when I'm ready.'

'We'd better give you a lift. You'll be safer.'

'I have other things to do in town.'

'Don't you understand, Olympia? Your luck will run out some time.'

She understood and wasn't impressed. She got up and started walking. This was one stubborn dame.

22

'Shadow them,' Diamond instructed Ingeborg even as Olympia was clicking across the tiled floor towards the hospital exit, trailed all too obviously by Johnny Getz. 'See where they go. And stay sharp, Inge. The gunman is still around.'

'Don't you want to be part of it?' she asked him.

'I'm too large a target.' He didn't admit he had other business. He was uncharacteristically shy to admit what it was. Usually he would have shared his plans with Ingeborg, but she didn't need to know about this. Left alone, he finished his coffee before strolling out to look for a taxi.

He knew he was visiting one of Bath's larger properties high on Sion Hill when all he could see from the road were treetops above a redbrick wall a mile long. Eventually the monotony was broken by a pair of stone stags facing each other on piers supporting extraordinary ten-foot-high speared gates through which a white gravel drive appeared to go on for ever. When the taxi turned, the gates opened, courtesy of an infrared beam.

The gatekeeper's lodge to the right was no larger than the average town hall.

All the way from the hospital, the driver had been talking about the need for a revolution but now went silent, no doubt thinking he'd picked the wrong passenger. Beyond a long line of hornbeams, a herd of deer stopped grazing and stared at the taxi as if they only ever saw Rolls-Royces. On the other side of the drive, the lawns looked fit for a royal garden party and gardeners on ride-on mowers were making the bands of green even lighter. After that, tall hedges masked the view and ran for about fifty yards before opening to a paved parking area the size of Trafalgar Square, but empty except for a scattering of small cars that must have belonged to staff. And a private helicopter. When you live in the back of beyond, how can you survive without your chopper?

Ahead was a sunken garden with a circular lily pond and six fountains playing around a larger set-piece, a sculpture of lifesize maidens frolicking in the spray, their buxom figures not unlike Lady Bede if you dared to imagine her in the buff.

Diamond paid the driver, who, from the way he slammed the door and made the tyres screech, had expected a better tip. Bring on the revolution.

The house on the other side of the pond was equal to the build-up, three storeys high and ten bays wide, with a six-column pedimented portico, all in the local stone. The ground dipped at the back, allowing stunning views across the city. From the grandeur of the front you had a sense that there had to be unseen extra wings the other side, together with an orangery, an infinity pool and a theme park.

Virginia Perkins, builder's daughter from Mile End, had come up in the world.

Wishing he'd changed into his good suit, Diamond took the path around the sunken lawn, stepped between the stone griffins each side of the entrance and pressed the bellpush.

213

How would he justify this visit? Almost always, witness interviews were of his own making. This one was by invitation – an invitation with a hint of more in store than a drink and a chat. He hadn't yet worked out what Virginia Bede was about. She moved in high circles, was experienced with men, attractive and flirtatious. Was that her way of networking? Or was she sending out other signals? He was telling himself he needed to find out. He'd checked that she really was a bona fide member of the ethics committee, but he wanted to discover why she had fastened on to this investigation and was following it so keenly.

A young man in blue livery opened the door, waved Diamond in with an elaborate hand gesture you would only ever see in the court scene of *Swan Lake*, offered to take the trilby, had the offer turned down and was done for the day.

The interior didn't disappoint. The entrance hall, three bays wide and big enough to stable a family of dinosaurs, echoed to his footsteps on the tessellated floor. Enclosing it was an imperial staircase probably designed by Robert Adam, double sets of red-carpeted and white-pilastered stairs as wide as a street curving gracefully upwards to meet on a landing with a flower arrangement that wouldn't have disgraced a royal wedding.

From between the fluted Corinthian columns to the left appeared a silver-haired man in a dark suit. 'Detective Superintendent, welcome to Bede Hall. Virginia won't be long. Would you care for a drink?'

'Thanks, but I'll wait.'

Diamond took this to be Lord Bede and wished he'd armed himself with a few facts about the family, but from the way the guy showed him into an anteroom, dipped his head, took a step backwards and left, the second guess was that he was the butler. If so, addressing her ladyship by her first name had been odd – unless the modern aristocracy preferred informality.

Left in a modestly sized, richly furnished and panelled room, Diamond picked a magazine from a selection on a table. The cover picture was a Cessna Citation private jet standing on a runway with a background of palm trees. Along the fuselage in large letters was the word *Exorbitant.*

A happy chance to see the publication Olympia worked for, or was it delivered to every stately home in Britain? It was printed on top quality paper and was bulky enough to have a spine with the title printed along it. Predictably, he had to flick through scores of adverts for luxury items before finding the contents page. The main feature was a guide to buying Pacific islands. Someone had studied it already because the pages lay flat when he opened them and they gave off a faint smell of cigars. None of the main articles had been contributed by Olympia, but her name appeared inside a box at the foot of the back page entitled *The Exorbitant Team.* The only other name he knew was top of the list, Jock Scoular, proprietor.

'You caught me off guard, Peter. I haven't finished doing the flowers.' Virginia was in the doorway holding a vase of red roses. If they had any scent at all, it wouldn't stand a chance against her own. 'I was counting on your being at least five minutes late.'

'Want me to step outside again and take a turn around the pond?'

She rocked with laughter as if it was the funniest thing she'd heard all week. She was in a flimsy pale pink creation that glittered with each quiver of the hips. 'Come through and get a drink. I thought we'd use the blue reception room.'

He dropped the magazine on the table. 'Is there a choice?'

For some mysterious reason this caused more merriment. Had she been at the bottle or was she nervous?

Another young man in uniform was waiting inside with flute glasses of champagne on a silver tray. Virginia took two and handed one to her visitor before dismissing the servant with a flap of the hand. She told Diamond, 'I think I'm safe alone with you.'

'I'll take that as a compliment. How long have you lived here?'

'Six years. It's not what I would choose, but Clifford's family have been here for ever, so I try and make the best of it. Cheers.'

'Clifford being Lord Bede?'

'The seventeenth, yes. One to sixteen are on the walls staring down at me whenever I take any notice of them. It's obvious I get up their noses.'

He looked around the room.

'You won't see them here,' Virginia said. 'They're in the long gallery upstairs. These are recent acquisitions, my own choice.' She pointed to the portrait of a woman above the fireplace. 'That's the best thing in the room, a Thomas Lawrence. We know it's one of his because of his handwriting on the back. "Be pleased to keep this from the damp and sun." Isn't that sweet? Instead of signing his work, Lawrence left care instructions. I collect him because he lived in Bath as a youth.'

Interesting, he thought. She wasn't just marking time until she inherited Lord Bede's estate. She was investing in art and she seemed to know what was worth collecting.

'Who's the lady?'

'Unknown, more's the pity. Are you interested in art?'

'I know what I like,' he said.

This caused another peal of laughter. 'Don't we all? But I was speaking of art.'

'So was I.'

She pinched her lips into a shape of amused disbelief. 'Speaking for myself, there are things I'd rather be doing than collecting artworks, but needs must, as they say.'

'Who else have you got?' Her double-meanings were catching.

'Are we talking artists now? I haven't worked out how to take you. If you're really asking who I collect, there are plenty. Bath was a honeypot for painters in its heyday, at least a hundred and fifty of them.'

'Gainsborough?'

Her blue eyes held his for a long interval and suddenly the conversation got serious. 'What makes you mention him?'

'Things have moved on since you were last in the incident room. He's part of our investigation now.' He decided to tell her about the discoveries inspired first by Jean Sharp's close inspection of the photo and then Leaman's. There was no point in being secretive when she was at liberty to shadow the investigation. By sharing information he hoped to learn why she was so keen to be involved. 'None of this is certain, but it fits a lot of the facts.'

'Intriguing.' But she spoke the word flatly without meaning it, and he was certain everything he'd just said was already known to her. 'However, it's a lot to deduce from a photograph, isn't it?'

'Agreed,' he said. 'It's still circumstantial and I doubt if we'll prove anything for sure.'

'Why the excitement, then?'

'Because if we think this is a Gainsborough canvas, then maybe Seppy Hubbard and other interested parties think the same. Their behaviour seems to bear this out. Do you follow me? We don't have to prove Gainsborough painted the thing. What's important is whether people believed he did.'

'Clever.'

'Seppy went to London and visited an expert who did a cleaning job on the canvas and revealed what was underneath all the paint.'

'Something special, I hope?'

'We don't know. But I visited his daughter Ruby in hospital this morning and she confirmed that he believes it's genuine. If it is a Gainsborough and Seppy has it in his possession, he's even more at risk than he was already. It's no surprise he's vanished. He could be dead.'

'Does Ruby think so?'

'She's extremely worried. She knew all this before she was shot. That's why she hired Johnny Getz to find him.'

'The private eye?' She paused, studying Diamond's face. 'Is he any good?'

'I have my doubts. He found out about the London expert, but all he needed to do was latch on to Ruby's friend, Olympia.'

'Can Olympia be trusted?'

'These are questions I'm trying to answer. She's smart, ambitious and fearless. A journalist. She could easily walk into trouble. One of my team is tailing her as we speak.'

'You've got yourself some tense situations to resolve. I appreciate your telling me so much.'

'But you knew it already.'

She reddened. 'What makes you think that?'

'The way you listened to what I was saying just now without any sense of surprise.'

'I'm monitoring the case,' she said, lowering her eyes and rearranging the chiffon folds. 'I try to keep up.'

'So you won't mind if I ask you about that? You offered to tell me more about your sources.'

'Where did you get that idea from?' As if remembering that fierceness didn't become her, she turned flirtatious again. 'Are you sure that wasn't just a ruse to be alone with a handsome man?'

He was becoming irritated. 'You promised to tell me how you keep tabs on us.'

'Promised, no. I gave no guarantee. I may have hinted that you'd find me more forthcoming on home territory. I could have meant something entirely different.'

Her archness grated with him. He didn't delude himself that she fancied him. If she knew so much about the way things operated in CID she'd know he was in a long-term relationship. She was playing the flirt to defuse the conversation. 'Who's your source, Virginia?'

'Haven't you guessed?'

'My boss, Georgina?'

'Top of the class. Now let's relax and get to know each other better.'

'What made you pick the antiques shop inquiry?'

She wasn't pleased by his persistent questioning. 'You're starting to bore me, chuck, and that's not a good way to go. Fetch me another glass and I might forgive you.'

He picked one from the tray the servant had left behind and handed it to her and she answered the question that bored her.

'My husband, bless him, is struggling with dementia. Well, he's given up the struggle, doesn't relate to me any more and needs full-time care, so if I want to lead an intelligent life I'm forced to look elsewhere. Not the most altruistic reason for joining the ethics committee, but it's the truth and there's nothing more ethical than honesty. Police headquarters provided me with a list of all the ongoing investigations and pictures of the senior officers.'

'Really?' He prickled at this breach of confidence – and then remembered that his picture was on the police authority website along with many others. And in a glossy brochure as well. Security protocols had long since been sacrificed to the great god of public relations.

Lady Bede shared another confidence. 'I enjoy the company of men – mature men – and there's no harm in that. I'm not going to tell you which of you top policemen is the best looker, but now you understand where I'm coming from.'

He understood more clearly. She'd spoken candidly and it was starting to sound like the truth.

'Very well.' She picked up the thread again. 'If you came here expecting to talk shop, let's get it out of the way. I do have some sympathy for you trying to make sense of it all, a dead burglar in an Egyptian coffin, a missing shop owner, his daughter shot and in hospital, a gunman popping off shots at all the witnesses and now a centuries-old art mystery. So much to puzzle over. And to top it all, a private eye in competition with you. It would give me sleepless nights if I didn't get sleepless nights anyway.'

'That's tough.'

'The insomnia? I don't let it get me down. Instead of counting sheep I count men.'

Diamond smiled at that. 'I have no problems sleeping. I'm a detective by choice, so I enjoy a case that needs some brain-fag, but I can switch off at the end of the day.'

'And what is your brain telling you about this one?'

'That everyone is holding something back, you included.'

'That's a first. Nobody ever accused me of hiding my intentions.'

'You could hide other things in a big house like this. Do you own any Gainsboroughs yourself?'

'Unfortunately, no. But not for want of trying. They don't often come on the open market.'

'But you know what they're worth?'

'Nobody does until the bidding ends. You're up against a legion of nameless billionaires on the ends of phones. A full-length portrait of a woman fetched six and half million in a sale at Christie's ten years ago and it wasn't thought to be a major work. If *Mr and Mrs Andrews* or *The Blue Boy* came up for sale I could sell the house and grounds and still fall short in the bidding.'

'Your husband wouldn't be too happy.'

'Clifford?' she said, shaking her head. 'He wouldn't have a clue, poor old darling. He doesn't know a hawk from a handsaw.'

'He's living here, presumably?'

'In the gatekeeper's lodge, with a team of devoted carers. It may sound unfeeling, but he's better off there. I spent a small fortune making it comfortable for him. He's happy. Before I thought of that solution, he'd taken to wandering about the house and getting lost. Completely forgot where he was. You've no idea how big the place is. He was missing all night once. I had all the staff searching for him. We found him in the morning curled up in the dumbwaiter like a dormouse and fast asleep.'

'Does he have any other family?'

'No. He's the last Bede on the necklace, as he used to say to me when we were courting – as if I cared about inheriting the family fortune.'

Come off it, lady, he thought. Your whole married life has been about finding richer and richer husbands.

She motored on. 'This bloody Alzheimer's makes one

despair. He led a blameless life, church every Sunday, didn't gamble, smoke or drink, ate the right food, exercised, paid his taxes and he ends up like this. I won't sell the place while he still lives here, although I do have power of attorney. But you don't want to hear about my situation. Who's behind the killing and mayhem?'

'If I knew, I'd pull them in for questioning.'

'You must have your suspicions.'

'Plenty, but no certainty.'

'Is the gunman just a hired hand?'

'That's the way it seems.'

'Can't you set a trap? Arrest the blighter and make him lead you to the real villain?'

'I wish it were so simple. The way criminals operate, he won't know who is paying him. He's made so many cock-ups, he may be history already.'

'Dead?'

'It wouldn't surprise me. He's more of a liability than a solution – if indeed it's a "he".'

'Ha,' she said. 'Aren't you even sure of that?'

'Witnesses mention a slight figure.'

'No use looking at me, then.' She took a step towards him. 'Unless you'd like to.'

Nothing was going to divert Diamond, certainly not this seduction routine. 'As an art collector, would you buy anything in a car-boot sale?'

'I might if it interested me, but I'd be extremely wary.'

'And then if an expert cleaned off the excess paint and said it appeared to be a genuine old master, the right materials, the right style and so on? Wouldn't that set your pulse racing?'

'I'd want to know the provenance and there doesn't seem

to be much. You said this one can only be traced as far back as the 1940s?'

'To a mews building once owned by Gainsborough.'

'Gainsborough left Bath in 1773. How many years is that?'

'Two-fifty, give or take. But as the picture was painted over and used as a palette there won't be any records.'

'All that time, lying about in an outhouse? You can't tell me someone wouldn't have slung it out as rubbish. I can't see it ever coming to auction. Ten to one it's a forgery and not particularly clever either.'

'Seppy seems to have rated it.'

'I don't wish to be unkind, but Seppy sounds to me like a wishful thinker, a romantic at heart.'

He smiled. 'Now you put it like that . . .'

'Mind you,' Virginia said, 'I wouldn't want you to think I'm unromantic myself.'

Here we go again, he thought.

She wasn't giving up. 'You talked about my pulse racing. Believe me, it doesn't take much to make it race at Grand Prix speeds and I'm not talking about fake works of art. Your glass is empty.'

Definitely time to beat a retreat. He had a perfectly happy relationship with Paloma.

He replaced his glass on the tray. 'Such a pity I'm in the middle of a day's work. I must call a cab.'

23

'The only reason I tolerate you,' Olympia said, seated beside me in the cab she'd called, 'is that when you pushed me into that holly bush you may have saved my life.'

'Not a bad reason,' I said, choosing to ignore the sour grapes that came with it. I'd just bummed a lift with her, so I had to sound friendly.

'And to be frank,' she went on, 'I'm not even sure you *did* save me. It's quite possible the gunman aimed to miss. He could have been hired to put the frighteners on me.'

'Who knows?' I said, biting back my annoyance.

She seemed to realise she was being unjust. 'But for one brief shining moment you acted like a gentleman and bought me a coffee to get over the shock.'

'I needed coffee myself,' I said in case she took me for a soft touch.

The driver was taking us the quiet way into town, down Weston Lane and past the golf course.

'Why me, Johnny?' Olympia said in a rare sign of nerves. 'Why did he shoot at me when I'm a minor player?'

'There's a Ross Macdonald quote that sums you up. "She was trouble looking for somebody to happen to."'

'That's garbage. Ross who?'

'Don't tell me you reached this point in life without

224

encountering the greatest private eye series ever – Lew Archer.'

'Him?' she said, looking down her nose. 'I'd cash in six of him for one V. I.'

'Never heard of him.'

'Sexist,' she hissed at me. 'V. I. Warshawski is female, Sara Paretsky's sleuth. Welcome to the twenty-first century, Mr Rip Van Winkle. I'll give you a V. I. quote. "Never underestimate a man's ability to underestimate a woman." Says it all.'

I knew Olympia was a feminist. I knew she was good with words. I should have known she was a reader as well as a writer. Not wishing to be scattergunned with quips from female private eye writers, I moved the conversation on. 'Where exactly are we heading?'

'Relax. We're dropping you in Kingsmead Square,' she said. 'You can find your way home from there.'

'No thanks,' I said. 'In case you hadn't noticed, I'm shadowing you. I'll finish up where you do.'

'I'm on a job, Johnny.'

'All the more reason for me to tag along. And I'm not the only one.'

'What?' Her eyes gleamed like freshly minted coins.

'Take a look out the back. See the yellow Ford Ka? It's been behind us like it's on a tow rope all the way from the hospital. Unless I'm going blind it's being driven by Diamond's blonde sidekick.'

'Ingeborg?' She twisted around for a good look. 'Yikes, you're right. What does *she* want?'

'A slice of the action, same as me.'

'She won't get it.' She leaned forward and told the driver. 'Change of plan. Do you know Westmoreland Street?'

He did.

And so did I, although I hadn't been there yet. Lucky's place. She'd decided to abort her mission and return to base.

'It's make-up-your-mind time, Johnny,' she told me. 'If you don't want to end up south of the river with nothing to do, you'd better speak up and we'll drop you where you can walk home. You won't be welcome where I'm going.'

I didn't need telling. My ribs still ached from the kicking Lucky had given me last time we met. But I had a plan of my own. 'I'll link up with Ingeborg and tell her the fun is over for today. She'll want to quiz me, so she'll drive me back to Kingsmead Square.'

'True to type,' she said. 'Scrounging lifts from all and sundry.'

'I'll be doing her a good turn. She could waste hours sitting in her car waiting for you to show.'

And that was what happened – almost. The cab stopped outside a shabby terraced house in Westmoreland Street. While Olympia was paying the driver, I got out and made sure the yellow Ka had pulled up fifty yards behind us. I waved to Ingeborg and marched down the street to join her.

She lowered the window. 'What the hell is going on?'

'You want to get a different-coloured car.'

'Okay, clever clogs. You spotted me. Why has she come here?'

'It's where she's living. She wants us to think she's going to spend a quiet night in front of the telly. Why don't I get in your car and you can drive off and make it look like we called off the hunt?'

She thought about that, torn between telling me to get lost and taking my brilliant advice.

'You're too bloody obvious, parked here,' I added.

'Get in, then.'

She revved up and drove past the house and found she was faced with a dead end and no turning room. The main railway ran along the bottom of Westmoreland and barred all progress. How humiliating. She had to reverse the whole way she'd come, watched by Olympia, who was standing by the door of the house with her lips curved in amusement.

We ended up in Westmoreland Drive, which was a scruffier version of Westmoreland Street. Talk about the mean streets of San Francisco. Bath is not without its eyesores. But at least we managed to back the car into a space.

'Where was she aiming to go before you muscled in?' Ingeborg asked.

'I didn't find out. She'd spoken to the driver before I got in.'

'Didn't you ask?'

'She wouldn't have told me. She gives nothing away. She's a woman of mystery.'

'And you're a crap detective.'

Why do I get it in the neck from every attractive woman I meet?

I refrained from saying a CID sergeant who tailgated a taxi for three miles in a yellow Ka wasn't exactly spy material. 'She'll wait until she thinks it's safe to go out again. Shame there isn't a bar here. I could use a whisky.'

'I wouldn't want to leave my car unattended in this street for long,' Ingeborg said. 'Besides, we might miss her if she goes out again.'

'Don't you worry about that,' I said.

She looked at me in astonishment for a full five seconds before the penny dropped. 'Cool. You've bugged her.'

'This crap detective is better than you thought.'

227

'How did you manage that?'

'Trade secret.'

If I'd known we had more than two hours to kill I would have gone looking for that bar. Ingeborg turned on the sound system, disco deep dives as far as I could tell. I'm into bass-boosted hard rock myself and didn't dig her tame, tinny stuff at all. But there was no need to talk about the weather. I checked my phone every few minutes to see if Olympia was on the move.

Finally, when the light was fading and so was I, something showed on the screen. I said in a Cape Canaveral monotone, 'Lift-off. We have lift-off.'

Ingeborg cut the music and switched on the engine.

By my reckoning there was only one way out of Westmoreland Street. It was a dead end, right? Olympia needed to pass the road we were parked in, whether she was on foot or on wheels. We were facing the right direction ready to go. It wasn't as if the road was busy. Nothing had moved in the past half-hour.

We waited.

We'd had the lift-off and the rocket hadn't shown.

Impossible.

After a long minute, Ingeborg said, 'Where is she?'

'I don't get this,' I said, staring at the street map on my smartphone. 'She left the house, but I've lost her.'

'Already? You're joking.'

'Makes no sense.'

'Nobody has come by.'

I slammed the damned phone against my thigh. Didn't smarten the phone or me.

Another minute passed and suddenly out of nowhere contact was restored.

'How did she do that?'

To my surprise and mystification the tracker was showing she was on the other side of the railway. She must have got there by broomstick.

I showed Ingeborg. 'She's clean away.'

'If she can get there, so can we,' she said. 'Does she own a car?'

'Not to my knowledge. And I can't see her as a cyclist. She's got to be on foot.'

'Is there a bridge over the railway?'

'A tunnel under is more likely.'

'Give me your phone.' Miss Cool double-tapped with two of her slim fingers on the street map to zoom out, studying the line of the railway track. 'This must be where the tunnel is, only two streets away. Westmoreland Road.' Then she blinked and frowned. 'Isn't that where we are?'

'We're in Westmoreland Drive and Lucky's house is in Westmoreland Street. Westmoreland Road is different. God help the delivery people round here.'

'But how did she get where she is?' Miss Cool no more, Ingeborg slapped her forehead with her free hand and said, 'Birdbrain. I know. I saw when we got to the end of her street and had to reverse. It didn't register with me. There's a footpath leading off to the left, an alley almost hidden by bushes and running beside the railway. She must have gone through there on foot and walked as far as the tunnel.' She dropped the phone in my lap and glanced into her wing mirror, preparing to pull out.

'Don't,' I told her. 'Cut the engine. If she's walking, we do the same. She'd spot your car right away.'

She saw the sense in that. We both bundled out and started running. We turned the corner of Westmoreland Street. No need for stealth here. As we passed Lucky's house, I thought I saw a familiar face at the window, grinning.

Just as Ingeborg had said, the start of a footpath came into view to the left of the brick wall that blocked off the road from the railway. She was striding out ahead of me like the pacemaker in a world-record attempt and I knew exactly what was going through her head. She'd hate confessing to Pete that she'd lost Olympia.

The path took us for about five hundred yards and opened out to a main road. On our right was the tunnel under the railway, big enough for a bus to pass through. I was gasping by then. Ingeborg, who probably worked out daily on a running machine, was breathing like a baby. As soon as we were through the tunnel, I said, 'Hang on. We'd better check her position.'

Good thing I did, because the phone showed me Olympia was only two hundred yards ahead. At Ingeborg's pace we would have caught up with her in the next minute.

'What road is this?' she asked.

'Lower Oldfield Park.'

'Oldfield Park is where Ruby lives.'

You won't believe this. In all the time we'd been sitting waiting, neither of us had grasped the significance of our location. I hadn't made the connection between Westmoreland Street and Oldfield Park. Yet here they were, facing each other across the railway.

It's strange. I've lived in Bath for the greater part of my life and I hardly ever venture south of the river and the railway. You don't unless you need to. There's nothing except suburban sprawl, outdated industries, empty churches and street after street of boring houses. All the sites worth visiting are in the centre and on the northern slopes.

Before, when I visited Ruby, I'd used a different route.

If you recall, I cycled to Oldfield Park and met her at the station. Ingeborg and Pete had made their own way there.

Poor navigators as we were, we morphed into scouts on the trail, stepping out cautiously, alert for a sighting of our quarry.

'What's she up to?' Ingeborg said. 'Ruby's still in hospital. There's no sense in visiting her flat.'

'There's every sense if she wants a private look round,' I said.

'She's not going to find anything. The place was done over the same night she was taken into hospital. Anything of interest will have been taken.'

'She'll have a reason.'

'Keep out of sight. Don't stray into view.'

Ruby's flat was in a side road near Oldfield Park station. We were fast approaching the corner.

'Don't show yourself,' Ingeborg said.

I was quietly amused that this normally tough police sergeant was fussing like a mother on the day her five-year-old starts school.

I didn't speak. I had my face pressed to a lamppost. But I could see Olympia's tall figure on those impossible high heels moving up the street towards Ruby's place. No question now that she was going there. The only uncertainty was how she would get in, and it was soon resolved when she stepped up to the door, reached into her bag and took out a key. I remembered Ruby had her own entrance from the front. Olympia – supposedly her closest friend – looked right and left, let herself in and closed the door after her.

'She's inside now,' I informed Ingeborg. 'We can get closer.'

I spotted a wall about a metre high opposite the house. It was the boundary of overgrown grounds in front of a disused chapel. Excellent cover. From behind we'd have a viewpoint better than the front stalls of the Theatre Royal.

Olympia would be occupied inside the house, so there was little chance she'd be staring out of a window. We stepped out brazenly, covered the distance to a wrought-iron padlocked gate, climbed over and waded through the undergrowth. In a stalking situation you don't complain about brambles scratching your legs. We picked our vantage point and crouched out of sight in thick bracken and elder behind the wall.

Cue another wait.

Across the street, a light was turned on upstairs.

'Are you going to book her when she comes out?' I asked.

'What for? She didn't break in. She's committed no offence.'

'We want to know what she's up to.'

'We'll speak to her.'

More minutes went by.

'Pete will be so pissed off he wasn't here,' I said. 'He misses all the action, poor sap.'

'Don't knock my guv'nor,' she warned me.

'I wouldn't do that. I value my link with you lot. Every private eye from Sherlock Holmes to Matt Scudder needs a line into the factory. Sam Spade had his tame sergeant, Tom Polhaus. Philip Marlowe had Officer Randall from Central Homicide. It comes with the territory.'

She stared at me as if I'd announced I was Elvis's love child. 'You really believe in this tripe, don't you? You live it.'

'There's worse tripe than crime fiction.'

'I don't dispute that, Johnny, but the private-eye era is buried in the past and mostly in another country, another continent. I can't see how you function in twenty-first-century Britain here in Bath, for Christ's sake.'

'So what am I doing with you up to our necks in stinging nettles behind a church wall if it isn't sleuthing?' I said. 'This is my client's home being invaded. It's really happening, ducky.'

She couldn't answer that. She said, 'It doesn't even smell like fresh growth. I'm wondering if one of us has trodden in something.' She raised her leg and inspected the tread of the trainer she was wearing. And then looked at the other. 'Not me.'

I scraped each shoe against the rough stone of the church wall. 'Nor me.'

But as I lowered my leg I hit my heel against a solid object. The sound was something between a thud and a clang.

'What was that?'

'Somebody slung an old petrol can over the wall, I guess.' I used the flash on my phone to show her.

But it wasn't a can. It was a crash helmet. I lifted it up and saw it was in very good nick. 'Funny thing to find in a churchyard.'

'Some so-called friend playing tricks,' Ingeborg said. 'People are so mean. This will have cost a bit.'

'We could leave it on top of the wall.'

'Not now.' She looked across the street. 'Drop it. The light's been switched off.'

Presently Ruby's front door opened and Olympia emerged, took a cautious look to each side and closed it behind her. She was holding a large rope-handled bag she hadn't carried before.

'Let's go,' Ingeborg said to me.

We quit the churchyard jungle, climbed over the wall, crossed the street and confronted Olympia before she'd gone a few steps.

'Hi,' Ingeborg said. 'Do you mind telling me what you were doing in there?'

'Eek, where did you come from?' she said, as if we were extra-terrestrials.

'Never mind. Answer the question.'

She started to say, 'It's no business of—' but Ingeborg cut her off.

'It's my business as a police officer. May I see what's in the bag?'

Olympia had got over the first shock and was dealing with a second, eyeballing me. 'What's he doing here?'

As if I was the guilty party. Well, sucks to that. 'You were nosing around in my client's flat. I have a right to find out why.'

That took the wind out of her sails. Tamely, she handed the bag to Ingeborg. 'See for yourself.'

I was half expecting Seppy's picture, even though the contents looked more bulky than perpendicular.

Ingeborg put her hand inside and took out a pink pyjama jacket and gave it to me to hold. Packing material, I thought. She delved in again and drew out an unopened pack of white knickers followed by a couple of T-shirts, some bras, jeans and socks. An awful lot of packing. By the time the last item, the pyjama bottoms, came out, I needed both arms to hold it all and I was feeling as stupid as if I'd nicked the lot from a neighbour's washing line.

Ingeborg handed me the empty bag. I stuffed everything back.

'You collected these things for Ruby,' Ingeborg said to Olympia, making it more of a statement than a question.

'If you think I was stealing them from my lifelong friend, you need brain surgery yourself,' Olympia said. She'd had time to recover her poise. 'Can't you tell they're not my

234

style? No disrespect to Ruby, but I wouldn't be seen dead wearing pink pyjamas. She asked for fresh clothes and I'll take them to her.'

'She gave you her key?'

'No. I have a spare. After the break-in, I took charge. Someone had to. I tidied up and got the locks changed. She knows I can come and go and she doesn't mind. This place is only a short walk from where I'm staying.'

'We needed to be sure,' Ingeborg said. 'We had no information you were visiting the house.'

'Since when have I been put on probation? I don't have to report my movements to the police.'

'It's been burgled once.'

'I'm not even sure of that,' Olympia said. 'They broke in and opened cupboards and drawers, but they didn't bother with valuables like her rings and earrings. There was money in the living room, still there. They were after the painting. Whether they found it, I have no idea.' She held out a hand for the bag and I handed it to her. 'And now am I free to leave or do you want to take me to the police station and throw the book at me?'

Ingeborg said she was good to go and apologised for the inconvenience we'd caused her.

I'm not sure how she managed it, but Olympia gave us a virtual V-sign with her rear view as she marched off.

'We cocked up badly there,' I said.

Ingeborg wasn't wholly sure. 'The bag of clothes could be a clever alibi.'

'It's a pity,' I said. 'I'd built up a good rapport with her.'

'We all know you're God's gift to women.'

I ignored that. I'd been called worse. 'Will you be driving back through town?'

'Before I do, I'm going to pick up that crash helmet,'

she said. 'It's too much of a coincidence that it turns up right opposite the house. I intend to run some tests on it.'

We returned to the churchyard, heaved ourselves over the wall once more and retrieved the helmet.

'That pong is still about,' I said as an ugly thought popped into my head. 'I'll take a look around.'

I didn't need to go far. The source was in a patch of bracken barely a couple of strides from the place where we'd been. A short guy in leathers with a bullet hole through his forehead.

24

Don't try this at home, folks. If you want to fire a bullet through your own forehead, it won't be a neat hole in the centre. That's too much of a stretch. For that, you'd need an arm longer than a gorilla's and a double-jointed wrist. It was obvious to me that the dead man in the churchyard hadn't killed himself.

Someone had popped him.

The shot was fired from close range, two feet or less. How do I know that? It's my job. You can't hack it as a private eye unless you master the basics.

The key to understanding entry wounds is gunshot residue, or GSR, as we call it in the trade. This is the extra shit discharged from the barrel with the bullet when the gunpowder explodes, mainly hot gases and bits of burned and unburned powder. If the muzzle is in contact with the skin the gases leave a star-shaped pattern, not pretty, but telling its own tale.

But when the gun is fired from six inches to two feet away, little particles of gunpowder get embedded in the skin, stippled neatly around the entry hole. That's what happened here.

I didn't spill any of this gun science to Ingeborg. She knew her stuff. She'd be insulted. All her energy was focused on taking charge of a murder scene. All cops know the drill.

You call for assistance and you seal the scene. She had her phone to her ear already. While she was giving them our location, I bent the rules a little, held my nose with my left hand and patted down the dead man's clothes with my right. As I expected, he had practically nothing in his pockets. His handgun wasn't on him. His killer must have taken it away.

It was obvious to me that the dead guy was the short-sighted gunman Pete had joked about. Or was he the constipated owl? This two-eyed loser had fired shots at Ruby, Olympia, Lucky and me and failed to kill any of us.

My first look at the face the crash helmet had hidden from me up to now was a let-down. It meant zilch to me. I judged the age at forty-five. Sallow, balding, unshaven, with maybe enough reddish hair above the mouth to rate as an attempt at a tash – though I wouldn't bet my house on it. Thin-cheeked, slack-jawed, showing he hadn't been near a dentist in years. Eyes still open, giving the dead man's stare, unimproved by catching some colour from a late afternoon Somerset sky. Not an attractive specimen of humanity, but nothing to strike fear into anyone else.

'You shouldn't have touched him,' Ingeborg said as she pocketed her smartphone.

'Too late,' I told her. 'I didn't disturb anything.'

'Get this in your head, Johnny. I'm in charge here.'

'Be my guest.'

'A patrol car will be here in under five minutes.'

'If the message went out to all cars, we'll have six or seven eager for some action,' I said. 'They all want a break from dealing with confused old people and noisy teenagers.'

'There's more to policing than that,' she said. 'A major incident can happen any time.'

'Like Pete asking you to fetch him a coffee?'

'That wouldn't be an incident. It would be meltdown.'

'I keep forgetting your stripes.'

'Well, don't.'

The *nee-naw* of the first responder reached our ears.

'Are you thinking what I'm thinking?' I said.

'That he's our gunman? Almost certainly. How long would you say the body's been here?'

'A couple of days, going by the flies and the smell. I guess he was holed up waiting for a chance to take another shot at Olympia. When was he last seen?'

'The day before yesterday, out at Limpley Stoke,' she said.

'Olympia's cottage. He was desperate to kill her, going everywhere he could think. She can feel safe now.'

'From what I've seen of her, she's pretty fearless anyway.'

'I'll second that. There's another good thing about this.'

'What's that?'

'One less item on Pete's to-do list.'

'Far from it,' she said. 'There's a bigger item now – a gunman who really can shoot to kill.'

I was right about the patrol cars. Two arrived together, beacons flashing, and a third wasn't far behind and then the inevitable gawpers started streaming out of the houses across the street. Ingeborg made sure they kept the other side of the wall. The plods stretched some crime-scene tape along and it looked like *Line of Duty* – if you had a good imagination.

The scene-of-crime van was next to arrive, followed soon after by Pete in a private car driven by his deputy.

'The pleasure of seeing you is wearing thin, Mr Getz,' the big man huffed as soon as he had hauled himself out.

'It's only thanks to me that you have a crime scene at all,' I pointed out. 'I found the crash helmet and we put two and two together. Isn't that right, Inge?'

She couldn't disagree. 'Roughly speaking, yes.'

'I don't know what you were doing here in the first place,' Diamond said to me.

'Working,' I snapped back. 'That's my client's house across the street, remember?'

'All too well. You kept us waiting outside for twenty minutes. How do I get where you are?'

I wasn't sure what he meant. Did he dream of quitting the force and becoming a private eye? Then I saw that he was eyeing the wall.

'The quick way is over.'

He scowled. It's one thing for a trained athlete like me to lever myself over, quite another for a sack of potatoes.

'There's also a gate,' I said.

'Where's that?'

I pointed, waited for him to take a few steps towards it and called out, 'It's padlocked.'

He got over the undignified way, his back to the wall, hands flat to the top, raising his arse high enough to sit there, draw up his legs, rotate and let himself down the other side.

His slim deputy, Chief Inspector Halliwell, was over like a cat.

The SOCOs were already at work, photographing the body.

'Where's the access path?'

Ingeborg showed him.

He stood over the body like a big-game hunter posing beside his kill, but it was Halliwell who recognised the dead man. 'That's Wally Knox. He's been around for years. Small-time criminal, in and out of jail. Shoplifting, mugging, nicking cars. You must have come across him, guv.'

'He's new to me,' Diamond said. 'I don't know every scumbag in the area.'

'I can picture him nicking a scooter,' Halliwell said, 'but I'd never imagine him as a gunman.'

'Somebody did, mistakenly. How about you, Mr Getz? Have you had any dealings with this man?'

I shook my head. 'My work is mostly at the high end of the scale.'

'Let's see his record,' Diamond said to Ingeborg. She was already checking the PNC.

'It's like Keith says. Petty larceny, handling stolen goods, stealing a vehicle.'

'If he's well known locally, it shouldn't be difficult to find out where he's been lately and who he met. Do you know what I'm going to say?'

'I'll raise a team,' Ingeborg said.

25

So we found the dead gunman. When I saw 'we', I'm being modest. Shucks, why should I be modest? No one else will blow my trumpet. Here's the plain truth. If it hadn't been for me hitting my foot against the goddamn crash helmet, he'd still be lying there rotting.

The top brass, Pete and his sidekick Halliwell, didn't stay long. They'd seen enough. Ingeborg was under orders to find Wally Knox's contacts, so she wasn't going to hang around either. She offered me a lift, which I turned down. I had a gut feeling there was more to be discovered, and I was right, but not in the way I expected.

The white overalls took over. One of the SOCOs told me if I was going to stay their side of the wall, I'd better get into a forensic suit. He'd seen me talking to the others and mistook me for a plainclothes officer, or he'd have told me to piss off home. My guess is that he thought asking me to struggle into a forensic suit would have the same result. I called his bluff by asking him for one and putting it on. Then I sat on the wall and watched them do their fingertip search.

I was glad of a chance to catch up with myself. Now that Wally Knox had been totalled in a cold-blooded shooting, this whole case had got more serious than I expected. For me, it was still a missing father job, but the chance of Seppy being left alive had shrunk like a jellyfish in the sun. With my client Ruby back in the world of the living and likely ready to break my balls to get the right result, I needed a breakthrough. But what if all I found when I broke through was her daddy with a hole in his head?

It was at this low point that a voice behind me said, 'Did we meet in the incident room?'

Female, easy on the ear. I turned my head, and she was easy on the eye as well and much my age, but either the years had treated her more kindly than they'd treated me, or she was a dab hand at making herself up. The eyes were her outstanding feature, such a deep blue you could have called them violet, topped with long dark lashes she'd definitely grown herself. She was a smart dresser, too, in a fedora, suede jacket, pink skirt and white boots.

I had to think how to answer the incident-room question. I'd never been allowed inside the Corn Market. It was clear she took me for one of the police because of the paper suit I was wearing. So I said, 'I'm sorry, but my memory has gone walkies today.'

'I'm Virginia.'

'Of course,' I said, pretending the name rang a bell. 'What brings you here, Virginia?'

'A little bird told me there was an incident. May I sit up there with you?'

I looked at the spotless pink skirt. I looked at the grimy lichen-covered top of the churchyard wall. She must have known what she was letting herself in for. 'If you like.'

'Help me up, then.'

Her hand was baby-soft and warm.

And her climbing action was prettier than Pete's. I was treated to a flash of thigh and a nudge from her breasts.

'Oops. Sorry.'

'I'm not,' I said, razor sharp. 'It didn't trouble me.'

The scent that came with her almost knocked me off the wall. We sat there like two pre-revolution Russian royals watching the serfs toiling in the field up to their chins in nettles. The corpse on view in the flattened part under our noses didn't trouble the Grand Duchess beside me at all. Her perfume neutralised the smell.

'I didn't catch your name,' she said.

'I'm Johnny. I do remember that.' Generally, I produce my business card at that point, but she thought I was police and I couldn't disappoint her.

'And are you in charge, Johnny? I don't see Peter anywhere.'

I took note that she was on first-name terms with the head honcho. 'You just missed him. Are you interested in crime?'

'Not crime *per se.*'

For me, *per se* was a conversation stopper. I hadn't the foggiest what she was talking about.

She tried to help me out. 'You see, I'm deeply interested in the ethical dilemmas the job puts in the way of you police professionals. Can you sleep at nights?'

'Not a problem,' I said, wondering where this was going. Ethical dilemmas? What planet was she on? 'A slug of whisky helps. How about you?'

'Me?' She wriggled her legs in amusement. 'My sleeping habits don't come into it. If you really want to know, I lie awake thinking of things.'

'Ethical dilemmas?'

'No.' She laughed and said, cool as you like, 'Sensual things. I'm married to an older man. Twenty-five years older. We don't sleep together any more.'

This had turned awfully personal and I wasn't sure why.

Maybe she thought it was amusing to hit on a cop who could lose his job if he did anything about it. If she'd known I was freelance she would have watched her words more. A PI doesn't turn down a good offer. Take one of my heroes, Travis McGee, in the John D. MacDonald books. There are twenty-one in the series and I can't think of any when he doesn't get laid. But before you ladies call Travis and me sexist pigs, I'd better point out that it's always in a good cause. The guy appreciates and understands women and helps them understand themselves. Even Sue Grafton wrote that she envied the generation just discovering Travis McGee. Me, I discovered him before I ever went out with a girl. I envied McGee and I still do. Give me the chance and I can be a mentor, too.

Virginia must have sensed where my thoughts were drifting because she changed the subject. 'Who's the dead man?'

'Him?' I said. 'Almost certainly the gunman who's been scaring people. Wally Knox, a no-hoper.'

'No hope now, for sure. Who killed him?'

'We aren't naming anyone yet.'

'But you have your suspicions, I expect?'

'Sure,' I said as if I'd never been more certain, 'but I won't say without firm evidence.'

She laughed and clapped her hands. 'Perfect. There's your ethical imperative coming into play.'

She was hooked on this garbage, so I played along. 'I only bring it out for gorgeous ladies like you.'

She elbowed me in the ribs. 'You seem to have an alternative set of values, you wicked man. But you were telling me why Wally was shot.'

'Was I? He failed on the job.'

She smiled. 'Like Cliff.'

'Who's Cliff?'

'My husband. Poor dear, he tried his best to stay fit and capable. He was a lifelong non-smoker and wouldn't drink anything stronger than rosehip tea. Swam half a mile every morning. Took all the vitamins. They didn't make any difference. At fifty, he was a spent force. For my sake when we married he tried Viagra – but that's another story. In short, it didn't work for him – and in short doesn't work for me either.' She nearly fell off the wall laughing at her own joke. 'So Wally Knox was a flop, too?'

'In another way.'

'Obviously. He was put down because of it.'

'And because he knew too much.'

We sat watching the search for at least ten minutes more, flirting like crazy. Leastways, I think we were. She kept on about ethics, telling me at one stage that I was postmodern, which I took as a compliment because she nudged me again and rested her hand on my thigh and said she'd enjoy deconstructing me.

The fun was interrupted by a shout from one of the searchers, who had found the scooter lying on its side in dense bracken – surely enough to confirm that Wally had been the lone gunman. It was a black Vespa with the reg plates covered over.

'You'll be wanting to tell Peter,' Virginia said. 'He'll be so excited.'

'Unlikely,' I said. 'He doesn't show his feelings much.'

'Speaking of feelings,' she said. 'I've lost all sensation in my bottom. I'm not used to sitting on stone walls. Be a gent and help me down, would you?'

'Gladly.' I swivelled and jumped down on the street side.

'Close your eyes,' Virginia said. 'I can't do this decently in a skirt.'

246

I did what she asked and presently felt her hands on my shoulders. She expected me to grasp her waist, and I didn't pass up the chance. I slipped my hands inside the suede jacket. She was no sylph, but nicely built for a woman in her mid-forties. I'd call her cuddly. Rudolf Nureyev would have made a better job of bringing her down to earth, but he didn't work in a forensic suit with his eyes shut. 'Can I look now?'

'Wait.'

I felt her lips touch mine. 'Thank you, Johnny. Let me give you a lift back to the police station.'

That would ruin everything.

I thought fast and told her my duty was done for the day. She was just as fast.

'In that case you'd better unzip.'

But she was talking about the forensic suit.

'True.' I peeled the thing off and stepped out of it.

'Now you must come for a drink at my place.' It sounded like a command and I didn't disobey.

I wasn't expecting the uniformed chauffeur and the Rolls-Royce waiting up the street. I wasn't expecting the ride to Sion Hill and the palace she lived in. I wasn't expecting the butler serving the vintage champagne. I stayed grounded by thinking myself into chapter one of *The Big Sleep*. I was every bit as cool as Philip Marlowe visiting Sternwood Hall. She was Carmen Sternwood, give or take a few years and some extra inches round the waist, but, heck, I'm five inches shorter than Marlowe.

In a room she called the anteroom we swapped small talk for a bit. She told me about the ethics committee and how she hooked up with Pete's investigation. She knew at least as much as I did about the suspects. She wasn't in this to pass the time.

247

Then she really freaked me out by saying, 'You're a fraud, Johnny. You're no more a cop than I am. You've been stringing me along. I gave you the chance to call Peter Diamond and tell him the scooter was found and you avoided it. What's your game?'

She had me by the short and curlies. My granny used to tell me no one was ever ruined by speaking the truth. 'No game,' I said. 'I'm a private eye. Ruby Hubbard hired me to find her father.' I took out one of my cards and handed it to her.

'"Gets results"?' she read aloud. 'That's a joke. Seppy went missing almost a month ago and you haven't a clue where he is. Is she paying you by the hour? Is that the reason you're dragging it out?'

'Hey,' I said, 'gimme a break. I work alone. I'm not the Pinkerton agency.'

'That's obvious. And now she's in hospital, you're stacking up the overtime. I do know something about ethical behaviour and you fall well short. I took you for a gentleman and it turns out you're a freeloader.'

I may have deserved a kicking, but not for falling short of Virginia's high standards, so I gave some back. 'I haven't lied to you – not once. I just didn't correct what you were saying. As for ethical behaviour, ferchrissakes I'm a private eye. The reason people use me is I bend the rules and I'm proud of it. I do stuff Pete Diamond and his cronies would get sacked for. It's tough in the real world and you need tough guys to sort it. So don't preach ethics to me.' I nearly told her to stuff her ethics where the sun never shines, but there's a little of the gent in me, however hard I try.

'You live by a different code from the rest of us, is that it?' Virginia said, quite pink from the exchange.

'Right on.'

'Putting yourself above the law?'

'Like it says on the card, I get results.'

'That's your moral imperative? To me, it sounds immoral – or do I mean amoral?' A wide smile spread across her face. At least she was human enough to laugh at herself. 'Doesn't really matter, does it? The only thing that matters right now is whether you'll come up to my bedroom and make passionate love to me.'

Quite some switch. And quite some challenge. We private eyes have certain things in common, like an office, a gun, a bottle of scotch and, hopefully, a client. But when sex is on offer, we're all different. Mike Hammer would be halfway up those stairs already. Travis McGee wouldn't hesitate. Sam Spade would earn the right by beating up the baddies first. Philip Marlowe would say something witty and leave. Lew Archer is too world-weary to care. Spenser is a one-woman man. Easy Rawlins isn't as easy as he sounds. He goes in for serious relationships. And don't start me on the female eyes.

So it was my call.

I'll level with you. In all my life I'd never had an invitation like that and I was up for it.

My only worry was the set-up. This was still Sternwood Hall. I'd met the butler. I'd met Carmen. Where was General Sternwood?

'Is it safe?'

'What do you mean – "Is it safe?"' Virginia said with a puzzled pout.

'Is your husband at home?'

'Clifford? I told you – he's past it.'

'Won't he object?'

'He won't know. Did you see the lodge as we drove through the gate? He lives there with his carers.'

'Is the butler still about?'

'*Coronation Street* is on. He'll be glued to the TV below stairs.'

'I noticed he called you "my lady".'

'He stands on ceremony. I don't insist on it. With your sleuthing skills, I thought you would have known I'm Lady Bede. Doesn't make a jot of difference in bed. I still have needs.'

'I had to ask.' I took her hand and she squeezed my fingers hard. She'd made her pitch and now it was up to me.

We crossed the tessellated floor of the entrance hall, stepped up the grand staircase and walked the gauntlet of the long gallery of Lord Bede's ancestors, lords and ladies of all ages, three hundred years of them. Virginia took no notice of the disapproval in their eyes. I felt it like a hail-storm.

Her bedroom was at the end, so vast that the four-poster bed looked like it needed friends. A crystal chandelier, all very traditional. Huge stone fireplace smelling faintly of wood ash from winter log fires, currently filled with a fragrant lily arrangement. Four huge windows along one side overlooked the estate. Curtains big enough for cinemas. Two sofas, three armchairs, four wardrobes and more pictures than I cared to count. Good thing they were land-scapes and seascapes, not more members of the Bede family.

'You can have the dressing room on the left. Mine's the other one,' Virginia told me.

What do I want with a dressing room? I thought. I didn't bring pyjamas. All I could do was undress. Clearly that was what she meant. I was glad to find a fresh white bathrobe behind the door.

I guessed Virginia would take longer than I would.

What I needed most was a smoke. There was a shower

here and towels, a choice of colognes and mouthwash. I figured I could clean up afterwards, so I took the pack from my pocket, lit up, sat on the toilet seat and puffed away like every self-respecting private eye once did. Who remembers Humphrey Bogart without a cigarette? Sam Spade rolled his own. Philip Marlowe was a pipe-smoker. But in the twenty-first century, a quiet smoke is the next thing to peeing in the street. It isn't done.

I puffed away and felt the benefit. Virginia had her needs. Well, so did Johnny.

The fag end was the problem. They float. They won't always flush away.

For the moment, I left it on top of the toilet tank.

I stripped, showered, picked the Sauvage spray from the line-up on the glass shelf under the mirror and made myself even more manly before donning the bathrobe. In one way, all this pampering was good for my confidence. In another, it made me think I wasn't the first. Or the second. Or the twentieth.

I slipped my feet into the slippers that matched the bathrobe, checked my face in the mirror and just before leaving the dressing room remembered the cigarette butt. Handily, there was a large asparagus fern in a tub near the door. I picked up the fag end, separated the fern fronds – and found a collection of cigar butts of various sizes standing up from the soil like a strange form of fungus. With much to think about, I dropped my dog-end among them and stepped into the bedroom.

I was alone, bollock-naked under the bathrobe. Only now did it cross my mind that this could be a honey trap. I wasn't armed. I'd left my trusty shooter at the office. Get real, Johnny, I told myself, a honey trap would mean you're in a spy story. You're mixing your genres.

Where was it best to be found when Virginia made her entrance? Draping myself on the bed like a Roman emperor didn't seem right. I crossed to one of the huge windows and stood looking out, legs slightly apart and one hand across my middle like a certain French emperor who was no slouch as a lover. I could see lawns, a lily pond and fountains with statues, the silver Rolls-Royce Phantom we'd arrived in, a yellow helicopter and the white drive stretching for about a mile. Somewhere too far off to be seen was the owner of all this, tended by his carers in the lodge. The poor old peer had no idea what was about to happen in his ancestral home.

Not a good thought to have when you want to be at your virile best.

Then Virginia was in the room in a pale blue diaphanous gown that she slipped from her shoulders and allowed to fall on the floor and Lord Bede went straight out of my head.

It was a long night with short bouts of sleep between sessions of parallel parking and I can't tell you much about it because my memory is a blur. We'd started early in the evening, remember. At one stage, I guess about 9 p.m., Virginia left the bed, went to the door and pulled in a hostess trolley stocked with freshly grilled fillet steak cooked rare, baked potatoes, mushrooms and tomatoes and more champagne on ice. The butler must have been under instructions to have it delivered on the hour.

I remember asking in jest if this was extra fuel for the night ahead. I was expecting to enjoy the well-earned meal, get dressed and go home. A giggle was Virginia's answer.

Twelve hours later the cooked breakfast was left outside.

As we sat up in bed sipping coffee, I tried to think up

252

an original way of saying, 'How was it for you?' I do appreciate encouragement. Finally, I asked, 'Did we meet those needs of yours?'

'For the time being,' she said, giving nothing away.

'I don't think I can offer any more today.'

'No problem,' she said. 'We can take a sauna together and see if that revives you. It often does.'

The voice of experience.

'I'm talking about pressure of work,' I lied. 'I must put in some hours on the case I'm investigating.'

'You're a workaholic.'

'And you're' – I hesitated – 'amazing.'

I left soon after. She told the chauffeur to drop me in Kingsmead Square. I was hoping the stylists in Shear Amazing would see me step out of the Roller and revise their opinions of me, but they were busy chatting. I dragged myself upstairs, crashed on to my sofa bed and slept the rest of the day.

26

Peter Diamond wasn't a churchgoer, so it was a rare circumstance that placed him next afternoon in one of Sir Christopher Wren's historic churches in the City of London, St Mary Abchurch, off Cannon Street. He wasn't at prayer, even though he could have used some divine help. He was gazing up at the painted interior of an extraordinary dome – extraordinary because there were no buttresses. The entire weight was supported by four walls that were not symmetrical. Although the church was said to be square-shaped, no two walls were at right angles.

Carla Denison's sudden death needed probing. Whether accidental or intentional, it impacted on the case. He was here to inspect the scene for himself. Clearly if the funeral had already taken place, no one had seriously entertained the idea of murder. The Met weren't involved and he didn't want to ask for their assistance unless it proved necessary. So he had taken the train to London for this private visit to the scene, leaving the team well occupied following up the shooting of Wally Knox.

A large, smiling woman appeared with a tray bearing a teapot, cup, saucer, milk jug and sugar bowl. A diagonal sash across her chest proclaimed her as an FCC watcher.

'You should have a different label,' he said. 'You're an angel.'

'Only a friend,' she said, blushing. 'Friends of the City Churches.'

'Do all your visitors get treated as well as this?'

She laughed. 'You're lucky. Tea and biscuits are normally served after Holy Communion on Wednesdays, our one regular service of the week. This isn't a parish church, you see. City workers from the banks and the Stock Exchange come in their lunchbreak, or whenever they need to pray.'

He had an irreverent thought about stockbrokers praying for a hike in the market.

She gasped. 'Heavens above, I forgot the biscuits.'

Heavens above literally existed here. While the angel was gone, he took another look at the paintwork. The dome was forty feet across and the interior was decorated with angels and cherubs in adoration. He'd done enough home-work to know it had been painted more than three hundred years ago, probably by an English artist called William Snow, who had used oils on plaster. The highest part showed the sun's rays radiating from strange lettering picked out in gold that had an amazing luminous quality.

'You're going to ask me what it means,' his flesh-and-blood angel said when he'd picked a custard cream from the tin. 'It's the Hebrew for Yahweh, or Jehovah, as the Bible has it. Doesn't it show up wonderfully? Miss Denison was restoring the gold leaf when she had the accident.'

'Were you here the day it happened?'

She shook her head. 'She was alone. So dreadful. She was found next morning, but too late.'

'Too late?'

'She'd already joined the choir invisible.'

He had to think about that for a moment.

'A lovely woman, so talented and willing to talk to the likes of me about ordinary things like pets and shopping.

We won't get over this easily. The church has had some terrible disasters – the great fire of 1666 and the Blitz of 1940, and now this.' She made the disasters sound as if they'd happened over one weekend instead of nearly four hundred years.

He asked a pivotal question. 'How can you be sure she was alone?'

'It happened outside visiting hours. We have church sitters here most days until three p.m. After that we're officially closed. She had special permission to stay until daylight ended.'

'Outside visiting hours' didn't automatically mean she was alone, he told himself. 'Has anyone been here to investigate?'

'Three at least, to my knowledge. We had the coroner's officer, a policeman and someone from the insurance. That was before the scaffold tower was taken away. They each climbed up to the top – not at the same time, of course – and said there was nothing wrong with the scaffolding. They decided she must have been dazzled by the sun coming through one of the windows.'

He'd noticed the four elliptical window spaces set into the sides of the dome. They were the main light source for the Hebrew lettering. 'They're unusual.'

'Yes, I haven't been up there myself, but I can see how a sunbeam would hit you right in the eyes. The insurance man called it an act of God.'

'Bad taste,' Diamond said.

'Oh?'

'Considering where she was and what she was working on. Could anyone else have been here?'

'After closing time? I can't see how. The notice outside clearly states the visiting times.'

'But was the church door locked?'

'I shouldn't think so. Miss Denison had to come and go. She didn't spend the night here – except the night of the accident and she had no choice then, poor soul.'

'So it's not impossible someone could have come in quietly while Miss Denison was at work?'

'I suppose. You don't think . . .' She couldn't bring herself to complete the sentence.

'I'm a detective, ma'am. I have to get into the minds of some bad people. If she was restoring the gold leaf, she was at the highest point of the dome concentrating on her work.'

'Why would anyone wish harm to such a lovely person?'

'We don't know anything for certain. I came here to see if it was remotely possible anyone else was involved.'

'In church?'

'Even in church.' The exchanges had reached the stage when there was little more to be learned. He felt in his pocket for loose change and found a fifty-pence coin. 'Is there a box for donations? You've been extremely hospitable. I needed that tea.'

'Are you in London for long?' she said. 'The forecast isn't good. They're talking about showers.'

'I'm not worried by a few spots of rain.' He showed her the trilby he'd taken off for respect.

'You'll need more than that. If you'll step this way, I've got just the thing.' She headed towards the souvenir stall by the door.

Diamond trailed after her, already plumbing his brain for reasons not to buy an umbrella.

Sure enough she picked a large, old-fashioned, crook-handled brolly off the table. 'It's such a clever idea.'

When she sprang it open, he was forced to agree. A

brilliant design concept, the umbrella, black on the outside, had the dome reproduced in full colour inside, every detail sharp and accurate, even the four windows.

'Only thirty pounds.'

Thirty pounds was a hefty slice of his budget. He hesitated. Then he thought what a useful visual aid it would be. He could picture himself demonstrating it in the incident room and in Paloma's house. He took out his wallet.

'How generous. All profits go to church funds.'

Before leaving, he asked the angel, 'The coroner's officer, the policeman and the insurance man – did they get tea and a biscuit?'

'Oh, yes.'

'And did they leave here with umbrellas?'

She blushed a little, smiled faintly and there was something in her eyes she tried not to have there. 'They did.'

There's no such thing as free tea and biscuits, he reflected as he started along Cannon Street with his new umbrella.

It wasn't raining. There was hardly a cloud in the sky.

He hailed a taxi and asked to be driven to an address in Chelsea. He intended to pack as much quality time as possible into this rare visit to The Smoke. He'd served the early part of his career in the Met, but he had no nostalgia about the place. Those bad old days were best forgotten. If Georgina thought he was a loose cannon in Bath, she should have seen how he'd got results in his days with the Yard.

As he'd half expected, it wasn't a publisher's office where the taxi pulled up. It was a private address off the King's Road. He started walking towards an upmarket tower block before realising his mistake. Bairnsfather Tower was the other side, one of a crop of twenty-storey monstrosities skirting the river. The area was called the World's End and felt like it. The lift wasn't working and he had to toil up five sets of stairs. All he could see from the balcony outside were more high-rise buildings with brown-brick cladding. He checked again to make sure he was in the right place: *Fine Words, 57 Bairnsfather Tower, World's End, Chelsea, SW10.* Number 57 was the only flat that aspired to a name. A brass plate with FINE WORDS in Gothic lettering was screwed into the brickwork. Someone had scratched a word across it that was anything but fine.

He rang the bell.

No answer.

The blinds at the flat's only window were closed.

He tried a second time.

'Keep going, mate,' a voice behind him said. 'He's in bed. He'll have heard you.' The speaker was an old man with a face like a war zone and white hair trailing below his shoulders.

'Do you know him?' Diamond asked.

'I don't see much of him. He's an owl, isn't he?'

'An active night life?'

'Couldn't tell you about that, but he sleeps in every morning. Give it another press.'

Diamond did so. 'I think I hear something.'

'I'm off, then. Best of luck.'

The man who opened the door and said, 'Yes?' was in a black dressing gown and not much else. His feet were bare. 'Hirsute' described him best. Black curls down to his shoulders – and up to his shoulders from what could be seen of his chest. His eyebrows could have been plucked from the mane of an unloved rocking horse.

'Mr Jock Scoular?'

'It's not convenient.'

'I'm a police officer.' Diamond held out his warrant card.

259

'Avon and Somerset?' the man read aloud. 'Are you kidding?'

'Let's do this in a civilised way, sir. Would you kindly confirm your identity?'

'You got it right the first time. What do you want?'

'A chat about someone you employ. Can we do it inside?'

Scoular shrugged, turned his back and padded away, leaving his visitor to follow. No tea and biscuits here, Diamond told himself. Unprepared for the semi-darkness of the place, he felt his foot start to skid on the morning's mail delivery, a spread of letters on the doormat. Only his new umbrella saved him from an embarrassing tumble.

Picking his way more carefully to the doorway Scoular had gone through, he found himself in a living-room-cum-office. Desk, computer, printer, table stacked with issues of *Exorbitant* and large envelopes, a mug containing pens, some reference books and a revolving globe. Two chairs, one with a high back already occupied by Scoular and the other stacked with more issues of the magazine.

'May I move these?' Diamond asked, still scrupulously polite and willing to imagine how it felt to be disturbed from sleep by the police.

'If you want,' Scoular said. 'Will this take long? I haven't had my shower.'

'Not long.' He propped the umbrella against the front of the desk, shifted the magazines to the table and sat down. 'I'm here about Olympia Ward, one of your employees.'

'I wouldn't call her that.'

'What would you call her, then?'

'She's inflating her importance if she said she's staff. She's on a modest retainer.'

This wasn't the impression Diamond had got from Olympia. She dressed and acted as if she had money and status.

260

'How did you meet her in the first place?'

'At a casino I sometimes visit with the hope of mingling with my readers. She was the dealer at a blackjack table. Between games we got chatting and she told me she really wanted to break into journalism. She had no idea of my connection with the magazine. She was obviously bright, so I bought her a drink and heard her story. The next night I had some luck with the cards and was feeling good so I offered to help in a small way. As a croupier she was well placed to introduce me to potential readers.'

'There was no other motive?'

Scoular glared. 'Isn't a man allowed to encourage a young person at the foot of the career ladder without that kind of slur?'

'Do you employ anyone full-time at all?'

'No. I do the bloody lot – editing, advertising, design and distribution.'

'But not the content?'

'I commission all the articles I publish. My contributors are experts in their fields.'

'And is it all done from this room?'

'Get up with the times, officer. Publishing is an internet activity.'

'But you still have to get the copies printed.'

'That's the only part of the operation that isn't online, apart from mailing the brutes. What else do you need to know about Olympia? I can't tell you much because she's a minor player.'

'You came to Bath and took her for a drink at the Royal Crescent.'

'You heard about that? She'd left London and was trying to go freelance. She wanted to pitch an idea to me, a possible feature for the magazine.'

'The unknown Gainsborough?'

Scoular pulled the front of the dressing gown closer across his chest as if he felt a sudden draught. 'You're well briefed.' It was more accusation than compliment. He'd turned crimson, a pleasing sign of life from a presence as bloodless as an algorithm.

'Isn't this known as a scoop in your profession?'

'A scoop of shit in all probability,' Scoular said. 'These stories of masterpieces turning up in car-boot sales generally are.'

'But you needed to know.'

'My readers do. If it's genuine, with a real prospect of coming on the market, they expect to find out before anyone else. That's the USP of my magazine: privileged information. Any of my readers may want to negotiate a private sale before it gets to auction.'

'Is that why you took all the trouble to go to Bath and treat her to a drink?'

Scoular shot him a foul look. 'You're making me sound like a predator. A newly discovered Gainsborough would be an exciting prospect. I couldn't ignore the possibility, unlikely as it was.'

'And how much was she able to tell you?'

'Most of it was hearsay from a friend. Her friend's father, actually. I told her candidly it wasn't nearly enough. I needed provenance, which she couldn't supply, expert opinion of the sort she wouldn't find in Bath and hi-res photos she couldn't obtain. She hasn't started writing the story as far as I know. She's extremely ambitious and still thinks she's going to be an overnight sensation with this.'

'Were you trying to put her off?'

'Of course not. There's a small chance the picture is kosher. But she has to be professional about it.'

262

'So you told her to redouble her efforts?'

'She needs no encouraging from me. I advised her to treat it like a top secret, which she patently failed to do.'

'I didn't hear it from Olympia,' Diamond said in her defence. 'We got there through dogged detective work.'

'Why are you here, then? Have I been set up?'

'That's unlikely. There's more at stake than your reputation.'

'Thanks,' Scoular said with irony.

'We agree on one thing. Everything about Olympia suggests she really believes this is her breakthrough as a journalist.'

'But someone further back in the chain could be pulling a fast one.'

'That's another matter.'

'What do you want me to do about it?'

'Play along with it for the time being, but be careful. Several people have been shot at, including Olympia.'

Scoular gripped the front of his dressing gown again. 'I don't like the sound of this at all. She definitely blabbed if the crime world knows about it. My readers are respectable people. They won't go near anything dodgy.'

'The super-rich?' Diamond said, his voice rising in disbelief, trading some irony of his own.

'There's no need for sarcasm.'

'Ask them how they got their money. Not at the blackjack table, unless they own it, which they probably do. Certainly not from doing an honest day's work like you and me.'

'You're talking like a Marxist.'

'I'm a policeman, not a politician. I mean the super-rich guys I can't touch because they latch themselves on to the people who wield the power. I don't blame you for finding a clever way to earn a modest income from them, but don't tell me they're white as snow.'

He actually felt a touch of sympathy for Scoular, peddling investment opportunities to zillionaires, working late into the night and making a pittance for himself. The bitterness was evident in every sentence the man spoke. What a contrast between their lifestyles and his.

'I'll let you get to your shower,' Diamond said. 'I've got the picture, thank you.'

Scoular made a strangulated sound deep in his throat that worked its way uncomfortably upwards and outwards through his teeth and turned out to be an unthinkable event: laughter. He'd thought of something funny. 'If you've got the picture,' he spluttered, 'you're a dead man.'

Diamond grinned and got up.

'Don't forget your umbrella,' Scoular added. 'I hope it's bulletproof.'

27

The final call of Diamond's London trip was to a Chelsea address only a short walk from Scoular's tower block, but a world away in every other respect. Cheyne Walk, home to the super-rich and famous, and possibly some of the ultra-rich readers of *Exorbitant*. Musicians from Vaughan Williams to Mick Jagger had lived here; actors from John Barrymore to Laurence Olivier; artists from Dante Gabriel Rossetti to Gerald Scarfe; and a host of the well-heeled who stayed anonymous to dodge the limelight.

The terraced front had nineteen windows on five levels overlooking the street and the Thames. Only one side of the street was built on. Over the years, the influential residents had seen off any number of attempts by planners to spoil their view.

You entered Carla Denison's studio rooms by first persuading someone inside by answerphone to open the gate before you could approach the front door. Diamond had already made an appointment. He announced his name and waited. The gate inched inwards as if it hadn't made up its mind if it wanted to admit an overweight detective. He checked his watch. He'd made this appointment in advance. The front door was opened with more certainty by a middle-aged woman soberly dressed in a navy jacket and skirt. She spoke his name, just to be sure she'd heard right over the intercom, and said, 'I'm Daphne Pinero.'

'I don't mind Peter.'

But Daphne Pinero minded. She wasn't ready for that degree of intimacy. 'Come in then, Mr Diamond. I don't know where you can hang up your hat and umbrella.'

'I'll survive. Good of you to turn out for me like this.'

'Yes,' she said. 'I hope it won't take long. I have a mountain of paperwork at the office.' The office was the bank appointed as sole executor for Carla Denison's estate.

'Let's get started, then.'

'I don't know what you expect from me. I've started making an inventory for the valuation, but the technical side of her work is outside my experience.'

'Mine, too,' Diamond said. 'I'm sure we'll make some headway between us.' In truth, he wasn't sure at all yet. First impressions didn't promise a productive relationship. 'I'm only interested in her artwork. Is there a studio?'

'Upstairs. We had quite a debate in the legal department as to what to call it, studio, workroom or lab. It's a bit of all three.'

He could imagine lawyers filling their well-paid time like that.

They started up a wide carpeted staircase. 'I expect you've been doing this all week, showing people round.'

'Actually you're the first. We have a duty to be careful. If you were from the Met, I'd insist on seeing a search warrant, but I assume if you came all the way from Bath, it's for a legitimate reason.'

He didn't go into that. They'd reached the landing. Miss Pinero showed him into a large room dominated by three studio easels, each taller than Diamond. Above them, powerful-looking lights on adjustable arms. To the right, a long bench with taps and a deep sink. Ranged along the surface, enough machinery to track a Mars landing. Diamond hadn't a snowball's chance of understanding any of it.

Then he spotted something he could name, thanks to John Leaman. It was among a group of items on a tray. 'That's a headband magnifier.'

Miss Pinero softened a little. 'Really? I wouldn't have known.' She took out her phone and thumbed in the name.

'Used by modellers and stamp-collectors.' He milked his bit of knowledge some more.

'I've amended the inventory. Thank you. The things on the tray were brought back from the church where she was working at the time of her accident.'

'I was there this afternoon.' He stepped up for a closer look. Brushes, a hand torch, sheets of gold leaf, tubes of paint, a palette, bottles of oil and a domestic item he recognised at once. 'Did you get a note of the hairdryer beside it?' he asked, getting his confidence up. 'She would have used this to speed up the drying when she was doing her restoration work.'

'Actually,' Miss Pinero said, icing over again, 'it's a hand-held spectrometer. If you look at the blunt end, there's a small screen.'

His big mouth again. 'Long time since I used a hairdryer,' he said, passing a hand over his head.

She didn't smile. 'She kept the instruction leaflets in a lever arch file on the bench. The large machine to your left is a Raman spectrograph.'

'Roman?' He thought of the 'What have the Romans ever done for us?' routine from *Life of Brian*, but had the sense to keep it to himself.

'Raman,' she repeated, as if to a deaf man. 'The inventor.'

267

'You can tell I'm out of my depth already.'

'In simple language, it's a kind of X-ray machine.'

'I'll settle for that.'

'It gives readings of the fluorescence given off by the pigments used in paintings without in any way damaging the surface. It shows you hidden images right down to the first marks made by an artist beneath the layers that came after.'

'Did all these machines belong to Carla Denison?'

'They were nearly all gifts from the manufacturers. She was such an expert in her field that companies benefited from her discoveries. She was often in the technical journals explaining the methods used by great artists. She was able to demonstrate that many of Van Gogh's pictures covered earlier work he discarded.'

'This is where I get interested,' Diamond said. 'Not in Van Gogh, but Gainsborough, a particular canvas she worked on recently.'

'It won't be here,' Miss Pinero said without an ounce of pity. 'We listed the paintings she had in store for analysis. Some major names, but nothing by Gainsborough.'

'I wasn't expecting to find it,' he said. 'I'm hoping there might be some record of it.'

'If there is, it will be in one of the three filing cabinets. She was well organised.'

'May I look?'

'In the cabinets? I'll unlock them. They're arranged alphabetically.'

Heart-rate rising, he crossed the floor before she did. To get more light he adjusted the blinds at the window beside the filing cabinets and got the view from the back of the house, the one the residents wouldn't enjoy – the seven tower blocks and connecting walkways of World's End. The neighbours nobody mentioned.

The first cabinet was A to G. He opened the bottom drawer and checked the tabs. There was no file for Gainsborough.

'Shit.'

'Not there?' Miss Pinero said, unfazed.

'Pardon my French. No.'

He wasn't giving up yet. He went through the rest slowly in case the file was in the wrong place. They were all meticulously sorted. He pulled out a folder filed under Gauguin to see what might have been included. It was stuffed with notes and photos.

'Plan B, then. May I see her computer?'

'I'm afraid not. It was taken away to be examined by an expert. The software is encrypted. I'm not sure if he's found a way into the system yet.'

'I came here with such high hopes.' He closed the drawer with his foot and got a dark look from Miss Pinero. But he was getting her measure. He didn't need to grovel. He crossed the room to look at a calendar planner pinned to a cork board. 'This may be helpful.'

The columns were well filled even at weekends, testimony to Carla Denison's heavy workload. In the slot two days after her death there was an entry marked '3 p.m. Olympia Ward'. He smiled. He'd never thought Olympia's name would be a comfort. He ran his finger across and found an appointment some weeks earlier for Mr S. Hubbard, the third of three for Seppy spaced twelve days apart.

Off the top of his head he asked, 'Can I look in the second filing cabinet?'

'I can't think why.'

'But can you think why not?'

Clicking her tongue in annoyance, she stepped across and used the key again.

If what he wanted was there, it would be in the top drawer, under H.

H for Hubbard.

And it was – a fat file for Seppy. He felt like hugging Miss Pinero. He could have waltzed her around the studio floor like Yul Brynner with Deborah Kerr in *The King and I*. He removed the folder and took out a set of at least twenty 8x10 colour prints.

'This could be the jackpot.'

The photos were a record in sequence of Carla's work on the canvas, beginning with the original multicoloured mess in its art nouveau frame. The second and third were enlargements of the thumbprint in the corner and the narrow strip Leaman had recognised as an ear.

The X-ray spectrometer had come into use in the fourth. A ghostly head and shoulders large enough to fill the canvas were revealed through the layers. Diamond's throat dried with excitement. He would have loved to share this moment with the team. Jean Sharp and John Leaman deserved to be here.

The next photos were straight shots of the picture. By slow stages, Carla had begun removing pigment and keeping a photographic record as she worked. A process that must have taken more than a week could be seen in seconds.

Too impatient to work through them all, he lifted out the last and took it closer to the window. Seppy's find of a lifetime, a strikingly sharp portrait of a youth in a large white collar fitted to a pale blue jacket with the sheen of satin. Face square on, the boy stared out with a confident, almost mesmeric look. A patch of his dark brown hair had been combed over his forehead, not enough for a fringe and too much to be called a kiss curl. The rest of the hair was long, spreading either side of the collar. He had a finely formed mouth, the lips a bold shade of red, the cheeks pink enough to have been rouged, yet there could be no question that he was male, moody and ready to take on the world.

Such subtleties could only have been rendered on canvas by an artist of exceptional talent.

'It's extraordinary,' Miss Pinero said, forgetting that lawyers don't enthuse about anything. 'He's almost alive. I can't think why it was covered in all that paint.'

Diamond, lost for words, shook his head.

'What else is in the file?' Miss Pinero asked.

He hadn't got round to that. He placed the batch of photographs on the filing cabinet, picked up the folder again and took out what looked like a report of twenty or more closely printed pages. It was headed *Oil on canvas, property of Mr Septimus Hubbard*. He opened it several pages in and knew at once that the text was beyond comprehension – his, anyway. At the mention of spectroscopic signatures and X-ray diffraction his brain shrieked for mercy.

'I'm lost already,' he said.

'Isn't there a summary? Any report worth reading should have a summary.'

Top of the class, Miss Pinero. He turned to the opening page and found a digest he had a fighting chance of understanding:

Mr Septimus Hubbard, the owner of a Bath antiques shop, asked for an opinion of an oil on canvas 17½ x 14¼ ins (44.5 x 36 cm). The client had noticed a small fragment of what appeared to be an earlier work under flaking layers of paint apparently applied randomly. Although it was in a twentieth-century art nouveau frame, the plain-weave linen canvas was clearly much older and the condition of the wood stretcher bars bore this out. Dense concentrations of pigment and some obvious running of the oil medium suggested the canvas had been put to use as a palette for mixing colours. Thumbprints in the right lower corner appeared to confirm the palette theory.

Analysis of the overpainting showed it to have been mixed with linseed and poppyseed oil. The pigments were consistent with those in use in the mid-eighteenth century, notably Prussian blue, lead white, vermilion, burnt sienna and Cologne earth.

Terahertz imaging revealed a head and shoulders figure at the subsurface painted directly on the grey priming and this was confirmed using X-ray fluorescence. When consulted, the client asked for all layers obscuring this image to be removed. A gel containing slow-acting solvents was used and the process took more than a week.

The subject, when fully revealed, was a front view of a youth wearing a white Van Dyke collar and the top section of a pale blue jacket. Blurring of detail in the clothing suggested that the artist was interested mainly in achieving a likeness. The face, by contrast, was precisely rendered. The painting appears to be a preliminary study from life for a larger, more finished portrait. The artist may have treated the result as a mere aid and discarded it afterwards and used the surface for mixing colours.

The model bears a marked resemblance to the sitter for Thomas Gainsborough's celebrated work shown in the 1770 Royal Academy exhibition and popularly known as *The Blue Boy*. The colours and general shape of the clothing, although loosely suggested, match the larger portrait. If such a link were confirmed, the value would be significantly enhanced. As to verifying its authenticity, the picture met each of the tests applied: the condition of the wood and canvas; infrared imaging of the preliminary sketch; chemical analysis of the pigments; and the spectroscopic signature of the artist's use of colour and paint-bonding oils. Moreover, the quality of the brushwork will stand comparison with the best of Gainsborough.

The main impediment to authenticating the work is the lack of provenance. But if the artist himself used the canvas as a palette, as seems clear from analysis of the over-painting, and it was put in store and lost to view for two and a half centuries, there can be no provenance in the normal understanding of the term.

'Even I've heard of *The Blue Boy*,' Diamond said. He handed the report to Miss Pinero. 'Have a read if you want. I need to get my head around this.'

He wouldn't be sharing what had triggered his memory – his passion for old films. In a Laurel and Hardy short called *Wrong Again,* the famous painting had been stolen and the pair mistakenly supposed it was a horse called Blue Boy. They found the horse and tried to reunite it with the painting's millionaire owner and claim the reward. In the confusion at the end, the police arrived with the recovered masterpiece and all became clear – except that in the rush for the exit the painting got knocked over.

He still needed reminding what the real thing looked like. His smartphone remedied that. From what he could make out on the small screen, a boy in his early teens in a blue satin suit with a large lace collar was standing against a mainly brown landscape and overcast brown sky that set off the colour of the jacket, cape and breeches.

True, you can't appreciate a work of art reduced to the size of a playing card, but Diamond wasn't impressed. No young lad he'd ever known would be seen dead in such a fancy outfit. The Blue Boy's left arm was propped defiantly on his hip and the right held a large black hat with a cream-coloured feather plume. There's no accounting for taste.

Scrolling down, he learned that the original was almost lifesized. It had been housed for the last hundred years in the Henry E. Huntington Library and Art Gallery, San Marino, California. The price the railroad tycoon had paid was a world record for any painting. Eat your heart out, Leonardo da Vinci. In 1921 *The Blue Boy* was top of the pops.

It would never grace Diamond's wall. His idea of art was a film poster of *The Third Man*.

Because he had the phone in his hand, he checked his inbox and read a message from Keith Halliwell. It should have come with a burst of zither music.

'This has been hugely helpful,' he told Miss Pinero – and meant it. 'But duty calls. I must get back to Bath by the next train.'

28

I woke to the sound of a vacuum being pushed around the salon downstairs. The hairdressers had already shut up shop for the day. The cleaner always took over at 7 p.m. My head was telling me I had important work to do, but what? The brain works even when you sleep, processing stuff and making sense of things you didn't fully take in at the time. My office was screaming for a tidy and a dust, but it had been screaming for six months. A more urgent duty was hollering to me if I could only hear it. Something Virginia had said. I had a feeling it was to do with our conversation on the church wall when she'd mistaken me for one of the cops. All that toe-curling stuff about Cliff, her elderly husband, and how Viagra hadn't worked for him. She was letting me know why she was hitting on a stranger she'd just met. Her needs, as she put it. Let's be clear, though. I wasn't just any available man. My good looks go without saying. Don't underrate my animal attraction, even dressed in a forensic suit.

My fuzzy brain was telling me I'd learned something that tied in with my investigation, but what?

I got up, shaved, cleaned my teeth and showered. Under the shower, everything clicked. The grey matter earned its keep. I cast my thoughts all the way back to that Tuesday morning Pete and I first went into Seppy's antiques shop and discovered the body in the mummy case.

The adrenalin stirred and fizzed.

That was the Eureka moment. I had a mission. I would return to Sternwood Hall, or whatever Virginia called her stately home, but not for the reason you're thinking. Not for more of the same.

Not having eaten since breakfast, I picked up a Big Mac and a black coffee before hailing a taxi and telling the driver to take me to Sion Hill.

'You're not planning to eat that thing in my cab?'

'It's for later.'

'Because if you so much as rustle the bag, you're out.' With that clear, he became Mr Nice. 'Sion Hill, you said. Anywhere in particular, squire?'

'I'll tell you when we get there.'

It was already getting dark. We drove by way of The Circus, Brock Street and Cavendish Road to the high point of Sion Hill and passed the shut gates of Virginia's estate. Lights were on in the gatekeeper's lodge. I let the taxi run for another fifty yards and told the driver to put me down.

'Are you sure, mate?' he said. There was nothing to be seen in the headlights except the high brick wall stretching along the empty road.

'I'm so sure, I'm about to take a bite from my Big Mac if you don't unlock the door.'

I got out and paid him. After his rear lights had vanished, I sat on the verge and wolfed my supper – or was it breakfast? Then I strolled towards the gates. From out in the moonless night I heard the chilling scream of a vixen, followed by the answering bark of the dog fox. How did I know? I'm a townie. We got foxes too.

I used the flashlight app on my phone to check the wall. The top was out of reach unless you were a basketball pro. Common sense told me not to risk climbing the gate. It was sure to be alarmed. What does a hard-boiled dick do with a nine-foot wall to get over? I faced it like a high-jumper eyeing the crossbar, except I wasn't eyeing anything. I'd be jumping in the dark. I couldn't light up the wall because I needed both hands free. Going by memory, I made the run, slammed my foot against the brickwork as high as I could and took off. I got a handhold on the top, pulled with the arms and pushed with the legs, hoisted myself up, wriggled over and landed on my feet without breaking an ankle.

Not bad for a shagged-out forty-four-year-old.

No alarm bells sounded. No bullmastiffs sank their teeth into me.

My first task was to see inside the lodge. Like everything else about this estate, the building just inside the gate was big in scale, big enough to house a small army of gate-keepers.

I crept forward confidently – until without warning a bank of halogen lights came on. I'd triggered a motion sensor.

I hit the ground like a panel of sheet metal.

Did I panic? Did I hell! Moments like this are meat and drink to a professional. I knew security lights are programmed to bathe the area in brilliant light for one, five or ten minutes and then switch off again. As long as no one came out to see what was wrong I would be okay. But I needed to be alert. I reached under my chest for my handgun – and cursed. In all the excitement, this professional had forgotten to pack his piece.

No sound came from inside the lodge. I counted to sixty and nothing changed.

This may sound odd, but the only sure way to get out of range of security lights is when they are on full beam. If you stay where you are and wait for them to go off, you'll trigger the system again when you move in the dark.

In full view of anyone interested enough to watch, I squirmed towards an area I thought might be safe and lay still again.

The lights dimmed. They must have been on the five-minute setting.

This side of the house seemed more promising. Active security cameras have small red lights around the lens visible in darkness. The cameras at the front were live. None were visible along the left side.

I raised myself off the ground and crept forward. I'd noticed a waist-high window with drawn venetian blinds. The light was on in the room behind them. If I could get close, I might be able to see between the slats. People don't often shut blinds completely.

I was on turf, so I could creep close without making any sound. At the window, I couldn't see much through the slats, but there was a space on the left where the blinds didn't quite cover the glass. Inside, a man in an armchair was watching TV.

Lord Bede?

Unlikely.

Even from the back, he didn't look like an old guy needing carers. For one thing, his right leg was hooked over the arm of the chair, more the body language of a teenager than a seventy-five-year-old. For another, there was a small table beside him with a beer can on it. To cap it all, he was holding a cigar in his right hand. Virginia had told me Clifford Bede was a lifelong non-smoker who drank nothing stronger than rosehip tea.

There wasn't time to reflect because someone grabbed my shoulder from behind, swung me round and kicked me in the stomach. As I doubled up in shock and pain, an uppercut struck me below the jaw.

If you've ever read a Loren D. Estleman, you'll know what I mean when I say I'm an Amos Walker fan. Amos is a hard man, the Vietnam vet who joined the Detroit cops and got thrown out of police academy for punching someone in the shower. He set up as a PI and his whole career is peppered with punch-ups. All in good causes, natch.

Bath Spa isn't anything like the hardboiled city Detroit was when Amos was toughing it out, so I don't get much practice fist-fighting, but believe me I was ready to go. My attacker had split my tongue with that uppercut and I could taste the warm blood, which only made me more mad. I moved in close, kneed him in the groin, pummelled his ribs and heard a satisfying grunt of pain with each hit.

This is the real deal, Johnny, I told myself, so go for it and sucks to the Queensberry rules. I was about to headbutt the guy when I felt my collar grabbed from behind.

There were two of them.

The second was big, seriously big. I sensed his size without seeing him and I had the feeling we were not going to get along. His grip on my jacket had already burst the seams under my armpits. He could have lifted me with one hand. Instead he pulled me against his body. The top of my head was below his jaw, well below, not far above his belt.

Seeing I was helpless, the smaller guy threw a free punch at my face that I managed to ride by turning my head.

'Leave it, jerk,' the big man said. 'We got him.' With that, he threw me to the ground and pinned me there with what felt like an elephant's foot on the small of my back. 'Get his belt off.'

I didn't like the sound of that. There was nothing I could

do to stop it. The jerk knelt on the backs of my thighs, unfastened my favourite leather belt with the silver bullet buckle and pulled it clear of the loops on my jeans. In the faint light from the window I could see it dangling. I thought I was in for a flogging.

Instead, the giant said, 'You know what to do.'

'Fasten his arms?' the jerk said.

'Get on with it.'

I felt my wrists tugged together.

'Not like that,' the giant said. 'Above the elbows.'

So my biceps were forced together behind my back and the belt was wound around them a couple of times and buckled hard. Great for improving the posture, but not the way I care to spend an evening.

'Move,' the giant told me, removing his boot from my back and giving me an encouraging prod.

I struggled upright and faced his middle. From the little I could see of his face by bending my head as far back as it would go, he had the lantern jaw and gorilla brow typical of the condition of abnormal growth.

'Where to?'

He made a movement with his head towards the front of the lodge, so I stumbled in that direction. The hero of this story had become a quivering wreck. What a turna-round. One minute he'd been Amos Walker in *Every Brilliant Eye*, the next he was the cowardly lion in *The Wizard of Oz*.

The jerk rang the doorbell.

After some time, it was opened by the guy I'd seen draped all over the armchair. He looked peeved at being made to move. A strong smell of cigars wafted out into the night air. He was in slippers, pink cord trousers and a black T-shirt with the words ANYTHING BROKEN MUST BE PAID FOR.

'Do I know you?' he said to all three of us.

'Security, sir,' the giant said. 'We caught this person acting suspiciously, peeking through your window.'

'Really? Who is he?'

I spoke up. I'd been racing through my mental case notes and everything made sense. 'I'm Johnny Getz, the private eye hired by Ruby Hubbard to find her missing father Seppy. I believe I've just earned my fee.'

What a moment! There are times when I need to remind myself I'm one of life's winners, because whoever is in charge up there puts me through the grinder. Finding Seppy was sudden and wonderful, better than waking from that dream when you're on a sinking ship in a shark-infested sea and the last lifeboat has left without you. Don't get me wrong. It was no accident that threw us together. If you've followed my story carefully, you'll have worked out how smart sleuthing brought me to his doorstep at that moment in time. Credit, please, where it's due.

Seppy was all I'd expected, urbane, affable and forgiving, the sort of guy who steps up to open doors for ladies. He would have shaken my hand if it hadn't been clamped behind my back. He sized up the situation at once and told the giant to release me.

'Is he safe?' the giant asked.

'He's family, or the next thing to it,' Seppy said. 'Please untie him at once. Then I suggest you gentlemen get back to your duties and look for real trespassers.'

The giant nodded to the jerk, who gave me back my arms and my belt. The blood started exploring my veins again and gave me gyp.

The security men lingered, hopeful of a tip. They wouldn't be getting one from me. Seppy waved them away and they stood scowling. Seppy closed the door.

'Come through, my dear fellow.' He waved me into the

281

room with the armchair and the TV. I could now see three more armchairs and a sofa, bookshelves, tables, framed cartoons on the walls and a retro cocktail cabinet with the flap down and the lighted bottles and glasses on view. 'What will you have? A gimlet, I should think. Isn't that the drink the detective orders in Victor's bar in *The Long Goodbye*?'

Had I died and gone to heaven? Seppy was a Chandler fan. 'A straight scotch would go down a treat if you have one.'

He reached for a bottle. 'I'm well provided for. Lady Bede sees to that. Have you met her?'

Had I met her?

Watch it, Johnny, I told myself just as I was starting to relax. This is the charm offensive. You're about to step into a minefield. 'Yes, we met.'

He poured me a large malt whisky in a chunky Waterford glass. 'It's through Virginia, as I call her, that I heard about you. She's been acting unofficially as my own special agent.'

And that's not all, I thought, going by the cigar butts I'd found in that dressing room. 'I know she has a line into the police, being on the ethics committee.'

'Perfectly placed to let me know what's going on. After the calamitous incident in my shop I chose to vanish from the scene, as I'm sure you deduced. She told the rozzers straight out she's taking a special interest in the case.'

Rozzers? That wasn't out of Chandler. More like Peter Cheyney. I hadn't heard the term used in real life.

'Cool.'

'I also get to know how my darling daughter Ruby is progressing. The police have monitored her from the start. She's almost ready to leave hospital now, but I'm sure you know more than I do. You've been extremely loyal to your client, continuing your investigations even when it seemed she might never recover.'

'My job is more than just the fee,' I said, not missing a chance to buff up my reputation. 'When I take on a case, I see it through to the end, whatever happens.'

'Spoken like a true private eye.' He took another cigar from his pocket. 'You don't mind? I assume you don't smoke these things yourself. How did you get on to me?' He cut the cap with an oval-shaped guillotine and used a match to light up. More smoke drifted upwards to thicken the cloud already trapped by the ceiling.

'One thing and another,' I answered.

How did I get on to him? I could have told him he was holding the reason in his hand, but explaining how the trick is done is not smart. He'd be unimpressed hearing about the cigar butts I'd remembered seeing on his untidy desk in the antiques shop – and under the fern in the dressing room. Not many people chain-smoke cigars. 'I never believed you were dead, or I wouldn't have taken the case.'

'You're ahead of the police. From all I've heard, they're in two minds as to whether I'm dead or not. I didn't want to get into this situation. I'm afraid I was in a blue funk after killing the wretched thief who broke into my shop.'

This was it, the raw truth we'd all busted our guts to discover.

'You were spending the night there?'

'Sometimes I sleep over. I have an old horsehair chaise longue upstairs, where the customers don't go. The blighter made a frightful noise forcing the front door. He was about as subtle as an elephant in a supermarket. But who am I to criticise? I completely lost control. I saw red when this jobsworth started rummaging through my property.'

'Enough to make anyone mad,' I said.

But Seppy didn't need my sympathy. He was well into his

story, as if he'd been waiting weeks to spill it. 'He was there for a reason. I knew what he was after, but that's by the way. As I was saying, the red mist came down. I acted stupidly and crept downstairs and cracked him over the head with the first thing that came to hand, which was a plaster bust of Julius Caesar. Killed him outright when all I meant was to stun him.' He paused and shuddered at the memory. 'There wasn't much blood, but he was a goner and no mistake. I can't even claim I did it in self-defence. And then I made things worse by concealing the body. I panicked, you see. It wasn't easy lifting him into the Egyptian coffin even though he was a small fellow, but I thought hiding him might delay the investigation, and apparently it did.'

'No question,' I said. 'The cops called to the break-in must have been at the end of their shift. They missed a bucket-load of clues. They sealed the place and a whole week passed before Pete Diamond and I went in with Ruby to look. By then, the trail had gone colder than outer space.'

'It gave me time to sort myself out,' Seppy said. 'I decided to head for the hills, so to speak. Well, Sion Hill, anyway. Virginia had been suggesting for some time that I moved in with her. She was only too happy to install me in the lodge.'

'What about Lord Bede? Wasn't he living here?'

He shook his head. 'That's what we agreed to tell anyone who noticed the lodge was in use. Actually, Clifford has a suite in the main house at the end of east wing. He's senile, but well looked after. Virginia is fond of him, I'm sure of that. It's just that she's a much younger woman with phys-ical and emotional needs he can't supply.'

Those needs. I knew exactly what he meant and was careful not to say so. 'How did you first meet Lady Bede?'

'She came into the shop one afternoon some months

ago looking for vases – she arranges the Bede Hall flowers all on her own – and there was an immediate spark between us. I sold her a very fine majolica jardinière and pedestal and she asked if I could deliver it, so I did, the next day. When I got there I was bowled over by my first sight of Bede Hall. I don't know if you've ever visited the house itself.'

'I feel as if I have,' I said, spotting another tiger-trap. 'It's online. Magnificent.'

'Well, Virginia will make any excuse to serve champagne, so I was treated to some and she told me about her situation and made it rather obvious she found me attractive and the next thing we were in the sack.' He put the cigar to his lips and blew out a huge proud plume of smoke, then added modestly, 'Nothing like that has ever happened to me before.'

'I know what you mean,' I said.

'Since then, we've never looked back. She can't get enough of me. My only concern is whether I can match her energy.' He smiled. 'Between ourselves, there are times when I say I have a headache.'

Like last night, for instance, when I stood in for you, I thought to myself. If my experience was anything to go by, I had to admire his stamina. 'But you haven't moved into the main house?'

'No, the present arrangement suits us both. I'm well hidden from any visitors Virginia has, I can smoke here to my heart's content and she says it adds spice to our encounters when I visit. Like a gigolo.'

A less likely gigolo than Seppy was hard to imagine, but I may have been jealous.

'Don't you miss the shop?'

'Would you, in my shoes?' Seppy said with a wink.

285

The fact that he was wearing slippers and looked as sexy as the wreck of the *Hesperus* didn't enter into it, except in my twisted mind. 'Definitely not.'

'You're right, though,' he went on blithely. 'My business is in an absolute mess. I haven't even dared go back to my house. I can't do anything about it when I'm supposed to have disappeared. The worst part is being out of touch with Ruby. I was appalled when I heard she'd been shot in the head. I wanted to visit the hospital, but Virginia insisted there was no point because she was in a coma. Now she's on the mend, I'd like to hug her and let her know I'm alive and well. But as soon as I break cover, I'll be arrested and charged with manslaughter, concealing a body and obstructing the police and God knows what else.'

'I don't suppose they'll press charges,' I said.

'I wish I had your confidence.'

'They'll know you can afford the best lawyers – or Lady Bede can.'

'Virginia? She could be in trouble, too. She could be charged with harbouring a criminal. And other people have lost their lives. It's a hideous mess, Johnny, and all of my own making. Let me top you up.' He got up and fetched the whisky bottle.

I didn't discourage him.

'Now that you've caught up with me, I suppose you'll turn me over to the law.'

'The thought hasn't crossed my mind,' I said, and I was speaking the truth. 'My job was to track you down and that's what I've done.'

'How much is your fee?'

'It's not up to you to pay it.'

'I'll double it if you draw a line under this and say nothing to the police.'

Tricky. 'It's out of my control,' I said. 'I doubt whether Pete Diamond will let me walk away as easily as that.'

Seppy leaned on me some more. 'When I say double it, I mean you get triple the amount. The original fee plus my contribution. I can afford it. I'm in the money – and I don't mean Virginia's money.'

Whether he meant to, I've no idea, but he'd given me an opening. 'Are you talking about the Gainsborough?'

I shocked him so much that his mouth popped open like a pedal-bin and the cigar fell in his lap. The red-hot end finished face down on his flies. If he hadn't leapt up from the chair he would have been pleading headaches to Virginia for the foreseeable future. The smell of scorched corduroy showed what a near thing it was. A hole had burned right through and his underpants were showing. The pink trousers were a write-off.

Meanwhile, I'd picked the butt off the carpet. 'Do you want this?'

He shook his head. 'Long time since I've done anything as stupid as that.' He sank into the chair. 'How do you know about the Gainsborough?'

'It's no secret any more,' I said. 'Just about everyone in Bath knows, not to mention London.'

He was more crushed than a piece of roadkill. 'Ruby must have talked.'

I shrugged as if I hadn't the faintest idea who had talked. It's a golden rule that you don't dish your client.

Seppy had made up his own mind. 'She will have spoken to her friend Olympia. I'm so disappointed in her. I suppose it was too big a secret to keep to herself. I can only hope and pray she's kept the picture safe.'

Kept the picture safe? Now it was my turn to be gobsmacked. 'Was Ruby taking care of it?'

He gave a nod. 'I had the good sense not to keep it in the shop once it had been cleaned and restored. I'm certain that's what the thief was after when he broke in and opened the safe.'

'If the thief knew, your secret was already out.'

'Certain people had to know. Carla Denison, who did the restoration, for one, but I'd trust her.'

'She's dead.'

'I heard. A tragic accident.'

'Tragic, yes. An accident? Who knows?'

His face creased. 'Oh dear, this gets worse and worse.'

'You must have visited her more than once.'

'Indeed. A charming lady, brilliant at her work.'

'This was before you went into hiding?'

'Weeks before. I bought the canvas at a car-boot sale and noticed there was a thin band of finely executed painting under all the muck. I knew the right person to approach. I'm not a beginner in the world of antique art. She was as intrigued as I was by my discovery. She was prepared for a forgery and amazed when it turned out to pass all the tests – the paint, the canvas, the wood and, of course, the workmanship. She was willing to stake her reputation on its being genuine.'

'How did you plan to cash in?'

'You mean how *do* I plan to cash in?' He'd recovered enough from the cigar episode to rub his hands at the thought. 'Before I do anything, I'll have to find a way of returning to the human race with as little fuss as possible, and that won't be easy. Then I hope to convince one of the big London auction houses I'm a respectable citizen and put the picture up for sale. Their experts will want to take a good look at it first, but as it had Carla's seal of approval and she was respected by everyone, I don't anticipate any trouble. She said it was almost certainly a study for *The Blue Boy.*'

Another juicy detail no one had shared with me. 'Makes a difference, does it?'

'A trifling difference of several million.'

'You can afford a new pair of trousers.'

He grinned. 'It's impossible for me to say how much it will fetch. An unfinished sketch called *The Blue Page* was sold by Sotheby's in New York for over three million dollars in 2016. It seems to have been painted after 1770, when *The Blue Boy* was done. Mine is a preparatory study, a finished work with a striking resemblance to the masterpiece, so it's infinitely more collectable.'

'And more valuable.'

'Many times more.' He grinned. 'A humble antiques dealer hardly dares dream of something like this.'

'Does Lady Bede know you're about to become a multi-millionaire?'

'I told her. It's only right she should know when she's shared so much with me. She'd love to buy the picture herself, but I'm not sure her funds will run to that. The upkeep of Bede Hall must be a staggering drain on their income.'

'Will you give up the shop?'

'I intend to employ a manager. I wouldn't want to close it. I'll move out of here, but remain in Bath. I'd hate to hurt Virginia's feelings after all her generosity.'

'Visiting when the need arises?'

His eyes twinkled. 'As and when.'

'A gigabuck gigolo.'

He laughed. 'That's absurd.'

We wittered on about his spending plans for the next half hour before it was obvious he had nothing more to add, so I thanked him for his kindness and phoned for a taxi.

I'm a thick-skinned guy. In my job, you have to be. But as I was driven off and Seppy stood waving in his doorway, I felt a right turd for failing to tell him Ruby's flat had been burgled the night she'd been taken to hospital. If the precious Gainsborough hadn't been swiped, I was a banana.

29

'Listen up, people. This is for your ears only.'

At short notice, Diamond was briefing his team. Chances like this were precious. He didn't want Lady Bede listening in. Or his boss, Georgina. Or that pest Johnny Getz, who hadn't yet wormed his way into the incident room but was capable of it. Not one of that trio had been told about his trip to London. His trusted colleagues had covered for him and now he was sharing what he'd learned.

At heart, he'd always been a showman. He liked pulling rabbits out of hats. So he held the umbrella like a staff and didn't open it until the finale. He spoke about his visit to the city church where Carla Denison had been working at the time of her death and how her body was found one morning below the scaffold tower; about Jock Scoular's humble home in World's End where he'd learned first-hand the story of Olympia Ward's progress from casino croupier to pushy journalist; and about Carla's hi-tech studio where he'd inspected her Seppy Hubbard file and discovered the sensational truth about the canvas bought in the car-boot sale.

At the mention of *The Blue Boy*, phones were out and scrolled in earnest.

'Yikes, it's world famous,' Paul Gilbert said.

'The real thing is,' Ingeborg Smith corrected him. 'Seppy's find is an early study for it.'

'Still worth a fortune, I bet.'

'Worth killing for, obviously,' Keith Halliwell said.

Which was the opening Diamond wanted. 'Two or three killings. We've had three deaths for sure. Mark the safe-cracker, Wally the gunman and Carla the restorer.'

'They weren't all homicides, were they?'

'Weren't they? The safecracker was bludgeoned with a heavy object, the gunman shot through the head.'

'No argument about that,' Halliwell said.

'And the picture restorer fell,' Ingeborg said. 'We've been through this. It was an accident. She didn't jump and she wasn't pushed.'

'Hold on, Inge,' Diamond said. 'I've been there, seen the ceiling – and I was about to say "got the T-shirt". In fact, I got something better.'

Showtime. He held the umbrella high and pressed the catch. Everyone knows how a brolly works, but there's still a childish satisfaction at seeing one snap open. He gave it a twirl before angling it to show his audience the interior.

Ingeborg said, 'Yay.'

Gilbert said, 'Cool.'

Halliwell brought his hands together twice over.

Even solemn John Leaman smiled.

'This is the view I had yesterday, standing in the aisle and looking up,' Diamond said. 'You can just about see where Carla was at work, right at the top, above the clouds and the sun's rays, applying fresh gold leaf to the Hebrew word for God. Lower down are cherubs and angels dancing in praise. Lower still in more subdued colours there's a sort of frieze meant to look as if it's stonework with sculpted figures.'

'Cornice,' Leaman said, ever ready with obscure infor-mation. 'It looks to me like a *trompe l'œil* cornice.'

'I won't argue with that,' Diamond said, 'but I want you all to notice the four large circular windows. Those are real.'

'They look elliptical from here,' Leaman said.

'Give me a break, John. The point is that they provide the daylight that lights up the dome. My arm is aching. I'm going to pass this round and you can each get a closer look.' He handed the umbrella to Jean Sharp. 'The placing of those windows is important. The coroner's officer and the insurance guy believe Carla Denison must have been dazzled by a low ray of evening sunlight coming through one of the windows. They say she lost her balance and fell. I'm not convinced. Anyone tell me why?'

Ingeborg saw the point at once. 'If she was working at the highest point of the dome, there's no way a sunbeam could have reached her.'

'Right on.'

'Vertigo,' Leaman said.

'What?'

'Vertigo. She wouldn't have to be dazzled by the sun to get dizzy.'

'She'd been working there for days. Why should she suddenly get an attack of vertigo?' Diamond said, huffy at having his show interrupted again. Before Leaman could respond, he said to the team, 'I'll tell you something you don't know. I'm at an advantage here because when I visited Carla's studio I was shown a tray filled with items of her equipment they brought back from the church. Paints, brushes, gold leaf. And among them was a torch, a simple hand-torch, or so I thought when I first saw it. But it wasn't.' He dipped his hand in his pocket and took out a cylindrical object looking like a torch, switched it on and pointed it upwards at the rafters. A small circle of light appeared up there, flitting between the beams.

'A laser pointer,' Gilbert said.

'Right. This is one I borrowed from Paloma.' He switched it off and held it in the palm of his hand, another party trick performed. 'It's a low-power job, under five megawatts, that she uses when she's lecturing. Even so, you don't point it in people's eyes. On the way back from London, I thought about what I'd been shown and I called Miss Pinero, the woman who showed me the studio. She confirmed that the torch thing was a laser pointer and a powerful one, with more than one battery.'

'You think someone shone it at Carla and dazzled her?' Ingeborg said. 'Nasty.'

'I didn't believe the sunbeam theory,' Leaman said. 'This makes better sense. She was vulnerable up there.'

'But why?' Gilbert asked. 'She wasn't a threat to anyone.'

'She was,' Leaman said. 'She knew too much, obviously. She'd done her work on the Gainsborough and Seppy dispensed with her.'

'Seppy?' Ingeborg shrilled in disbelief. 'Why would *he* want her dead?'

'I told you,' Leaman said. 'He was covering his tracks. We've all got used to calling him Seppy – as if he's a pet lamb or something – when in fact he's an evil, grasping killer. He stands to make millions from the picture. He's a collector. You have to understand the mentality of these people. An adult life devoted to acquiring antiques in the hope that one day he'll come across a real bargain – a Ming vase or some such. Well, he got lucky. A genuine Gainsborough.'

'We can agree on that – at least, I think we can,' Ingeborg said.

Leaman wasn't stopping to debate the finer points. 'He gets the picture cleaned up and authenticated and then he's got a security problem, so he takes to sleeping over in his shop. And one night there's a break-in. Seppy panics, brains the guy with a plaster cast and kills him. In a real state now, he shoves the body out of sight in the coffin and goes into hiding. All bets are off. He's terrified of being arrested and missing the chance to cash in. As a man on the run, he can't deal with the big auction houses. His best hope is to sell to some billionaire with a castle stuffed with old masters. People like that exist outside James Bond films, they really do. He just needs to know how to contact them. Who better to ask than Carla? He takes the risk of travelling to London to see her again. She's at work on the church ceiling by now. What he doesn't appreciate is that she has a reputation in the art world. So when he tells her his story, she wants none of it, even when he offers her a bribe for names and contact details. He's messed up again. When the body in his shop is found, as it surely will be, the police will appeal for information and Carla, the upright citizen, will feel it's her duty to tell all she knows. Do I need to go on?'

The room had gone as silent as a prayer.

The first to speak was Halliwell. Something needed explaining. 'Where would he have got the laser? He wouldn't have brought it with him.'

'The guides in some of the big churches use them to pick out the fine details high up,' Leaman said as if it was common knowledge.

'It was there already? I can believe that,' Diamond said. He'd had more time than the others to ponder the significance of the laser theory and Leaman was right. Seppy ticked all the boxes as the prime suspect – motive, means, opportunity. Find him and you'd find the killer. 'Has anyone called the hospital to ask about Ruby?'

'She isn't there any more,' Ingeborg said. 'She went home yesterday.'

'For fuck's sake. I wish someone had told me.'

Ingeborg gave a soft sigh. No use telling the old grump he obviously hadn't read his texts while he was in London all of yesterday.

'If she's out, she'll think of nothing else but finding her father. We need to speak to her. Inge, you'd better come with me. Is your car nearby?'

The meeting was cut short. A pity, because he had more to tell them about his visit to Jock Scoular and what he'd learned about Olympia, not to mention his find in the filing cabinet in Carla Denison's studio.

He was chuntering all the way to Oldfield Park.

The shiny new keyplate on Ruby's front door was a reminder that the lock had been changed. She was in no rush to come to the door and when she opened it she didn't appear ready to invite them in. The chain was on and the gap was about three inches. They couldn't even check how she was dressed. There was only a glimpse of the chilli-red locks. She'd covered the wound and the shaved patch with a yellow scarf. 'Yes?'

Diamond was in control of himself. He was the soul of discretion. 'You know me, Ruby. Peter Diamond. We met in your father's shop and I visited you in hospital. And you remember Detective Sergeant Ingeborg Smith.'

'Have you come to tell me something?'

'It's more a matter of what you need to tell us. Can we come in?'

'I've got nothing to say to you.'

'You sound stronger than when we last spoke.'

'My head is better, if that's what you mean. I really don't have time to stand here talking.'

'Is anyone in there with you?'

'No.'

'Then you'd better let us in. We're investigating the shooting and your burglary. We need to speak to you about both.'

She could scarcely refuse. She sighed and released the safety chain and they followed her upstairs. She was in a navy trouser suit with silver buttons over a yellow blouse that matched the headscarf.

The bedsitting room had changed little since they were last there. A large floral quilt covered the bed, the wardrobes were closed and the low table was empty except for the wine bottles coated in candle wax. Ruby scooped up two china mugs and carried them to the kitchen area.

'Had a visitor already?'

She didn't pick up on Diamond's remark. Standing in the kitchen doorway as if she didn't want anyone investigating the state of the fridge, she asked, 'What exactly do you want from me?'

Getting any answer was like chipping stone with a mustard spoon. 'Was it a horrible shock, coming back yesterday and finding your flat had been broken into? Or had Olympia told you what to expect?'

'She texted me.'

'When – yesterday?'

A nod.

'After she knew you were coming home? She hadn't said anything while you were recovering in case it distressed you?'

This time the answer was no more than a sigh of annoyance as if he needn't have asked.

'Thoughtful of her. And she had the lock changed so you'd feel safe. Have you checked what was taken?'

'I don't have anything worth stealing.'

'That may be true, but the thief wasn't after your property, was he?'

She didn't move a muscle.

'I'm going to make a wild guess that the only thing stolen was an item belonging to your father – the picture he bought at a car-boot sale that turned out to be the find of a lifetime.' He smiled. 'Well, not such a wild guess when I've spent as much time on this case as I have. He asked you to take care of it for him because he thought no one would guess it was here. Am I right?'

She shrugged and sighed and it was good as a yes.

'Where was it – the top of a wardrobe? Under the bed? There aren't many hiding places in a bedsit.'

She looked up at the ceiling.

Diamond pressed on. 'Doesn't really matter where it was, does it? The thief found the picture and got clean away. What a good friend Olympia is, saying nothing to you about the burglary. You'd have been out of your mind with worry.'

The irony passed without comment. She wasn't being drawn on anything.

'The Gainsborough is the only item that was taken, right?'

With impatience, Ruby said, 'Now you've cleared that up, can you leave me in peace? I've nothing else to say.'

'I'm surprised to hear that,' Diamond said. 'Each time we've spoken before, you were worried sick about your father. This morning, not a word. What's changed?'

She looked startled and this time put together an answer. 'Nothing has changed. I've given up hoping you'll find him. I've lost all confidence in your lot.'

'Ruby, that isn't quite true, is it? I'm willing to believe the last part, about losing confidence in us. We haven't been much help. But when you say nothing has changed, you're wrong. I saw in your eyes as soon as we arrived that something has changed. You don't need our help any more because you've had news of your father. You had a visitor before we arrived. I saw the coffee mugs and I saw how quick you were to snatch them up and put them in the sink. You're standing there in the doorway as if you're guarding the crown jewels and it's only two recently used mugs. The visitor wasn't your father, I'm sure of that. Seppy is still on the run. No, it had to be Johnny Getz, the detective you hired to find your father. What's the betting he was here to collect his fee? Personally I wouldn't rely on anything that man says – unless he can prove it's true.'

She couldn't resist blurting out, 'Well, you're wrong about that. Daddy is alive and well. I spoke to him on the phone half an hour ago.'

'Ah. Mr Getz delivered.' He swallowed a large chunk of injured pride and turned to Ingeborg. 'Well, that surprises me.'

A slight smile from Ingeborg. She'd been silent up to now, letting the boss prise out the truth, and he didn't need help.

'And what did Seppy have to say?' he asked Ruby.

'Nothing to interest you.' This young lady had a thousand ways of saying 'no comment'.

'We need to know, Ruby.'

'It was personal.'

'Personal, but friendly?'

'He's my own daddy, for God's sake,' she said in a burst of emotion. 'Why shouldn't he be friendly? All he said was how worried he'd been, wanting to know how I'm feeling and telling me to rest up. Does that satisfy you?'

'So there's no ill-feeling about the picture?'

'Why should there be? It wasn't my fault it was stolen.'

Shaken, self-righteous and petulant, she was in denial, failing to admit she must have leaked Seppy's secret to her best friend.

'Was it mentioned at all?'

'Not once.'

'You're not telling me he's lost interest in his precious picture?'

'What's done is done,' Ruby said.

'Did he tell you where he is?'

'No, and I didn't ask him. I honestly don't have the faintest idea. Now will you leave me in peace?'

He was inclined to believe her. Seppy had made one huge error in entrusting his daughter with his secret. Blood ties and loyalty are easily confused. The chastened father wouldn't risk another leak. He'd made contact again, and now his conscience was clear.

He exchanged looks with Ingeborg. She gave a small shrug meaning she, too, thought there was no more to be gleaned.

They left Ruby. Whether they'd left her in peace was an open question.

Outside in the car, Ingeborg said, 'Where to, guv?'

'With reluctance,' Diamond said, 'Kingsmead Square. A hairdresser's called Shear Amazing.'

30

We all have our ways of saying 'case closed'. Sue Grafton's ultra-efficient PI, Kinsey Millhone, will write a report dealing with all the fine points needing explanations in the narrative, but other sleuths reward themselves. James Lee Burke's Dave Robicheaux will share a crawfish Louisiana-style with his buddy, Clete Purcel, on the deck of his houseboat in New Iberia. And James Crumley's C. W. Sughrue will amble into Mahoney's Bar and Grill in Meriwether, Montana, and get stonkered. Me, I banked Ruby's cheque and called at Waitrose for one of their chocolate indulgent cakes. I'm a recovering chocoholic always willing to lapse for a special occasion.

I wouldn't want anyone to think I grossed out on that cake. I cut it into twelve slices and shared them with the stylists downstairs, making sure they knew I'd had a major success. I'm a generous guy, but that doesn't make me a fool. Word of mouth is a powerful driver in my kind of work. Each of those gossipy girls chats to eight to ten clients in a day and if half of them mention what a fantastic detective the guy upstairs is, it's cheap, targeted advertising.

With the two last slices of the cake on the desk in front of me, I sat back in my chair and allowed myself to ponder a brilliant future. Success breeds success. Mysteries are being hatched every minute, but that's not the same as getting a knock on my door. A process as sure as natural selection guarantees that eventually some troubled client will come asking for help. The only flaw in the reasoning is that natural selection isn't quick, so even a brilliant private eye spends most of his time waiting. Especially in Bath.

I was dozing off when the knock came. I raised my chin off my chest and rubbed my eyes.

'It's open,' I shouted. 'Just turn the handle.'

What a let-down.

The face that looked round the door was Pete's. He squirmed in like a ferret and reached for a slice of cake before I could move the plate. 'You must have known I was coming, Johnny,' he said, spitting crumbs.

His peach of a sergeant, Ingeborg, followed him in, but didn't make a grab for the last slice.

'A cup of something to wash it down wouldn't come amiss,' Pete said. 'It feels like a long day already.'

'You're in the right place,' I said.

'Good.'

'You've got a choice of three coffee shops in the square.'

He blinked like a toad in a sand heap. 'Don't you have a kettle here?'

Actually I do, but I wasn't getting it out for a gutso who helped himself to my cake. My feet didn't move from the desk. 'The professionals make it so much better.'

I saw his eyes widen and slide towards Ingeborg. I saw Ingeborg's eyes narrow. No way would the super-cool detective sergeant run that kind of errand for him or anyone else. The moment passed. Pete had finished his first slice and was eyeing the last. 'Ruby told us you found Seppy.'

'It's true.'

'You should have told me.'

'Ruby is my paymaster,' I said. 'She had the right to know first.'

'It's a police matter.'

'Pete, my friend, if you cast your mind back to the start of all this, you and I divided the labour. I was to find Seppy and you were to sort out the rest.'

'Three murders and several shootings,' he said. 'You got off lightly.'

I hit him with a stinger. 'The difference is that I delivered.'

'So where is he?' Pete asked, unable to defend his failure. 'Where can we find him?'

'Not a million miles away, but he won't talk to you.'

'It runs in the family. I've never got much out of Ruby. Are you going to tell me where he is, Mr Getz, or shall I do you for obstruction of justice?'

'Why the formality all of a sudden? I notice you call me Johnny when you steal my cake.'

He turned to Ingeborg. 'What do you think? Shall we read him his rights?'

'Better not try,' I said. 'I don't like threats.'

His mean eyes made a slow survey of my office. 'I could get you evicted from here, no problem.'

'That's another threat.'

I could tell he wasn't giving up. He's a stubborn cuss and mean enough to do what he says.

I was in a fix. Virginia Bede would call it an ethical dilemma. I'd as good as promised Seppy I wouldn't reveal his hideout. My brilliant future was on the line. Sorry, Seppy. No contest.

Pete got a real shock when I told him his man was up at Bede Hall. His jaw dropped like the tailgate of a furniture van.

'Lady Bede's place? Are you sure?'

'So sure that I spent an hour with him last night.'

'I find this hard to believe.'

'Disbelieve it, then. Makes no difference to me.'

'We'll go there right away,' Pete said. 'You'd better come, too.'

'He won't welcome it.'

'He can go to hell.'

'He's headed there anyway – or so he thinks. Shall I call him to say we're coming?'

'Jesus, no. This is a raid.' Saying which, he reached for the last slice of cake, but Ingeborg steered his arm away.

'We don't want you combusting, guv,' she told him.

We couldn't possibly have crammed Pete into the rear seat of Ingeborg's Ford Ka, so muggins rode in the back. What a good thing Sion Hill was barely two miles away. Diamond used the ride to grill me about the line of inquiry that had led me to Bede Hall. I opted not to dent his admiration by saying how I worked it out. I was tempted to boast a little about my night of passion with Virginia, but discretion won out.

'It's far too boring to go over,' I lied. 'A PI's life isn't what writers would have you believe. Ninety-nine per cent of the time it's as thrilling as the view from inside a coffin.'

'You can do better than that, Johnny. What took you there in the first place?'

'A taxi.'

'Don't try me. Someone tip you off?'

'Give me a break.' I tapped my head. 'It's all deduction.'

'Have you met Lady Bede?'

'Didn't I tell you? She cleans my office three days a week.'

I saw Ingeborg's face light up in the mirror. Pete wasn't amused.

304

I suffered his dumb questions all the way to Bede Hall. A bright sun dazzled us through the treetops along Cavendish Road like an enhanced interrogation technique. I was almost ready to roll over and tell all when the long brick wall loomed up. As we came to a stop outside the gate, Pete asked, 'How did you get inside?'

'Over the wall.'

'You're quite an athlete,' he said, sarcastic son-of-a-bitch.

'And then I was beaten up by the security staff.'

'Is any of this the truth?'

'I still have the bruises to prove it.'

'How did you get away?'

'Seppy appeared in the nick of time or I would have ended up in intensive care. I told him who I was and he called off the heavies.'

Pete decided to try the official way through the gates, using the answerphone. I don't know who was on the other end, but the word 'police' did the trick. The gates inched inwards and we drove through.

'Hold on,' I told Ingeborg as she started to go through the gears. 'We don't need to go all the way up the drive. Seppy is in the lodge.'

'Not according to my information,' Pete said. 'Lord Bede lives in there with his carers.'

'That's horsefeathers,' I informed him. 'Lady Bede puts that out to fool people like you.'

So we halted and got out. This time, the giant and the jerk didn't materialise. The lodge still looked huge, but not so scary as it does after dark.

Pete, the master-planner, instructed Ingeborg to cover the back door in case Seppy made a run for it. She disappeared round the side.

He approached the front door and rang the bell.

I was making myself inconspicuous behind a laurel bush.

'Stand beside me, Mr Getz,' Pete said. 'I haven't met him, but he'll recognise you.'

That's what scared me. Seppy would see me standing next to the cop and know I'd grassed him up. He could be armed.

'This is your show,' I called back. 'I'm staying out of it.' But I made sure I was close enough to hear every word.

He turned away from me. He must have heard footsteps in the hall.

Shock horror.

It wasn't Seppy who opened the door. It was a woman in a blue healthcare tunic.

Pete's whole frame tensed. He introduced himself and said he'd come to meet Mr Septimus Hubbard.

The carer shook her head. 'You must be mistaken. Lord Bede lives here and he's not receiving visitors.'

He gave a half-glance in my direction. 'I was told Mr Hubbard was here last night.'

She shook her head. 'I've never heard of him. You must have got the wrong address.'

'Would you mind if I look inside?'

'That's out of the question. Lord Bede is confused as it is, without having policemen wandering through his home. If you want to take it further, I suggest you speak to Lady Bede in the main house.'

Lord Bede may have been confused, but not as much as I was. After the front door closed and Pete marched back to me, puce with rage, I thought he was going to lay into me. You hear a lot about police brutality. Ingeborg wasn't in sight.

'What are you playing at, you dickhead?' he yelled at me. 'I told you Lord Bede lives here.'

'Pete, I swear to you Seppy was here last night. I went

in. I shared a drink with him. We spoke for more than an hour. This is some kind of trick.'

'Yeah? The shabby trick you pulled to cover your butt. You concocted the story about finding him. It was a lie. You conned Ruby into parting with your fee. That's fraud and you won't get away with it. And I'm bloody sure you banked the cheque already.'

I was too freaked out to speak. Of course I'd banked the cheque, but it didn't mean I'd conned Ruby.

Then Ingeborg appeared from the back of the house. 'Heard your voice, guv,' she said. 'I should think most of Bath heard it. What's happened?'

He told her the whole sorry tale, adding a few choice remarks about the fly-by-night I was. I won't repeat them here.

Ingeborg – what a fab cop! – got the point straight away. 'But Ruby told us she spoke to Seppy on the phone. She must know her own father's voice. He's alive and well, even if he isn't here.'

Pete reddened and turned murderous. 'Where the hell is he, then?'

I found my voice again. 'He can't have gone far. He'll be up at the house. It's big enough to hide a football team of missing fathers.'

I'm going to give Pete his due here. He was willing to listen. 'In the car, everyone. We'll see if you're right.'

I could have quit there and then, called a taxi and left them to their manhunt, but I'm not sure they would have allowed me.

Cooped up on the rear seat, I racked my brains for an explanation. All we'd seen was a woman dressed as a nurse. We didn't know for sure who was inside the lodge. I couldn't believe Lord Bede and his carer had been moved in overnight just to provide a cover story for Seppy. I was starting to ask myself if Lord Bede existed at all. The old guy must have been around when Virginia married him and staked her claim to all his riches, but who would know if he was already dead and buried? I hadn't seen him. Pete hadn't seen him. We only had Virginia's word that he was still breathing. Ugly questions hung in the air.

The lady of the house was waiting for us at the end of the drive when we pulled up in a vast area used for parking limos, four-by-fours and the odd helicopter. What a fancy crib this was. Fountains playing, a lily pond and the great pile that was Bede Hall, no doubt built from a million tithes paid by humble peasants who could have been your ancestors and mine.

In a pink creation with see-through shoulders and arms, Virginia greeted us with hands spread in front, as if our arrival was all too much for her. 'I'm triply honoured. Two of my favourite gentlemen and a gorgeous young lady.'

Pete introduced Ingeborg.

'Of course, I know you,' Virginia said to her. 'I've watched you at work, keeping all those men civilised in the incident room.'

'We don't have much time,' Pete said. 'Seppy Hubbard was seen here last night. As you know, he's a wanted man. Is he in the house?'

'Seppy?' she said, as if he'd just named Albert Einstein. 'Where did you get that idea from?'

My reputation was on the line, so I spoke up. 'I was with him last night in the lodge. He told me he's been hiding here ever since his shop was broken into and he killed a man. You know it's true, Virginia.'

Now she had an ethical dilemma of her own. 'I'll say this. I'm positive he's not the villain you all seem to think he is. Seppy is a gentleman through and through.'

There are no flies on Pete. He spotted this for the admission it was. 'You've met him, then?'

Her hand covered her mouth, but the words had already escaped. 'I've known him a long time. I'm a regular customer at his shop.'

I said, 'The friendship runs closer than that, Virginia. Seppy told me about the day he delivered the majolica jardinière to Bede Hall and you drank champagne with him and what happened after. He's in love with you.'

Emotion overwhelmed her. Tears streamed from her eyes. 'Did he tell you that? He's a sweetie. I can vouch for him. He's been staying with me ever since he got in trouble.'

'In the lodge?' I said.

'Yes.'

'We called there a few minutes ago and a carer came to the door and said Lord Bede lives there.'

She gave a nervous laugh. 'That was a little charade we arranged, I'm afraid. Seppy said this morning he expected some unwanted visitors would come calling now that he's been found. One of Clifford's carers was posted in there to answer the door.'

Pete was shaking his head in disapproval. 'By "unwanted visitors" you mean the police. And you're on the ethics committee.'

'I'm as much in love as Seppy is.'

'You joined the committee so that you could report back to him how the investigation was going?'

'Was that so reprehensible?'

'It wasn't ethical.'

'But I really have contributed. My title unlocks many doors. Georgina Dallymore couldn't contain her excitement when I offered my services.'

309

'That I can believe,' Pete said. 'Where is Seppy now? We need to speak to him.'

'He left more than an hour ago.'

'*What?*'

'He said he had an important meeting in Bath that would put everything right. He wouldn't say any more.'

'God help us. So you don't know where?'

'No. I offered to drive him, but he insisted on calling a taxi.'

'He could be anywhere.' He looked right and left for aid. He was at a loss.

I took out my phone. I'd had a neat idea. 'It's eight minutes to twelve.'

'How does that help?' Pete asked bitterly.

'Most people arrange meetings on the hour. We could be looking at twelve noon.' I shifted to the tracking app. 'Olympia is on the move.'

'How do you know that? Have you bugged her?'

'Naturally,' I said.

'You sly bastard.'

I said, 'If a meeting is planned, Olympia will know about it. She's currently in Gravel Walk, heading towards the Royal Crescent.'

'There's no way we can get there in under eight minutes,' Pete said in a frustrated rasp.

Then Virginia said, 'We can use the chopper.'

31

The last hour had been bruising for Peter Diamond, but he was playing the long game. Johnny Getz had been an irritant right through this investigation. Even now, having found Seppy and pocketed his fee, he wasn't going away.

Fortunately there was a bigger fish to fry. The killing, the shootings and the art theft were down to one perpetrator. Diamond had long had his suspicion and now knew for sure who it was. He knew the motive and the means. He'd worked out how the various opportunities were engineered. He still needed proof that would stand up in court.

He was in two minds whether a helicopter would help. The others were more bullish. Then he remembered that the residents' lawn in front of the Royal Crescent – a well-maintained level surface within the curve of the famous terrace – was a natural helipad. Virginia was already on the phone to one of her staff. 'Get aboard, boys and girls,' she said as soon as the call was made, 'My pilot Esther will be with us directly.'

Only a billionairess could have her own helicopter pilot on call. And as owner of the plane, Virginia meant to ride with the investigators. How could they object? No use telling her the mission was dangerous.

Before boarding, Diamond gave Ingeborg confidential instructions for what was to come. She listened with her customary calm. You wouldn't have known he'd said anything of interest unless you saw how her eyes dilated.

They bundled inside the six-seater Sikorsky S-76 already standing on the launchpad. It was a long time since Diamond had used this mode of transport. His main memory of his last flight was that it had been so noisy the passengers had been supplied with earmuff headbands. But when Esther powered the twin turboshaft engines, it became obvious that the cabin was soundproofed.

No time for pre-flight checks. The helicopter lifted, tipped its nose briefly to allow the rotor blades to grip the air fully, and was up and away.

For a minute or so, they adjusted to the sensation of being airborne and the sight of Bath's terraced slopes beneath them. Then Diamond prepared the others for what was to come. 'There can only be one reason Seppy has broken cover. He was nicely holed up in Bede Hall. This is all about the Gainsborough he discovered, the find of a lifetime, as he called it. Nothing else is worth the risk of getting caught.'

'Pete, my old chum, the Gainsborough's gone,' Johnny said as if to a three-year-old. 'It was stolen. Seppy knows that.'

'Yes, and the person who stole it wants to cash in.'

'Olympia?' Johnny said in disbelief. He checked his phone again. 'She's heading for the Crescent, I'll give you that.'

'She could be heading for a long stay in prison by the sound of things,' Virginia said.

Johnny shook his head. 'She's smart. Ruby trusted her and so did I. Why would she do such a thing?'

'Art theft is a crime on its own,' Diamond said. 'I've never understood why people do it. Steal a famous painting and you give yourself a major problem making it pay. Right, it's worth a fortune, but you can't put it up for sale. Everyone knows it's hot, it's stolen goods. You can't break it up or melt it down like jewellery. You might steal it to order. That's John Leaman's theory.'

Johnny seemed to like the sound of Leaman's theory. 'Nick the Gainsborough for some rich nutter who wants to own it. They exist.'

'You can ransom it,' Diamond went on without pause, 'but as soon as you try, you put yourself at more risk.'

'Is that what's happened here?' Johnny said. 'Is Seppy so desperate to get his picture back that he'll part with ransom money?'

'Are you asking me?' Virginia said. 'He said nothing to me about this. He's not a rich man.'

'You could bankroll him,' Johnny said.

'Oh, come on. I have my standards.'

Nobody spoke.

Through the windows, the countryside changed from looking like a relief map to a more structured perspective as the aircraft started its descent. The spectacular curve of Bath's most famous landmark was already visible, the rich amber stonework enhanced by the green of the lawns.

'The only thing about arriving by chopper is that everyone sees us coming,' Ingeborg said.

'They'll be inside the hotel,' Diamond said.

'Not for long.'

The Sikorsky banked left and dropped altitude.

On the cobbled road in front of the Crescent, tourists were looking up and taking photos. The novelty in the air took all the attention from John Wood's audacious masterpiece. More people streamed from the hotel doorway to see what was causing the noise.

'This could work in our favour,' Diamond said to Ingeborg. 'Be ready for action.'

They were hovering above the lawn now, creating a draught that had the watchers holding on to their hats.

In front of the dense magnolia that grows up the hotel wall, a dense crowd of hotel guests and diners had collected. The least they could expect was a film star or a royal stepping down from the helicopter.

The rotor blades snapped the air with a changed sound prior to touching down.

'Keep watching the entrance,' Diamond said.

Just before Esther lowered the Sikorsky to ground level there was a disturbance between the columns of the hotel doorway as if someone was pushing for a better view. Heads turned in annoyance. The same person – in casual clothes and baseball cap – forced a way through and started sprinting towards Brock Street at the east end of the Crescent.

'That's him, Inge,' Diamond said before the helicopter touched down.

Ingeborg swung the cabin door open, jumped out, hit the ground with such force that she tipped forward and flattened her palms on the turf. Apparently unhurt, she sprang up, vaulted over the iron fence and gave chase.

Johnny seemed to decide no private eye should pass up the chance of some action. He exited the plane and dashed after her.

All this was played out in front of the astonished onlookers.

Diamond and Virginia alighted with more dignity and stood staring after the two pursuers. A man called out to ask if they were shooting a film.

Towards the back of the crowd, Diamond spotted Olympia standing with two others. 'Is that Seppy in the striped blazer?' he asked Virginia.

She shaded her eyes from the bright sunlight. 'Oh, yes, poor lamb. I can't tell you who the others are.'

'His daughter Ruby and her friend Olympia. Would you like to join them? I must see whether Ingeborg made an arrest.'

He didn't vault over the railing as the others had done. He strolled as far as the gate. And then he started running.

Two shots had come from the direction of Brock Street. The echo bounced off the tall buildings making it sound like more.

He sprinted. He found a burst of speed he hadn't needed since his rugby-playing days. He couldn't keep it up for long.

More shooting up ahead.

When he turned at the end of the Crescent he saw a figure lying still in the centre of the road. Johnny, obviously hit. Lines of blood from a head wound were streaming along the ridges between the cobbles.

Diamond couldn't stop.

He ran past, heart thumping more from alarm than exertion. Had Ingeborg been hit as well?

No one was in sight. He could see all the way up Brock Street. It was long, straight and empty.

To his right were two huge trees bordering the lawn below the Crescent. Behind them were more railings and, beyond the railings, Gravel Walk led down the slope, around the back of Brock Street and into the centre of town. They must have run down there.

Gravel Walk, where, days before, the drive-by shooting had taken place.

His first sight when he turned the corner was a pair of struggling figures on the ground.

Inge had got her man.

He ran forward to assist, but there was no need. She had handcuffed the gunman and was kneeling astride him. 'He was out of bullets, guv,' she said. 'He tried to fire more and the gun just clicked. I tackled him and threw it out of reach over there.'

He barely glanced at the prisoner. He knew who it would be. He'd known for sure after his trip to London. He took out his phone and called first for an ambulance and then back-up.

'That was incredibly brave.'

'Johnny's the brave one,' Ingeborg said. 'When the shooting started, he grabbed me and pushed me into a safe place behind a car. He saved my life, but I think he took a bullet.'

'Are you hurt?'

'I'm okay,' she said. 'A few bruises I'll feel later, I expect, that's all. I try to keep fit, as you know. It paid off today.'

'Such bravery,' he said again.

The sound of an approaching siren so soon meant someone else had phoned for help before Diamond's call went through.

Ingeborg stepped out into Brock Street to meet the ambulance and make sure they knew where Johnny was lying.

Diamond grabbed the gunman by the collar and got him upright: Jock Scoular, now a cringing parody of the grouch who had spewed arrogance in the World's End flat. The eyes were watery with self-pity and the left cheek twitched.

'Did I kill the guy?'

'Do you care? You shot him in the head. He wasn't moving when I came past.'

'I panicked.'

'You messed up at every stage.'

'Is he police?'

'You'd better start praying he survives.'

More sirens sounded. A patrol car and a second ambulance appeared from Upper Church Street, opposite Gravel Walk.

Ingeborg spoke to two uniformed officers and showed them where she'd thrown Scoular's handgun. They would mark it and leave it in position for the scene-of-crime team to deal with. The pathetic, bowed figure was marched away and locked in the rear of the police car.

Diamond and Ingeborg stepped over to the first ambulance. Johnny had been put on a trolley and wheeled into the back.

'Does he have a chance?' Diamond asked a paramedic.

'He's not dead yet, but he isn't conscious either. Is he one of yours?'

'In a way, he is.'

The paramedic climbed in, the door was shut and the ambulance left.

When Diamond and Ingeborg returned to the Royal Crescent Hotel, they found Virginia, Olympia, Ruby and Seppy seated at a round table in the garden with drinks and alfresco sharing-dishes funded by Lord Bede – although he would never know it.

'You both look as if you need a pick-me-up,' Virginia said in her uniquely pick-me-up tone. 'Pull up a chair and tell us what happened.'

They both asked for beers and while these were being fetched, Diamond told everyone what had happened.

'Will Johnny live?' Ruby asked.

'It's touch and go. No one can say.'

'He's a bloody hero,' Ingeborg said, without meaning to be so literal.

'I've said some hard things about him that will come back to haunt me,' Diamond said.

'He'd understand, guv. He wasn't always complimentary about you.'

317

The waitress arrived with the beers. Diamond emptied most of his glass before recovering enough of his poise to deal with some unfinished business. 'So Jock Scoular is on his way to a police cell, but that's not the end of the story, is it? This has been as tough a case as any I've had to deal with. It should have been straightforward, but each of you made it more complex through your actions.'

'Really?' Virginia said. 'I don't mind putting my hand up to some flimflam in a good cause, but tell us more.'

'Don't make light of it, Lady Bede. I'm talking about excessive secrecy, self-serving guile and downright lies. You all had a personal part in the mess we had to untangle and now's your chance to come clean.'

A sticky moment. Everyone except Ingeborg swayed back from the table and avoided eye contact with him.

'Let's start with you, Mr Hubbard, or Seppy, if I may.'

Seppy shifted uneasily in his chair. Virginia, seated next to him, put her hand over his.

'We haven't met until now,' Diamond said, 'and I'm not sure how Mr Getz got on your trail and tracked you to Bede Hall. You've been central to our inquiry and I feel as if I know you well enough for some plain speaking. I won't go over the story of your find of a lifetime and how you were smart enough to spot it and get it cleaned up. You shared the good news with your daughter Ruby and asked her to take care of the picture for you, a perfectly sensible security arrangement. Just how sensible became clear when your shop was broken into. Then it all went belly-up. You hit the burglar, Mark Rogers, so hard with the plaster cast that you killed him. And instead of reporting the incident, you hid the body and went into hiding, courtesy of your friend Lady Bede.'

Seppy seemed content to stay silent, but Virginia wasn't.

'Can't you see it from Seppy's point of view, Peter? He panicked and who wouldn't? He was already on tenterhooks about the news of the picture leaking out before he could get it to auction.'

'I'm sure that was in his mind,' Diamond said, 'but he added fuel to the flames through his conduct, and you aided and abetted him.' He raised both hands to stop a verbal reaction. 'I'll get to you in a moment. Let's deal with this in sequence. Seppy vanished and made no contact with Ruby. She was out of her mind with worry when he disappeared, so desperate that she hired a private eye to find him. Isn't that so, Ruby?'

He was rewarded with a nod and a flush of blood to the face, but no response and he wondered if he was in for another session of stonewalling.

'Mr Getz very properly called me in,' he went on, still eyeing Ruby, 'but we didn't get the full truth from you. You failed to tell us anything about the Gainsborough you were guarding for your father – out of loyalty, I suppose.'

This unexpectedly earned an explanation from Ruby. 'I told you Daddy called it the find of a lifetime and that was true. I thought that was all you needed to know. He'd put his trust in me.'

'Yes, and you'd already betrayed him by sharing the secret with your friend Olympia and triggering a whole extra layer of wrongdoing.'

'I thought it wouldn't matter. Really I did,' Ruby said. 'I was excited for Daddy. I needed desperately to tell someone and I knew what a boost it would give Olympia. It all got out of control.'

'You paid for it with a shot to the head and then you were out of it and events took their course.'

Olympia was quick to say, 'So it's all down to me, is it?

I was offered a scoop and I pitched it to my boss and got it approved. Is that a crime?'

'No,' Diamond said, 'but withholding information is, and every one of you is guilty of that. In your case, Olympia, you could have saved us days of painstaking investigation by telling the truth about the Gainsborough.'

'It was my scoop,' she said. 'You can't expect a journalist to chuck away a story as big as that one.'

'When people were getting killed and shot at? Get real,' he said. 'You knew the picture had been stolen from Ruby's flat and you said nothing to us.'

'Put yourself in my shoes,' she said. 'If I'd told you then, I'd have faced questions about when I first knew it was a *Blue Boy* study. Ruby had told me and pledged me to secrecy and she was fighting for her life in hospital. There's such a thing as loyalty to one's closest friend.'

'Which you ignored by pitching the story to Jock Scoular.'

'But it was in Jock's interest to keep it quiet until the story went to press.'

'And we all know how he reacted to the news,' Diamond said.

'Do we?' Virginia said. 'I have no idea what he hoped to achieve.'

'Before we get to him, I haven't finished with you, Lady Bede,' Diamond said.

She looked at him over her gin and tonic. 'It wasn't "Lady Bede" when you were drinking my champagne.'

'You volunteered for the ethics committee knowing you were harbouring the missing man we wanted to interview.'

'He was a dear friend in trouble who needed a bolthole. That's all.'

'Not quite all. You monitored my investigation and got the inside story of the limited progress we were making.'

'That wasn't unethical,' she said. 'I wasn't telling all and sundry what was going on. I was doing it entirely for Seppy's sake, bringing him news of poor Ruby.'

'And much more.'

'But never in front of the servants.'

He had to smile. 'And you lied about Lord Bede being housed in the gatekeeper's lodge.'

Seppy spoke up while still hanging on to Virginia's hand. 'She did that for my protection. I can vouch for everything Ginny says.'

She gave him a smile. 'I'm an accessory in any crime Seppy is guilty of, a self-serving, conniving bitch.'

Seppy made sounds of dissent that were drowned out by Ruby taking up the theme. 'And I'm to blame for stupidly talking about the picture Daddy asked me to keep for him. It was supposed to be a secret and I couldn't resist sharing it with Olympia. I knew what I was doing. I told myself it would give her a scoop and help her career but if I'm completely honest I was so excited by Daddy's find that I couldn't possibly keep it to myself. I had to tell someone and see their reaction.'

Olympia said in a more measured tone, 'All this soul-baring is so depressing. I'd better put up my hand as well and get it over with. I'm as responsible as anyone because Jock would never have found about the Gainsborough if I hadn't pitched my feature article to him. I loaded it with eye-watering stuff about sale prices and how this was a completely unknown work. All I was thinking of was getting my scoop into print when really I was stoking up his greed.'

'He needed money badly,' Diamond said, ready, finally, to turn the full focus on the real culprit. 'He was deep in gambling debts. You'd met him first in a casino, hadn't you?'

'Long before I came to Bath. I was running a blackjack

table and he was a minor player who kept coming back. You can easily spot the ones who are addicted.

'One of his neighbours told me he sleeps in every morning because of the late nights. I put two and two together when I saw the place he lives in.'

'Did you go out with him?' Ingeborg asked Olympia.

She pulled a face. 'You're joking, I hope. It was never like that. Oh, he chatted me up, thinking, I guess, that he'd get lucky at the table, but that's how some guys are. He liked to boast about the magazine and the fabulously rich people who read it. Jokingly I said I'd like to be on his staff and he said all I had to do was find an exclusive that would give his readers the chance to get richer. When Ruby told me about the Gainsborough, I thought I'd found it.'

Diamond had heard enough to charge each one of them, but he wouldn't. He could see the bigger picture. 'You're all minor offenders compared to Scoular. He was an extreme case, a gambling addict, as you say, living in a London tower block and dreaming of escape, driven by envy of the fat cats who read his magazine. When he heard about the unknown Gainsborough, he thought this was heaven-sent, his ticket to a life of luxury. He came to Bath and hired a safebreaker to steal the thing before it got on the market. Being almost skint, he couldn't afford the best. Mark Rogers came cheap, made a mess of the break-in and got his head bashed in. Incidentally, Seppy, you needn't lose any more sleep. Nobody is going to prosecute you.'

Seppy sighed with relief and Virginia reached for his hand and squeezed it.

Diamond said, 'It was typical of Scoular's poor planning that the picture wasn't even in the safe at the time. But he wasn't giving up. He found another lowlife called Wally Knox, supposedly a gunman. The idea was to eliminate everyone who knew how the picture had been acquired. It went well at the start – from Jock's point of view, anyway. Wally shot at you, Ruby, and put you in hospital and broke into your flat the same night and came away with the Gainsborough. Scoular was over the moon. Stupidly he was only beginning to think this through. Seppy and Ruby were out of it, but there were two others who knew about the picture.'

'Carla Denison, who did the restoration,' Virginia said, 'and Olympia who'd first told him about it.'

'Right. He got lucky with Carla. When he caught up with her, she was at the top of a scaffold tower working on a church ceiling after normal visiting hours. He picked up a laser pointer and directed the beam at her eyes. She fell forty feet and was killed.'

'That's evil,' Ruby said.

'And then he had you to dispose of.' Diamond made eye contact with Olympia. 'He set up the meeting with you here in the Royal Crescent, supposedly to give you the green light for your article but really to allow Wally Knox to eliminate you in a drive-by shooting. Fortunately for you, Johnny was with you and saw the danger before you did.'

'Saved my life,' Olympia said. 'That's two of us he's saved.'

'Added to which, Wally was no gunman,' Diamond said. 'He missed. He was told to do the job properly next time, or else. But Wally was a real loser. He turned up at your cottage in Limpley Stoke after you'd moved out. He almost shot Lucky instead. Then he set himself up in the church-yard opposite Ruby's flat, meaning to pop you when you came to collect things for Ruby. But by then Scoular was through with Wally. He came to Bath armed with his own gun and shot him point blank. From now on, he'd do his own dirty work.'

'But he had the picture,' Virginia said.

'Yes, and he couldn't think how to cash in. His only hope of selling a stolen Gainsborough was to find some Mr Big who secretly hoarded valuable works of art. He knew such people existed and he might have reached them through his magazine, but Olympia's article still hadn't been written. He was stymied. I tracked him down to his cheap Chelsea flat on the wrong side of the King's Road, supposedly to get some background on you, Olympia, and the bitterness oozed out of every pore. I came away convinced I'd met the source of all the mayhem.'

'Couldn't you arrest him?' Ruby said.

'Without firm evidence, no.'

Then Seppy found his voice. 'You've got more than enough to convict him now. Did you know about him coming here today?'

'Only at the last minute. He must have got in touch with you to set up the meeting here.'

'He contacted Olympia,' Seppy said.

'Got it. He didn't know you were still about. What exactly did he say, Olympia?'

'That he wanted another meeting at the Royal Crescent to give me fresh information about the painting. He was unusually pleasant – quite friendly, in fact. He wanted the article written for the next issue.'

'So how was it you also invited Seppy?'

'I'd heard from Ruby, so I knew where he was. I thought Jock would want to meet Seppy and hear first-hand about how the painting was discovered. It was a chance to bring them together. Jock said he'd think about it and get back to me.'

'And he did?'

'Later that evening. He said it was a good plan to meet

and he had good news for Seppy. I asked if he knew the picture had been stolen and he did. He said the good news was that he knew where it was and how to get it back.'

'For a hefty share of future profits, no doubt. He was unable to fence it, so he'd decided to cut his losses and pose as the middle man offering it back to its rightful owner. Some cheek.'

'He didn't exactly say that,' Olympia said, 'but I guess that's what it came down to.'

'There wasn't time to discuss it,' Seppy said. 'The moment he heard the chopper outside the hotel he got up and fled. He probably thought it was the police.'

'It was, sweetie,' Virginia said. 'Our chopper coming to the aid of the law.'

'What worries me,' Seppy said, 'is where the picture is.'

'It will be in London in his flat,' Diamond said. 'I look forward to seeing it myself.'

'It's Seppy's property, remember,' Virginia said. 'He bought it fair and square and paid for it to be cleaned. But he isn't going to sell it. I told him I can find a bit of wall space for it in Bede Hall.'

Seppy gave a broad, besotted grin. His future was spoken for.

Diamond turned to Ingeborg. 'Are you really feeling okay? We'd better get you home. I'll call a taxi.'

'My car's at Bede Hall.'

'Give me your key and I'll take care of it. I can drive a bit when push comes to shove.'

32

'I'm outta here,' I told the nurse.

'No chance, Sunny Jim,' she said. 'You have stitches in your head and you lost several pints. Doctor says you stay overnight.'

'You can't hold me against my will.'

'A jab in your backside can. Behave yourself.'

This should not be happening, I told myself. It was never in the script for me to end up in hospital with a bandaged head and a tube in my arm. Sure, I'd been shot, but I was breathing. I was well enough to know I survived. Getting plugged comes with the territory. Any self-respecting shamus expects to crash the car, be beaten senseless, driven over, coshed, savaged by guard dogs and shot at least once per book. He'll bleed, burn, bruise and fracture, but no way does he end the story in the sick bay. Can you imagine Lew Archer flat on his back having his blood pressure taken? Sam Spade without a cigarette? Mike Hammer on the commode? It ain't gonna happen. Those dicks take every kind of punishment and still stand tall on the last page.

I must have drifted off, because the next thing I knew I had a visitor.

I saw who it was and said, 'I didn't know you cared.'

Pete took a deep breath. 'It chokes me to say this,

Mr Getz, but I do care. I care more than I ever thought I would. I've been on a learning curve these past few days. Actually more like a switchback. At the end of the ride, I've decided you can't be the flake I took you for.'

'Can I have that in writing?' I said. 'I'd like to frame it and hang it in my office.'

'No. There are limits to my lovable nature.'

'Big of you to say so, anyway. You got your man, then?'

'You and Ingeborg did.'

'Is Inge okay?'

'A few bruises. I won't complain if she's late in tomorrow. What are the medics saying about you?'

'Nothing wrong with me.'

'Apart from a hole in the head?'

'It isn't even that. Parted my hair, that's all. The doc who stitched me up said the injury is superficial and before you say another word I'll say it myself. Superficial sums me up.'

Pete shook his head. 'I won't say anything of the sort. You saved Ingeborg's life today. That was brave. There's nothing superficial about you, Johnny. You're the real deal.'

An End Note from the Author

These days I live too far from Bath to visit locations as often as I would like. Fortunately I can count on the willing help of two Bathonians, my author friends Liza Cody and Michael Z. Lewin. At my request they visited and photographed Beehive Yard and the Corn Exchange. They also made a recce of the back of The Circus from Circus Place and were spotted looking over a wall by a police patrol car that returned for a second look at them, an incident that went into Chapter 19 with some fictional embellishment. I am relieved that Mike and Liza escaped without even a caution.

Some beautiful and authoritative books have been written about Gainsborough's years in Bath, notably *Gainsborough: a Portrait*, by James Hamilton (Weidenfeld & Nicolson, 2017); *Gainsborough*, by Michael Rosenthal and Martin Myrone (Tate Publishing, 2002); and *Gainsborough in Bath*, by Susan Sloman (Yale University Press, 2002). The story has benefited from them and I apologise for all the liberties I have taken to suit my plot.

I know some readers enjoy visiting the settings in these books, most of which are real, but I must make clear that Seppy's antiques shop is an invention; Bede Hall does not exist; and if there is a hairdressing salon in Kingsmead Square called Shear Amazing, it's a sheer amazing coincidence.

PL